MAKING HER MINE

MAKING HER MINE

MONICA MURPHY

Cover design: Enchanting Book Designs

Editor: Rebecca, Fairest Reviews Editing Services
Proofreader: Sarah, All Encompassing Books

PLAYLIST

"AUGUST IS A FEVER" - ella jane
"West Coast Love" - Emotional Oranges
"7 Things" - Miley Cyrus
"Dancing With Our Hands Tied" - Taylor Swift
"The Jackie" - Bas, J. Cole, Lil Tjay
"Your Love" - The Outfield
"Jade" - Monsune
"Hello?" - Clairo, Rejjie Snow
"California" - Berhana
"My Love" - maye

Find the rest of the **MAKING HER MINE** playlist here:
https://spoti.fi/3ILK3YK

PROLOGUE

Beck

*S*eventh Grade...

"Go! Go! Gooooo, Big Blue!"

As the cheer team keeps chanting those words, I concentrate on them, the sound of their voices, the roar of the crowd in the stands firing me up. When I'm playing football, I feel like I'm a part of something. Something special, something that I care about—and so does everyone else.

We've won all of our games this season, but today's game has been tough. This team is bigger. Stronger.

More intimidating.

As I'm about to walk out on the field, Dad grabs me by the back of my jersey, stopping me.

"Watch yourself out there, son." His gaze, his entire expression is serious. "They're big. Bigger than you."

I check out the opposing team's offensive line, who are already on the field, before I turn to face my dad, who's also one of our coaches. He usually doesn't say this kind of thing to me. He doesn't worry about me on the field. He's always told me I can handle myself out there, and it's true. Nothing stops me. "They don't scare me."

His lips form a straight line as his gaze returns to the field, his brows lowering. "Just—be careful."

His words echo in my head as I run onto the field and get into position as a defensive lineman. It's the second quarter and we only have five minutes on the clock, but I'm not scared. Even as I stare at the guy opposite me, who I swear is twice my size. Our youth league is composed of seventh and eighth graders, and my dad is right, a lot of those eighth graders on the opponent's team are huge.

At my school, I'm big for my size, but I'm only in the seventh grade. These dudes practically look like men.

"Gonna tear you fuckin' apart, you little prick," a guy from the opposing team mutters at me.

Dang. We shit-talk on the field all the time, but I've never had someone say he was actually coming for me.

I ignore him. Dad always said that's what's best. My older brother Jake says it too—though who is he to talk? He's a total shit-talker and gets into fights all the damn time. I've heard Dad and Mom talk about him when they didn't know I was around. They say Jake has anger issues.

Not me. I'm the easygoing Callahan. The one who gives them no trouble. Agreeable yet fearless.

We stare at each other for what feels like minutes, though it's probably only seconds. My heart starts to race and I mentally tell it to slow down. My breathing accelerates, and I recognize the signs.

I'm on the verge of having an asthma attack.

Not now, I tell my body, trying to take a deep breath. I used to have asthma attacks when I was really little, but I haven't had one since that time I got strep last winter and couldn't breathe. This is my mom's biggest fear. Dad always reassures her I'm fine. Healthy. Made for football, a natural athlete.

"With asthma," she'd always stress, earning a guilty look from Dad.

I refused to let it prevent me from playing the game that I love. Football is in my blood. My dad retired from the NFL as a Super Bowl winning quarterback, and my brother and both of my brothers-in-law currently play professionally. It's a part of my family.

It's a part of me.

The play is called, and without thought, I'm lunging forward, straight at the kid who told me he was going to tear me apart. I shift my right shoulder and knock into him, a growl escaping him just before he angles his body, just so, and blocks me.

At the same time, another player on his team plows right into me, sending me straight to the ground.

I'm flat on my back, a strangled sound leaving me as I stare up at the blue sky. I try to inhale, but it's like nothing happens. My lungs tighten to the point of pain, and I can't breathe.

I can't breathe.

Whistles are blowing, and on our side of the stands, people are booing. I hear my dad yelling as the one who threatened me laughs.

"Take that, little Callahan," the jerk says, just before he kicks my shin and struts away.

The crowd in the stands boos and whistles their displeasure.

Air sticks in my lungs and my chest squeezes. My entire body starts to tingle and I close my eyes, trying to fight the sudden dizziness. I'm not even moving.

Why am I dizzy?

My throat tightens as my panic rises. I recognize the feeling, and while my past asthma issues don't help, that's not the issue.

I got the wind knocked out of me.

Dad kneels by my side, his worried gaze meeting mine. "You okay, Beck?"

My lips part, but no words come out. Just a low groan. I try to nod, but it turns into a shake.

No. I'm not okay.

"We need a medic!" The panic in my dad's voice is unmistakable, which makes it even more of a struggle for me to breathe. I close my eyes and try to force myself to swallow, but it doesn't work.

It's as if my lungs are paralyzed, and it takes everything I've got to form actual words.

"I-I c-can't b-b-breathe," I stutter, feeling stupid.

"Calm down, son. You're going to be okay. Are you hurt anywhere else?" He seems afraid to touch me. Probably concerned if he moves anything that's injured, he could make it worse.

I croak out a sound, my stomach aching. My lungs burning. I know I'm breathing, or else I wouldn't be experiencing any of this. I'd be blacked out or, ya know—freaking dead.

That thought only makes everything worse.

My heart is beating so hard, I'm pretty sure it's trying to escape my body. I try to sit up, scratching at my helmet strap, because it feels too tight and I make a noise, tugging on it.

Dad bats my hands away and takes my helmet off for me and it's as if I can finally take a semi-decent breath.

"You all right?" Dad runs his hand across the back of my

head once I'm sitting up. I look around, seeing how my team-mates are all kneeling at various spots on the field as they wait for me to get up. My mom's not in the stands anymore. Instead, she's standing behind the chain-link fence that sepa-rates the bleachers from the field, her hands clutching the top of the waist-high barrier, worry written all over her face.

She's standing behind the cheer team, and I spot Addison Douglas in the middle of the row of girls, watching me care-fully. Her lips are parted, a stray strand of dark hair that escaped from her ponytail blowing across her face.

I focus on that familiar face. She's pretty. My friend. My secret crush since last year. No one knows how much I really like Addie—and that includes Addie herself.

To her, I'm just Beck. Her friend.

My eyes never stray from her as my father helps me to slowly rise to my feet. As he continues to help me hobble off the field, the entire crowd erupts into encouraging applause, and my teammates push to their feet as well, surrounding me once I'm on the sidelines. All of them ask me if I'm okay at practically the same time, overwhelming me.

I nod, but otherwise say nothing. I'm too embarrassed. My lungs still burn. My stomach hurts from where that kid slugged me right in the gut with his shoulder pad. He put all of his weight behind it when he ran into me. Those dudes were big. They mowed me over, just as the one promised.

My coaches fuss over me, but I tell them I'm all right. I just want to sit on the bench and pretend I'm invisible.

"Beck."

I glance over my shoulder to see my mom approaching, and I sort of fall apart.

Which is a whole other level of humiliating.

But I can't help it. That scared me—when I said I wasn't scared of anything.

She sits on the bench next to me and I can tell she's

restraining herself, rubbing my shoulder when I know she wants to give me a big hug. I want nothing more than for my mom to hug me and tell me it's going to be okay, but I'm thirteen. I don't need my mama.

Even though, deep down, it still feels like I do.

The clock runs out, and it's halftime. The cheer team is about to go out and perform and usually I'm unable to watch since the team huddles in the end zone and our coaches give us a speech.

This time, though, they let me stay on the bench, and I get to watch Addie perform.

They dance to a popular song, but they're not that good. Addie is so tall that she's kind of awkward when she moves, especially with her long arms and legs.

But she's got a smile on her face through the entire dance and when they get into formation to do a stunt, she's right in the back, spotting the girl they throw up in the air.

"Addie looks good out there, huh?" Mom says, making conversation like everything's normal.

While I'm sitting on the bench with my mom, like some sort of baby, still struggling to get a full breath.

The cheer team eventually finishes and leaves the field, their metallic pom-poms in their hands, the girls in my class smiling at me as they walk past, including Addie.

"Hey, Beck. You all right?" she asks in her sweet voice.

She comes to a stop in front of us, her wide smile as bright as the sun.

"I'm okay," I admit grudgingly.

"Those guys hit you hard. I saw it all." Her smile fades. "Did you lose your breath?"

I nod.

Her expression turns sympathetic. "I've had that happen before. It's the worst."

"Yeah." I shrug.

Her smile reappears. "Well, good luck for the rest of the game!" She shakes her pom-poms and runs away.

"Aw, she's so nice. I've always liked Addie," Mom says once she's gone.

"Uh huh."

"Do you guys still talk? I remember when you used to have play dates."

"I'm too old for play dates," I mumble, hating how she makes me feel like a little kid.

"I know." Mom leans against me. "I'm just saying you two used to be so close."

"Not anymore." Sort of, but not really.

"She's getting so tall," Mom continues, "and pretty too."

"I guess." I hang my head, not wanting my mom to see my face.

She always figures me out. And I don't want her to know how I feel about Addie. That would be so embarrassing.

"Hey, you seem like you're breathing pretty good now." Mom lowers her voice. "You need your inhaler?"

I furiously shake my head. "Please don't give it to me. I'm okay. Really."

The look of doubt that she casts in my direction annoys me, and I avert my head, checking out the cheer team yet again.

My gaze zeroing in on Addie, like usual.

She smiles, our eyes locking, and offers me a quick wave. I do the same, holding my hand up before I turn back around and face the field. My lips are curved into a faint smile, the wind blowing through my hair as I take a deep breath.

The first real breath I've taken since those two jerks took me down.

Guess I didn't need my inhaler after all.

I just needed to see Addie Douglas smile.

CHAPTER 1

ADDIE

*L*ate summer before senior year...

THE NIGHT STARTED out like any other. I got off work at eight, right after the sun set. I contemplated going home and taking a quick shower but realized that would probably take too long. And what if something happened at the party before I even got there?

I didn't want to miss a thing. Not tonight.

Instead, I went with my friends Emma, Tori and Lexi to the grocery store, where we picked up snacks. Someone else was bringing the booze, so we didn't have to worry about it. I'd already loaded up the trunk of my car with a couple of pillows, blankets and even a sleeping bag. I like to come fully prepared.

We live in a small town, so there aren't many places to party. During the summer, the local lake is full of tourists, so we avoid it. Plus, the majority of us work there—like me. I work practically full time at the fountain at Mitchell's Landing, and by the time I'm off my shift, the last thing I want to do is hang out at the lake. Why would we want to party with our friends at the same place we work?

No thanks.

Instead, we go up Bayshore Road, deep into the woods, where the air is cooler and the elevation is higher. Where there are a lot less people and the sheriff deputies leave us alone. There are remote campgrounds up there, not many people know about, and someone from our high school—and even the rival one—will "host" a party almost every weekend. That's the way it's always been done with the upperclassmen at my high school, and we're just carrying on the tradition.

Tonight, Beck Callahan is hosting.

And you can bet your ass I'm going to be there.

We've been flirting with each other for years, not that anything has happened between us. We send each other mixed messages—and maybe some blunt, throw it all out there messages too, though we've never acted on anything. We've kept things between us firmly in the "just friends" territory for all these years. It started in middle school, this unspoken attraction between us. I've always been afraid to cross the line because I consider Beck a friend—and I didn't want to ruin our friendship.

Did I mention that Beck is my gorgeous, hot friend who's funny and smart and athletic and oh wait—did I already say he was hot?

Yes, Beck Callahan is the hottest, most popular boy in our class.

What does he see in me?

Apparently something because, like I said, we've been flirting with each other, especially last year. There was one little problem though.

Two little problems.

He had a girlfriend—still does, actually.

And I had a boyfriend.

I'm not a cheater. Neither is Beck. We might've had an almost kissing incident in a bathroom at a party last fall, but we were interrupted and nothing happened.

Thank God. I was fully prepared to go for it, and I'm pretty sure he was too. Things haven't really been the same between us ever since. Our friendship has been rocky, full of distance, and I took advantage of that separation and threw myself into my relationship with Jonah.

My now ex-boyfriend.

At first, things were great between us. Jonah is funny. He made me laugh, we had a lot in common, which meant we could keep up conversation with each other, and my friends embraced him wholeheartedly.

But he's on the drumline and part of the marching band, and I swear, the band kids stick together hardcore, which means they looked at me as some sort of interloper once I started dating Jonah. None of his friends—and they were all in band too—seemed to like me much. I felt like I was trying too hard to be accepted, and I hated that.

Eventually, we started to become annoyed with each other. Little things bothered me. I wouldn't rush to text him back. I was running out of things to say—and so was he. He'd spend more time with his friends than me and I'd get upset. Until I broke up with him, right at the end of our junior year. He didn't protest or try to convince me to stay with him either.

Jonah was done too.

I'm grateful I didn't do much with him beyond heavy make-out sessions where we would grope each other. I might've given him a hand job once.

Okay, there's no 'might have.' I totally gave him a hand job, and it was awkward and I felt completely inept. He was just so insistent and really wanted a blow job, but I wouldn't cave, no matter how much he begged.

And he kind of begged.

Okay, again, he *really* begged, because boys are desperate sexual creatures sometimes and they can't help themselves. That's what my mother told me when I was fourteen and couldn't imagine letting a boy touch me naked.

Honestly, the only boy I've ever thought about touching me naked is…

Beck Callahan.

Maybe it helps that I never actually believed we could be anything beyond friends. He's out of my league. Out of my universe. Not that I think he's better than me, or that he acts like an arrogant asshole. We have a lot of those at school, and Beck has every reason to behave like a cocky jerk.

But he doesn't. He's a nice guy. The perfect, all-American kid who does well in school, is liked by his peers and the teachers and faculty, is an excellent football player and is really, really attractive. The boys want to be his friend, and the girls want to win his heart. There are so many people clamoring for his attention at all times, there is no way he would actually want to be with me. He has so many options to choose from and I would never be one of them.

There's one little secret I've always kept to myself, and not even my very best friend, Emma, knows about it. It's a big one, and I barely like to admit to myself.

When Jonah and I would kiss, it was…nice, but I never really felt any spark. Jonah was a decent kisser, though I don't have many others to compare him to. But there was never any real chemistry between us, not on my side at least. I didn't see him and want to immediately jump him, which is how Emma describes her feelings toward whatever current boy she's lusting after.

The only spark I've ever felt—and again, I've told no one this—is with Beck.

Beck and his sweet smiles.

Beck and the way he always calls me "Adds".

The way he watches me.

The things he says.

He has a girlfriend, who makes me feel inferior in every single way possible, because she is everything I can never be. Sasha Rodriguez is a year older than us, and she's beautiful. Shiny brown hair and big brown eyes. A smile that dazzles everyone who sees it. An athletic yet curvy body that I secretly envy—let's face it, I envy so much about Sasha. She's smart and popular and everyone respects her. She's also poised and a complete overachiever. In other words, she's total goals for a girl like me.

She's also nice—no one can say anything mean about Sasha, without sounding like a jealous bitch. She's kind to everyone, including me. I've been in leadership with her since my freshman year and we've always gotten along.

They were *the* couple on campus, like something out of a movie. Two beautiful people gravitating toward each other. Of course, they made sense when they got together. When she started dating Beck, I wanted to hate her but I couldn't. It's like hating Cinderella or Bambi. You can't hate the sweetest Disney creatures.

Once she got accepted to UC Davis, things noticeably shifted between Sasha and Beck. She'll be attending school three hours away and he's still going to be here. With his strenuous football schedule, they won't be able to see each other much. I'm sure her class schedule will keep her busy too. They'll be experiencing different things without each other, and I don't know how they're going to be able to maintain their relationship. It's possible, but it won't be easy.

If their relationship is serious, if they really love each other, then they can make it work.

But will they?

I can't help but wonder if Beck and Sasha had sex. I mean, come on. Sasha's gorgeous and Beck is too, and they're both full of surging hormones, so I'm guessing that's a big fat yes. They've most likely done it hundreds of times—and I can guarantee she feels a spark every time Beck so much as looks at her. Plus, she's a year older. She's probably not as scared as some people.

Like me.

Jonah pushed for it, especially near the end of our relationship, but I always said no. It just didn't feel right, giving my virginity to him. I cared about him, but I wasn't *in love* with him. And speaking of Jonah...

"Oh God, there's your ex," Emma utters under her breath, just as we come out of the snack aisle of the local grocery store.

I hear what she's saying, but it's as if I have no comprehension of it until I practically run into him. "Oh, sorry. Uh, hey."

God, I *would* be the one to almost run into my ex in the grocery store—while he's with another girl. Humiliating.

"Hey." He's got his arm around Serena Lewiston's shoulders. She's in band with him. Cute girl. Wears glasses. Really short, with light brown hair that flows far beyond her shoulders and a bright smile.

Which she is currently directing at Jonah.

"How are you?" I ask, my voice light and airy, as if I'm simply running into an old, beloved friend.

Emma jabs me hard in the ribs with her elbow, but I ignore her. Why shouldn't I make pleasant conversation with my ex-boyfriend?

"I'm good. Great actually." He squeezes Serena's shoulders, and she finally tears her gaze away from his face...

To send me a withering look, her smile fading fast.

I don't acknowledge her.

And she doesn't acknowledge me either.

"Good. Great." I nod and smile like a dope, which earns me another jab from Emma.

"You guys going up to Bayshore tonight?" Jonah asks, as he and Serena start to leave us.

"Maybe! We might have better prospects though," Emma answers for me, practically yelling at them as they walk away.

"Why did you say that?" I ask wearily, once they're out of earshot, glancing down at the various chip bags I'm holding in my arms. I'm sure I look ridiculous. Still a little messy from getting off work, wearing my Mitchell's Landing T-shirt and a pair of dirty black shorts stained with ice cream.

"Because I hated that smug look on his face as he stood there with his new band ho and basically rubbed her in your face," Emma says, indignant as she marches past all the checker lanes and heads straight for self-checkout. I follow after her, wincing when she says, "You know those two are fucking."

I really hope no one heard Emma say that.

"Serena isn't a ho. She's nice. She was one of my lab partners in biology freshman year." I glance around the store, looking for our other friend. "Shouldn't we wait for Tori?"

"She's around here somewhere. Don't worry about her. She'll text us." Emma waves a dismissive hand and starts ringing up her purchases, which aren't many. "And Serena is a *total* ho. Don't you think they're doing it?"

I look over my shoulder to see if Jonah and Serena are nearby before I answer her. "I have no idea."

"He basically had his hand on her tit, so I'm guessing yes."

Emma pulls her debit card out of her wallet and inserts it into the card reader. "Men. They're ridiculous."

"I love that you're so pissed on my behalf, but I really don't care who he's with or what they're doing." And I mean it.

Really.

As a matter of fact, I'm evaluating my emotions right now after running into Jonah and Serena, and I'm realizing that... okay fine. It bothered me a tiny bit, seeing them together, hanging all over each other.

But not enough for me to want to cry or freak out.

She sends me a look that says, *bullshit.* "Please. He's a dick who pushed you for sex and when you wouldn't give it to him, ran right out and found someone else who would."

Ouch. I mean, Emma isn't wrong.

"He wasn't the love of my life." Emma gets out of my way, so I can scan my bags of chips. I wonder if Jonah and Serena thought I was going to eat all of these, when that was definitely not my plan. "It wasn't that difficult to break up with him either."

"You cried. A lot," she reminds me. "So yeah, it was a little difficult."

I pull out my debit card and pay for my items. "Whatever. I'm over it—and him—now."

"Good." She grins as I put away my wallet and then scoop up my bags of chips. "Let's find you a new boy to focus on. Tonight."

I slowly shake my head, both of us coming to a stop when we hear Tori yelling for us to wait for her. "No thanks, I'm not looking for a new boyfriend."

Wouldn't mind basking in Beck's attention tonight, but he'll probably be too busy with Sasha. Plus, since he's hosting, everyone will want to talk to him. We're seniors now, and he's the big man on campus.

I'm sure plenty of people will be surrounding him tonight. I probably won't even get a chance to get close enough to say hi.

"Oh, come on. It's our last year in high school." Emma turns to Tori as she approaches. "Don't you want a boyfriend during our senior year?"

"Hell yes," Tori says as we all start to head out of the store. "Isn't that every seventeen-year-old girl's dream? Cute boy on her arm for the entirety of senior year? Someone she can go to all the events with? Take photos with?"

Tori lives and dies by social media, so what she's saying doesn't surprise me at all. "I just want to have a fun senior year. If that involves a guy, cool. If it doesn't, still cool."

Emma and Tori send each other a knowing look as we approach my car.

"Whatever," Emma says, rolling her eyes when I glance over at her. "Keep telling yourself that."

I laugh, mentally brushing her words off. I'm not going to let her get me down, and I know that's not her intention. She's just watching out for me, and I appreciate that. "I just want to let loose and have fun tonight."

"You have been working a lot this summer," Emma points out.

"I know. And I don't want to worry about how I look or what I say because that's exactly what will happen if I try to talk to some random guy." I unlock the doors with the keyless remote and slide into the driver's seat. Emma takes the passenger seat and Tori is in the back.

The moment the doors are shut and I start the engine, Tori is clutching herself and giggling as she falls to the side.

"What's your problem?" I ask her, our gazes connecting in the rearview mirror.

"Want to see what I picked up at the store?" she asks.

Emma turns to look at her. "You didn't buy anything."

"You're right." I see her giant smile in the rearview mirror. "I didn't."

A weird feeling settles over me and I pull out of the parking spot so fast, the tires squeal, making the girls squeal too. "Don't tell me you stole something."

"Okay fine. I didn't." Tori digs in her oversized bag, pulling out a bottle of cheap vodka. "I, uh…picked this up on the way out."

"Oh my God!" Emma starts clapping, a giant smile on her face.

I groan. "You're lucky you didn't get busted."

"No one was paying attention to me. It was so easy to just slip the bottle into my bag, I almost couldn't believe it." Tori shrugs. "At least we got something just for ourselves to party with tonight."

"This is the cheap stuff," Emma says, inspecting the bottle after Tori hands it over to her. "You could've at least got the more expensive kind. It goes down a lot smoother."

"So picky. Be glad I got what I got," Tori says, taking the bottle back from Emma with a faint glare. "You gonna drink tonight, Addie?"

Most of the time I don't, especially lately. Volleyball practice is kicking my butt and the season hasn't even officially started. Yet Tori and Emma show up at practice after a hard night partying always fresh and ready to play. Going to practice hungover sounds like a nightmare.

But thankfully I don't have practice for the next two days. Partying in Bayshore means that most of us stay the night in our cars. Some people even bring tents. It's the perfect way to stay safe, get drunk and not have to worry about driving until the next morning.

"Definitely," I say with a nod and a grin, letting their mood carry me.

I pull into the parking lot of a shutdown restaurant, just

outside of town, and change my clothes, pulling on a pair of black leggings that make my butt look good and my favorite hoodie I bought over on the coast a couple of summers ago. Then we're on our way, ready to party.

We make the twisty drive up Bayshore Road, the music on full blast and the car windows down, since the mountain air gets cooler and cooler the farther up we go. We're all singing along at the top of our lungs with the songs playing, and Tori already has the vodka bottle open, she and Emma taking swigs from it. I tell them to put the vodka away because I could totally get busted with an open container in the car, but they don't listen to me.

Not like we pass many cars going up this road, so I guess we're okay.

By the time we pull into the campsite, it's fully dark and I can see the tiny flicker of a campfire in one of the designated spots. There's a group of guys standing around it, all of them tall and broad, and I can only assume they're members of the football team.

Wonder if Beck is with them.

"Hey, give me a drink," I say to Tori before we get out of the car.

She hands over the bottle with a grin. "Be careful. It's fiery."

I take the bottle from her and sip from it, grimacing. Then I take a couple of swallows, earning cheers of encouragement from my friends.

"Look at you," Emma says with admiration, when I hand the bottle over and wipe my mouth with the back of my other hand. "You'll be drunk in no time."

"That's the goal," I say with a faint smile, though I don't want to get sloppy drunk. Just feel a pleasant buzz that'll make it easier to witness Beck and Sasha together.

Plus dealing with Jonah and his new girlfriend slobbering

all over each other requires all the alcohol I can get my hands on.

We exit my car and slowly make our way over to the clusters of people. There's a group standing by a car we walk by, passing a joint among them. Another group is kicking back in chairs they brought, every single one of them clutching a beer can and their heads tipped back in laughter. I spot the guys around the fire, one of them facing the site entrance, his gaze landing on mine as I draw closer.

It's Beck.

And he's alone. No girlfriend by his side.

Hmm.

He smiles at me and I smile in return, trying to ignore the butterflies fluttering in my stomach.

We've known each other for a long time, Beck and me. Our older siblings are part of the same friend group, so that brought us together in the first place. Plus, we're in the same grade, and we've been in the same classes most of the years of elementary and middle school. We were actual friends when we were kids, and sometimes he'd come over to my house, or I'd go over to his.

Ah, the Callahan house. I haven't been there in a long time, but I love his parents. They're always so nice and welcoming. And I love his sister Ava and brother Jake, who are good friends with my sister and her husband, Diego. In high school, they were a tight-knit group.

I wouldn't call Beck and I tight-knit. We don't even really share the same friend group. We've had classes together in high school and we talk. There were a few moments last year, where I wondered what his motive was when it came to me.

But he's with Sasha. And for a while, I was with Jonah. We've never really been on the same page.

We still aren't. He's taken and I'm single.

Typical.

Beck says something to one of his friends and then walks away from the fire. Pretty sure he's making his way toward us.

Toward *me.*

I go completely still, my heart tripping over itself when I realize that, yep, he's coming to talk to me.

"Wait a minute," Emma says, her voice low as he draws closer and closer. She sends me a quick look, before returning her attention to him. "Hi, Beck."

He stops in front of us, his gaze flitting to Emma, then Tori, before landing on me. "Hey ladies." He doesn't look away from me.

And it's like I can't look away from him either.

"Hi, Beck," Tori says, toasting him with her vodka bottle before she takes a sip. "Thanks for having the party tonight."

He chuckles and the rich sound reverberates somewhere deep inside of me. "Thanks for coming."

His gaze still doesn't stray from mine. And I stare at him like a lovestruck idiot, unable to speak.

"I brought ice chests and they're over there." He waves his hand toward his car. "If you want something else to drink besides Tori's vodka."

She is currently cradling said vodka bottle like it's her baby, which is a little weird.

"There's beer, White Claws and other stuff. Oh, and tequila." Beck returns his attention to us, slipping his hands into the front pockets of his shorts. "Whatever you ladies want, you're more than welcome to it."

There is not much I want. Maybe just him?

Okay, yeah, no. Can you imagine if I said that to him? He'd probably laugh his ass off. Then go tell Sasha and make her hate me forever.

Speaking of Sasha...

"Where's your girlfriend?" I ask, wishing I could slap my hand over my mouth the moment the words are out.

His expression doesn't change, but I see a flicker in his gaze. "She's out of town. Went to meet her new college roommates for the weekend."

"I bet she's so excited to start at UC Davis!" Tori is gushing after taking another big swig of vodka. "You're going to miss her, huh, Beck?"

"Yeah, sure." He shrugs, his expression impassive. Giving away nothing.

Why do his words sound so falsely positive?

"Come on." Emma takes my hand and starts walking. I have no choice but to follow her, Tori right behind us. "Thanks again, Beck."

She drags me away before I can say anything else to him and it takes all of my power to yank my hand out of her grip. "What was that about?"

"I should be asking you the same question." Emma doesn't stop until we're standing in front of the three ice chests that Beck just mentioned to us. She sends me a sly look. "I think he likes you."

I burst out laughing to cover up my nervousness. "He does not."

"He so does! He always has." Emma flips the lid open on one of the coolers. "I always wondered why he didn't just go for it with you."

"Because we're friends. He has a girlfriend," I stress, reaching for a White Claw nestled in the melting ice. I crack it open and take a sip. "I'm not his type."

"What do you mean by that?" She grabs a White Claw too and slaps the cooler lid down before she opens her drink.

I spot Tori talking to the group of guys by the campfire, laughing when one of them tries to steal the vodka bottle out of her hand. Pretty sure it was Dom, Beck's best friend. Tori has crushed on him since the end of junior year.

"I don't know." I shrug, taking another sip of my drink as I contemplate what to say. "We've just never made anything happen between us. Something always gets in the way, and I'm okay with it. We're just meant to be friends, I'm thinking. Plus, we're on totally different planets."

"Sasha's leaving soon. How long will their relationship last once she's at UC Davis? I know I wouldn't stick with my still-in-high-school boyfriend, even if he is Beck Callahan," Emma says.

I just nod in agreement. I can't imagine them staying together, but maybe Sasha knows a good thing when she's got it. Maybe they're madly in love. After that time in the bathroom last year with Beck, he's never really tried to make a move on me again. I'm guessing he realized Sasha meant too much to him to ruin his relationship with her by sneaking around with me.

Not that I would've let him sneak around with me. I'm not that kind of girl. Sasha is my friend.

"Okay, don't make it obvious, but when you can, check out what's happening at the fire," Emma murmurs.

I frown. "What do you mean?"

"A certain someone is watching you." Emma smiles to herself as she keeps drinking.

My heart in my throat, I play it casual as I glance around the campsite, taking in all of the people I go to school with. Half of the senior class is here, which isn't saying too much since our school is small. There are a few juniors here too, as well as even a couple of sophomores who have no business being at this party.

Like, who let them come? If I was an incoming sophomore at this party, I'd be terrified, no joke.

Finally, I glance over at the boys standing around the fire, spotting Beck immediately. He's so tall and broad, it's hard to miss him.

My gaze eats him up as I start at his legs and keep going up, up, up. Until I see his face and can tell he's watching me.

Watching me check him out.

Oh my God.

I quickly turn away to find Emma facing me, an amused expression on her face. "Girl, you were so obvious right now."

My cheeks are hot. "Can you blame me?" I ask weakly.

"No, I can't. He's fire." She laughs and steps toward me, curling her arm through mine. "Should we walk over there?"

"Oh, hell no." I furiously shake my head. "I'm fine right here."

"You just need more liquid courage," Emma says, before she drains the rest of her White Claw. "Let's grab another one."

"If you say so."

Doesn't matter the amount of liquid courage I consume tonight, I probably won't get a chance to talk with Beck. Not that I should. He's taken.

Even if Sasha's not here, I have no business talking to him —*flirting* with him.

Thinking about him as something more.

No business whatsoever.

CHAPTER 2

⚜

BECK

I'd been weirdly nervous since the moment I showed up at Bayshore, hoping like hell Addison Douglas would show up. My friends convinced me to "host" this weekend's party at Bayshore, telling me they knew a bunch of people would show if I were the one inviting them.

Which I did. I invited everyone I could think of and I also sent out a mass invite on my private story on Snap and IG. It worked. There are a lot of people here tonight already and I'm sure more are still coming. The only one who wasn't able to make it?

My own damn girlfriend.

I get that she's facing a lot of life changes, and unexpected opportunities are coming at her continuously. Like meeting up with her new roommates at Lake Tahoe for the weekend. One of the girl's families vacations there every year in a giant cabin, and they invited the roommates in order to come meet one another. There are four of them total, which means that Sasha has three new friends I won't really know, and it's...

Weird.

I let my gaze wander around the guys standing at the fire, all of them my friends. Members of the football team. Guys I've known a long time, and trust with my whole heart. There's Liam, who's interested in a girl that's here tonight, though he won't reveal exactly who she is.

My best friend Dominic is totally hot for Tori, the girl currently lugging a cheap-ass bottle of vodka around with her like it's her pet. Marcus is chilling with us, though he's got his eye out for his side-piece, Monique.

Ugh, Monique. She's always trying to be someone's side-piece. She's tried to get with me multiple times, but I've never been interested. She has no loyalty to anyone.

Sighing, I take a sip from my beer, my gaze snagging, yet again, on Addison. Addie.

Adds.

My middle school crush—hell, I've *always* had a little crush on her since I was twelve, but she always friend-zoned my ass, which I never understood. When it came to me and what I thought was my obvious interest in her, the girl was clueless. Or maybe I was really freakin' bad at dropping hints that I was totally into her.

Not sure what it was, but we could never get on the same page, much to my regret.

The beginning of my junior year, I got together with Sasha, and Addie found a boyfriend too, that weenie Jonah who's in the band and thinks he's some drum playing rock star.

Gimme a break.

I heard Addie broke it off with him right after school ended. I never found out the reason why, and it's not like I can ask around and find out. People might get suspicious, considering Sasha and I are still together.

Draining the rest of my beer, I go grab another one, Sasha on my mind, as usual. But not in a good way. Things are tense between us. We haven't been getting along lately, and I blame it on her life changing so much. She's leaving soon, and what does that mean for me? For us? I sound like a selfish ass, but I really don't want a long-distance relationship, especially during my senior year of high school.

I also don't think I want to be in a relationship with Sasha any longer. I haven't wanted to be with her for a while, since prom. She got so drunk on the night that was supposed to be our first time, there was no way I could have sex with her. Not when she was half passed out in the hotel room we were staying in. Instead, I put her to bed, still wearing her dress, and went to Dom's hotel room, where we partied and I got fucking wasted.

The drunker I got, all I could think about was seeing Addie at the dance that night, beautiful in a sky-blue dress that sparkled in the light. She wore her hair up, showing off her pretty neck, and I wished I could've been the one who danced with her. Instead, it was Jonah's arms that were around her as they swayed to the music. The way he looked at her. How she smiled up at him.

It about killed me.

Because I was a gentleman and wouldn't take advantage of her in her trashed state, Sasha got pissed. We've been at odds ever since, though you'd never guess it, considering the public persona we've been putting on. Her graduation night, we were all smiles out on the football field, my arms around her, her beaming in her cap and gown. The minute the photo ops were done, she ditched me for a "seniors only" party at a house someone rented for the night on the lake.

There was a rumor I heard that she kissed someone else that night, but she denied it to my face emphatically.

Whatever. I almost don't care if she kissed someone else. It would give me the perfect excuse to end it with her, once and for all.

My gaze wanders to Addie yet again, who's laughing at something Tori said before she takes a big sip from her White Claw can. Her long legs look sexy as hell in those leggings she's wearing.

Everything about her is sexy as hell.

Addie showing up tonight with her best friends changed my mood. I wonder if she'll talk to me.

I wonder if I can get her alone.

I hang with my friends and all we can focus on is the upcoming football season. We're finally good, on top of our game, since we're seniors, and after a decent season last year, we're ready to dominate this fall. I offer my opinions while sipping my beer, not wanting to get too drunk tonight. Nothing good comes from that. My parents know I'm here, and they know what we do up at Bayshore. I'm their fourth kid, and all of my siblings did the same thing before me, so they're not completely clueless. As long as I'm safe and don't do anything stupid, they're okay with it.

Well, I don't know if they're actually *okay* with it, but they prefer that I'm honest with them versus sneaking around and lying to them.

I keep it real with my parents, for the most part. Ava is the sneakiest one of the bunch, though honestly, from what I remember, Autumn was sneaking around a lot with Ash back when they were in high school too. I was just a kid and didn't really care. Jake's been pretty straightforward, I think. So maybe it's more of a girl thing?

I don't know. I've always been open and honest with my parents, especially my mom. We're close. But I'm close to my dad too.

People would probably make fun of me if they knew how close. Or they'd be blown away by how much I tell them, though I don't care.

It works for us.

More and more people show up as the night goes on. A few of them bring alcohol, but Dom has a solid connection. Some guy he works with just turned twenty-one and I gave him some cash, and he hooked us up with a decent variety.

Someone else brought their mini speaker and they're playing music from a solid playlist that has some bangers on it. My friends start showing off the drunker they get. Saying stupid shit. Doing stupider shit. Dom grabbed a saw out of the back of his truck for some reason and is taking down a little pine tree that stands nearby, while guys from the football team are encouraging him.

Pretty sure he could get in major trouble for that if a park ranger showed up, but I can't imagine that happening right now.

I'm quiet, listening to everyone talk, while biding my time, not wanting to go over and talk to Addie too soon. Stupid, but I don't want to push. Or make a fool of myself. Everyone thinks I've got my shit under control since I'm popular or whatever, but I'm just as insecure as the next guy, especially when it comes to Addie.

She has no idea how much she means to me.

The girl is clueless.

We're about two hours into the night when I spot her talking with my friend, Liam. Just the two of them chatting it up near a cluster of giant rocks. I can't stop looking at them. To the point that Dom nudges me, jolting me out of my trance.

"You say something?" I ask him.

"I asked if you were going to stop staring at her and just go over there and start talking." Dom shakes his head before tilting it in Addie's direction. "Grow some balls and do it."

"I've got a girlfriend."

"Who's leaving you soon. You told me so yourself, you want to break up with her," Dom points out.

I wince, sipping from my beer. I did tell him that. I've said it a few times. I send Dom a quick look before my gaze goes back to my friend and my crush. "Please tell me Liam isn't interested in Addie."

"I have no idea if he is. That guy doesn't tell me shit," Dom mutters with a shake of his head.

"Me either." Unease fills me as I watch them talk, Addie laughing at something Liam says.

Shit.

"Addie Douglas is open game right now, Callahan. And Sasha's not here. Go talk to her." Dom chuckles.

"It's not like that," I say irritably, hating how he called her open game.

"Then what is it like? Because you've been staring at Addie every time I've caught you in the same room as her for months. Don't bother bringing up Sasha either. I know what's really going on with you two." Dom smirks.

I send him a dirty look. "That's not true. I don't stare at Addie."

It's definitely true, but I don't want to admit it to him.

"Whatever, man. You stick with Sasha who treats you like shit most of the time, when you can bag whoever you want. And that girl over there? The one talking to Liam? She will want you. I see her sending you the same kind of looks you send her so…"

"Really?" I hate the hope in my voice and I clear my throat to hide it. "I don't believe you. Besides, she's talking to Liam."

"Only because you won't talk to her." Dom gives my shoulder a shove, which sends me toppling a bit. And I'm a big guy, though so is Dom. "Go. Say hi. Tell her you want her body before Liam beats you to it."

"I can't do that." I shove him back, annoyed, and he laughs at me, the asshole.

"Why the hell not?"

"I have a girlfriend, asswipe." Annoyance fills me and I try my best to push it away. "What if she's the girl Liam likes?"

"It's on him that he doesn't tell us what's up. Right now, she's fair game, my friend. I say go for it." Dom inclines his head in their direction.

I'm not fair game, though. I'm with someone else, and I don't cheat.

Turning away from him, I head to where Addie and Liam are standing. She's staring up at him as he continues talking, nodding and smiling as if what he's saying is so damn interesting, and I stop right next to her, not saying a word.

Liam pauses mid-sentence when he spots me, his expression turning decidedly unfriendly. "Beck. Hey."

I flick my chin at him in greeting. "What's up?" I glance over at Addie to find her watching me, the faintest smile on her pretty face.

"Hi," she says to me, her voice low.

Inviting.

Liam glares at me, as if I'm infringing on his territory, which is some straight-up bullshit if you ask me. "Mind if I talk to Addison privately for a minute?"

His hesitation is obvious, his gaze cutting to Addie's for a brief moment before he returns his attention to me. "Sure. No problem." He turns and leaves in a literal cloud of dust, which I would find amusing any other night.

But not tonight.

"I think you might've scared him," Addie says once he's gone.

"Why would I scare him? We're friends." I settle on the edge of one of the rocks, a fantasy forming in my head. One where Addie sits on my lap and slings her arms around my neck. I'd put my arms around her waist and kiss her, right in front of everyone.

I wonder what she tastes like.

I've wondered that for a long-ass time.

"You mow guys down on the football field." She waves a hand in my direction. "You're intimidating."

"You think I'm intimidating?" I raise my brows, surprised.

"No, I don't think so. But everyone else might." She shakes her head, her lips curling into a barely-there smile. "You don't scare me, Callahan. I knew you back when you got the wind knocked out of you at a youth league football game, and you cried for your mom as they carried you off the field."

Shit. I remember that. A humiliating, adolescent moment. "You were there?"

"Heck yeah. I was on the youth cheer team that one year, remember?"

I do remember. Back when seeing girls in short skirts didn't do much for me.

Times have definitely changed.

"Why'd you quit?" I ask her.

"My mom said I needed to choose—volleyball or cheer. They're both huge commitments. I liked volleyball a lot more so that's what I stuck with. Really, I just wanted to be like my big sister," she says, referring to Jocelyn.

What I've heard from Jake and Ava is that Jos was a great volleyball player in high school, but I'm pretty sure Addie's better.

"Don't we all?" I scratch the back of my neck. "I got into football because of Jake. And my dad, of course."

"Of course. Your dad is an NFL legend. And your brother is on his way to becoming a legend too." Addie smiles, not fazed by my dad's fame whatsoever—or Jake's. Most people who go to our high school aren't. Drew Callahan is a fixture on the football field since he's been coaching the varsity team for years. They're used to seeing him around.

And Jake went to our high school—he's not the only pro

football player to graduate from here. My sister Autumn's husband Ash Davis went pro, and Addie's brother-in-law Diego Garcia plays for the NFL too. They were both coached by my dad, which is totally cool.

"You're a great volleyball player," I tell her, and I'm not just saying it either. "I've watched you play a few times."

"More like most of the time." I chance a look at her and the glow in her eyes is freakin' mesmerizing. "I like how you football guys always show up to our games."

"You do the same for us," I say with a shrug. A lot of my friends from the football team will attend the volleyball games with me, only because I convince them to. Plus, it's a great time for all of us to be social in the stands, which we never get to do since we're always at practice or at a game. Though really?

I'm just there to watch Addie.

She always looks damn good in the uniforms. The tight-fitting tops and the short shorts that show off her long, toned legs.

My gaze drops to those legs, appreciative of the leggings she's wearing.

"Athletes taking care of each other then?" she asks.

"Yeah, for sure." I glance around before I return my attention to her, my gaze snagging on her blue eyes and how she's looking at me right now. As if she might be…

Interested.

I'm probably just getting my hopes up.

"You wanna go sit somewhere and talk?" I ask her out of nowhere.

That wasn't very smooth, but it's the best I've got.

"Aren't we doing that right now?" She laughs.

"Yeah, but maybe…somewhere more private?" Oh fuck, where am I going with this? Not like I drank a lot, so it's not alcohol that's making me so bold. This is some risky shit, considering Sasha's not here and all kinds of people are, who'll report back to her.

"Um, sure." She ducks her head, tucking a thick strand of brown hair behind her ear. "Where are you thinking?"

"My car, maybe?" We glance over at my SUV and realize there are tons of people standing around it, drinking and laughing. Not a one of them is paying attention to us. "Or maybe not."

"How about my car?" she suggests.

I raise my brows. "Do you mind?"

She slowly shakes her head. "No. Plus, it's getting kind of cold standing out here. I'll grab a blanket from the trunk and we can chill in my car."

I tell myself not to get excited, but chilling in Addie's car while we're sharing a blanket sounds promising as hell.

You shouldn't even be thinking like this. Don't be an asshole. She's your friend. That's it. You have a girlfriend. Even if you're not into her anymore, you need to break things off with Sasha. She's a nice girl. You've had a great relationship, but now it's over.

Make it official before you do something stupid and Sasha finds out.

Ignoring the very practical voice in my head that sounds suspiciously like my mother, I follow Addie to her car, noting how dark and desolate it feels the farther out we are from where everyone's clustered together. She unlocks the doors and goes to the trunk, lifting the lid to grab a couple of blankets out of it before she slams it closed.

"You come prepared," I say as I approach the passenger side of the car.

"I don't like freezing my ass off out here," she says with a laugh as she opens the driver's side door.

I copy her, opening the passenger side and climbing inside. I immediately push the seat back to accommodate my long legs, and I let out a huff of surprise when she tosses a blanket at me, hitting me in the head.

Pulling it away from my face, I glance over to find her smiling at me.

"Sorry," she says, not sounding sorry at all.

"Uh, thanks?" I shake the blanket out and drape it over me, noting how it's pale pink and dotted with white hearts. "It's so…cute."

I make a face, which only makes her laugh harder. "It was my Valentine's Day present this year."

I'm about to shove it off me in disgust.

"—from my mom," she finishes.

I find her gaze again to check if she's playing me.

She's just smiling, looking pleased with herself.

"How sweet." I nod toward the blanket currently sitting in her lap. I'm just damn grateful the blanket I'm using didn't come from her ex. "Where'd you get that one?"

"My sister got it for me for Christmas a couple of years ago." She shakes out the pale blue blanket, so it covers her bottom half. "Kind of one of our school colors, you know?"

"Sure." I lean back in my seat, glancing up at the ceiling to see she has a sun roof. "Hey," I slide the cover open, exposing the glass, "we can see the stars."

"We can, huh?" She hits the start engine button on her Honda and slides open the window partway, letting in a whoosh of cool air. She shivers, pulling her throw blanket up to her chin.

"We can shut it if you want," I tell her, not wanting her to freeze. That was half the reason why she wanted to come to her car and talk to me in the first place.

I mean, maybe it could have something to do with me, but maybe not. I'm not getting my hopes up. Addie has me in the friend zone for sure, where I deserve to be.

"No, this is fun. We can lean back our chairs." She does exactly that, so she's practically laid out flat on the seat.

I run my eyes over her, lingering on all my favorite parts, though I can't see much thanks to that damn blanket covering her. She turns her head toward me, an expectant look on her pretty face. "You going to join me?"

I immediately go into action, putting the seat back until I'm pretty much horizontal, my knees practically hitting the dash. I try to get more comfortable, tugging the blanket over me, but fail. Addie stretches over the console, grabbing the edge of the blanket and pulling it into place so I'm mostly covered. "There you go," she murmurs as she settles back into her seat.

I stare at her for a moment, at a loss for words. Swallowing hard, I jerk my gaze to the window above us, staring at the stars in the black sky. In the distance, I can still hear the music playing, though it's more the throbbing of the beat versus the actual song. There are people talking, but I can't make out what they're saying.

It's as if we're locked away in our own little world.

"I'm glad it's clear tonight," Addie says. "We can see the stars."

"Yeah." That's all I can manage to say. I'd rather stare at her instead of the sky.

I wonder what she'd do if I scooted closer and took her hand in mine.

"Don't they feel like you can reach out and touch them?" She stretches her arm out, the blanket falling, her hand drawing closer to the open window above us. "I sound silly."

She's about to drop her arm, but I take my chance and grab her hand, interlacing my fingers with hers. "No, you don't," I say, my voice serious.

Her hand is much smaller in mine and I sweep my thumb across hers, nice and slow.

Fuck, I feel that touch deep inside me, and I immediately want more.

Addie turns to look at me, and I realize our faces are close. Really close. Our hands still interlocked. My gaze drops to her mouth and all I can think about is kissing her.

That's it. That's all I want. To lose myself in Addie's lips.

"Oh my God!"

CHAPTER 3

ADDIE

I nearly jump out of my skin when I hear a loud thump against my window. I tear my gaze from Beck's to see Tori standing there, her hands braced on the glass, her expression...

Green.

That's when she opens her mouth and vomits all over the driver's side window and door.

"Oh shit." Beck lets go of my hand and jumps out of the car, then ducks back in to wave at me. "Come out this side."

I do as he says, taking his hand and letting him pull me out. I'm not a delicate flower. Meaning, I'm no dainty girl who weighs nothing. I'm solid, thanks to all the volleyball playing over the years, and I know I could be considered heavy, especially compared to other girls.

Beck just hauled me out of my car with a gentle tug of his hand, as if I weighed nothing, which is pretty impressive.

And I don't know what was about to happen between us just then, right before Tori threw herself at my car and puked all over it, but I think...

I think he was staring at my lips.

Like he was contemplating kissing me.

Nah.

No way. He wouldn't do that. He's with Sasha. They're in love or whatever. We're just friends.

So why did he take my hand?

Pushing all confusing thoughts dealing with Beck out of my head, we round the car together to the driver's side and find Tori hunched over, saliva streaming from her mouth in a long string. The smell hits me and I wrinkle my nose, glancing up at Beck to find him standing there frozen, with a vaguely horrified expression on his face.

"Addie," Tori groans, blindly reaching out to brace her hand against my car, her palm smacking right into the vomit. "Help me."

I bolt into action, going to her, not sure what to do first. It's one of those overwhelming situations where there's so much going on, I don't know where to start.

"Beck." I turn, offering him a faint smile. "I have a couple of bottles of water inside the car. Will you grab them for me?"

"Will do." He runs off, seemingly glad to be given a task.

He probably is. This is a nightmare. The last thing I expected to do tonight is clean up Tori's vomit off my freaking car. And where's Emma anyway?

I carefully step around the vomit, though I feel my shoe landing in some anyway, as I approach Tori. "You okay, Tor?" I ask softly.

She shakes her head, lifting it so I can see into her bloodshot and watery eyes. "I feel disgusting."

"Even after puking?"

Tori makes a face, closing her eyes. "Please don't say that word."

"We need to get you cleaned up."

Beck chooses that moment to appear with three, mostly

full, bottles of water gathered in his arms. He hands one over and I take it, cracking it open and immediately splashing the side of my car to wash off the vomit.

"I'm so sorry," Tori says, and I swear she sounds like she's crying. "I didn't mean to do that to your car."

"No more cheap vodka for you," I mutter as I take the next bottle and twist the lid off, washing off the last remnants before I reach for the door handle and open it. I bend down and hit the lever to open my trunk. "Can you grab a couple more waters from the trunk, Beck?"

"Sure." He goes to grab some and comes back with two unopened bottles. "You have an entire case in there."

"You never know what could happen." I shrug as I crack the lid and then hand it to Tori.

She takes it and drinks from the bottle greedily, finishing almost half in a few swallows.

"Slow down," I tell her. "You don't want to throw up again."

"I keep a case in my car too. Learned it from Jake," Beck continues, sounding impressed.

I smile at him, wishing I didn't have to take care of my friend. There is so much I don't know about this boy and I want to learn *everything*.

"Oh God." Tori at least whirls away from the car this time, throwing up on the ground. It hits with a loud splatter and my stomach turns.

Dang. And this night held so much promise.

Too bad it's ruined now.

* * *

ONCE I HELP Tori get cleaned up and Beck helps me get her into the back seat of my car, where she promptly passes out, we go in search of Emma, who I find sitting with a smaller group of football players near the fire, her gaze locked on Marcus, her ex-boyfriend from the beginning of our junior year.

"Hey," I call to her. She glances up when she hears me, her eyes widening slightly when she spots who's standing next to me. "We should probably go."

Emma's face falls. "I don't want to go yet. The night has barely begun. And we always stay the night."

I go to her, lowering my voice as I kneel beside her. "Tori threw up. She's passed out in the back seat of my car."

"Let her sleep it off then," Emma whispers, her gaze snagging on Marcus as he gets up and walks away. The disappointment on her face is clear. "I was just talking to him until you interrupted me."

"Sorry. Thought you'd care that our best friend barfed all over the driver's side of my car," I say, rising to my feet.

Emma starts laughing. "Oh God, really? Wish I would've seen that."

"No, you really don't." I glance around when I realize Beck is nowhere to be found. Where'd he go? "I think I'm going to take her home."

"Are you sober?"

"I am now." Cleaning up someone else's puke will sober you up right quick. "And I really don't want to stick around."

Emma snags my hand and yanks me back down, so I'm kneeling beside her once more. "Saw who was by your side earlier. Beck. What's up with that?"

"We were just talking." I shrug.

The look she sends me is shrewd, as if she has me all figured out. "Uh huh. You trying to start something with him? Don't forget he's still with Sasha."

I don't really like the tone of her voice or the look on her face, as if she thinks I'm making a huge mistake. Worse, she's making me feel like I'm wasting my time—which I so am, meaning I don't need the reminder. "Are you trying to start something back up with Marcus?"

Her expression shutters, closing right up. "Of course not."

Marcus is her Achilles heel, the one who got away. The one she regrets losing.

"Don't forget he's with Monique." Sort of. They flirt. I think they even hook up on occasion, but they don't really commit to each other.

She's my secret archnemesis, who used to be my sort of friend. The girl who chased after Beck every chance she got when she knew at one point, I was trying to chase after him too. In middle school.

Ah, those were the days.

They were awful.

Emma makes a face, then waves her hand, dismissing my words. "They're not together. They just hook up on occasion."

Yikes. "And you're okay with that?"

"Once he's back with me, he won't feel the need to be with Monique anymore." The smirk on Emma's face is downright triumphant. "I hope you don't mind that I'm staying."

"Where are you going to sleep?" I ask.

"Don't worry about me. I'm sure I can stay with Marcus in his car. And there probably won't be any sleeping going on either." She laughs.

Guess she has no problem hooking up with him, even though what she really wants is a commitment from Marcus.

Whatever.

I head back to my car, not surprised at all when I spot Beck pulling away from his group of friends to come talk to me.

"Are you leaving?"

"Yeah, I need to get Tori home before she pukes in the back seat of my car." I wince.

He grimaces. "Not gonna lie, that was fuckin' gross."

I can't help but laugh. Beck doesn't curse much around me, though I know he has a mouth on him. I hear the way his friends talk—and the way he talks when he's with them.

"It was so gross," I agree. "She's passed out right now."

"You sure you can't stay a little longer?"

Oh, I definitely want to, but I can't leave her back there.

Can I?

"Beck!" screeches a familiar female voice.

We both turn to see—oh good lord—Monique approaching.

Beck stiffens, his entire mood shifting. "Hey."

She comes right up to Beck, placing herself in between us as she throws her arms around him in an exuberant hug. He barely touches her as he returns it, his hands lightly patting her back before they spring away from her.

"What are you doing, talking to Addison?" Monique sends me the evil eye and I glare at her in return. "Where's Sasha? Doesn't she usually keep you on a tight leash?"

From the stormy expression that suddenly appears on Beck's face, that was the wrong thing to say.

"No, she doesn't keep me on a tight leash," he says through clenched lips. "I can talk to whoever the fuck I want."

"Oooh, so feisty." Monique laughs. "I find it weird, how you two are always hanging out together, when Beck has a girlfriend. I'm sure Sasha won't like to hear that you were in Addie's car earlier."

Damn it. Of all the people to see that, it had to be Monique.

"We've known each other a long time," Beck says, his

voice full of irritation. "Our families are friends. We were just talking."

"Tell that to your girlfriend, who's not here tonight." Monique grins, and that does it.

I'm out of here.

Whirling away from the two of them, I march back to my car, checking on Tori to find she's kind of awake, a water bottle clutched in her hand, her face pale, but at least it's not green anymore.

"You want to leave?" I ask her.

"Yeah," she practically groans. "I still feel awful."

"I'll take you home then. I don't mind." I'm about to shut the door, but she says something, making me pause.

"I'm sorry. I'm totally ruining your good time, huh?" Her gaze meets mine, her expression pained.

I glance over my shoulder, watching with disgust as Monique continues talking to Beck. He doesn't even notice me. Instead, his attention is completely focused on her.

Turning back to Tori, I smile at her. "You're not the one ruining my good time," I say, just before I slam the door.

That's Monique.

Oh, and Beck too.

CHAPTER 4

BECK

"What the fuck, Callahan? Why'd you pull that stunt with Addison a couple of nights ago?"

I turn to find Liam standing in front of me, his hands on his hips and a ferocious glare on his face.

He's pissed, and I know exactly why.

But I decide to play dumb.

"What are you talking about?" I ask with a frown, scratching my temple.

It's Monday afternoon and we're currently taking a short break during football practice. School starts Thursday. We're playing a scrimmage game Friday night at home, but those don't count. They don't even let us put a score on the board.

I hate scrimmage games. Why can't they just let us play for real? It doesn't have to count toward the season, but no. That's not how we do it before the season kicks off.

Doesn't really matter though, because I'm always keeping track of the score in my head.

"You know what I'm talking about. Saturday night at your little get-together." The last three words are said in a snide tone, and I can tell Liam is actually put out. "You asked to talk to Addie alone and just pulled her away from our conversation, like you own her or some shit. You've already got a girlfriend, so stop stealing hot chicks from your friends."

Hey, he let her go, so it's kind of on him. Not that I tell Liam that. Instead, I shrug, trying to play it off. "I had stuff to tell her."

"Really? Well, whatever. I'm staking my claim." The look on Liam's face is pure determination.

"Staking your *claim?*" My voice rises, and Dom chooses that moment to approach us, concern etched in his features.

The three of us have been close since freshman year. Dom and I have been best friends since middle school and we met Liam the first day of high school football practice, immediately taking him into our friend group. We're tight. And we've never fought over the same girl.

Until now.

Not that I can fight over Addie. I'm still with Sasha. We were supposed to get together Sunday night after she came home from Tahoe, but she never called me to let me know she got home.

Considering I planned on breaking up with her last night, I was fucking bummed. But it's going to happen.

Soon.

"Everything cool here, dudes?" Dom asks.

Liam doesn't even look in his direction, completely ignoring Dom's question. "Yeah. I'm staking my claim. I've been interested in Addie ever since she broke things off with Jonah. You and Addie have known each other a long time, I get that you two are friends. But I actually *like* her."

The words, *I like her too*, hang on the tip of my tongue, just dying to get out. I part my lips, almost ready to say it when Dom interrupts.

"What's up with Monique hanging all over you?" he asks me.

Shit.

Liam's brows shoot up. "What the hell, bro? It's not enough that you already have a girlfriend yet you steal Addie away from me for the rest of the night. But then you go and flirt with Monique too?"

We all know Monique flirts with every guy on this team. Every guy in our class. Pretty much every guy in the junior class too. And once she runs through all of us—which she's real close to doing—she'll probably check out the sophomores. Maybe even the freshmen.

Yeah, she's that girl. The one who won't settle down with just one guy when there are a whole bunch of others she can talk to and flirt with. I'm not slut-shaming Monique—my mama beat that out of me eons ago, as did Ava—but damn, the girl is the worst.

Doesn't help that she's not particularly nice either. She's never been that nice—her ego is too big. Yeah, she's gorgeous and she's got a nice body, but that only gets you so far. She might've been trying to hang all over me Saturday night, but I was shoving her away from me as much as possible. I'm not interested in her.

I never have been.

"It's nothing. You know how she is," I say, trying to brush the moment off.

"Looked like something to me," Dom says, wagging his brows and smiling like this is one big joke.

I glare at him. Liam glares at me.

"Well, I'm saying it again in case you forgot—I'm staking my claim on Addie. I'm interested," Liam says, his words only for me. "I've liked her for months."

"Huh. Yet you never managed to tell us who you were

simping over until just now," Dom points out. "Kind of lame, if you ask me."

"Fuck off," Liam tells him, and not good-naturedly either. "I don't need you two ganging up on me."

Before I can say a word in my defense, Liam stomps off, heading for the offensive line, who are all standing clustered together with their coach, who looks ready to launch into a huge speech.

"What's his problem?" Dom mutters once Liam's out of ear shot.

"He's mad I supposedly stole Addie away from him Saturday night." I turn my glare onto Dom. "That was your idea, by the way."

Dom shrugs, his expression pure innocence. "How were we supposed to know he has a thing for Addison? He hasn't told us shit. That guy always keeps his feelings to himself."

Whereas Dom loves to blab his feelings to anyone who wants to hear them. I love my best friend. He's loyal, and I can trust he's always got my back. We don't keep anything from each other for the most part, but I've never really talked much about my feelings for Addie with him. They've always felt too...special.

Okay that sounds lame as hell even in my head, but I can't help but feel that way.

And that's exactly why I keep my feelings about Addie mostly to myself—kind of like Liam.

"What am I supposed to do?" I turn to face Dom fully, my voice low. "Just let him stake his claim and back off from her?"

Just the idea of letting Liam have his chance with Addie sends a sharp spear straight into my gut. It's that fucking painful.

"First, you've got Sasha, so you can't say shit until you end things with her." He pauses for only a moment. "You're planning on ending things with her, right?"

I lower my voice. "I was going to break up with her last night when we got together, but she bailed on me at the last minute."

"About damn time." Dom holds his hand up for a high five and I slap it halfheartedly. "Get rid of her and then you can pursue Addie."

"I can't do that if Liam is into her." Just saying those words makes me feel miserable.

"Wait a minute. Doesn't it kind of matter what Addie thinks about you two assholes?" Dom points out.

"Probably." A ragged exhale leaves me. The problem is I have no clue what she's thinking. We've danced around each other for years, the attraction between us always right there, growing and growing.

At least it was for me.

Was it for her?

And now here's Liam 'staking his claim,' like some sort of gold mining prospector. I remember learning that shit in the fourth grade when we studied the history of California, so I know what I'm talking about.

Well, Addie isn't a piece of property he can claim. She's an actual human being with thoughts and feelings, and we're not even taking those into consideration.

Oh, and I'm a complete dick to insert myself into this situation when I already have a girlfriend. Doesn't matter that I plan on breaking up with her next time I see her, I have no business thinking I have a chance with Addie when I'm still with Sasha.

I'm an asshole. If my mother knew I was thinking like this, she'd probably call me an asshole to my face.

I stew over the situation for the rest of practice. To the point that I'm extra aggressive out on the field and take out a few guys on my team when I ram my body into theirs. I'm surly and noncommunicative and every time Liam glances in my direction, he has a knowing look on his smug face that tells me he's aware of what's bothering me and he likes that he's the cause of it.

Such a bunch of bullshit.

"Callahan, get your ass over here," my dad hollers at the end of practice, just as I'm grabbing my water bottle from where I left it beneath the bench.

I take a long drink before I snap the lid closed and jog over to where my father is standing on the sidelines, a stern expression on his face.

A face I look a lot like, though not fully. My brother Jake is more my dad's clone. I'm a solid mix of both my parents with some throwback genes in there, making it so nobody can figure out exactly who I resemble.

"What's up?" I ask, once I'm standing directly in front of him. The rest of the coaching staff is already leaving, so it's just the two of us. Considering he's my ride home, I don't understand why he just doesn't talk to me when we're in his truck and headed back to the house.

"Son, you need to be careful out there." His voice and his expression are both so damn serious, I start to feel remorseful about my behavior out on the field. "You're a lot stronger compared to some of those guys and I don't want you hurting anyone."

"Got it. Sorry," I say with a single nod, my voice clipped.

Dad tilts his head to the side as he considers me. "Something bothering you?"

"Nah." I shrug, trying to play it off. "I'm fine."

"You were good out there today." Reaching out, he settles his hand on my shoulder, giving it a shake since I have my practice gear on. I remember when I was little and absolutely idolized him. There was no one better than my dad. Who else could say their father played professional football and won a couple of Super Bowls?

Not very many kids. Not any of the kids at my school could make that claim, and it made me feel special. I played football because of my dad and my brother. We both wanted to be just like our dad growing up.

Jake's playing professionally and my dad is always saying I could do the same, if I really wanted to. I'm not a quarterback like them, but I have the potential. I just need to bulk up more if I want a shot, but I don't know if either of those things are possible.

I'm not so sure I want a shot, though. Is that what I want to do with my life? Play football in college and go on to play in the NFL, if I'm lucky enough?

It's dangerous, especially being a defensive lineman, which is a position I was drawn to since I was a little kid. I had no problem mowing kids down on the field, and I was always big for my age. I'm not as big as a lot of the pros, though I'm fast—and fearless. The position is risky. I could get hurt and destroy my career.

Not sure if I want to take that risk.

"Thank you," I tell him as his hand drops. Dad's getting older. He's just as lean as he was when he was playing professionally, but he doesn't have as much muscle. Plus, he's got gray hair at his temples, though Mom constantly tells him she thinks the grays are sexy.

I always roll my eyes and pretend I didn't hear her say that.

"I still can't believe that you're taller than me," Dad says, after he grabs his bag and slings the strap over his shoulder and we're walking side by side to the parking lot. "You and Jake both."

"Face it, you're a shrimp, Dad." I'm teasing him. He's not a shrimp, but shit, I'm almost six-foot-five. Jake is closer to six-four, so I just barely stand taller than him.

Which irritates the shit out of my brother, not that he would ever admit it out loud.

"What the hell ever," he mutters, though he's grinning. "You ready for Friday's scrimmage."

"Ready to kick some ass." We scrimmage the same team every year. Le Grand is a solid team, but for the most part, we always manage to come out on top.

"As always," Dad adds, his attention zeroing in on my friends who are clustered next to Dom's giant-ass truck. "I'm surprised you're not going to hang out with them."

He tips his head in their direction.

"I might still. You never know." It's not like I want to continue the conversation with Liam, but I do need to know what's going on inside his head. And clarify the possessive statement he made about Addie.

The more I think about it, the madder I get.

"Yo, Beck, we're going to Pete's," Dom calls as my dad and I draw closer. He's referring to a local restaurant that serves the best cheeseburgers and chicken strips in the area. "Wanna come with?"

I glance over at my father who's already nodding. "Go with them. Have fun. You've only got a few more days until school starts."

"Thanks, Dad." I hand him my bag full of my football gear and give him a quick slap on the shoulder before I leave him for my friends, who are all watching me expectantly.

With the exception of Liam. He's too busy tapping away on his phone.

Texting Addie, maybe?

Jealousy rises, which makes my temper rise as well. But I tamp it down, telling myself to chill the hell out. I have other things to take care of before I can worry about Liam with Addie.

Like end things with Sasha.

* * *

WE PLACE our orders at the front counter at Pete's Place and find a giant table, where we're all sitting at now, involved in both one table-wide conversation about football and the upcoming season, as well as separate, more one-on-one conversations. Like the one I'm currently having with Dom.

"Hey, watch out for Monique, okay?" His brows shoot up.

I take a giant gulp of my Dr. Pepper before I speak. "You know I'm not interested in her. I shoved her off me as quick as I could."

"Guess she's coming for you this year?"

"When is she not?" A chuckle slips out, and I'm trying to treat the moment lightly, but I still hate how Dom mentioned it in front of Liam earlier.

Dom laughs. "Just—keep her away from you. Marcus might not like it."

Right. Because Marcus and Monique hook up on occasion. They have all summer. "Trust me. He can have her."

"You sure? She gives it up easy," Dom reminds me, like that's what I want.

No thanks.

I shake my head. "I'm not interested in that."

"Why the hell not? *Everyone's* interested in that." Dom laughs, and I glare at him.

"Not me," I say firmly.

"Aw, Mr. Serious. Always looking for a long-term girlfriend, not a girl who's DTF." When I send him a confused look, he explains himself. "Down to fuck."

I roll my eyes, grateful when the girl at the counter calls

my order number. I go grab my tray of food—a cheeseburger *and* chicken strips, plus a boatload of fries—and make my way back to the table. I settle into my seat and start eating, ignoring everyone around me.

"Better watch yourself, Callahan. You're eating enough for three," Liam says, making other guys at the table laugh and say stupid shit with him. "Don't wanna get fat. The ladies might not like it."

I set my cheeseburger in the paper-lined basket it came in and send Liam a death glare from across the table. "Fuck off, bro."

Liam laughs, though there's nothing humorous about the sound. This guy is my friend, yet he's acting like a complete dick right now. All over a girl? I mean, I get it. Addie's pretty damn special, but he doesn't even know her. "I bet Monique won't like it if you get soft in the middle."

The entire table goes quiet, all eyes on Marcus, who's sitting on the other side of the table and a few chairs down.

He appears completely unaffected though. He's too busy stuffing his face full of fries. It's only when he swallows that he announces, "Fuck that ho. She's too busy trying to grab onto every dick she sees. I'm tired of it."

Laughter erupts and someone even high fives Marcus. I drop my head, concentrating on my early dinner, pissed that Liam called me out about Monique.

"What about Sasha?" someone else asks. "Bet she'd be pissed if he got fat."

I glare at the kid. His name is Danny. He follows Liam everywhere he goes because they both warm the bench together for most of our games. "You better watch what you say."

"Yeah, watch it, fucker," Dom adds.

"Leave Danny alone. Both of you," Liam says, rushing to

his bench-warming buddy's defense. "Worry about Sasha and I'll worry about Addison."

I hate that he said her name. That he gets to worry about her and I don't.

Conversation goes on around us, but Dom and I are quiet, ignoring them. I pick at my food, my appetite leaving me.

"That was a dick move, what Liam said," Dom finally mutters, so only I can hear him. "He's on your case."

"Yeah, he is." I wipe my fingers with a napkin and take a sip of my drink before I continue. "He must really like Addie."

Which makes me feel like shit. Maybe Liam was right, and I shouldn't have pulled her away from him so I could talk to her like I did Saturday night. But shit, I had no idea Liam even liked her—pretty sure none of us did, or that she was the girl he was waiting to show up at the party.

Exactly like *I* was.

Damn. This is all kinds of messed up.

"You two need to talk it out," Dom says. "Like for real. He can't just walk up to you and call dibs. That's some bullshit."

"Is it though? I can't call dibs on her. I'm with Sasha."

"You said you're ending it."

"I am, but I haven't yet." I pick up a chicken strip, wrinkling my nose at it before I let it drop back into the basket, my appetite now completely gone.

Why didn't I think one of my friends would eventually realize just how great Addie is? It's hard not to like the same girls. Sometimes we even eventually date the same ones, since our school is so small. The field is only so big, meaning our choices aren't varied.

No one from my friend group has tried to date Addie, though. She went out with Jonah, the band geek, most of our junior year, so I guess no one bothered even thinking about her.

Clearly that's changed, thanks to Liam. It's senior year and we're all aware of the potential prospects. Though I don't view her that way.

"Maybe I should let him shoot his shot and see what happens," I say, my voice purposely casual. Inside though, I'm a mess.

What if he shoots his shot and fucking succeeds? And I'm left longing for Addie while she's with someone else?

No. I can't do it. Not again. I can't stand by and let someone else have a chance and not take my own.

"What if they get together? How are you going to feel then? You going to just stand by and let it happen?" Dom asks.

"I don't know what to do." I shrug, feeling helpless.

And that's not an emotion I experience often.

Except when it comes to Addie. For some reason, that girl always has me twisted up. Feeling helpless and stupid.

It sucks.

CHAPTER 5

ADDIE

"Okay, you need to spill," Tori says, the moment she barges into my bedroom. I knew she was coming over, so it's no surprise that she's here.

I glance up from my perch on my bed, where I'm curled up beneath one of my endless throw blankets I keep in here. Mom and Dad blast the air conditioner all summer long and it's always freezing in our house. "Spill what?"

There are all sorts of things I could spill about. Beck. Liam. I need to know exactly what she's referring to first.

Tori shuts the door and joins me on my bed, lying down next to me so her face is practically in mine, her brows arched and her gaze knowing. "You haven't mentioned Beck Callahan once to me since the party. I'm starting to think he's your dirty little secret."

Ha, in my dreams.

"I haven't mentioned him because there's nothing to say. He has a girlfriend." I roll so I'm lying flat on my back, staring up at the ceiling.

"They haven't broken up yet?" Tori sounds confused.

I sit up quickly, shocked by her question. "No." I draw the word out. "Were they supposed to break up?"

She sits up as well, her expression shifting, and I swear she's trying to appear innocent. "Not that I know of."

"Then why did you say that?" I ask, skeptically. I think she's hiding something.

Tori shrugs. "I thought you two were looking extra cozy Saturday night. He wasn't trying to make a move on you?"

"No," I say firmly. "We're just friends. Remember?"

"Right. Okay." She nods. "I also saw you talking to Liam."

"Yeah. He's nice." Now it's my turn to shrug. "He's been texting me."

"What! Really?"

I glance over at her, noting her shocked face. "Yes, really. Why? Do you know something I don't?"

Tori slowly shakes her head. "Of course not. I just—I don't know what I'm trying to say."

I remain quiet, wondering at her remark about Beck and Sasha breaking up. In my dreams that happened, but it's not like he'd want to rush into another relationship—with me.

Clearly, I must be dreaming.

"I've got news." When my gaze finds Tori's, she smiles. "I've been talking with Dom."

I bump my shoulder into hers. "No way."

She nods, excitement making her practically vibrate. "Yes. We were talking Saturday night up at Bayshore and I was a little drunk, you know?"

"More like a lot drunk," I remind her.

"Yes, oh my God, I made an absolute fool of myself, barfing everywhere, but I don't think he saw it, thank goodness. He found out though. And then he texted me Sunday morning on Snap, asking if I was feeling okay." Her expression turns dreamy. "Isn't that sweet?"

"Who told him you threw up? My car was parked pretty

far away from everyone and no one else was with us." Except for Beck.

Sitting in my car, staring at the stars, my hand in his.

The look on his face...

Like he was thinking about kissing me.

I've had more missed opportunities with Beck than any other human on the planet, I swear.

"Beck was." The sly smile on her face is obvious. "This is why I asked you what's up. Even in my drunken state, I noticed who was with you in your car."

"Nothing happened," I tell her, and I see the apology in her gaze.

"I interrupted you guys, huh? I'm so sorry."

"You don't have to apologize. Nothing can happen. He's got a girlfriend, remember?"

Tori's eyes are huge as she studies me. "If I tell you something, can you promise to keep it a secret?"

My heart starts to hammer against my ribs. "Of course."

"Dom told me Beck wants to end things with Sasha before she leaves for college," Tori admits.

This news should not make me happy, but I can't help it.

It does.

"Why does he want to break up with her?"

"Things haven't been good between them for a while, I guess. Beck wants to be a free man for his senior year. Not that I can blame him," Tori says. "And think about Sasha. Why would she want to go away to college and leave behind her high school boyfriend? That's kind of lame."

When Tori wrinkles her nose, I can't help but laugh, and she joins me.

"What will you do if he breaks up with Sasha?" Tori asks me once our laughter has died.

"What can I do? I'm kind of talking to Liam."

Tori's eyes go wide. "Is it official? Man, he moves quick."

"Of course not. It's only been a few days," I tell her, my tone a little chastising. Tori always jumps to conclusions, but I don't mind. She's always so sweet and positive, and lots of fun to hang out with.

Lately, she's been more fun than Emma, who's always in a bad mood. Everything bugs her. She's never happy—with herself or with any of us.

It wears on a person, always being in a bad mood. It wears on the people around her too.

"Tell me about you and Dom," I say to Tori, desperate to change the subject.

She's had a minor crush on him since the end of our junior year, when he walked by her in the hall and whistled at her, calling out, "Nice legs."

That was it, she was done for. She's set her sights on him and no one else ever since.

"We've been texting all week," Tori says excitedly. "Just normal conversation stuff. He hasn't asked me out or anything like that, but I get this feeling…like why would he keep talking to me if he wasn't interested, you know?"

I nod, my smile pasted on my face while my heart drops into my stomach.

I wish it was Beck who was texting me and not Liam.

I think he's interested in me.

And while Liam is nice and we've been chatting via text on Snap and DMing each other on Insta the last few days, I don't really feel anything when it comes to him beyond friendship. Though Liam is cute, not gonna lie. Dark blond hair that's a little too long. It curls around his face, getting in his eyes so has to shake it back. Deep brown eyes and a nice smile. If Beck wasn't around, I would totally go for it.

But Beck's around. Meaning, I don't want to go for it.

My phone dings and I check it to see a text from Emma. "Emma will be here in a few," I tell Tori.

"Cool." Tori nods, hopping off the bed and going to the backpack I didn't even see her drop by the door. "I brought a bunch of options for tomorrow."

She brought clothes and Emma is supposed to as well, so we can give each other a live and in-person fit check on our first day of school looks.

Tori's already trying on stuff when Emma walks into my room, her attitude breezy as she tosses a shopping bag onto my bed.

"I only brought one outfit," she says.

I frown. "Why?"

"Marcus and I were on FaceTime last night and he helped me pick my outfit." Her smile is full of confidence. "We're basically back together."

"Oh my God, that's so exciting!" Tori jumps up and down, clad only in jeans and a bra. She gushes as per usual, asking all of the proper questions while Emma answers her with the haughty casualness of someone who's very comfortable in her current position.

In other words, Emma thinks she's got Marcus exactly where she wants him, which is probably true. I have no idea what it feels like, to have that much confidence when it comes to relationships with boys. Even when I was with Jonah, I was always a little nervous and unsure. Worried I might do something dumb.

I remain quiet as Emma goes on about Marcus. The way she talks about him, I'm guessing they had sex at Bayshore Saturday night. Not like she's flat-out giving Tori vivid details, but she's alluding to it. The minute Tori starts talking about Dom and what's going on between them, I can tell Emma's tuning her out.

I love my best friend, but sometimes she can be selfish. Like now. If we're not talking about her and her latest relationship, she doesn't care what anyone else has to say about their life.

And that kind of sucks.

"I heard a rumor," Emma declares, once Tori's tried on a variety of shirts and has finally decided on one. "About you."

I turn to face her when I realize she's talking about me. "What did you hear?"

"That you and Liam have been talking a lot lately."

My gaze finds Tori's real quick—she appears ready to burst, like she can't contain what I told her earlier—before I return my attention to Emma. "We've been texting, yeah."

I purposely keep my voice calm. Level. Like it's no big deal.

Really, it's not a big deal—not to me.

"Marcus told me Liam really likes you," Emma continues.

She sounds like we're in the sixth grade and just discovered boys.

"We've been texting over the last few days," I admit.

"I've heard." She smirks at Tori, who laughs extra loud, making me wince.

I withhold the sigh that wants to escape and check out my outfit in the full-length mirror in my room. I'm wearing mom jeans and a tight-fitting black top that's cropped, but my jeans are so high waisted, only a sliver of skin is revealed. Hopefully I won't get dress-coded.

"Your outfit is so cute. Love the jeans. Are you trying to impress Liam?" Emma asks as she walks up behind me, looking at my outfit in the mirror.

"Just trying to find an outfit I feel confident in for the first day of school tomorrow." I'm being honest right now. I don't care what anyone else thinks of my outfit.

I'm just doing this for me.

"Rumor has it Liam is going to ask you to wear his jersey for next week's game," Emma says.

"Oh my gosh, I didn't even think of that. I hope Dom asks

me. Then we'll all be able to wear jerseys on Friday together! All three of us!" Tori starts bouncing up and down again, clapping her hands like an overexcited seal. I can't help but laugh, though Emma seems annoyed.

It's customary for football players to ask the girl they're interested in/dating to wear their jersey on game day. It's a big deal for girls to walk around the halls at school, flaunting their boy's number on their chest. I can't deny that it's kind of a big deal, and something I've always wanted to do but...

It's not Liam's number I want to wear.

God, why did Beck still have to be with Sasha?

I hear a notification come through on my phone, so I check it and see a text.

Liam: **Ready for school tomorrow?**

Me: **I guess so. How about you?**

Liam: **For sure. I'm there pretty much every day thanks to football practice so I'm used to it.**

Me: **I'm there every day for volleyball practice so same.**

Liam: **I always forget you're on the volleyball team.**

Hmm, that's kind of annoying. Volleyball is important to me.

Me: **We have a real shot at being league champions and even going to states.**

He doesn't respond and I go about my business, shedding my clothes and pulling my tank and shorts back on. Emma and Tori do the same and I realize we got together to "pick out outfits" just as an excuse to hang out.

One last night together before we're seniors in high school. Our last year together before we go our separate ways.

Our last shot at being a kid. To enjoy all of those things you only experience in high school. Football games and rallies and dances. Being goofy with your friends you've known forever. Crushing on boys and partying all night at Bayshore and falling in love for the first time.

High school is a time for plenty of firsts. Some I've experienced.

Some I haven't.

Some I'd prefer to experience with a certain someone, but he belongs to someone else. Still.

And from the way things are looking...

I'm not sure if it's ever going to happen.

CHAPTER 6

BECK

*I*t's not easy, breaking up with someone. When I broke up with Cadence McWilliams in the eighth grade, she cried before I could barely get the words out. Literally burst into tears when I told her one day after school that I didn't think we should be together anymore.

That was tough.

She bad-mouthed me to all of her friends—to anyone who would listen to her, and that made me so mad, I decided to avoid girls for a while. Who needed them when you've got your friends, video games and football?

I sort of went out with a girl our sophomore year. We texted a lot. She asked me to the Sadie Hawkins dance, and, of course, I said yes. We had fun that night, but we sort of drifted apart after that. All of my friends were getting with girls, some of them having sex or at least taking things pretty far, but not me.

I didn't get it. What was wrong with me that I couldn't get a girlfriend? Some of them could barely approach me. Others were too forward—like Monique—and I wasn't interested. Still others treated me like just a friend.

Addie, for instance. A guy can be friend-zoned only so many times. I figured that's all she wanted so I left her alone. I left girls alone in general.

Until the beginning of my junior year when Sasha Rodriguez was in my environmental science class. We sat at the same table and started talking—a lot. In the beginning, I was clueless. Then one of my friends told me she liked me and I couldn't believe it. Sasha Rodriguez was the most popular girl in school, and a year older. What could she see in me?

Apparently something because we started hanging out together more and more until it turned into a full-fledged relationship. Being with Sasha at first was weird. Our conversations weren't very deep. She laughed a lot. Sometimes too much. Like, why did she feel the need to do that? But then I'd shut up her laughing by kissing her, and that worked.

It was fun and casual between us for a long time, until it wasn't. Now it just feels like an obligation. I'll always have a soft spot for Sasha, but could I consider her my first love? No, not really. I care about her, but it's not love.

What the hell is love even? I'm not sure...

I'm not even Sasha's first love. She had a serious boyfriend her junior year, went out with Jayden Mansfield who was a senior when I was a sophomore. He dumped her when he went away to college.

And now I'm dumping Sasha before *she* goes away to college. I feel kind of shitty about it, but come on. She's not into me. She's got other things to focus on now.

I just pulled up to her house and am headed up the walkway, because no way am I going to be a chicken shit and break up with her via text. All of my friends told me I should. They've all broken up with their past girlfriends via text or

Snap or whatever, which I think sucks. Be a man. Tell her to her face what you're feeling.

I jog up the porch steps and hit the doorbell, standing there impatiently waiting for her to answer. I feel antsy. Like I could come out of my skin. I just want to get this over with and move on with my life.

Finally, I hear the lock turn and the door opens, Sasha standing there in black shorts and a UC Davis T-shirt. "Beck. Hey. Want to come in? No one's home."

Her dark eyes flare with interest, like I'm going to let her drag me into her house so we can hook up. She's either completely clueless or in utter denial.

"Uh, can we talk outside?" I ask, scratching the back of my neck.

She frowns and pulls the door shut behind her. "Sure."

Her parents have a nice house. They actually live in the same neighborhood as Addison's family, and the Rodriguezes have this really big front porch with big pots of flowers everywhere as well as a couple of wrought iron chairs with a round table in between them. I settle in one of the chairs and Sasha takes the other, her gaze finding mine from across the table.

"You have fun in Tahoe?" I ask.

She never let me know she was home. I found out only because I saw her location via Snap Map. I'm the one who had to reach out to her first, which fuckin' sucks.

At least her expression is contrite. "Yeah, I did. I'm glad I went. I really got to know my roommates."

"That's awesome," I say with a faint nod.

"How are you?"

I meet her gaze, never looking away when I say, "Not good."

Her frown deepens. "Why not?"

I'm starting to wonder if she's being deliberately clueless.

"This…things are changing, Sasha. I barely saw you this summer, and now school is starting back up. I'm busy with football. It's taking up a lot of my time, and you're leaving for college soon."

"I don't leave for another month," she says, her expression wounded. Pretty sure she knows what I'm about to say, but I'm thinking she believed she'd be the one to do it first.

"I think—we should break up." I lean back in my chair, an immense sense of relief settling over me once the words are out.

Her mouth drops open, as if she's shocked by my statement. "Are you serious?"

It takes everything inside of me not to roll my eyes and yell out, *oh come on.*

"Yeah, I'm totally serious. You're not into me anymore. You're too busy hanging out with your friends, and making plans for your future, and I get it. That's what you should be doing. I'm still in high school. Why would you want to be with me when you're about to start at a college that's three hours away?" I ask her.

She watches me, quiet for a moment. As if she needs the time to absorb my words.

"You'll find someone new. You're pretty and smart and everyone likes you. Eventually you'll meet some guy at college and forget all about me," I continue on.

"Maybe I'm not ready to meet some guy at college," Sasha protests, crossing her arms in front of her, a pout on her face. "Maybe I'm perfectly happy with you."

I tilt my head to the side, contemplating her. "Come on, Sasha. Be real with me right now."

"I *am* being real with you. You always treat this relationship like it's one-sided when I have feelings too!" She throws her arms up in the air, clearly frustrated. "Is it because we never had sex? You know that was more of a *you* problem than a *me* problem."

Frustration fills me and I glare at her. "Sex has nothing to do with why I'm breaking up with you, Sasha. And I can't believe you're still pissed that we didn't have sex on prom night. Let it go. You were too drunk. No way was I going to have sex with you like that."

"No other guy would care, Beck. Seriously, it's like you're a saint. The perfect golden boy at school that all the girls want but can't touch. Funny how that works out, since you never bother trying to touch me, and I'm your freaking girl-friend! Ever since that night happened, you haven't been interested in me. Don't bother trying to deny it."

"That's not true," I start, completely ignoring her words, but I shut up when she shoots me an irritated look.

"It is true, and you know it. Are you saving yourself? Is that it?"

I squirm in my seat, uncomfortable with her line of questioning. She's not wrong. Once that night happened, I was sort of done with her, but not quite ready to end things. I thought I'd get over it. Get over how she yelled at me the morning after for leaving her alone, like what I did was a bad thing. Memories of how drunk she got that night hit me, one after the other. She was so sloppy, hanging all over any guy who'd look at her at the dance, and it filled me with anger. We'd made all of these plans. Prom night was going to be a major point in our relationship—we were about to take it one step further, and there was no going back.

Instead, she got trashed and laughed at me when I'd try to get her to calm down or sober up. I had to practically carry her to our hotel room and we argued. She even tried to leave, but I wouldn't let her. Eventually she passed out on the bed, completely blacked-out, thanks to all the cheap-ass flavored vodka she drank.

Just remembering that night leaves me with a sour feeling in my stomach. Sasha was awful that night. Guess I never recovered.

"Or is that you're not interested in having sex with *me*? Ever." Her voice is flat.

I avoid her question. "We've grown apart."

"Maybe you've found someone else." Her tone and her expression are both accusatory.

"No way," I say vehemently. "How could you say that?"

Now it's her turn to ignore my question. "I think I know who it is, too."

Unease slides down my spine. "What are you talking about?"

"It's Addison Douglas, isn't it? You've always had a thing for her. Pretty sure she has a crush on you too," Sasha says, her eyes narrowing. "Someone told me you two hung out up at Bayshore Saturday night."

Fuck me. Who ran their big mouth to my girlfriend? I can't imagine any of my friends saying anything. No way in hell would Addie tell her. I don't think they even speak to each other outside of school. Maybe one of Addie's friends? Or...

Oh shit. Maybe Monique?

It would be just like her to do something shitty like this.

"Well?" Sasha says snottily. "Is that it? Are you going to run off and get with Addison next?"

"You know she's just a friend—"

"Ha! Please. That's what you all say. 'Oh, she's my friend, that's it.'" Sasha leaps to her feet and points at me. "Did you fuck her?"

"What? No, of course not. I'm with you."

"Not anymore. You just broke up with me." Sasha crosses her arms once more. "Her family lives two streets over. You going over to her house after you leave here?"

Damn, Sasha seems downright jealous of Addison, which is crazy. She's leaving for college in a month. She could have any guy she wants. Why is she acting like this?

"No, I'm not going over to her house. It's not like that between Addie and me. Like I said, we really are just friends."

Sasha rolls her eyes. "Whatever. I hear she's talking with Liam Thatcher anyway, so good luck with that."

Word travels fast around here. Sasha doesn't really hang out with my crowd. She's already graduated for the love of God, yet she knows all the gossip. About me and Addie. Addie and Liam.

"Who are you talking to?" I ask her.

"None of your business." She tilts her head up, her nose in the air. "You'll regret this."

"Regret what? Breaking up with you?" I ask incredulously. I doubt that.

"Don't sound so pleased with yourself. I was the most popular girl at school. All the boys would've killed to get with me, yet you reject me every chance you get. Something's wrong with you, Beck. Like you're some sort of weird prude —are you studying for the priesthood maybe?"

She laughs at her own joke and I stand, looming over her.

"I used to really like you," I say, my voice low. Her laughter dies as she stares up at me. "As a friend. As my girl-friend. I thought we could remain in contact after this, but maybe not. You're just bitter now. And mean. Have fun at Davis, Sasha."

"You're a dick, Callahan!" she yells after me, as I practically run down the porch steps and sprint toward my car. I can still hear her yelling as I climb into my 4Runner and slam the door, muffling the sound of her screaming as she appears on the steps, her mouth moving, but I can't hear the words.

Thank God.

I start the engine and press my foot on the gas, revving

the engine. That annoys the crap out of her and she starts down the stairs, marching across the lawn and headed straight toward me.

I shift into drive and get the hell out of there, glancing in my rearview mirror at the last second to see her standing on the sidewalk, shaking her fist into the sky.

Well damn.

That was fun.

Not.

CHAPTER 7

ADDIE

*I*t's late. Past eleven and I can't sleep. As if I'm a little kid excited about going back to school tomorrow. Though I wouldn't call myself *excited* over starting my senior year.

More like anxious. Nervous.

Things are going to be different. It's my last first day of school as a kid. Jonah and I are no longer together. Liam is interested in me, and while I like texting with him, I don't necessarily think he's my type.

Emma is being weird, which I don't get. Yet Tori is more supportive than ever.

There's a shift in the air. I can feel it. Is it a good shift or a bad one?

I'm not sure yet.

After scrolling through TikTok for the last hour, I switch to Instagram, going into my search and looking up Beck's profile. I scroll through the photos like a pathetic stalker, frowning when I realize it's mostly football shots. There is a photo of him with his dad and brother. Then more football.

There's a photo of him holding his niece Kenzie—Ava's daughter.

Not one photo of Sasha is anywhere on his feed.

I sit up, the comforter falling to my lap as I go back and search Sasha's name, pulling up her profile. Her profile pic was a photo of her and Beck. Now it's a photo of her looking extra cute on a boat in the middle of a lake, sunglasses on and a big smile on her face.

I get out of IG and open up my text messages, ready to text Emma first, but realizing she'll probably turn the conversation toward herself. I text Tori instead.

Me: **Did you hear anything about Sasha and Beck breaking up?**

She answers immediately.

Tori: **Nooo. Have they?**

Me: **Go check out their IG.**

I impatiently wait while she looks over their profiles. Eventually she responds.

Tori: **DUDE I THINK THEY BROKE UP.**

Me: **Right??? She's off his profile and he's not on hers.**

Tori: **And did you see her story? What a thirst trap.**

I immediately go check it out. It's a boomerang video of her in a tank top that's scooped so low her tits are practically falling out as she leans into the camera, her eyes closed while she's sticking her tongue out. I watch it a few times, noting how her makeup is perfect and her hair looks amazing as usual. She posted it only an hour ago and it's captioned, "So bored."

Me: **Total thirst trap.**

Tori: **She wouldn't post like that if she and Beck were still together. They're through! OMG!**

She sends me a string of bug-eyed emojis.

I shouldn't be excited. A breakup is tough. I wonder who broke up with who? I hope Beck isn't suffering.

Tori: **You can console Beck through his tough time.**

She basically stole the thought right out of my head.

Me: **We're friends.**

Tori: **With the potential for more.**

Me: **I'm kind of talking to Liam.**

Tori: **Please. If it's Liam vs Beck, I'd tell you to go for BECK. That boy is fire.**

Now she sends me a string of fire emojis.

And she's not wrong. He's fire. Sweet yet hot. Great on the football field. Stacked with muscles. Flat abs and thick thighs and pretty blue eyes. Oh, and that mouth...

Me: **Fine. He's fire.**

Tori: **You've already got the in with him too. You should go for it!**

Me: **What if he's traumatized by the breakup?**

Tori: **He didn't seem so traumatized over Sasha when he was hanging out with you Saturday night.**

That meant nothing. Yes, he grabbed my hand, but come on. It was a friendly grab. He was still with Sasha then too.

Me: **That's different. They were still together Saturday night.**

Tori: **Yeah, but she was in Tahoe acting the ho while Beck was with you in your car.**

Me: **You make it sound so scandalous. And you shouldn't call Sasha a ho.**

Tori: **Um...I heard a rumor...**

Me: **What did you hear???????**

My phone rings, indicating a FaceTime call from Tori. I answer it to find she's sitting in bed in the dark, the phone illuminating her face and making her look a little freaky.

"Too much to type out. Thought I'd just call you," Tori says.

"What rumor did you hear? And from who?"

"My sister! She's so well-connected." Paisley is going to be a sophomore, and she's more popular than her big sister. She was homecoming princess of the freshman class. She's on the cheer team. Everyone knows Paisley. "One of her best friend's is Jayden Mansfield's little sister, Callie. Her brother has been home for the summer, working with their dad and she overheard him talking to his friends, telling them he was going to Tahoe to hook up with Sasha over the weekend."

Oh shit. That is some good, steamy tea. "Are you serious?"

Tori nods. "Paisley swore me to secrecy, but it'll eventually get out. Can you believe it? She really was ho'ing around in Tahoe. She's a Tahoe ho."

I can't help but giggle, and I tell myself to stop. "I'm guessing she probably broke up with him then, if she's hooking up with Jayden."

"Nope. I just texted Dom and asked about it, and he said Beck broke up with her," Tori says, sounding triumphant.

That puts an entirely different slant on the situation. Did Beck find out about her getting with Jayden behind his back? I'm sure that made him mad—and upset him too. Beck has always had a good heart. Was he in love with her and she just stomped all over it?

"You need to swoop in, my friend. Snap that boy up and make him your senior year boyfriend," Tori says encouragingly.

"I can't just swoop in. He literally just broke up with his girlfriend. He's probably all down and out," I say.

"What better reason to be a good friend for him and console him during his troubling times?" Now it's Tori's turn to giggle.

"I don't know." A sigh leaves me. "I'll feel bad."

"Now is not the time to let your guilt drive you. Look at Emma. She goes after what she wants, whenever she wants it. And she snagged Marcus."

"Who I'm sure will still be talking to Monique on the side. That girl has him ensnared," I say, way too truthfully.

It's always been Emma and me first. We would confide in each other about everything. Stand up for each other, no matter what. We have lots of dumb private jokes, and we don't have to say a word to each other yet somehow know what the other is thinking just by sharing a look.

Lately, though, we've been drifting apart. She's become more secretive, especially this summer. I worked a lot so maybe that made a difference, but still.

I feel closer to Tori right now. Her support feels unconditional, as a friend's support should be, but Emma has been snarky and judgmental.

"Marcus is funny and I like talking to him, but I don't think I'd want him for a boyfriend," Tori admits.

"He's kind of awful," I agree, suddenly desperate to change the subject. What if Tori tells Emma we were talking about her and Marcus and we think he sucks? She'd lose it. "How are things going between you and Dom?"

She can barely contain the smile on her face. "Good. Wonderful. Awesome. I can't wait to see him at school tomorrow. How about you and Liam? Or are you going to forget all about him, thanks to Beck being a free man?"

"I don't know what to do," I admit, because it's the truth.

Stick with Liam? Or try to see if something happens with Beck?

"You know what I love about this situation?" Tori asks me.

"What?"

"You have options, girl. Solid ones." She grins, and I have to agree.

For once, I do have options.

Things are suddenly looking up.

* * *

First day of school and it's the typical scene. Lots of familiar faces and some new—most of them young and petrified, since they're the incoming freshmen. I'm hanging out by Emma's car, Tori and I chatting while Emma and Marcus are wrapped up in each other.

"Didn't Monique post a photo of her and Marcus with him licking her neck just last week?" Tori asks me, rolling her eyes.

"Yeah." I glance back in the couple's direction when Emma squeals as Marcus nuzzles her neck. "Looks like that's his thing."

Tori laughs. "Maybe he has a fetish."

"Who has a fetish?"

We both turn to find Liam standing in front of us, a friendly smile on his face.

"Oh nothing. No one," I tell him, waving my hand dismissively. The last thing I want to talk about is fetishes with Liam. I barely know him.

He blatantly scans me from head to toe. "Looking good, Addison."

"Thanks." I don't know if I liked how he just checked me out, but I go with it. He has such an expectant look on his face, I realize quickly that he might be waiting for a compliment in return. Hmm. "You look good too. I like your shoes."

Liam kicks out his foot, showing off the new Vans he's got on. "Thanks. Just got them."

We're all rocking our new back-to-school clothes. I don't get as many as I used to when I was a kid, but Mom always takes me shopping a few weeks before school starts and I pick out a few things. "I just got my shoes too."

I lift my leg, showing off my white-on-white Nike Air Force 1 shoe to Liam, but he's not even paying attention, too busy glancing around, as if there might be better prospects appearing.

"You want to get together tonight?" he asks when he returns his attention to me.

I can practically feel Tori vibrating with excitement at him asking me out, which points out the complete nonreaction I'm currently having. I mean, it's cool that Liam is asking me out, but...

I don't know why I'm not excited.

"I have practice after school," I say.

"So do I," he says. "How about after? We can go pick up something to eat. Hang out."

His expression is expectant, and I look at him—really look at him. He's tall, though not as tall as Beck. The shaggy, slightly wavy dark blond hair that's always falling in his eyes is kind of cute. He's attractive, but being in his presence doesn't make me feel all tingly, and I'm not having that butterflies-fluttering-in-my-stomach feeling like I do when I'm with Beck.

But he seems nice enough. Maybe I need to get to know him better first. How can I know him better if I don't do things with him? Hang out with him?

"Okay." I nod. "Sure."

He breaks out into a huge smile, just as the warning bell rings, indicating we need to head for our first class. "Great. I'll text you later and we can meet up."

The moment he's gone, Tori is on me, grasping my arm and giving it a shake. "This is so great. You're going on a date with Liam!"

"Shh." I don't want anyone else—namely Emma—to hear. "It's nothing. Just dinner."

"That's a date," Tori says with a giant smile. "I'm excited for you!"

I smile and nod, wishing I was as enthusiastic as Tori.

But I'm not.
Because he's not Beck.

CHAPTER 8

BECK

First day of school and I'm finally top dog.

Kind of a stupid way to think, I know, but I can't help it. It's hella hard to feel on top of anything when you're the baby of the family. I'm the last Callahan, and trust me when I say that all my older siblings let me know it on a regular basis. Plus, I've been compared to one or all of them at some point in my life, even my sisters. They've all "been there and done that" and I'm the one who's just coming after them, scraping up the leftover pieces where I can.

I'm used to it. It's cool. But every once in a while, I think to myself, what about me?

Here, right now, is my time.

I remember having this same 'rule the school' feeling in the eighth grade and my friends and I reveled in it, as fourteen-year-old boys will do. We were obnoxious as hell and ran that campus like we owned it, which we thought we did.

I'm definitely going to do the same thing again this year too. I've *earned* this spot.

My class load this year isn't too strenuous. Not like I'm going to skate by my senior year, but at least it's relatively easy. My friends and I have already compared our class schedules, so I know who's in what class with me for the most part—with one exception.

Addie Douglas.

I have no idea if she's in any of my classes or not, and like a complete ass, I haven't talked to her since the party at Bayshore. Though what was I supposed to say?

Hey, it was fun sitting with you in your car. Don't know what got into me, holding your hand like I did when I had a girl-friend at the time, but I got rid of her so...want to go out sometime?

Yeah. I'm sure she'd respond well to that.

Besides, I was busy the last few days. Football practice kicked my ass. Thoughts of how I needed to end things with Sasha also preoccupied my time. After our breakup, she blocked me everywhere she could, but my friends sent me the video she posted on her private story the night we split. Looking all sexy and shit with her tits in the camera.

Whatever. If she wants to find someone new, I could give a damn. I'm over her.

Completely.

So yeah. It wasn't a good time for me to reach out to Addie.

Until today. Today, I'm ready. I'm single. She's single. I need to make a move before Liam beats me to the punch.

The asshole.

The way I hear Liam talk about her at practice, they're texting on a daily basis. He's gone so far as to say that they're officially talking—which is code for them speaking with each other exclusively. When that happens, usually a couple are on their way to actually being together.

If that's the case, Liam moves fast.

And I'm completely fucked. Yet again.

First period I have English and Addie isn't in there, which

isn't a surprise. She's in honors English and I'm in college prep.

Second period is American Government, again no Addie.

The entire morning, I don't see her. Every passing period between classes, I'm looking for her familiar dark head, those pretty blue eyes and the smile that gets me every time I see it, but nope.

I don't see her, and it's fucking depressing.

By the time lunch arrives, I'm feeling dejected. Down and out. Hopeless, even.

I should've realized a long time ago I can't get my hopes up over this girl. Something always gets in the way. We're never on the same page, and I'm getting impatient.

Maybe I should just give in to Liam and be done with it.

We all go off campus and grab McDonald's—not the lunch of champions, but we've waited the last three years to be seniors, so we can leave school for lunch, and we're going to celebrate. Liam is with us, along with most of the seniors from the football team.

Guess he's not so official with Addie that he has lunch with her. I make a point not to sit with him so I don't have to listen to him talk about her. It's easier that way.

By the time lunch is over and we're back on campus, we only have two periods left. I walk into my World Religions class to find Addie sitting at a desk with no one else nearby, her lips curled in the faintest smile as she watches something on her phone. There's not a friend of hers in sight.

Not a friend of mine in sight either.

Excitement filling me, I stare at her, taking in the tight black top she's wearing and how it reveals a bit of skin. Nothing too scandalous, just her lower back, but it's enough to have me curious.

But then again, when it comes to Addie, I'm always intrigued.

About everything.

Deciding to just go for it, I approach her desk, plopping into the chair right next to hers. "Hey, Adds."

She glances up from her phone so quick I'm afraid she just gave herself whiplash. "Beck. Hey."

Her voice is breathy. Almost like a whisper. Maybe she's surprised to see me? I don't know.

"Hi." I smile at her like a dope and stare, while she does the same thing, her lips curling, her nose scrunching a bit.

Adorable.

"I'm so glad you're in this class. None of my friends are. They all took it last year," she says, glancing around.

The class is filling up quickly, mostly with juniors.

"I had friends in this class last year too. My schedule wouldn't allow it, and I wasn't going to take it, but Ava pushed me to," I tell her.

"Yeah, Jos said the same thing. She loved this class." Addie's smile grows. "How is Ava?"

"Great. She's spending a lot of time with your sister." Eli Bennett and Diego Garcia—my sister is married to Eli and Addie's is married to Diego—both play for the Seattle Seahawks. "Always chasing after kids."

"Jos is doing the same. I wish they lived closer," Addie says, her voice full of longing.

"Me too."

My mind suddenly fills with images of the two of us going to Seattle together to see our sisters. That would be fun...

But, of course, I'm dreaming big time because this girl views me as a friend and that's it, though I'd give anything to change her mind. She's too busy talking with Liam to see me as anything other than the guy she's known for what feels like forever. Yeah, we might have chemistry, but it's never enough for her to act on. Maybe it's not enough for me to act on either, considering I never really fuckin' do.

I think of that one time in the bathroom at that party last fall, when I almost kissed her. The timing was awful. I was with Sasha and Addie was with Jonah and damn it, I'm not a cheater. The guy interrupting us by knocking on the bathroom door right before my lips touched hers was the only thing that prevented it from actually happening.

I came this close to cheating on Sasha and I might've not been able to forgive myself. Addie might've viewed me differently too. That would've ruined everything between us.

Thank God it didn't actually happen.

But then again, I wish it had happened because at least I'd know what Addison tastes like. And right now, that is the biggest question lingering in my mind.

What do this girl's lips taste like? How would she feel in my arms? A perfect fit? What would it be like to have her melt against me, whispering my name when I keep kissing her, her fingers in my hair, my hands on her waist, sliding down to her ass—

"Maybe someday our families should go up together and visit them," Addie suggests, her sweet voice interrupting my increasingly dirty thoughts.

About her.

"Yeah, maybe." Doubtful, but it's fun to dream.

"How's your first day of school going?" she asks, changing the subject.

"Better now that I see you're in this class with me." I probably shouldn't have said that, but I'm shooting my shot, just like that fucker, Liam.

Her cheeks turn the faintest shade of pink. "I'm glad you're in this class too." She ducks her head, her lips still curled up. "I'm sorry about what happened Saturday."

I frown. "What about it?"

"I don't know. We were talking. Things were good. Then Tori had to show up and puke all over my car." She lifts her head, her expression vaguely pained. "So gross. She feels terrible about it. She even asked me to tell you she's sorry."

I laugh. "She doesn't have to apologize, even though it was gross as hell."

Addie wrinkles her nose again. "It was so gross. I told her she owes me."

"She does. You were a good friend, helping her get cleaned up."

"I couldn't just leave her standing there puking." It's her turn to laugh, and I soak up the sound, basking in her presence. Noting how her eyes glow, and when she moves to tuck her hair behind her ear, she sits up straighter, my gaze dropping to her chest.

She's got nice tits. I stare for only a second before I look away, almost relieved when the teacher walks in. Mrs. Hardison has taught at this school for years. She's practically an institution in her own right and everyone goes quiet when she starts talking.

I send a quick look in Addie's direction, just because I can, and find her already smiling at me. Makes me feel like we share a secret and I smile in return before I look away.

The next fifty minutes drag on, even though I'm genuinely interested in the class subject. I'm just itching to talk to Addie again, wondering if I should ask her about Liam and what they're up to.

Is it any of my business? I'm tempted to make it my business because I want to know what the hell is going on with those two, but I also don't want to come across as too pushy.

Damn it, I can't win with this girl. Seriously. She twists me up and leaves me overthinking my every move. With Sasha, it never felt like that. Maybe because I didn't really care. I just went for it.

With Addie, I care. Maybe too much.

Dad always said things should be easy. If they're complicated from the get-go, they might not work out.

Is that what's happening between Addie and me? Are we so complicated that it will never work out between us?

Damn, I hope not.

By the time class is over and the bell is about to ring, I'm leaning back in my chair, sprawling my legs in front of me as I take a deep breath and stretch my arms above my head. I glance over to catch Addison watching me and she quickly averts her head, like she's embarrassed she got caught.

Good. This makes me feel like we're on more of a level playing field.

The bell rings, but I don't immediately toss my stuff into my backpack and make for the door. Neither does Addie. I send her a questioning look. "What's your next class?"

"TA for Hardison," she answers.

"No shit? Me too." Usually, they don't schedule a bunch of teachers' aides during the same period for the same teacher, but I know Hardison has a heavy class load, so maybe she needs more help?

And how lucky am I, that Addie will be with me as a teacher's aide? Just the two of us…

"Beck, Addison, could you come up here please?" Mrs. Hardison asks us.

I shove my crap into my backpack and head up there while Addie takes a little more care with her stuff before she slides everything into her backpack carefully. I probably should've waited for her. Mom would've given me a minor speech about manners if she were here.

"Being it's the first day of school, I have nothing for you to do," Mrs. Hardison says, not wasting any time. "You can go to the library if you like. That's where all the TAs go if their teachers don't have any work for them to do."

I glance over at Addie who's nodding. "That sounds good," she says.

"You can head straight over there tomorrow as well." Hardison glances down at her planner on her desk, flipping through the pages. "It might take a few weeks for me to actually have projects for you two to work on, so I'll keep you posted. Quite handy having you both in my sixth period class as well."

"Sure is," I tell Hardison with a smile and she grins at me in return.

"I remember having your sister in this class," Mrs. Hardison starts.

Okay, here we go. The Callahan legends who came before me. "Oh yeah?"

"She ditched a lot." Hardison frowns, making me laugh.

"Guess Ava wasn't so perfect after all," I joke.

"I was actually referring to your oldest sister, Autumn. That girl…" She shakes her head. "She'd run off with Ash Davis every chance she got."

"And look at them now," I murmur. He's an NFL legend. They're married with twins. Doing pretty well if you ask me.

"Yes, look at them now," Hardison agrees. "I loved your sister Ava. She always wrote such thoughtful papers."

She drones on about my siblings for a little while longer before Addie and I finally make our escape. The hallways are already mostly empty, thanks to everyone being in their last class for the day, so it almost feels like we have the school to ourselves.

"Do you deal with that a lot?" Addie asks me once we're out of the classroom.

I send her a look. "Deal with what?"

"Teachers comparing you to your brother and sisters."

"Yeah." I groan a little. "It sucks. Everyone always has something to say about Jake. Or Autumn. Or Ava."

"You're the baby of the fam," she points out. "It happens to me with Jocelyn but not too much. There's a gap between us that wasn't filled with other siblings like yours is. Some of them forget about her—with the exception of my volleyball coach, of course."

"Does your coach compare you and Jos a lot?" One of the math teachers at school is the volleyball coach and she's amazing. The girls' varsity volleyball team seems to kick ass every year. "Always going on about how great your sister was?"

I don't hear that from my dad, because he thinks Jake and I are both great—he has to, he's our father. But the other coaches on staff? Some of them were around when Jake was playing and yep, I hear the comparisons from them all the time, even though we play different positions.

"At first, yeah, only because she didn't know me and I hadn't proved myself to her yet. As time went on though, she started to respect me for who I was and how I played. I'm a different player compared to Jos," Addie explains, as we leave the building and head toward the hill for the library.

"Better?" I raise my brows.

Addie shrugs. "Different." She's quiet for a moment. "Coach has mentioned before that I'm better, yeah."

"Knew it." My tone is assured, my gaze on the library ahead of us as we keep walking, a faint smile curling my lips.

She nudges me with her elbow, a spark igniting from that simple touch. "You're cocky."

"You like it," I throw back at her, making her laugh. "Especially if it has to do with *your* athletic abilities."

"True." Her laughter grows and it makes me want to keep on doing it.

Seeing her smile. Making her laugh.

Knowing I'm the cause of it.

We approach the double door entrance to the library and

I rush ahead of her, opening the door for her. She walks past me into the building with a murmured thank you, and I subtly inhale, drawing her scent into my lungs. Trying to keep a straight face and not let on what I'm doing, though damn, her scent makes my knees weak.

Lame but true.

There's hardly anyone in the library and we find a smaller table to ourselves, the two of us settling in across from each other, me dropping my backpack at my feet while she sets hers on top of the table.

"Do you have homework?" she asks me.

I slowly shake my head and lean back, sprawling my legs out much like I did earlier in Hardison's classroom. "Nah. Do you?"

"I do. English. I have to write a short paragraph," she says as she unzips her backpack and pulls out a notebook.

"That sucks. It's the first day. It should be a crime for teachers to give kids homework on the first day of school," I protest.

"I agree, but I had a summer reading assignment." She pulls out a battered paperback of *To Kill a Mockingbird*. "And now we have to write an intro paragraph for the essay we'll eventually be assigned."

"Damn, I'm glad I'm in regular English. Meyer doesn't give us summer reading assignments," I mutter, sitting up straight once more and resting my arms on top of the table. Addie's arm is resting on the table too, and it would be so easy to reach out and touch her. Draw my finger down the length of her forearm, see if goosebumps would rise.

"You have practice after school, right?" she asks after she sets the book on the table.

"Always." I nod. "You do too, right?"

"I do. We have our first game next week. At home."

"What day?"

"Tuesday."

"We'll be there," I say firmly, mentally reminding myself to tell the guys on the team we need to show up.

Her smile is faint. "I appreciate that, but you don't have to go. I'm sure you're tired after being at school all day and then two hours of practice."

"It's no problem. I don't mind, and neither do the guys," I reassure her.

"Well, thank you." Her smile is faint. "My team loves it when you guys show up."

"That's why we're there. We all gotta support each other." Well, I'm supporting her. I don't know what everyone else's motive is.

"Why aren't you in P.E. right now?" Addie asks.

"How do you know I usually have P.E. seventh period? Keeping tabs, Adds?" I raise my brows, teasing her.

She blushes prettily, her cheeks the faintest pink. "I remember when you had to switch into my history class last year because they added that conditioning class for the team seventh period. Not because I'm stalking you." She reaches across the table and jabs her finger against my forearm, just like I was tempted to do to her only a few minutes ago.

I wish she'd touch me longer, though I take it as a good sign she wants to touch me at all.

"Admin changed it up. Something to do with the schedule and how they couldn't accommodate the entire football team having their conditioning class during seventh period anymore. We're conditioning in the early morning, before school starts—only the upperclassmen. They call it a zero period." It's only for thirty minutes, just enough to get the blood pumping, and it's held on Tuesday, Wednesday and Thursday, so it's not too bad.

"Lifting weights and all that?"

"I need to bulk up," I tell her.

Her gaze drops to my shoulders. My chest. Her eyes linger there, as if she likes what she sees. "Aren't you bulky enough?"

That she notices makes me want to flex, but I withhold the urge. "Never. My goal is always to crush my opponents."

"You've been doing okay with that for a while." She reaches out and touches me again, her fingers drifting across my forearm before they slide up, lightly tapping against my biceps. Faint goosebumps break out, and I wonder if she noticed. "You're pretty strong, Callahan."

"Glad you noticed, Douglas," I tease her, though my voice is rough. Disappointment crashes over me when she drops her hand.

But damn, she just willingly touched me. Again. I feel like we're middle schoolers who don't know how to flirt, but this is kind of a big deal. Or maybe I just feel the need to grab onto every seemingly meaningful moment between us and clutch it tightly.

Fuck, I'm ridiculous.

"Hey. What are you guys doing back here?"

We both look up at the sharp male voice to find…

Shit. Liam standing at the head of our table, glaring at both of us.

Glaring at me.

CHAPTER 9

ADDIE

I smile up at Liam to hide the annoyance I feel at him just showing up out of nowhere. I liked being alone with Beck in the back of the library, tucked away. Just the two of us having a conversation.

Fine, we were flirting. And it was so easy with Beck. Not awkward and weird like it feels with Liam.

I don't know what possessed me to reach out and touch him.

Twice.

But I have zero regrets. The boy is firm and muscular and it is an absolute pleasure to test all that firmness and his muscles. His bicep was rock hard.

Rock. Hard.

I don't think there's an ounce of fat on the guy, and my fingers literally itch to touch him again.

Everywhere.

"We're both aides for Hardison," Beck says to Liam, his voice casual. Easygoing, like nothing bothers him.

But I noticed the flash of irritation in his eyes when Liam spoke—and I'm sure the accusatory tone of his voice didn't help matters. I also see the way Beck holds himself, his shoulders tense, his entire body stiff.

HIs body language is telling me he might feel threatened by Liam, but I thought they were friends. In fact, I *know* they are. Are they possibly angry at each other for some reason? Liam is currently glaring at Beck like he might want to blow his head off, which sounds incredibly dramatic, but I don't think I'm too far off the mark.

These two clearly have beef.

"Isn't that convenient," Liam practically snaps before turning all of his attention on me. "I was going to ask you when we went to dinner later tonight, but—want to wear my jersey tomorrow?"

I gape at him, shocked at the whiplash change of subject, how he just flat-out asked me in front of Beck with no finesse whatsoever. Actually, Liam sounds pissed. "Um…"

"It's not even a real game tomorrow," Beck adds, my gaze going to him to see he's slowly shaking his head. "It's a fuckin' scrimmage, Thatcher."

The boys stare at each other as if they're in a standoff and they're waiting to see who draws their gun first. The air practically ripples with tension.

It's the weirdest thing.

"What do you say, Addison?" Liam directs his attention to me, a smile on his face, but I can tell it's a little forced. He's still mad.

And I can practically feel the anger rolling off Beck in palpable waves.

"Sure," I say weakly, ignoring Beck when he swivels his head my way. I can feel his gaze on me and it makes me nervous. "I'd love to."

"Good. I'll bring my jersey tomorrow and give it to you before school starts. Maybe we could meet for breakfast first," Liam says, sending a smug smile in Beck's direction.

We have late start every Friday, meaning school doesn't begin until nine-twenty and lots of people meet for breakfast so they can hang out. Jonah and I used to meet up for breakfast last year when we were still together.

But the whole point of late start Friday is to sleep in, so I'd always beg off of meeting before school started because… what can I say.

I like my sleep.

Plus, I didn't want to run into Beck and Sasha anywhere.

God, I annoy myself sometimes.

"We can discuss it later," I tell Liam.

"Tonight at dinner?" He sends a look in Beck's direction, who's currently watching me.

"Sure," I say weakly. When Liam doesn't budge from his spot at the head of the table, I keep talking. "Why are you in the library anyway?"

"Oh, I'm an aide in the office this period. Had to run something to Miss Smith." She's the librarian's assistant.

"Probably should head back to the office before they send out a search team," Beck practically bites out.

Liam ignores him, offering me a soft smile instead when he says, "I'll see you after practice, okay?"

"Sure." I smile in return. "See ya."

"Bye, Addie."

Once he's left the library, it's as if all the tension bleeds out of Beck. His shoulders relax and he slouches in the chair once more, kicking his legs out. I like it when he does that. He's so long. And broad. It's like he's everywhere at once and I can't help but wonder what it would feel like, to be completely surrounded by him. To have him hold me. Crush me to his chest. Press his mouth to mine—

"Rumor has it you two are officially talking," Beck says, sounding like a sullen little boy who just got his favorite toy taken away.

Hmmm.

"Well, we're talking, but I don't know if it's official…" Liam has never said anything about it, and I'm not about to bring it up because honestly? I don't want to be officially talking to Liam.

I'd rather be official with the bonehead currently sitting across from me at this table.

Though if I'm being real right now, I've been a complete bonehead as well.

"You're really going to dinner with him tonight?" Beck asks, his eyes narrowed as he contemplates me.

"Yeah, I really am." I smile.

Beck scowls.

Realization dawns.

Beck Callahan is…

Jealous.

"I thought you two were friends," I say, because I want him to explain himself and why they're acting like they're not.

Beck shrugs. "Kind of. Lately he's been a prick."

"Uh huh." I nod, contemplating him. Wondering if I should try and push his buttons.

Yeah. Maybe I should. Just a little.

"Liam is really nice." I press my lips together, waiting for his response.

"I'm sure," Beck mutters.

"We've been talking a lot lately."

"That's great." He glances toward the front of the library, like he's bored with our conversation.

"He even FaceTimes me," I say, just to rub it in.

Liam FaceTimed me once. Just to show off his shoe collection. He talked about himself the entire time.

Beck winces and grips the back of his neck, his gaze sliding to mine. "Sounds kind of official to me."

"I'm not sure if I'm interested," I admit.

He goes completely still at that truth bomb. "What do you mean?"

"I mean exactly what I said." I shrug. "Liam is nice. We talk a lot. But I don't know if I'm interested in him in…that way."

"You're going to dinner with him. And you might wear his jersey tomorrow."

"For a *scrimmage game*," I stress, barely able to contain the smile that wants to burst through. "That doesn't really count, remember?"

Beck never breaks eye contact, some of that tension easing away once more, and his bluish-green eyes sparkle. "Nah, it doesn't count at all. Such bullshit. They don't even let us keep track of the score."

"I know. And why not? Who cares?" I roll my eyes.

"I don't know why. But I always keep score." He taps his temple with his index finger. "Up here."

We stare at each other for a little while in silence, and I'm so tempted to say something. Anything.

What about me?

What about us?

We'd make a good couple...right?

I'd wear Beck's jersey in a heartbeat. For a scrimmage, for real games, for all of it. I'd paint his number on my face and jump up and down in the stands every time he was on the field, screaming his last name as loud as I could.

I can envision it all now.

But can he?

Does he want to?

I don't know.

The jealous thing though? That's real. He doesn't like the idea of me with Liam, but is he that good enough of a friend that he won't play interference and ruin Liam's chances with me? If that's the case—which it might be—then that's so sweet. Beck Callahan is a good guy.

I want him to be mine.

And maybe that's why I'm putting so much on this. Maybe Beck isn't jealous at all. Maybe he could give two shits about me.

Nahhh, as he would say.

I'm pretty sure he likes me.

"Can I offer you some advice?" he asks, his deep voice knocking me from my thoughts.

I slowly nod, unable to look away from his eyes. I knew they were beautiful, but they are extra swirly with color this afternoon.

"Watch out for Liam. He's my friend but sometimes—he doesn't treat girls well," he admits gruffly.

Is he just saying that because he doesn't want me with Liam, or is he speaking the truth? "Thanks for the advice."

"You're welcome. Just watching out for a friend," he says before he tears his gaze from mine and stares at the table.

My heart sinks. *Friend.* I hate that word.

Especially when it comes to me and Beck.

* * *

"GIRL, you can't concentrate for shit today," Emma yells to me after I serve the ball like absolute crap, yet again.

"Thanks for the reminder," I call back, annoyed at her for pointing out all my faults, though deep down I know I'm overreacting. Usually, she's so supportive of me, but I've noticed that she's become more competitive since practice this summer.

This is our senior year. We all want to look good. I get it. But she doesn't need to show off or call out my faults to make herself look better.

"You're doing fine," Tori whispers to me, always encouraging. "You're probably tired because of the long day at school. We need to get used to it. That's what my mom always says."

"For sure," I tell Tori, smiling faintly at her. "And thanks."

This time, my serve is good and aimed right at Emma, who's standing on the other side of the net. She bumps it neatly, sending it over to our side, right at Tori, who bumps it as well, the ball flying high into the air before another teammate sends it back over the net.

We keep it up, playing cleanly, until ultimately, it's Emma's turn to screw up.

Looks like she can't serve today for shit either, but I'm respectful enough to keep my mouth shut.

Once practice is over and we're exiting the gym, Tori stops Emma and me, excitement glowing in her brown eyes. "Let's go down to the football field."

Emma nods, her smile growing. "I'm down. We can watch the boys practice."

"That's what I was thinking," Tori says excitedly.

Though there's nothing clever about us sitting in the bleachers watching the football team practice. Hopefully, they're out on the field.

"What do you think, Addie?" Tori asks me.

I shrug. "Sure. Why not?"

"Oh, don't act like you don't care." Emma bumps her hip against mine. "We know you want to go watch Liam get all sweaty out on that field."

I laugh. Nod. Smile.

Though I'm not imagining a sweaty Liam. More like a sweaty Beck.

We stash our backpacks in our cars and then walk over to the field, Tori talking a mile a minute, and it's all Dom this and Dom that. It's kind of cute, how excited she is over him, and I'm so happy for her.

"Are you two 'official' yet?" Emma asks, her voice casual.

I send her a sharp look but otherwise say nothing. She knows they're not, so why she has the need to ask, I don't know. To make Tori feel doubtful?

If so, that's messed up.

"No." Tori's smile falters slightly. "But I'm sure we will be soon!"

"He seems totally into you," I reassure her.

"And what about you and Liam?" Emma asks, her head swinging in my direction.

"We're not official," I say. "We're not even officially talking. But—we are going to dinner after practice."

Tori and I share a quick look. I haven't mentioned him asking me to dinner at all today. Neither has Tori. But I can't keep it from Emma.

Emma's mouth hangs open and she reaches out, giving me a not so gentle shove. "What the hell? You're totally holding out on me! Dinner? That's a date, my friend."

"That's what I told her!" Tori crows, pressing her lips together the moment Emma glances over at her, a mixture of anger and hurt on her face.

"Oh, so you already told Tori but not me?" Her tone is accusatory.

"Tori was there when it happened," I admit, biting my lower lip.

"And when exactly did it happen?" Emma asks.

"This morning. Before school started," Tori says.

Emma doesn't speak the rest of the walk over to the football field, and neither do Tori and me. I feel like shit for not telling Emma about it sooner, but I know she would've made a big deal out of it and possibly said something in front of Liam and the other guys, and I didn't want to hear it.

Maybe I didn't want Beck to find out either.

Guess Tori didn't want to, either. I don't want Emma to think we're leaving her out of stuff, even though it sort of seems like that's what we're doing.

Making me feel even shittier.

Once we arrive at the football field, we find it super busy. The cross country team is jogging around the track. The band has taken up a small corner of the field, practicing the fight song over and over and over again, and the football team is circled around the coaches as Drew Callahan himself is yelling instructions before they spread out into formation, preparing to run through a play.

We settle on the bottom bleachers, the heat from the August sun baking into my skin. I can't wait until it's the end of September, or even better, the beginning of October and that sun isn't as intense. Football games early in the season are the worst.

"They look good," Tori says, as she leans into me ever so slightly.

"Yeah, they do," Emma says, as she leaps off the bleacher and goes to the waist-high chain-link fence that surrounds the entire track and field. "Looking good, Marcus!" she screams, her hands cupped around her mouth to amplify the sound.

Marcus whips his head toward the sound of Emma's voice, making a gesture like he wants her to quit yelling. Which she does, but she doesn't come back and sit with us yet. She's too busy calling out to one of the cross country boys, who stops to talk to her. His name is David, a senior who's perfectly nice, but a bit of a stoner.

I'm sure the only reason Emma is chatting with him is to make Marcus jealous.

"What's wrong with her?" Tori asks me, her voice laced with concern. "I know you two have been friends way longer and you're really close, but she's been acting different lately. Or maybe that's just towards me."

"No, I've noticed it too," I agree, my gaze snagging on Emma. How she's leaning against the fence, her chest thrust forward like she's trying to get poor David to stare at her tits.

She probably is.

"She was mad we kept Liam asking you to dinner from her, huh?" When I glance over at Tori, I find her frowning at me so hard, her forehead is wrinkled. "I figured that was your story to tell, you know?"

"Yeah, I know. She'll get over it." I lift my gaze to the football field, where the guys are currently repositioning themselves on the field. I spot Beck easily, the way he's hunkered down into a squat, his big body lurching forward the second the play is called.

Tori wrinkles her nose. "You think she's giving it up to Marcus?"

"I'm positive she is." They were doing it when we were sophomores. Nothing's going to stop her now that we're older. I'm sure that's the first thing Marcus wanted from her.

"Dom told me he doesn't want me talking to anyone else." The look on Tori's face is downright dreamy. "And he didn't say it in some jerk-off, 'I'm in charge' way either."

"I'm sure you loved it that he got all possessive about you," I say, nudging her shoulder with mine.

She laughs. "I can't lie. I totally did. Does Liam ever talk that way to you?"

I hesitate, wondering if I should tell her the truth. "No, not really. It's too early for that, don't you think?"

"It's early for Dom and me too, but he's not holding back." Tori's eyes sparkle with excitement. "I like it."

"I'm sure you do." I turn my attention back to the field. "Liam asked me to wear his jersey tomorrow."

"Dom asked me to wear his! Right after lunch. He said the game tomorrow doesn't really count, though," Tori says.

"It's a scrimmage."

"Right."

We're quiet for a while, sweating in the sun as the boys move the ball down the field. The cheer team shows up, the girls standing right in the middle of the track, causing the cross country team to change their route. The coaches brought a speaker and start playing music while the girls start practicing what I assume is a future halftime routine.

"I sometimes wish I was a cheerleader," Tori says with a sigh.

"I was one in the seventh grade," I tell her, thinking of Beck and how I used to cheer him on back then.

When am I not thinking of Beck?

"It would be impossible to be on the cheer team and play volleyball," Tori continues. "So, no regrets."

"Same for me." The boys jog off the field for a break, many of them grabbing their water bottles and taking long swigs. Beck clutches the hem of his sleeveless T-shirt and lifts it up, wiping what I can only assume is sweat dripping off his jaw.

Gross, right? That's what I try and tell myself.

But my gaze drops to the slice of stomach he's revealing. Even from this distance, I can just make out the trail of dark hair that leads from his navel and disappears into the waistband of his shorts. His flat abs. His biceps flex, and he tips his head back when he drinks from the water bottle he just picked up, the strong column of his neck making me wish I could kiss him right there.

Even if he was sweaty and smelly, I'd do it. Press my lips to warm, salty skin, breathing in his scent. Feel the way his pulse picks up beneath my lips—

"I like Dom." A little sigh escapes Tori. "I'm glad we're

talking and I have a feeling we're going to end up together, which is so exciting. But…"

Her voice drifts and I frown, turning toward her. "But what?"

"Beck Callahan is so freakin' fine I can barely stand it. I mean look at him! He makes drinking water look sexy." Tori waves a hand in Beck's direction.

I can't help but laugh because I was thinking the same exact thing. "I know," I tell her with a wistful sigh. "I know."

CHAPTER 10

ADDIE

"Follow me over to Marisco's?" Liam yells as he approaches me in the parking lot.

I've been waiting for him in my car for the last ten minutes. Everyone else has pretty much left. I'm one of the last cars in the lot, besides Liam's old Toyota truck, sitting not too far from mine.

"Sure," I say as I roll the window up, watching him get into his truck. He's wearing the clothes he had on earlier today and I wonder if he took a shower.

God, I hope so. I really don't want to sit across from a sweaty, smelly boy while I try and eat my dinner.

And Marisco's? Everyone goes there because it's fast and cheap—and delicious—Mexican food. It's right next to the Starbucks in town. The entire strip of businesses and restaurants is always busy, filled with people from school, especially at lunch and after practice.

I'm sure we'll see someone we know. And everyone will see us together. By tomorrow, the word will be out.

Addison and Liam are a thing.

My mind drifts as I follow Liam out of the school parking

lot, remembering how Beck glanced over at me, his gaze narrowed and his face formed into a sexy scowl, when he saw Liam and I chatting directly after practice.

I used to get a little embarrassed when my friends would talk about how sexy someone was. I always thought it sounded so silly and completely over the top. And so...grown up. How could I think someone was sexy when I was only fifteen, sixteen, whatever?

Guess what? Beck Callahan is freakin' sexy. Everything about him just...ugh.

What am I doing having dinner with Liam when he doesn't make me feel even a spark of interest? One pissed-off glare cast in my direction from Beck Callahan and I'm ready to go up in flames.

Clearly, I'm doing something wrong here.

By the time we pull into the parking lot where Marisco's is located, there are hardly any spots left, which fills me with dread. This means all sorts of people are here. I spot more than a few familiar cars.

I'm climbing out of my car when Liam approaches, a contrite expression on his face. "Hey, I know I asked you to dinner, but I just realized I left my wallet in the boys' locker room."

Well, that was stupid. It'll probably be stolen by tomorrow, if he doesn't go get it now.

"You want to go back to school and get it?" I ask.

"Coaches are gone for the night. The locker room will be locked," he answers, shoving his hands in the pockets of his shorts.

"Are you asking me to pay for dinner then?" I ask, a little shocked that he would do this.

It's an accident, I remind myself. Not like he did it on purpose.

He makes a face. "I hate to do this, but I have no money on me."

"It's okay," I reassure him. "No biggie."

Relief spreads across his features. "Thanks for understanding, Addison."

"Sure." I shake my head. "No problem."

We start toward Marisco's and Liam walks ahead of me when he spots one of his buddies. A guy named Danny, who's a year younger than us, is standing in front of the restaurant, a giant burrito wrapped in foil clutched in his hand. Danny grins at him and they slap hands, Liam leaning in close to say something in his ear, making Danny laugh as he glances over at me.

What the hell is that about?

"Want to go inside and order for us?" Liam asks me, as I approach where he's standing with Danny. "I'll take four carne asada tacos."

I glance through the window inside the restaurant and see how busy it is. The line to order is long, and every table is filled, mostly with people from school. "Um, sure?"

"You're the greatest," Liam says, before turning all of his attention to Danny.

Reluctantly, I walk into the restaurant, baffled by how Liam is treating me. Like he doesn't give a crap. He didn't even say please or thank you when he gave me his food order —*that I'm paying for.*

I go to the back of the line and wave hi at a few people I know before I check my phone. Thankfully, the line moves pretty quickly, and there are only two people ahead of me when Marcus walks inside the restaurant, Emma by his side.

"What are you doing here?" Emma asks me before she tilts her head back and gazes adoringly at Marcus.

"I'm grabbing dinner with Liam," I answer. "Remember?"

"Oh. Right." She glances around. "Where is he?"

"Outside with Danny." Marcus jerks his thumb toward the entrance, his gaze meeting mine and a knowing smile curling his lips. "Tell me he didn't get you to pay for his dinner."

I frown. "What are you talking about?"

"Did he pull the, *I forgot my wallet* trick that he usually does?" Emma slaps Marcus' chest, and he glares at her before returning his attention to me. "Sorry. He's only done that like…once."

Uh huh. I get the feeling that I've been totally played.

Once I place my order, I go sit at an empty—but incredibly messy—table. I grab a couple of napkins and wipe the remnants off, glancing out the window. Liam is still outside, talking and laughing with Danny.

Why isn't he inside with me?

Emma leaves Marcus in line and joins me at the table, a sympathetic look on her face. "I'm sorry for what Marcus said. He's just joking."

I lean across the table, lowering my voice. "I don't think he's joking at all. I don't doubt that Liam has pulled this sort of stunt before."

Emma mimics my body posture, her brows lowered in concern. "What kind of stunt?"

"He said he forgot his wallet in the boys' locker room." I can just feel the doubt on my face and it's reflected in Emma's gaze. "I thought it sounded a little suspicious."

A sigh leaves her and she slowly shakes her head. "He doesn't come from the…best family."

"What's that supposed to mean? And how do you know this?"

"I've had him in a few classes over the years, and people talk. His parents divorced when he was little and his mom took off. His dad isn't the greatest. Left him home a lot when he was young, so he got into some trouble when he was fourteen, fifteen. They don't have a lot of money either, so maybe that's why he had to pull the *I forgot my wallet* thing," Emma explains.

"Then why did he ask me to dinner in the first place, if he couldn't afford it? That sucks." My gaze goes to the window, yet again, where he's still standing outside talking to Danny. And a couple of other guys have joined them too. "He's not even sitting with me or talking to me. This isn't a date. This is a guy using me to get a meal."

"Oh, don't judge him too quickly. He's not that bad," Emma says, glancing over her shoulder to also watch him through the window for a few seconds before she turns to face me once more. "Don't be surprised if Danny sits with you guys while you eat. He's been Liam's shadow lately."

Right on cue, Liam and Danny enter the restaurant, Liam smiling when he spots me sitting with Emma. They walk over to our table and settle in, Liam next to me and Danny next to Emma.

"Where's dinner?" Liam asks me, making Danny laugh.

I glare at him. "It's not ready yet."

"Cool." Liam flicks his chin at me. "Mind if Danny chills with us?"

Emma muffles her laughter with her hand.

"Only if Emma and Marcus sit with us too?" I meet her gaze. "You guys want to hang with us?"

"Sure."

"Great." I bare my teeth at all of them, irritated beyond belief.

Beck would never do this to me. If he asked me on a date, he'd actually take me on one. He'd buy my dinner. He'd pay attention to me. My ex was better than this guy. Jonah was fun. He always seemed completely into me, even when his friends were trying to convince him to dump me for a girl in band.

Those band kids really stick together. Just like the jocks stick with the cheerleaders and the smart kids all hang out. Typical high school behavior I guess, breaking off into our little groups.

Marcus makes his way over to the table, giving Danny a dirty look until he gets out of the chair that's next to Emma and goes to find another one.

"How's my girl?" Marcus asks Emma, once he settles into the chair Danny just vacated.

Emma kisses him right on the lips. "I'm good."

I watch them. The way they seem lost in each other's eyes. The possessive way Marcus touches her, as if he owns her. I don't know if I want all that, but I want something close.

Without worrying if my man is cheating on me because, let's face facts—Monique is for sure still in the picture. She'll rear her rotten head back in between their relationship and try to ruin things.

I'm glad Emma and Marcus joined us. They make things a lot less awkward. Liam goes to grab our food, only after Emma kicks him in the shin when our number is called. Once Liam brings the tray to the table, he shares his tacos with Danny while I eat my asada fries, batting Danny's hand away every time he tries to steal one.

What the hell is happening right now?

"I'm having a party," Marcus announces when we're almost done eating.

Liam leans over the table to high five Marcus. "Hell yeah. At your house? When?"

Marcus nods. "Tomorrow night after the scrimmage. My parents are gone all weekend, taking my sister to college. I have the place to myself."

"Do I get to stay the night?" Emma practically coos to Marcus.

He slips his arm around her shoulders, hauling her in

close. "Whatever you want, sexy. You can stay the entire weekend."

"Your parents going to be okay with that?" I ask Emma.

Emma shoots me an irritated look. "I'll just tell them I'm at your house."

"The scrimmage won't last long, which gives us more time to party," Marcus continues. "And my brother is bringing the booze, so we're good."

"Sounds like a bash." Liam kicks my chair leg, jolting me. "You want to come with me? We can ride up together."

I hate that he asked me in front of everyone. I have an audience, which makes me really uncomfortable, especially when I actually want to turn him down. And they're all watching me, waiting for my answer. Talk about awkward. "Uh…"

"We can ride up together, Addie," Emma suggests. "You can ride up with Marcus, Liam."

"I ain't taking this schmuck with me." Marcus points at Liam, who bats his finger away. "He can find his own ride."

"I'll take you up," Danny says to Liam.

The sullen expression on Liam's face tells me he's not happy with the situation but too bad. He really put me on the spot.

Thank God Emma saved me.

"I really need to get home," I say. "I have homework."

"On the first day of school?" Liam's brows shoot up. "Give me a break."

Danny coughs the word "bullshit" into his fist.

I think of what Beck said about me having homework, and how he teased me about it. At least he didn't make me feel bad. Unlike these jerks.

"I have to write that intro paragraph too." Emma turns to Marcus. "I should go."

"Come on. You said we could hang out for a little while

longer." He toys with the strap of her tank top, his touch almost intimate.

Emma pulls away from his hand. "You can have me all weekend. Come on, let's go."

We all toss our trash and walk out of the restaurant together, the warm evening air like a smack in the face after the chilly air conditioning inside. I head straight for my car, not even waiting to talk to Liam, when I hear footsteps coming from behind me.

Turning, I find Liam heading my way, Danny long gone. Marcus and Emma are in Marcus's truck, already pulling out of their parking spot.

"Addie, hey." He stops in front of me. "Sorry about what happened in there."

Is he really sorry? Or is he just sorry I got mad?

"It's fine," I say on a sigh, though it's totally not.

"I'll pay you back for dinner."

"The money isn't the issue."

Liam frowns. "There's an issue?"

I glance around the parking lot, wishing Emma hadn't left. "I don't know if I want to wear your jersey tomorrow."

"Why the hell not?" He rests his hands on his hips. "All because I forgot my wallet and asked you to cover me? I'll pay you back, I swear."

"Marcus mentioned you've done this sort of thing before," I admit.

He's quiet for a moment, his eyes darkening. "Marcus is an asshole."

"Look, whatever. Like I said, that's not the issue. I just think—we're moving way too fast," I say.

"Way too fast? Come on, Addie. Wearing my jersey tomorrow is not a big deal." He rolls his eyes.

To me, it feels like a huge deal. The problem? I don't want

to wear Liam's number. Not when there's another boy whose jersey I'd much rather wear.

But I can't sit around and wait for him forever either.

"Maybe next week," I say to Liam, my tone vaguely pleading. "Tomorrow's game isn't a real one anyway, right? It doesn't even count."

"You've been talking to Callahan too much," Liam mutters. "Fine. Next week. I'm going to hold you to it."

God, I hope not.

"Okay. See you tomorrow?"

"Yeah." He steps forward, grabbing hold of me and pulling me into his arms. I have no choice but to hug him, and while it's brief, it feels like—a lie.

Liam is not the boy I want to hug.

"Bye, Addie. See you tomorrow," he says after he lets go of me.

"Bye." I watch him head for his truck before I slip into my car, slamming the door and exhaling loudly as I lightly bang the back of my head against the seat. Dinner was a disaster. Liam was a jerk, I really don't like his friend Danny, and Marcus isn't that great either. The only person who came through was Emma, and she hasn't done that in a while.

I don't want to have that kind of experience again. I also don't want to give Liam another chance.

He's definitely not for me.

CHAPTER 11

BECK

I show up on campus, fighting the dread that wants to sweep over me. Hoping like hell a certain someone isn't wearing Liam's jersey. When I spot Addie with her friends at the school entrance, I can see she's wearing a navy Badgers T-shirt. Not a jersey, like her friends Emma and Tori have on.

The relief that surges through me nearly has me sagging.

Dom slaps me in the arm with the back of his hand as we make our way through the parking lot. "Happy Friday, asshole. Looks like your girl isn't wearing Snatcher's jersey."

I can't help but chuckle. Dom always calls Liam, Snatcher, and it makes him furious, which only eggs Dom on. "She's not my girl."

Yet.

"Uh huh." Dom pauses, but only for a moment. "Speaking of your girl, how's Sasha?"

"She's definitely not my girl," I say firmly. "And she blocked me on everything, so I have no clue what she's up to. Not that I care."

"I'm sure she did block you, considering who she's been

posting with lately." He sends me a look. "You want to know?"

I consider his question and realize it won't bother me if she's with some guy. I'm over her. I've been over her for a while. "Lay it on me."

"Jayden Mansfield," he admits.

"Her ex?" I'm kind of surprised. I had no idea they were still in contact with each other. "No shit?"

"Yeah. Guess they've been hanging out all week—hanging all over each other too."

"Girl moves fast," I mumble. Back with her first love, I shouldn't be surprised. I'm sure she's already had sex with him. That's great. Good for her.

Fuck. Not that I care, but she didn't even hesitate in getting back together with him. She didn't mourn the loss of our relationship one bit.

I've got no room to talk. I'm not mourning it either. Hell, I'm already plotting how I can get with Addie.

"I don't think Sasha liked being rejected by you, but fuck her, man. She sucks. Forget her." Dom inclines his head toward the three girls we're quickly approaching. "Focus on that girl instead."

"I don't know—" Dom punches me in the arm with what feels like all his strength, making me wince. "Ouch, damn it. What was that for?"

"I'm tired of the doubt, Callahan. You've been tripping over that girl for *years*. As long as I've known you, you've had a thing for Addison Douglas. Well, bro, your time is now. Fuck worrying about ruining your friendship with her, or with Liam. He didn't give a shit that you like her. Why should you give a shit if he likes her?"

"I don't give a shit." I rub my arm where he hit me, the fucker.

"You definitely give a shit about her, and if you guys end

up together and eventually break up, who cares about the friendship? We're graduating this year. You might never have to see her again, if that's your choice."

Why does the idea of never seeing Addie again make my gut clench?

"Make a move, son," Dom continues. "At the party tonight. After our scrimmage."

"What party?"

"Marcus is having a party at his house. His parents are out of town for the entire weekend and his older brother is supplying the booze. We're all pitching in money to help cover the cost. You in?"

"Marcus never mentioned it to me," I say, my gaze snagging on Addie and never wavering. That shirt fits her tight. The fabric stretches across her tits, making them look bigger than normal.

Or are they just that big? Damn.

"Don't be an ass. You're invited. So was Addie."

"How do you know this?"

"Tori told me. And speaking of..." Dom turns up the decibels, striding toward his newfound girl. "Ladies. Victoria."

He wraps her up in a hug and she squeezes him tightly, her arms around his middle. "Victoria? Really, Dominic?"

"We sound very official with the full names, don't you think?" He releases his hold on her to shift her to his side then slips his arm around her shoulders. "Looking good in my jersey, Victoria."

Her cheeks turn pink. Tori is cute. Average height. Long, golden brown hair. Warm brown eyes. A sprinkle of freckles across her nose and an engaging smile. She's looking up at Dom as if he can do no wrong and I wonder what that's like. To have a girl look at you as if you're her absolute favorite thing.

I may have been in a relationship with Sasha, but I don't remember her ever looking at me like that.

"Hey, Tori. Emma." I focus all of my attention on Addie. "Adds."

They all smile at me and say good morning. I tear my gaze from Addie to speak to Emma. "Where's Marcus?"

"Picking up Liam. I guess his truck broke down last night."

"Again?" The truck used to belong to his dad and it's in bad shape. It's given him trouble since he started driving it, and the repairs cost too much for him to afford.

"Yeah, Marcus said the truck is a piece of shit," Emma says, casting an apologetic glance toward Addie. As if she's talking bad about the guy Addie...

Likes?

Please tell me it isn't so. She's not wearing his jersey, which is huge. If she really liked him, that jersey would be on her, no matter what.

"It is a piece of shit," I readily agree. "He's made it work for him for a long time. Since sophomore year, when he first got his license."

Back when we were friends. I don't know when it shifted. Maybe over the summer. The last time he came to my house —I had a pool party celebrating the end of junior year—he kept making snide remarks about me being a rich boy. And while I can fully admit that yep, my parents are wealthy and I'm lucky I don't have to worry about money, I still didn't like how he acted. I've never flaunted my wealth in front of my friends. Most of the time, I share it with them.

It's like resentment toward me built up in Liam, to the point that he's not holding back anymore. He's just letting it all out.

And making me feel like shit about it.

"Are you ready for tonight's scrimmage?" Addie asks me

with a faint smile. "Notice how I called it a scrimmage and not a game?"

I smile at her. "I did. And yeah, I'm ready. I'm always ready."

"You're going to do great," she says. "We're going tonight. To watch you guys."

"You're driving all the way out there?" I raise my brows. Le Grand High School is a solid hour from our town.

"Yeah. I'm going with Emma. She wants to watch Marcus, and Tori wants to support Dom," she says.

"Who are you going to support? Liam?" I brace myself for her answer.

She wrinkles her nose and slowly shakes her head. "No, I don't think that's going to work out, though he still wants it to."

"I thought you two were talking?" I take a few steps closer to her, hoping she'll confess to me exactly what's going on between them.

"We sort of are. I don't know." She glances toward her friends, before grabbing hold of my wrist and tugging me a few steps away from them. Her fingers burn into my skin, sparking heat to flood my veins.

It blows my mind, how her simple touch affects me. Every single time.

"He asked me to go to dinner last night after practice, and it was a total disaster," she admits.

I shouldn't take joy in their disastrous date, but I can't help it. I try to keep my reaction neutral. "What happened?"

"He's just...I don't know. I followed him over to Marisco's and his friend showed up."

"Danny?" I ask.

"Yeah, that's the one. Anyway, when we got there, Liam admitted he forgot his wallet in the locker room."

"Really." My voice is flat. I call bullshit. He's always "forgetting" his wallet.

"Yeah. I mean, if he can't afford to take me to dinner, I don't care. But don't ask me to go out for a meal if you can't afford it, and then ask me to cover you. Plus, he stayed outside and talked to Danny the entire time I stood in line, and paid for his tacos—which he shared with Danny, I might add." She shakes her head, mild disgust on her face. "Thank God Marcus and Emma showed up so I could hang out with them. Emma saved me from having to make awkward conversation with just Liam and Danny, who third-wheeled on our date."

"Sounds like an...interesting night," I say, because how else can I describe it?

Addie laughs, the sound so pretty I just want to soak it up. "It was terrible. Seriously. He didn't text me last night either. Maybe he was embarrassed? I told him I didn't want to wear his jersey because we were moving too fast, but it was just an excuse."

It's as if my ears prick up like a dog's, eager to hear more. "An excuse for what?"

"I don't think I'm interested in Liam. Not like that. He's kind of—rude. And not very respectful," she admits. "I guess you were right when you warned me."

"He revealed himself that quick? Usually he moves a little slower than that," I tell her, fighting the excitement that's building inside of me.

"I didn't really like Danny. He's obnoxious. And if he's Liam's shadow like Emma told me last night, I don't think I want to deal with that, you know?"

"They're together a lot," I agree, as I glance toward the parking lot, where I see Marcus, Liam, and yep, Danny heading toward us. "Like right now."

Addie's gaze follows mine, her face falling a little when she spots them. "Great."

"I've got you," I tell her with a faint smile. "I won't let him say anything shitty."

She smiles up at me. "Thanks, Beck."

I realize I'm running on limited time. I won't be in class today because we're leaving early to head over to the scrimmage. "You going to Marcus's party tonight?"

Addie nods. "Are you?"

"Yeah. Maybe we could—hang out." I want to punch myself in the face for saying something so lame.

Her smile grows. "I'd like that."

Okay. Maybe I wasn't so lame after all.

"Hey, asshats," Liam announces as he joins our group. Talking as if we're still in the locker room, or out at practice. Does he realize he just called all the girls asshats too? The guy is an idiot. "What's up?"

"Your truck take a shit on you again, Snatch?" Dom asks with a chuckle.

Tori smacks him on the chest, murmuring, "Be nice."

Liam's good mood evaporates, just like that. "Yeah. Fucking thing is a hunk of shit. I need new wheels."

"If you'd work a job where you get actual hours, maybe you could find something," Dom says.

I feel like my best friend is giving Liam extra shit on my behalf, which I can't help but appreciate.

"Fuck off, Dominic. I'm not some rich asshole born with a silver spoon in my mouth, like Callahan," Liam says, sending a glare in my direction.

That glare intensifies when he realizes Addie is standing right next to me.

I hold up my hands in front of me in a defensive gesture. "What I'd ever do to you?"

"You were born. That's enough." He laughs, but it's a cruel sound. Danny high fives him.

They're both complete douches.

Addie sends me a look, one that tells me she sees it. And she agrees.

"Too bad you're not wearing my jersey today, Addison," Liam says as he moves to stand right beside her. "My number would look pretty damn good on your chest."

He actually leers at her tits and Danny joins him.

"Anything would look good on that chest," Danny adds.

I can't take it anymore.

"What the fuck, Thatcher? Leave her alone." I turn my glare on Danny. "You too, dickhead."

Danny snaps his lips together and backs away. He's scared of me. Helps that he's a puny junior who I could easily take out.

Liam though? He looks ready to throw down. "Fuck off, Callahan. You can't tell me what to do."

"Liam, get over yourself," Marcus interjects, sending me a look. "And cool down, Beck. I thought you two were supposed to be friends."

"Tell him to get away from my girl and we'll be good," Liam says, gesturing toward Addie, who is gaping at him as if he sprouted two heads.

"I am not your girl, Liam," she says firmly. "You can't claim me."

"Aw, come on Addie. You still pissed about last night? I can pay you back," he practically whines.

I'm actually embarrassed for the guy, having this conversation in front of all of us.

"I don't want your money," she says with a firm shake of her head. "And I definitely don't want you making public claims that I'm your girl. I don't belong to anyone."

"Yeah, Liam, ease up," Emma adds, coming to stand beside

Addie. "You keep this up and she definitely won't want to be with you."

He glances at all of us, Danny at his side. "What the fuck? Are you all conspiring against me? Did you get them all to hate me, Beck?"

"I had zero to do with this," I tell him, disliking how he's trying to pin this on me. "Pretty sure you're doing this all on your own, bud."

"Fuck you," he says to me before he storms off, Danny bravely sending me a dirty look before he goes chasing after his friend.

"Whoa," Dom says after they're gone. "That was kind of intense."

"Can't wait for my party tonight," Marcus says. "Better not start any shit with him, Callahan."

"Definitely won't," I say firmly.

But I can't control Liam, that's for damn sure.

CHAPTER 12

❦

ADDIE

Only the second day of school and I missed having Beck in sixth and seventh period, which is silly. The football team left early to travel to the scrimmage and I stared at his empty seat pretty much the entirety of World Religions, wishing he were sitting next to me. Wishing I could see that warm smile that appeared on his face every time he looked at me.

Am I stupid for thinking something could happen between us? I know for sure he and Sasha broke up, even though I haven't heard the confirmation from him directly. It doesn't matter though. She's making it pretty obvious via her Instagram stories she posts every night of her and her ex, Jayden.

Has Beck seen any of those videos? They're such a big fuck you to him, but he's never mentioned it. Not like he would.

Then there's Liam. He really showed his true colors to me last night and this morning, and it only took a week. He blew up at Beck for no apparent reason and he's just…not the kind of guy I want to go out with. Not even the kind of guy I want to talk to really.

It's unfortunate he's part of the guys' friend group, but if he keeps acting the way he has been, I get the sense he's on his way out. He just seems so angry all the time.

I don't want that kind of energy in my life. I'm trying to focus on positive things. Enjoying my senior year before my entire life changes and I become a so-called adult.

Once school is over, I go home to grab some things before me and Tori head over to Emma's, who invited us to get ready with her before we go to the game together. The girls are still wearing the jerseys to the game, but afterward, they're changing into "party attire," as Tori calls it.

"Gotta look hot for our boys," Tori explains, once we're all at Emma's house and contemplating outfit choices. I've already got my shorts picked out, but I still need to come up with a shirt to wear.

"Marcus says I always look hot," Emma brags, right before she bursts into laughter.

"Who are you cheering on tonight, Addie?" Tori asks, her expression innocent, but I think she knows who I'm cheering on.

The little sneak.

"I don't know," I say with a shrug. "Definitely not Liam."

"Oh my God, wasn't that awful? I don't know what's gotten into him," Emma says, shaking her head.

We talked about the incident briefly during lunch, but then Emma took off with Marcus and God knows what they did together when they disappeared for thirty minutes.

"You've given up on him completely, right, Addie?" Tori asks me as she pulls out an endless pile of various shirts from the bag she brought.

"Yeah, I never really liked him that much in the first place," I admit.

"Who do you like?" Emma asks, her tone vaguely accusing. "Because you certainly haven't mentioned it to me."

Here's my moment of truth. Should I admit it to Emma? She has to know. This has been going on between Beck and me for a while. And Tori figured it out quick. Plus, she's so encouraging.

I don't know if Emma will be as positive.

"I'm thinking...Beck," I admit.

"Yessssss." Tori bounces up and down. "I fully encourage this."

"Really?" Emma's voice is sharp and she trains her gaze on me. "Are you sure, Addie? You two have kind of done this thing before, and nothing ever comes from it."

This right here is why I didn't want to tell her. She discourages me every chance she gets.

"It's our senior year, right? We only live once and I may as well go for it," I say with a shrug, hoping like crazy she'll support me.

I don't like feeling as if I have to keep things from her, which is exactly how I've felt the past week. Not that she's paying attention to me or Tori. She's too wrapped up in being back with Marcus.

"I don't know..." Emma's voice drifts.

"Oh, stop being so discouraging. We only live once. If Addie has been lusting after Beck for years, she should totally try something with him now. If she never takes that chance, then she'll live with regret for the rest of her life. And that's not cool," Tori explains.

"So deep," Emma murmurs, her gaze going from me to Tori. "Feels like you two are talking without me."

I stiffen, but thank God, Tori says something first.

"You're always with Marcus." She shrugs.

Glad she beat me. I would've apologized, when I really have nothing to say sorry for. We're all friends, and we can't control it if she's hanging out with her new/old boyfriend instead of us.

I steer us out of that conversation and focus on getting ready, since we're running out of time. The girls basically force me to wear a pair of shorts that are almost too short. As in, my ass cheeks practically hang out of them and the hem is completely frayed. The sides have working zippers, and I wore the shorts when I went to the beach with my family and Emma over the summer. Mom about had a heart attack when she saw them on me, while Emma cheered me on for wearing them.

I pair it with a soft and faded green T-shirt, so I'm not going full-on skimpy. I've never been comfortable showing a bunch of skin, especially at a party. Sometimes people get drunk and get grabby.

Emma, on the other hand, has no issues with going skimpy to this party. She's wearing a black denim skirt that barely covers her ass and a freaking white tube top. It accentuates her tan nicely, but dang.

"Really, Emma?" Tori asks drolly when Emma models the outfit for us. "That's pushing it, even for you."

"What's wrong? I like it. Plus, easy access." She yanks her tube top down quickly, flashing us and making Tori and I squeal. "God, you two are ridiculous," she says after pulling the top back over her breasts.

"Marcus will die," Tori says.

"That's the point." Emma smirks at me. "And you're going to make Liam regret every decision he's ever made once he gets a look at you tonight."

"I don't want to do that." I glance down at myself. "Actually, I don't want him to notice me at all."

"Those shorts on your long legs are every dude's wet dream." Emma walks over to the full-length mirror propped against her wall and checks herself out.

"You look amazing," Tori reiterates as she tugs on yet another shirt, before going to the mirror to stand behind Emma, trying to see herself. "Don't make her feel bad, Em."

"I'm not trying to. Just stating facts." Emma shifts out of the way of the mirror so Tori can examine herself in her reflection. "I like that shirt best so far."

It's black and cropped and shows a lot of Tori's stomach. She turns this way and that, a small frown forming. "You sure I don't have back fat?"

"You're skinnier than all of us. Give me a break. I wish I was as tall as you guys. And had your tits, Addie."

I glance down at my chest before I return my gaze to hers. "What are you talking about? My tits are nothing spectacular."

Tori glances over at me. "They're pretty spectacular. I don't have any." She grabs hold of her smallish boobs to indicate just that, making me laugh.

"And mine are too big." Emma is practically busting out of that tube top. It's risky, wearing it tonight.

"We are going to a school," I remind her. "Are you sure they won't dress-code you?"

"How are they going to bust me for breaking dress code? I don't even go there." Emma laughs. "You worry too much."

And she doesn't worry enough, though I don't bother mentioning that to her.

"Should we be wearing Badger gear to cheer them on?" I ask.

"Nah." Tori shakes her head. "This game doesn't count, remember? We'll bust out the spirit wear next week when they play their first real game."

"True." I go to the mirror and check myself one last time. My legs do look really long in these shorts.

I hope Beck notices.

I hope Beck likes what he sees too.

* * *

BY THE TIME we arrive at the high school to watch the game, it's already halftime, which annoys me, considering I wanted to leave Emma's house an hour ago. We're late because of Emma, who took forever doing her makeup and hair when Tori and I were ready way before she was.

After we pay to get in, we go sit in the visitor section, waving at a few people we know, though the bleachers are pretty sparsely filled, mostly with parents and families. People won't travel for a scrimmage game and I'm sure everyone is thinking they can come to Marcus' party later and hang out there.

I don't blame them, but I enjoy watching our team play football—specifically Beck. He's so good out on that field. So intense and unafraid of anything. He charges forward every single time the call is made, plowing into the other team's players. Blocking them. Stopping them. Taking them down. It's fun to watch.

"I'm starving," Tori grumbles as we settle onto the hard metal benches that are hot to the touch, thanks to the blinding sun that is aimed right at us. "If we'd left like we originally planned, we could've stopped and got food."

"God, how many times do I need to apologize? Go check out their snack bar," Emma says, waving toward the building in the near distance. There's a line, so they must be selling something.

"I don't want to support their football boosters," Tori says grumpily, propping her elbow on her knee, so she can rest her chin on her fist. "My stomach is literally growling."

"You're such a baby," Emma says as she stands, rubbing her hands across her butt to wipe off any dust. "I'm going to go grab you something."

Tori sits up straight, beaming. "Thank you, Em."

"You want anything?" Emma asks me.

I shake my head and hold up my water bottle. "I'm good, thanks."

Once Emma is gone, Tori kicks out her legs so they rest on the edge of the bleacher below us. "I can't believe we came all the way out here just to go back to Marcus' house."

"You're just hangry," I tell her, knocking my shoulder into hers. "It was nice of Emma to get you something."

"She owes me for making us so late. We paid five bucks to get into the stadium and for what? To watch a lame second half, where they don't even keep score?"

"I'm sure they're winning."

"That's the problem though. We won't even know."

I go silent when I see our team jog back out onto the field. I spot Beck immediately by his number—sixty-four. Though he doesn't have a helmet on, so I definitely recognize his dark hair, the angles of his familiar face. His hair is longer than he usually wears it and he keeps pushing it away from his forehead as he walks the rest of the way to the sideline, Dom right beside him.

"Oooh, there are our boys." Tori sits up straighter, a big smile on her face as she lifts her hand to wave at Dom.

He spots her and smiles, nudging Beck in the ribs with his elbow. Now they're both looking up at us and I sort of want to die, yet I also want to bask in Beck's attention because, from the look on his face, I'm thinking he's pleased to see me.

It's the smile. The way his eyes light up. How he won't stop looking at me.

Makes me feel like I'm the only person out here.

"I don't care what anyone says. That boy is totally into you," Tori murmurs.

"Maybe," I say, not wanting to get my hopes up too high.

But yeah. I'm thinking Tori might be right.

Can't deny how excited that makes me feel either.

The last half goes by quickly. Emma and I share a hot dog while Tori completely demolishes hers. We cheer and scream every time one of our boys runs a touchdown in, which is often. Not that it matters, since there's no score, but we're having a good time yelling and carrying on.

By the time the game is over, we've completely slayed the other team. We run down the sideline of the field, Emma and Tori confident when they approach their boys they're here for, while I hang back, my gaze on Beck and no one else.

Not even Liam, who I can feel glaring at me as he stands with Danny, both of them eventually giving up and heading for the bus that will take our team home.

"Adds." Beck walks straight up to me, his hair sweaty and sticking every which way and there's a smudge of dirt on his cheek. "You came."

"I said I would." I smile up at him. "You played well."

"Even if it was a scrimmage?" His eyes gleam and I know he's teasing me.

"You guys definitely won," I reassure him.

"Oh I know. I was keeping track. Up here." He taps his temple again, like he did yesterday.

I can't believe that moment was only yesterday. It feels like a lot has happened. A lot has changed in the past forty-eight hours. Crap, I went on a date with Liam last night.

And it was awful. I don't even want to think about him right now.

"Damn those shorts make your legs look long," Beck says, his gaze appreciative as he scans me.

My skin grows warm and I suddenly feel shy. The shorts are totally pushing it. I'd get dress-coded immediately if I wore these to school. "It's hot," I offer up as a lame excuse.

"I'll say." He grins, looking so pleased with himself I can't help but laugh.

"Uh huh."

"I'm not complaining. You've got—really nice legs." He shakes his head. "That sounded stupid."

"No, it really didn't," I say softly, my gaze never straying from his. I want him to keep saying stuff like that. Maybe I should compliment him too. "I like your hair."

He runs his hand over it, making a bigger mess of the sweaty strands. "It's out of control."

"I like it longer." I wouldn't mind running my fingers through it. See if it's as soft as it looks.

"I was thinking about getting a haircut. My mom said I should."

"No, don't do it," I say way too quickly, my cheeks immediately going hot. "Not yet."

His smile grows. "I'll tell my mom you don't approve."

I sort of want to die right now. I also want to bask in his attention under the Friday night lights for a little bit longer. He looks so good in his uniform. Big and imposing.

"I want a photo of you two!" I hear Tori shout from behind me.

I turn to see her headed in our direction, waggling her eyebrows at me like some sort of co-conspirator. "You do?"

"Oh yes. I definitely do. Beck, stand next to Addie." Tori stops right in front of us, holding her phone out.

He does as he's told, slinging his arm loosely around my shoulders as he tugs me in close to his side. I go to him, sliding my arm around his lower back, surprised by how warm and solid he feels. "Like this?" he asks Tori.

"Perfect." I can tell Tori is taking a bazillion photos, and I feel my smile grow. "You two look cute together."

Okay, I want to die again.

"You smell good," Beck murmurs, low enough that only I can hear.

And now I want to die for a totally different reason.

"But you always smell good so this isn't a surprise." He

squeezes my shoulder before he lets go of me, stepping away. "I'll see you at the party, right?"

I nod, feeling weak. "Yeah."

"Who knows when we'll show up, since we have to ride the bus. Marcus' brother came to the scrimmage though, and he's taking him home," Beck explains. "I'm sure Emma will know when you can head over to his house."

"Oh, I'm sure." I wave at him like a dork. "See you soon."

"Bye, Adds."

The moment he's out of earshot Tori is squealing as she grabs hold of my arm and squeezes it so tight, it hurts. "Oh my God, you two are so adorable together! Wait until you see the photos."

I hold my hand out, wanting her to give me her phone. "Let me look at them now."

"Nope." Tori hides her phone behind her back. "You can look at them in the car."

"Where is Emma anyway?" I glance around the mostly empty field, not spotting her or Marcus.

"God knows. Maybe she's in a dark corner with Marcus, giving him a quickie hand job." Tori rolls her eyes and hooks her arm through mine, steering me toward the direction of the parking lot. "Come on, let's go wait for her by the car."

It takes Emma an extra ten minutes after we get to her car before she finally appears, which gives me just enough time to scroll through Tori's phone, looking at all the photos she took of me and Beck. Some of them are terrible. My eyes are closed or I'm making a weird face as she catches me talking.

But some of them are really good. We're both looking in the camera, standing so close, his arm around my shoulders and an easy smile on his handsome face. There's one photo in particular though, that I can't stop staring at. I'm smiling at the camera, but he's looking at me, his lips quirked up, his gaze eating me up while I'm completely oblivious.

"That's the money shot," Tori whispers to me as Emma heads our way. "Look at how he's watching you. That boy is in loooove."

I shove at her, making her laugh, and Emma wants to know what the joke is, but I keep it to myself.

I'm making Tori Airdrop every single one of those photos to me so I can keep them.

Forever.

CHAPTER 13

BECK

We show up to the party late. It's already in full swing when Dom and I pull up in my 4Runner. There are all kinds of people hanging out in the front yard, most of them with red solo cups clutched in their hands because Marcus' brother got him a couple of kegs for the party.

"Looks dope," Dom announces when I cut the engine. "What's the plan tonight?"

"What do you mean?"

"You've usually got a plan. Back when you were with Sasha and we'd come to some party with her tagging along, you'd always strategize with me before we went inside." He tilts his head to the side. "Is that over now that Sasha is out of the picture?"

I don't even remember wanting to strategize about anything. "Do you want to strategize?"

He shrugs. "Sure. My plan is—I'm going to work my hardest to get my hands in Tori's panties tonight."

I chuckle. "Okay."

"What about you? Whose panties are you going in search of?"

My mind goes to Addie in those shorts with the zippers on the sides. I want to test them, see if they work. And if they do, I want to see how high they go up, and what I might discover under those shorts.

"Addie's," I admit.

"That's my boy." Dom holds his hand up for a high five and I give it to him. "When you were with Sasha, you always talked to me before we went to a party about watching out for her drinking, remember?"

"Oh." I make a face. "Right."

I sort of forgot how drunk Sasha would always get. Sloppy. Messy. Angry. That was Sasha's mode at any get-together where alcohol was involved. Little miss perfect at school would turn into a raging bitch at parties if she consumed too much.

And she always had a way of consuming too much. That's why, eventually, I got Dom involved and he would help keep an eye on her when I couldn't.

"She's not your problem anymore, though. Thank God," Dom says. "Saw you taking photos with Addie on the field after the game. Tori planned all that, you know?"

"I want to see them." I want to keep a few too.

"I'll make sure she shows them to you." He reaches for his door handle. "Let's head inside."

We climb out of the car and I lock it, brushing a hand through my hair, hoping like hell it looks good. After what Addie said, I'm more conscious of how I look tonight. I wore my favorite North Face T-shirt and khaki Dickie shorts, a gold chain around my neck that my parents got me last Christmas.

"Nice jewels." Dom reaches out and slips his finger

beneath my necklace. I flinch before I swat his hand away. "Flexing the gold?"

"Marcus wears three chains around his neck," I say in defense of myself as we walk toward the house. I can hear music playing, and I wonder what his parents' neighbors think of this.

Hope we don't get ratted out to the cops and they show up, ruining our night.

"You bunch of pretty boys." He laughs. "I'm the guido who should be rockin' the chains. My grandpa has so many photos of himself back in the '70s with his hairy chest exposed and thick gold chains around his neck."

I don't bother saying anything in response. Dom is making me feel dumb for wearing the necklace, but I blame it on me being extra sensitive tonight. Too damn worried over what Addie might think.

The moment we enter the house and everyone shouts their greetings at us, my worry eases. Tori practically runs to Dom, wrapping him up in a big hug and nearly spilling her beer all over his shirt.

I glance around the crowded room, looking for Addie, and when I spot her, anger fills me when I see who she's talking to. Or more like, who's talking to her.

Fucking Liam, with Danny right by his side.

Moving through the clusters of people, I head straight for them, Liam spotting me first, a nasty sneer forming on his face.

"Coming to infringe on my territory, Callahan?" he practically yells.

Addie glances over her shoulder with wide eyes, relief filling them when she spots me. "Hey, Beck."

"Hey." I stand right next to her, my arm back around her shoulders in a protective gesture. "Are they bothering you?"

"Jesus, we were just talking." Liam rolls his eyes. "No need to get all territorial. Don't forget I was the one who took her to dinner last night."

"You mean you're the one who took advantage of her when she bought your meal?" I throw back at him, tucking her more closely to me. "Give me a break."

Liam's expression hardens. "Who the hell said that?" His gaze drops to Addie. "Did you tell him?"

I tighten my arm around Addie's shoulders. "Keep her out of this."

Liam's gaze flicks up to mine. "Why don't *you* stay out of this. We had a good thing going until you pushed yourself into the middle of it."

"Too late. I'm already in it." I smile, feeling like a smug asshole as I say, "Face it, Snatcher. You lost this round."

Liam rears back, his gaze narrowed. "You are such an asshole, Callahan. She's going to see right through your good boy act and when she realizes what she lost, I'm going to be long gone." He smacks Danny in the chest as he turns to leave. "Come on, let's go."

We watch them leave, Addie swooping out from under my arm, so she can turn to face me. "He lost this round? Does that mean you win?"

Oh shit.

Addie looks kind of pissed.

"I just said that to make him walk. And look." I wave a hand in the direction he took off in. "It worked."

She rolls her eyes. "I'm not some prize for you two to fight over."

"I didn't mean it like that." I grab her hand and pull her to me, noticing how she doesn't resist. "Come on, Adds. I don't want to fight with you. I'm sorry I said all that shit. I was just trying to piss Liam off, not you."

Addie contemplates me, her fingers curling around mine, making sparks shoot up my arm. What the fuck am I going to do if I actually get to hold her in my arms? Kiss her? I'll probably drop dead from pure fucking joy.

"I didn't know you had it in you to be so..." Her voice drifts.

"So what?" I tug her even closer, until her body bumps against mine. Marcus' house is pretty small and it's crammed with people, which means we're already standing pretty close. It's only going to get worse as the night goes on. But I'm not complaining if it means I get to be this close to Addie all night.

"Territorial," she says, her gaze scanning my face. "It's a new side of you I haven't seen before."

"I was just matching his asshole energy," I mutter.

She laughs. "You're not an asshole, Beck."

Liam was most definitely giving off asshole vibes though, the fucker. I'm done thinking about him.

I want to focus on the pretty girl in front of me instead.

Addie is giving me a different kind of energy tonight than usual. She seems more open. A little flirtier. Her gaze is warm and she's not pulling away from me. Our bodies are pressed together and our hands are still linked—it feels intimate.

I like it.

"What was he saying to you anyway?" I ask, reaching out and tucking a strand of dark hair behind her ear.

A shiver moves through her. I actually felt it. "He was just trying to convince me to give him another chance."

"Were you tempted?" My gaze zeroes in on her lips and stays there. They're lush and pink and so damn pretty.

Jesus, I'm getting carried away. And I haven't even had anything to drink yet.

"Not even close." Her smile is small. "I don't like Liam."

"Who do you like then?" I lean into her, fucking tempted to kiss her.

Not here though. Not now, in front of everyone. My first kiss with Addie needs to be special.

Private.

Her gaze lingers on mine. "I think you know."

"Guyyyyyyyys!"

We both jolt and turn to see Tori heading our way, a red Solo cup in each hand. "You don't have drinks! I brought these for you!"

I take one from her and so does Addie, who grimaces when the beer spills on her hand. "Thanks, Tor."

"My pleasure." Tori beams at us and glances around, before returning her gaze to me. "I want you to know that I'm not going to drink like I did the last time you saw me at a party."

"Good to know," I tell her before I take a sip of mostly foam.

"And I'm sorry if I freaked you out when I threw up everywhere. It was gross, I know." Her expression is solemn, and I almost want to laugh.

"It's okay, Tori. Really." I contemplate her. "Hey, I know how you can make it up to me."

"Make what up?" Tori frowns.

"When you threw up at my party." I lean against the wall behind me and take another sip of my foamy beer. "You can send me all of those photos you took of me and Adds on the football field."

"Adds? That's so cute." Tori sends Addie a knowing smile. "You don't need my help there—*Adds* can give you all of them. I Airdropped the photos to her earlier."

"Oh, so you've already got the photos, huh?" I smile at Addie.

She nudges me. "I can send them to you."

"You two are so cute in practically every single photo," Tori gushes. "You guys would make *such* an adorable couple."

139

"Tori, oh my God, stop." Addie's cheeks are crimson.

I laugh and shake my head. "Tori, I like you. And I like the way you think. Keep talking."

"See, Addie? I told you he likes you. Hey!" Tori yelps when Dom approaches her from behind, wrapping his arms around her. "Where's my beer?"

"You don't need any more beer right now. Pace yourself." Dom drops a kiss on her cheek. "What are you guys talking about anyway?"

"How cute they are." Tori waves a hand at me and Addie.

"They are pretty cute," Dom agrees, which earns him an eye roll from me. "You know what's not cute? How Marcus and Emma are fighting in the kitchen."

Addie frowns. So does Tori.

"What do you mean they're fighting?" Addie asks.

"It's just a little argument. Nothing too major. But it's over Monique, who just showed up." Dom makes a face. "I guess homeboy invited her."

"Oh shit." Tori's eyes go wide.

Addie groans. "I do not need the drama tonight."

"What do you mean?" I ask her.

"Emma will get drunk and she'll cry and I'll have to console her while she complains about Marcus and what an asshole he is for the rest of the night. All while I'll have to hold back saying to her, 'I told you so,' which a person never wants to hear," Addie explains.

"You just described that nightmare scenario perfectly," Tori says.

"Let's get out of here then," I say to Addie.

"What do you mean? You just showed up," she protests.

"I don't mean we'll actually leave. Let's go sit in my car for a while. Away from all the noise and people." I glance to my right to find Tori and Dom already wandering off, lost in conversation with each other. "What do you think?"

"I think that sounds nice." Addie smiles at me and I swear to God, my heart just skipped a beat.

I've got it so damn bad for this girl.

"That way Emma won't find you if shit really blows up between her and Marcus." I pause, realizing I sound like an asshole. "Unless you want her to find you. Because she's your best friend and all that."

"No, actually, I really don't want to be found by Emma," she admits with a wince. "Not tonight."

"Perfect." I smile and take her hand, interlacing her fingers with mine. "Then let's go."

CHAPTER 14

ADDIE

*B*eck grabs himself two bottles of beer and a cherry flavored Truly for me from the fridge in the garage before we escape Marcus' house. The air outside is still warm, but definitely cooler than inside, which is already packed with way too many people.

"Much better outside," Beck says as we walk toward his brand-new 4Runner. It gleams from the moon shining above it, and I'm about to go to the passenger side door when Beck slowly shakes his head. "Let's sit in the back."

"Okay."

I follow him to the back of the vehicle and he pulls out his key fob, hitting a button so the rear door slowly lifts up, revealing the back of his car. "This is nice," I tell him.

He sets his beer bottles on the floor before he pulls out the sliding deck and then leans inside, grabbing what turns out to be a blanket. He shakes it out and drapes it over the car's interior before he turns to me and holds his hand out toward the back end of his vehicle. "Have a seat."

"Why thank you." I settle on the edge, my feet dangling as I grab my Truly and crack it open. Beck settles in right next to me, the car dipping from his weight, his shoulder brushing against mine. "I like your car."

"Thanks. My dad wants to steal it from me." He twists the cap off the first beer and brings the bottle to his lips, taking a long pull from it.

I watch him drink in open fascination, not hiding my interest like I usually do. Something must be seriously wrong with me when I find the way a guy *drinks* is sexy.

But of course, it's not just any guy—it's Beck.

"What do you mean, your dad wants to steal it from you?" I ask, trying to focus on something else. Not the way Beck's neck looks with his head tipped back. Or how tempted I am to kiss him there. Breathe in his spicy cologne. Touch his soft hair…

"He wishes it belonged to him. We took it up a few trails over the summer and it handles great. Mom went with us once, but she clutched the grab handle the entire time, screaming how we were going to tip the 4Runner over." Beck shakes his head. "It sucked."

I laugh. "I'd probably do the same thing."

He glances over at me. "You don't like driving off-road? Going four-wheeling?"

"I've never done it before," I admit.

"I'll have to take you sometime," he says, his voice full of promise.

"Okay." I take another sip from my Truly to hide my giddiness.

We're quiet for a moment, both of us drinking, a warm breeze washing over us, ruffling his hair, so it falls across his forehead. My fingers itch to push it back, but I contain myself. Barely.

"I'm sorry Liam was bugging you earlier," Beck finally says.

"It's not your fault. I'm the one who went out to dinner

with him," I say, the memories of last night hitting me all over again. "It was so awful, with Danny tagging along and Liam barely talking to me. I don't understand him."

"I don't either. I wouldn't want anyone else with us if we went on a date." Beck glances over at me, his gaze serious. "I'd want to keep you all to myself."

The longer he looks at me, the warmer my skin gets, until I have to look away first, a secret smile curling my lips.

When I chance another look at him, I see he's got the same little smile on his face too.

"What's up with you and Emma anyway?" Beck asks when I remain quiet.

I frown at his change of subject. "What are you talking about?"

"Like you wanting to hide from her just now," he says. "Are you guys not getting along?"

"We always get along, it's just…" My voice drifts and I shrug then take another drink to stall for time as I think of how to put my feelings into words. "She can be very—self-absorbed sometimes, especially when she's in a relationship. And she's a little mean toward us when we don't give her the attention she wants. But I find her relationship with Marcus exhausting. They tried being together last year and it didn't work. Why do they think it's going to work now? He treats her terribly, and you know he's still hooking up with Monique. Or if he's not at the moment, he will be."

"Yeah. This is where I admit Marcus isn't so loyal when it comes to girlfriends," Beck says. "I don't know why he tries to be in a relationship when he always fails. He should just stay single and do what he normally does. Hook up with a variety of girls and not commit to any of them."

I wonder if that's Beck's mode this year, after being in a serious relationship for most of our junior year with Sasha. Crap, he only just broke up with her a few days ago. Maybe he thinks being in a serious relationship is stifling and he'd prefer to be single.

"I don't think Emma ever got over him when they broke up the first time," I continue. "She's still in love with him, and pretty sure he knows it. She'll do anything to get back together with him. Maybe even tolerate him cheating on her. God, I hope not."

"That sucks. Cheating sucks." Beck takes another swig from his beer. "I couldn't do it."

"Uh...we almost did," I admit, my voice so low I wonder if he can hear me.

But he heard me. His brows draw together as he turns to look at me. "What do you mean?"

"When we almost—kissed in the bathroom last year. At that party," I remind him. "You were with Sasha. I was with Jonah."

God, did he forget about that incident? If so, how embarrassing. I should've never brought it up.

His gaze drops to my lips, as if he's contemplating kissing me at this very moment. "Oh. Right."

"Right," I echo, wondering if that's disappointment in his voice.

"I remember that." He stares straight ahead as he shifts his position, making the back end of the 4Runner rock. "Here's the deal, Adds. I might've been with Sasha, but I thought about you. All the time."

I go still, my brain scrambling, trying to compute what he just said to me. "*What?*"

Beck slowly swivels his head to look at me yet again, his expression dead serious. "It's true. I fucking blew it all the time when it came to you. I don't know if I didn't come on strong enough or what, but I was totally into you. For like, years. And every time I would say something to you or act a certain way around you, you never caught my vibe or whatever."

"I didn't?"

He chuckles. "No, you didn't. You friend-zoned me every chance you got."

"I-I never meant to do that," I admit, feeling stupid.

Feeling like we just wasted a lot of time.

"You didn't?"

I shake my head. "That time when you asked me to help you find a gift for Sasha and we went to Urban Roots and you bought me that candle..."

"Yeah, that was a moment where I should've just admitted to you how I felt then," he says. "I thought you could tell. I bought you that candle, which was a way more expensive gift than the hat I got for Sasha. The way you kept sniffing it, I knew you liked that candle."

"I did. I still do. I haven't burned it yet."

"You haven't?"

"It sits on my nightstand. I like to smell it, but I'm afraid once I burn it and it's gone, I'll miss it." Oh does that sound stupid, but it's true. I'll miss the one gift Beck got for me.

The only gift Beck has ever given me.

"I'd buy you another candle," he says with a small smile.

"Promise?" I'm teasing him.

Flirting with him.

"Definitely." He drains the last of his beer before he sets the empty bottle behind him in the car. "Sasha and I weren't even together when you helped me out that time. I tried to ask you to lunch or coffee or whatever, but you turned me down. I figured that was it. You weren't interested in me beyond friendship."

My heart sinks. I knew I messed up that moment, but I didn't realize I messed it up that badly.

"You were trying to ask me on a date?"

He groans. "See? I fucked it up so bad, you couldn't even tell I was trying to ask you out."

"You didn't mess it up," I reassure him. "More like I'm totally clueless."

"Are you clueless right now?" His gaze finds mine again. "Or do I need to explain myself further?"

"I think I need you to tell me what you mean." I really need to hear him say the words.

To my face.

He scoots closer, his thigh pressing against mine, and I can feel the hairs on his leg tickling the outside of my thigh, reminding me of how very masculine he is. My chest aches and I realize I'm holding my breath, waiting for him to say something.

"I like you, Addie. I've liked you since the sixth grade." He dips his head, a single chuckle escaping him, as if he can't believe he just confessed that. He faces me once more, his expression so earnest. "I knew you didn't want to ruin our friendship, and I'm guessing you still feel that way but...fuck. That's half the reason why I'm drawn to you. You're easy to talk to, and you laugh at my jokes, when no one else thinks I'm funny. Sometimes it feels like you know me better than anyone."

My heart is hammering so hard, I swear it's going to burst out of my chest. I've been waiting for this moment for what feels like years.

And it turns out he has, too. I can barely wrap my head around what he's confessing to me right now.

Car lights suddenly flash across us and we both look in the direction of the vehicle approaching, the headlights so bright, I'm momentarily blinded. The car passes us by parking on the other side of the driveway and then the engine cuts off. All four doors swing open.

"I can't believe I'm going to a high school party."

It's Sasha who says that as she climbs out of the car.

"Please. You literally just graduated two months ago," says one of her friends, the two of them laughing.

"Oh shit." Beck's eyes go wide. "Come on. We need to hide before she sees me."

We scramble into the back of the car, Beck hitting the key fob so the hatch door closes, but the interior light above us is still on. Beck reaches up and hits the switch, shutting the light off, and we're shrouded in darkness.

We hear the crunch of footsteps on the gravel driveway and I glance over at Beck, who brings his finger to his lips, indicating he wants me to be quiet.

No problem. I'm not about to try and catch Sasha's attention.

"Look, Beck's here. There's his car," says another girl as they walk past the 4Runner. "You going to talk to him?"

Sasha laughs. "No way. He's just a little boy. Now that Jayden and I are back together, I know what it's like to be with a real man."

Ouch. That was such a bitchy thing to say.

"High school boys. They're the worst," says the friend. Her name is Laura. She graduated with Sasha. Meaning they're barely out of high school themselves.

"Right? Beck is a scared little baby. He'll probably be a virgin until he's in college. Maybe longer," Sasha says, her tone vicious.

The girls laugh and laugh as they keep walking, until we can't hear them any longer.

Well.

That was freaking awkward.

A sigh leaves him, once they're gone, and he leans against me, his arm pressed to mine. "She hates me."

"I think so," I agree.

"Talking shit every chance she gets," he mutters.

"Who broke up with who?" I ask.

"I broke up with her. She's leaving for college anyway, and we were losing interest in each other. Ever since prom night..." He goes quiet and shifts away from me, though I can still feel his warmth. His presence.

The back of the 4Runner might be roomy, but it's still pretty cramped with both of us crammed in here, especially Beck, since he's so broad.

"What happened on prom night?"

"I don't want to talk about it. Or talk about her. She's not worth wasting words on." He turns to me, his hand suddenly on my waist, his finger hooking into the belt loop of my shorts as he tugs me closer. "I have a question."

"What is it?" I'm breathless when he wraps his arm around my waist, his fingers at my hip, trailing down the side of my shorts.

"Do these zippers actually work?" He traces his finger down the length of one of them, until he's touching my bare thigh.

His quick change of subject has my head spinning. Or maybe it's the fact that his fingers are on my skin.

My thigh.

Whatever's happening, I can barely form words. "Y-yes. They do."

He shifts even closer to me, his fingers trailing along my neck. Across my jaw. Until he slips them beneath my chin, tilting my head up so our eyes connect. His are dark, his lips parted, before he presses them together and visibly swallows. "Stop me right now if you don't want this to happen, Adds. If you want to keep us as just friends."

When he touches the corner of my mouth with his thumb, my eyes fall closed and I part my lips. He slowly drags his thumb across my lower lip, as a shaky exhale leaves me.

"I've thought about this for a long time," he admits. "What it would be like, to kiss you."

He's killing me with his words. With the fact that he still hasn't kissed me yet.

I can hear and feel him shift closer. "You still haven't said anything yet."

I crack my eyes open to find him startlingly close. "I'm not stopping you."

There's no hesitation. He leans in, his mouth, almost but not quite, touching mine. I can feel the warmth of his breath, our noses brushing as he settles his hand on the side of my face, his thumb lightly pressing into my cheek.

He guides my face up, and our lips brush once. Twice, lingering for a beat. He pulls away first, only to return and kiss me again.

And again.

Tingles spread all over my skin and I part my lips. He does too, dragging his soft, full mouth against mine, pausing as he exhales slowly. Softly. I kiss him back, or maybe he kisses me. I'm not sure.

I can't tell anymore.

All I know is that I'm finally kissing Beck Callahan.

And it's just as good as I thought it would be.

CHAPTER 15

BECK

I forget all about the zippers on the sides of Addie's shorts. All I can concentrate on is her lips. How she parts them so easily for me, and I go for it, darting my tongue between them, touching hers before I retreat. Only to do it again. Until our tongues are sliding against each other, tangling together.

I can't get enough of her.

She scoots closer, her hand coming up to settle at my nape of my neck, her fingers sliding into my hair, tugging until it almost hurts. It's awkward as fuck in the back of my 4Runner and my legs are already starting to cramp up, but I can't worry about that right now.

All I can focus on is touching and kissing Addie.

It goes on for minutes. Our lips connecting. Breaking apart for only a moment, before returning to each other. I tilt her head back with a gentle shift of my hand, a soft sigh leaving her when I nibble on her lower lip. A quick, gentle bite.

I want to devour her. Explore her body with my hands,

touch her everywhere, but I'm careful. I don't want to push her too far, too fast.

But everything inside of me is repeating, *go, go, go,* like it's my new mantra, and to test things out, I brush my thumb just under her left tit, wondering if she'll push me away.

She doesn't. Not even close. She actually thrusts her chest into my hand, her arms tightening around my neck as if she doesn't want to let me go. Somehow, I guide us, so we're lying on the floor side by side, facing each other, our mouths still connected. My hand at the small of her back, holding her, but not pulling her too close.

I'm already hard. I don't remember responding this quickly with Sasha. Ever. But fuck, I'm willing to take it as far as Addie will let me. The question is…

Will she let me?

I break the kiss first, exhaling against her neck, and I feel her tremble. Brushing her hair out of the way, I drop little kisses along her throat, breathing into her ear before I press my mouth against it and tug on the lobe with my teeth.

She hisses in a breath when I bite her and I pull away, so I can look into her eyes. She stares at me, her lips swollen and damp, her breathing erratic.

I trace her lower lip with my index finger and she tilts her head back, closing her eyes as her lips part and she licks the tip of my finger.

Fuck. That was hot.

A jolt of electricity races through me, settling in my balls as I remove my fingers and return my lips to hers, my tongue thrusting, searching her mouth. She moans, scooting closer, her arm going around my waist as she grips the hem of my T-shirt.

I roll us over, so she's on her back and I'm above her, my chest pressed against hers, our mouths still connected. If I shift over her, she'll feel what she's doing to me and I'm not about to scare her. I don't want to push her too far either.

But it's like I can't help myself, and the next thing I know, I've got my hand beneath her shirt and on her bare stomach. My fingers tracing slow circles just above her belly button. Her skin is so soft and warm, and she smells so fucking good.

I can't get enough of her.

She curls her fingers around my shoulders and at one point, I think she's going to push me away, but instead, she pulls me closer, her palms sliding down my chest before she circles her arms around me, her hands sprawled across my back. I want to feel her hands on my skin. Pulling off my shirt.

Slow the fuck down, I remind myself.

It's hard, though, when I've got the girl of my dreams in my arms and she's so damn responsive. Every little sigh and whimper she makes is like a shock to my system, electrifying me. And when I slip my hand beneath her shirt to play with the lace that trims the bottom of her bra, she breathes my name into my mouth.

I end the kiss, blinking my eyes open, and she does the same. "You want me to stop?"

She slowly shakes her head, lifting up to press her mouth to my chin, dropping sweet little kisses that seem innocent along my jaw, but damn.

They don't feel *that* innocent.

I close my eyes, a wave of pleasure sweeping over me so intense, I can barely stand it.

This is what she does to me. How much power she has over me. My breaths come faster. Heavier. I swallow hard, trying to regain some control, but it's no use.

I'm this close to losing it.

All over her.

"I don't want you to stop," she whispers, once she gets to

my ear, and a deep, growling noise, I'm pretty sure I've never made before, leaves me as I grab her by the waist and forcefully position her, so she's lying directly beneath me. She automatically spreads her legs, accommodating me as I position myself in between them and her eyes fly open when she feels me pressed against her.

"Um…" She swallows and a little smile plays upon her lips, her eyes wide. "Wow."

I lean over her, pressing my forehead against hers as I thrust my hips, nice and slow. Fuck that felt so good, I do it again, vaguely worried I'll blow in my shorts, which would completely suck. "That's what you do to me."

Her gaze darkens and she slips her hand beneath my shirt, her fingers brushing against my abs, the muscles contracting from her fleeting touch. "Maybe you should take off your shirt."

I rise up so fast at her suggestion that I bump my head against the roof of the car. "Ow."

She laughs, her eyes sparkling as I rub the top of my head, drinking her in. She looks so pretty lying beneath me. Her cheeks are flushed and her hair is spread out everywhere.

Damn. I can't believe I've got Addie like this. I never thought this moment would happen.

I whip my shirt off as fast as possible, her eyes going wide as she drinks in my naked chest. She reaches out and settles her hand on my stomach and I close my eyes, wishing she was touching something else.

"Your abs are unbelievable," she whispers reverently as her hand drifts upwards, fingers lightly tracing the ridged muscle there. "Are you even real?"

"Yeah." My voice is rough and I grab her hand, bringing it to the center of my chest, letting her feel my racing heart. "Feel that? I'm pretty fucking real right now."

She lightly strokes her nails against my skin, and I close

my eyes, savoring the sensation of her touching me, my breath hitching in my throat.

I lower myself over her, tempted to pull her shirt off, but something tells me I should wait. I stare into her eyes, notice how flushed her cheeks are, her lips swollen, thanks to our kissing, and I touch her cheek. Trace her lower lip. "You're so beautiful, Adds."

She blinks, her expression full of surprise, and I wonder if anyone has ever told her that before. Did that asshole ex of hers ever mention it? Her beauty is all I can see. All I've ever been able to see since we were fucking twelve years old.

"Beck—" she starts, but I shush her, pressing my fingers against her lips.

"I've been watching you since we were twelve. I've been wanting you since then too, I just didn't know it. Or understand it."

Her eyes are wide as she listens to me, her lips trembling beneath my fingers.

"I don't want to push you into anything you don't want to do," I whisper. "We should probably slow down."

Reluctantly, I remove my fingers from her lips, our gazes still locked, my chest brushing against hers every time we breathe. She reaches for me, gripping my bare shoulders, her fingers digging into my hot skin, and I press my lips together to stifle the moan that wants to leave me.

"I don't want to slow down," she whispers.

I have no control over myself. Next thing I know, our lips are fused and my hands are beneath her T-shirt, cupping her tits, thumbs rubbing over satin and lace. The kiss we share is wild. All tongues and teeth and open, wet mouths. Our lower bodies grind against each other and the interior of my 4Runner is stifling hot.

She winds her legs around my hips and I thrust against her. Up and down. Up and down. Fuck, we're dry humping in the back of my car and it feels so good, I'm pretty sure I'm going to come in my shorts.

Addie reaches in between us, her fingers brushing against my dick and I can't help myself, I groan. The sound must embolden her because she does it again, her fingers curling around me, stroking. I push into her hand, an agonized sound leaving me and I'm sad as shit when her hand leaves me...

Only for it to slip beneath the front of my shorts, her fingers finding my cotton-covered dick.

Her boldness is a surprise. Addie's usually so subdued. Maybe that means she wants me as badly as I want her.

I roll us over, so we're on our sides, facing each other, and I reach for one of those zippers on the side of her shorts, testing if it works like she said.

It does, the fabric separating all the way up to the waist-band of her shorts. I break away from her lips, so I can stare at the exposed spot, her tanned, tone skin.

Is she wearing panties?

I decide to try and find out.

With shaky fingers, I settle my hand on the outside of her thigh, slipping my fingers beneath the parted denim, sliding around the curve of her bare ass. All the blood seems to surge to my dick when I touch her there, my fingertips finally making contact with the thin fabric barely covering her ass.

She's wearing a thong. Fuck, of course she is.

I grip a handful of flesh, making her moan, then I gentle my hold, lightly tracing her skin with my fingers, memorizing the lush softness. I tug her close, until our legs are tangled, and she hikes one leg over my thighs, opening herself to me. I slide my fingers down, brushing my knuckles against the damp fabric covering her pussy.

A whimper leaves her and I do it again. Rubbing her. Kissing her. She's touching me too. Pretty sure we're trying to drive each other insane, I swear to God, and when I sneak one finger beneath the fabric to find her molten hot and so damn wet, it's my turn to groan.

"Beck." She bites out my name on a moan as I continue exploring her folds, sliding my finger over her clit. I don't have much experience with this, but I can figure it out.

All I really want to do is make her feel good.

Somewhere I hear a ringing, but I ignore it. Instead, I dip my head and press my mouth to Addie's neck, breathing her in as I continue to stroke her. She moves with my hand, pushing her hips forward, as if she's seeking more, which is confirmation that she likes it.

The ringing starts again, a little louder this time, and I lift my head away from Addie's neck, listening. "Someone's calling."

"Ignore them," she murmurs, just as she gives my dick a firm squeeze.

My eyes nearly cross, her fingers on me feel so fucking good.

I try to do as she says and ignore it, but the phone literally won't stop ringing. And ringing.

To the point that I can't take it any longer.

"Where's my phone?" I remove my hand from her panties and rise up, her hand falling away from my dick as I check my pockets, finding it.

But I'm not the one with the ringing phone.

I spot Addie's just above her head, discarded at some point. I reach for it and hand it to her, just as the phone goes silent.

Only for the ringing to start yet again.

"It's Emma," she says with a groan, when she glances at her screen, her gaze going to mine. "Should I answer it?"

"Maybe." I pull away from her completely and lean

against the side window, trying to catch my breath. Calm my racing heart. My racing thoughts.

My extremely hard dick. I was so close to coming.

She stares at the phone screen for a few seconds more before she gives in and answers with a breathless, "Hey. Everything all right?"

I can hear Emma clearly, since she's practically yelling. And she sounds like she's crying. "Why haven't you answered your phone? Or my texts? Where are you?"

"I'm still here."

"Where?"

Addie's gaze goes to mine. "With Beck."

I smile at her, and she flashes me a nervous smile before she looks away, her voice lowering as she tries to calm Emma down.

I blow out a harsh exhale, closing my eyes as I tilt my head back until it hits the cool glass. If we would've kept that up, we might've actually had sex in the back of my freaking 4Runner.

And that's not how I imagined this night going. I was hoping something would happen between Addie and me, but I didn't think we'd take it this far.

Talk about getting out of control.

Eventually Addie ends the call and sends me a sympathetic look. "I need to go find Emma. I guess Tori is with her. She just sent me a bunch of texts complaining about Emma and how they need me."

"What's wrong?" I reach down, readjusting myself, hoping like hell my hard-on diminishes soon. My dick fucking aches.

"I guess she got into a raging fight with Marcus and now she's inconsolable." My eyes track Addie's every movement as she reaches down and pulls the zipper closed on her shorts.

Disappointment rises in me and I tell myself to calm down. I get it. She needs to go help her friends.

"What are they fighting about?" I draw my legs up, so they're bent at the knees, relieved my erection has started to deflate.

"Monique showing up." A sigh leaves her as her gaze skims over me, lingering on my still bare chest. "I need to go to them."

"Want me to come with you?" I grab my T-shirt and slip it back on, hating how awkward everything suddenly feels between us.

I can tell she's retreating. Focusing on something else. Her friend. Not me.

Not us.

Addie shakes her head. "No, it's okay. I should go."

Spotting my keys on the floorboard—they must've fell out of my pocket—I grab them and hit the button, the hatch door slowly opening. Addie scrambles out and turns to face me, raising her hand and waving at me.

"See ya."

She's gone before I can say a damn word and I thrust both hands in my hair, gripping the back of my head.

What the hell was that?

CHAPTER 16

ADDIE

I make my way back to Marcus' house on wobbly legs, my breathing erratic, my thoughts… Everywhere.

The night took a turn I didn't expect. Yes, I was hoping Beck and I would talk. Kiss. Something simple though. A sweet little make-out session maybe.

Instead, Beck admitted his feelings for me. Feelings that go way back. I can't believe he thought about me the entire time he was with Sasha. That he was trying to show me he liked me; yet, I was completely clueless.

I sort of thought he did, but always blew it off. I figured he was completely out of my league.

My heart still hasn't completely calmed down. I remember the look on his face when he leaned in and kissed me for the first time. How everything fell into place the moment our lips touched.

How everything became that much hotter once they did.

I did things with him that I never tried with Jonah. I touched Beck in places that usually made me nervous. I never felt like I was ready when I was with Jonah, though he always tried to talk me into it. The single hand job I gave him was awkward, uncomfortable—for me—and even a little disappointing.

With Beck, it's as if I became a different person. Bolder. Dare I even think it...

Sexier?

A secret smile plays upon my lips as I draw closer to the house. Beck told me I was beautiful. He held me as if I was made of glass. He slipped his fingers beneath my thong and touched me where no boy has ever attempted to touch me before.

More like where I never let anyone touch me before. I didn't want it to happen with Jonah—ever. Maybe I was saving myself for someone else?

"WHAT ARE YOU SMILING ABOUT?"

I stop short when I hear the familiar male voice.

Liam.

The very last person I want to see.

He's standing on the porch, and I'm pretty sure he's smoking a blunt. The strong scent of marijuana lingers in the air, and while I've partaken a time or two at a party or get-together, I'm not one to smoke weed regularly.

Not even close.

He takes a hit on the blunt, his gaze never leaving mine as he exhales smoke. At least he's alone. No tagalong Danny lurking nearby. But he is blocking my way into the house and from his stance, I'm guessing he's doing it on purpose.

I walk up the steps and stop in front of him, hoping I won't have to ask, but he doesn't budge.

Of course he doesn't. Why does he have to make things so difficult?

A sigh leaves me. "Can you move please? I need to get inside."

"Where've you been?" He crosses his arms, trying to look intimidating.

It's not working. I don't have time for this.

I try to duck past him, but he shifts with me, blocking my entrance. "Why weren't you in the house? Who were you with?"

His gaze roams over me, narrowing in on my face. I press my lips together, hoping he doesn't notice that they're swollen from Beck's kisses. I absently run a hand over my hair, trying to smooth it out.

I'm sure I look like I've been hooking up with someone—which I was.

"I don't really see how that's any of your business," I tell him, my voice firm. "Now get out of my way."

"So rude," he mutters as he does what I ask, moving away from the door.

Breathing a sigh of relief, I push open the door and stride inside the house, coming to an immediate stop.

There are so many people crowded in here. The living room is overflowing with people from my high school. So many familiar faces. Even a few unfamiliar ones.

Not a one of them is Emma or Tori.

I pull my phone out of my pocket and call Emma.

No answer.

I call Tori next.

She doesn't answer either.

Not surprising. It's so loud in here, I'm sure they can't hear their phones ring.

Glancing over my shoulder, I watch as Liam enters the house, Danny now by his side. In a hurry to get away from them, I push my way through the clusters of people congregated in the living room, heading toward the kitchen.

I'm on the hunt for my friends, but I can barely concentrate. All I can think about is Beck. His big hands on my body, his mouth on mine. When he kissed my neck, oh my God. His warm, damp lips. They're so soft. The boy knows how to kiss.

And all the other places he touched me...

"Oh! I'm sorry!" I run smack into someone, practically bouncing off of her, and when she turns, my mouth drops open in disbelief.

Of all the people I have to run into, it's freaking Sasha.

Her friendly expression falls, her mouth turning downward. "Oh. Hey, Addison."

"Hey, Sasha." I keep my voice even. Why am I running into everyone I don't want to see right now? First Liam, then Sasha?

My luck is terrible.

"So...where's your friend?"

I frown. "You mean Emma? I'm trying to find her."

"No. I'm talking about—" Her smile turns pained. "Beck. Where's he at? I know he's here. I saw his car. Is he trying to avoid me?"

A sigh leaves me. He is the last person I want to talk about with her. "I don't know."

"You two together yet? I told him you were more his speed." A giggle escapes her and my frown deepens.

"What are you talking about?"

"When we split up, I told him maybe he should try getting with you. You know, because you're more his speed, with that whole late bloomer thing he's rocking? I figure you're the same." Her smile turns saccharine sweet. "I'm surprised you're at this party since there's alcohol here, Addison. I never see you at these sorts of things. I always figured you were too scared to show."

The smile on Sasha's face never falters. It actually grows

brighter as she watches me, her gaze telling me she believes I'm some pathetic little creature who will never be as pretty or as popular as she is.

Or maybe those are my own insecurities talking. The girl is stunning, and of course tonight she looks extraordinarily beautiful. While I'm standing in front of her feeling like a mess. I can feel her friends' eyes on me.

Judging me.

But then I remember I'm a mess thanks to her ex-boyfriend having his hands and mouth all over me, and suddenly, I feel a whole lot better.

"Not sure what you're referring to with the whole late bloomer statement. As a matter of fact, I was just in the back of the 4Runner with Beck a few minutes ago." My smile is real as I remember exactly what he did to me—and what I did to him. "So thanks for the suggestion! Looks like it worked!"

I turn away from her, but not before I caught a glimpse of her shocked face and the way her mouth was hanging open.

Ha. She deserved that. Late bloomers? I didn't know she could be such a bitch.

I finally find my friends in the kitchen; Emma sitting at the counter with her head resting on her arms, Tori sitting beside her, absently rubbing her back. When we make eye contact, Tori's shoulders sag with relief. "There you are!"

Emma lifts her head and looks in my direction, her eyes rimmed red and her nose and cheeks flushed from all the crying. "Finally."

She sounds bitter. Annoyed. As if it's my job to be at her beck and call whenever she needs me.

Annoyance flashes through me, but I try to ignore it.

"Are you okay?" I ask once I'm standing next to them. Tori is behind Emma and she's furiously shaking her head, answering for Emma.

"Not really," Emma retorts, her eyes glassy with unshed tears. "I hate him so much."

"Who? Marcus?"

"He invited her here!" Emma wails, the tears falling again. "Why would he do that? I hate that bitch."

"Maybe we should go," I suggest, but Emma cuts me off with a single word.

"No."

A sigh leaves me and I send Tori a look. She gets the hint and walks with me over to the fridge, standing close to me as she whispers, "She's a mess. But she won't leave. She wants to confront Marcus and Monique."

"Are they together right now?" I ask, my voice squeaking. If that's the case, talk about ballsy.

"No. I don't know. I think he's with the guys. Dom texted me a few minutes ago that he was with him." A pouty expression forms on Tori's face and she stomps her foot. "I really wanted to hang out with him tonight, not babysit Emma while she cries."

I feel sorry for her because I've been in this exact position way too many times. "Go find Dom. I'll take over."

Tori frowns. "Are you sure? I hate to dump her on you."

"You've had to deal with her the entire night," I remind her.

Tori contemplates me for a moment, her gaze narrowing. "Where have you been anyway?"

My cheeks go hot. "With Beck."

"What? No." She grabs my arm and starts doing a little dance. I love how excited she always gets. Her excitement amplifies mine. "What were you two doing?"

"Uh…" I really don't want to say the words out loud. "Stuff."

"Good stuff, I hope."

"Oh yeah." This is so embarrassing.

"Oh my God! I love this! Okay." She pulls me in for a quick hug, releasing me just as fast. "You really don't mind if I go hang out with Dom?"

"Of course not. Go have fun. I'll take care of Emma."

Another hug and a few gushing words and then Tori's gone, pushing her way through the crowds of people, calling her new man's name. I can literally hear her, which makes me laugh.

But my laughter dies when I see Emma glaring at me from her spot at the counter.

"How can you laugh right now? My entire life is falling apart!"

I love my best friend, but she's so dramatic sometimes.

Most of the time.

I go to her, trying to be positive. "It's okay. Tori just talked to Dom and he said he had Marcus with him. He's not with Monique."

"I don't care. He invited her when he shouldn't have. He's a complete dick." She wipes at the almost dried tears on her face. "Where were you?"

"With Beck," I admit quietly.

Her face falls. "What about Liam?"

I want to roll my eyes but I hold back the urge. "You were there Thursday night, Emma. You witnessed it. Why would I want to be with him?"

"He's not that bad. You need to spend more time with him, one on one. Without Danny around."

I actually snort. "That's tough since they're always together."

"It's not that bad."

"It kind of is," I insist. "And why are you pushing Liam so hard on me? I'm not interested in him."

"Because he's so close to Marcus, and if you go out with Liam, we could double date." Her frown deepens. "And if you date Beck, his best friend is Dom and you'll always be with Tori. You two will eventually forget all about me."

Ah. She's jealous of me and Tori. I have been spending more time with her lately. Tori is much more positive than Emma. And supportive. She listens to me, and knows how to have a good time without making it all about her.

I feel terrible for thinking this but...sometimes I don't like hanging out with Emma.

Okay, a lot of the time lately, I don't enjoy spending time with my best friend. And while that makes me seem like a shitty friend in my head, I know the true shitty friend is...

Emma.

A sigh leaves me and I pull her in for a hug, squeezing her extra tight. "We could never forget you. We already spend a lot of time together."

"Because of volleyball. That's it." She's stiff in my arms so I let her go, frustrated. I don't bother arguing with her.

What's the point?

Emma jumps off the stool and pushes her hair out of her face. "I'm so over this party and everyone in this stupid house. Let's get out of here."

I frown. "Where do you want to go?"

"Anywhere but here. I can literally feel Monique's vibe, and I'm sick of it. Sick of her. Sick of Marcus. Sick of everyone. Let's go."

Before I can say a word, she exits the kitchen.

Leaving me no choice but to follow after her.

CHAPTER 17

BECK

I can't stop thinking about her.

Reliving what happened in the back of my car over and over. The taste of her lips. So soft and sweet. The sounds she made. How perfectly she fit in my arms. When I sunk my fingers between her thighs, how wet she was. How hot.

Fuck. I can't get over it. Being with Addison Douglas only amped up my feelings for her tenfold. But what did I expect? I was halfway gone over her already.

I never saw her for the rest of Friday night, though. At one point, I ran into Tori with Dom and tried to play it cool, asking if she knew where Addie was. The knowing smile Tori sent my way told me she talked to Addie but then she had to go and disappoint by saying Addie took Emma home.

I never got a chance to say goodbye.

After discovering Addie had left, I crashed on the floor in Marcus' room. Only to be woken up when he kicked me out around two in the morning. He was drunk as hell and had a girl with him, the dog.

And that girl definitely wasn't Emma. Nope, it was freaking Monique.

I got my ass out of there stat and fell asleep on the couch in the family room. Then hightailed it out of there the next morning, as soon as I woke up, and went straight home to sleep most of my Saturday away.

When I finally got up around three in the afternoon, groggy and out of it, I fumbled for my phone, checking to see if I had a text message from Addie.

Nope.

I took a shower. Jerked off to memories of us last night. Contemplated what I would say to her via text.

I want to see her tonight. Hang out. Maybe continue where we left off last night.

Would she be down?

Unable to resist my growling stomach any longer, I head down to the kitchen to find my mom in there, cutting up a bunch of strawberries.

"There you are," she says, as she watches me go to the pantry and grab my favorite cereal. "You slept most of the day away."

"I was tired." I take a giant bowl out of the cabinet and fill it almost to the top with cereal. Grabbing the milk out of the fridge, I dump a bunch in with my cereal, get a spoon and settle in at my usual place at the kitchen counter.

She watches me, seemingly amused. "You're always tired lately. Or hungry."

"It's been a busy week."

"It's going to be a busy year," she says, hesitating for only a moment before she asks, "How was the party last night?"

"Good." I keep my expression as neutral as possible, not wanting to give anything away, but I must.

My mother has always been ultra-observant of me and

my moods. Sometimes it's annoying as hell, especially when I want to hide my feelings from her.

"Something happen?" Her tone is innocent, but she's fishing for information.

"I uh—" Should I tell her? Ah, screw it. "I kissed Addie."

The knife lands with a clatter on her wooden cutting board. "No. *Really?*"

I shovel a bunch of cereal into my mouth and chew, contemplating how I should answer. She's always liked Addie. I don't think she views this as a bad thing. "Really," is all I end up saying once I swallow.

"That's so sweet." Mom is beaming. I think she likes this. "Are you two a—thing?"

"I don't know." I shrug. "Can't put a label on it yet."

She rolls her eyes but doesn't comment on my label remark. "Do you want to be a thing with Addie?"

"I like her," I admit.

"You've liked her for a while, huh?"

I duck my head and stare at the cereal floating in milk as I keep shoveling it in. I'm realizing cereal isn't going to cut it. I need something with more substance. "Maybe."

"I think she's a better match for you than Sasha," Mom says.

I glance up, watching her as she calmly slices strawberries, one after the other. "Why do you think that?"

"Don't get me wrong, I liked Sasha. She's a nice girl. But I always felt like you two wanted different things," Mom says, ever the observer.

"Yeah. I guess so."

"Do you think you're moving too fast, though? You did just break up with Sasha," Mom points out.

Yeah, I told her. I tell my mom lots of stuff, though I'm not going to confess what happened last night between Addie and me.

I can barely wrap my head around it myself. Still freakin' blown away at what we did do.

Which was a lot.

And I want more.

"No." I keep eating, so I can't talk.

"I'm assuming since you kissed her that Addie likes you too."

"Mom." That's all I say, and she clamps her lips shut, dumping all of her sliced strawberries into a bowl.

She's quiet as she works about the kitchen and I finish my cereal, checking my phone, staring at my text messages, which I don't have too many of. I'm sure all of my friends are still sleeping.

I wonder if Addie is.

Deciding I need to man the hell up, I open up our thread and send her a quick text.

Me: **Hey.**

No quick response. I go to refill my bowl with more cereal and milk, taking my time as I walk back to the counter and settle onto the stool.

Still no response from Addie.

Shit.

Once I consume two bowls of cereal and grab some Cheez-it crackers to take to my room, I head up there and start cleaning. It's a fucking disaster, and I know I'm going to hear about it from my parents at some point over the weekend, so I may as well beat them to it.

My phone dings with a notification as I'm piling clothes in a laundry basket and I check to see it's from Dom.

Pushing aside my disappointment that it's not Addie, I read his message.

Dom: **Yo, what are you doing? Party last night was lit.**

Me: **Cleaning my room. Yeah, it was.**

Dom: **Barely saw you tho.**

Me: **You were too busy with Tori.**

Dom: **Who were you busy with? Addie?**

I don't answer him. Not yet. I'm going to tell him about Addie and me, but I won't go into too much detail.

Dom: **Come on bro. Don't leave me hanging. You were with Addie, right?**

Me: **Yeah.**

Dom: **Knew it. Talked to Sasha last night. She's a jealous bitch, bro. She knew you hooked up with Addie and she was pretty fuckin pissed about it.**

Wait a minute.

How the hell did Sasha know about me and Addie?

Having zero patience for texting, I immediately call him.

"Be glad you dumped her," is how he answers. "That girl is straight-up mean. She was talking mad shit about you, bro!"

I ignore his mad shit comment. "How the hell did Sasha know I hooked up with Addie last night?"

"I didn't tell her about it because I didn't know about," he says. "She mentioned it to me."

This makes no damn sense. "So how did she find out?"

"Like I said, I have no clue."

"What exactly did she say?" I need clarification.

"Lemme think. I was kind of drunk. Nah, more like really drunk." He laughs and I grit my teeth together, frustrated. "Oh, I remember. She asked me where you were. I said I wasn't sure. She asked if you were with Addie and I pretended I didn't know what she was talking about."

"Okay." I draw the word out, hoping there's more to his lame-ass story.

"She heard you and Addie hooked up, but I don't know who told her, and she didn't mention a name."

"We did hook up," I admit.

"Ha! Knew it." His voice lowers. "How was it? Because her friend is kind of freaky."

"Tori?" I'd rather distract him and have him tell me about his adventures with Tori than give him any details about my experience with Addie.

"Yeah. That girl is up for anything." He chuckles. "I like that about her. She's fun."

"I like Addie," I admit. "And after last night, I really like her."

"Already forgot about Sasha?"

"Who?" I joke.

He starts laughing. "Okay, it's cool. I think you two make a good couple. You and Addie."

"Thanks."

"Tori says she wants to go out with you guys sometime soon," Dom says, his voice casual.

"Are you asking me on a date, dude?" I'm teasing him, and he makes a dismissive noise.

"You know you want it. But looks like I'm already taken."

We chat a while longer before I end the call and check my notifications.

Still no response from Addie.

I decide to go against everything I've been taught when it comes to pursuing a girl and I text her again, versus waiting for her to reply.

Me: **Did you tell anyone about us hooking up last night?**

I collapse on my bed, thinking about all the math homework that's due tomorrow night. I don't care. I can't concentrate. My brain is filled with reasons why Addie still hasn't responded to me yet.

All of them bad.

I fall asleep with my phone clutched in my hand, waking up when it buzzes, startling me. I check the time—it's already past five.

And I finally have a response.

Addie: **Sorry I didn't text you earlier! I've been at work, and I never get a chance to check my phone.**

I'm anxious, wanting to respond, but I bide my time when I see the gray bubble, indicating she's still typing. My heart is racing and I feel all twisted up inside.

All while waiting for a text.

Addie: **I don't remember telling anyone about us. Why?**

I'm not about to tell her because Sasha's talking shit about us. I don't need to bring my ex into our relationship. What if Addie gets mad? Or worse, it freaks her out and scares her away? I did just break up with Sasha, not even a week ago.

I can't wait for her to go away to college and get out of here.

Me: **No reason. How was work?**

Addie: **Busy. There are still a lot of tourists at the lake. We'll be busy until after Labor Day weekend.**

Me: **I bet you're tired.**

Addie: **Yeah. I had to be at work at nine. And I had a late night staying up listening to Emma complain about Marcus.**

Me: **That sucks.**

Addie: **Yeah.**

This conversation is going nowhere fast and I only have myself to blame. I decide to spice it up.

Me: **What are you doing tonight?**

Addie: **Nothing. I think Emma wanted me to come over.**

I start to respond when she sends another text.

Addie: **But I don't want to go over there.**

Me: **You should hang out with me.**

Addie: **And do what?**

My mind drifts, filled with the many things I could do with Addie.

Me: **Whatever you want.**

Addie: **You make it sound bad.**

Me: **What do you mean?**

Addie: **Like the good kind of bad.**

I chew on my lower lip, wondering if I should be truthful.

Me: **I can't stop thinking about last night.**

She's quiet for a while, which leaves me in bigger knots. To the point I start pacing around my room, just to burn energy.

Addie: **I can't stop thinking about it either.**

She sends a string of blushing emojis.

Okay, that's it. I can just hear my brother's voice right now, giving me advice on girls.

Take charge, little brother. Show her what you want—and what you want, is her.

Or maybe it was Eli who said that to me? He was always full of dating advice when he first got together with Ava and spent a lot of time at our house. And I ate up every word he said, believing it was true. Shit, I wanted to be him when I got older. Or at least a combo of Eli and Jake.

Me: **Want me to come pick you up?**

Addie: **Yeah. I need to get home and take a shower first. Can you come by around seven?**

Me: **I'll be there.**

I toss my phone on my bed, barely able to contain my excitement. I glance to my right, catching my reflection in the mirror. I'm grinning from ear to ear. I don't think I've ever looked this happy.

One thing is for sure—Sasha *never* made me feel like this. All giddy just at the mere thought of spending time with her. It wasn't unpleasant, being with her. But nothing compares to this feeling bubbling inside of me at the promise tonight holds.

With Addie.

CHAPTER 18

ADDIE

*B*y the time I get home, I'm rushing into the house and heading for my bedroom, shouting out a distracted, "I'm home," to let my mom know I've arrived.

I hear her footsteps coming down the hall after me, can feel her presence lingering in my bedroom doorway as I push open the closet door and look through my clothes, trying to find something to wear tonight.

With Beck.

The secret smile that plays upon my lips feels naughty, because my brain is filled with images of all the things we did last night.

What we might do tonight.

Will I let him take it even further? Or do I have any say in the matter? Not that he's pushing me into anything, but more like I can't control my body when it comes to him. I just automatically want to touch him. Kiss him. Explore him.

Everywhere...

I pull out a cute top that exposes a lot of skin, yet still somehow covers me up. Wearing this shirt won't be too obvious, will it? It was so hot today, and it'll be hot tonight too. It's only natural I'll want to wear something that's not so confining—

"What are you up to?"

I startle, a shriek leaving me when I hear my mom's voice. I forgot she followed me to my room.

Turning, I face her. She's still standing in the doorway, her arms crossed as she watches me. "Oh. Hey."

"Hi. How was work?"

"Okay."

"You make good tip money today?"

We split the tip jar there at the end of every shift change. "Almost fifty bucks."

"That's great. You can put it toward college."

"Uh huh." I withhold the urge to roll my eyes. She always says stuff like that, as if I might forget that I'm saving money for my future college tuition. I want to go away to college somewhere far from my hometown, though I want to stay in California. My dad is a lawyer who practices family law and does pretty well for himself, but my parents fully expect me to help contribute to my future education and living expenses. They want me to have a good work ethic and don't want to raise spoiled children.

A direct quote.

She nods toward the shirt on the hanger that I'm still clutching. "You going somewhere tonight? Hanging out with your friends?"

"Uh…" This is where it gets tricky between us.

Mom hated Jonah. Not that she hated *him* per se, more like she hated the idea of me having a boyfriend.

Okay, she *really* hates the idea of me having a boyfriend.

Having an older sister who was heavily involved with her boyfriend when she was so young terrified our mother. Jocelyn and Diego were serious. Madly in love. Everything was high passion all the time. The fights. The love. Having sex when they were really young—I think Jos lost her virginity to Diego when she was only fifteen? Or were they sixteen?

Whatever. It doesn't matter. She got pregnant when she was a senior in high school and while my mom has been extremely supportive and she loves Diego with all her heart now, it was a tough time back then. Mom had to learn how to let go of her first baby—my sister—and let her be an adult. A mother. Dad was supportive too, as best as he could be. But he was busy working all the time, and still is. A lot of what unfolded with Jocelyn fell on Mom.

After going through it, this meant Mom gave me plenty of speeches about saving myself for the right one and not to get too serious, too young. When I first started high school and the lectures ramped up even more, I took her words to heart. When you hear them all the time growing up, you can't help but let those words absorb into your brain and stick. No boy really interested me anyway. Not like that. I went out with Jonah because he was easy to talk to and I felt the need to have a boyfriend like everyone else.

But I didn't have a burning need to be with him. And I definitely wasn't going to have sex with him, no matter how badly he wanted to have it with me.

Mom's lecture actually worked.

"Uh…what? What's your plan tonight?" she asks, when I still haven't said anything.

"I'm going to hang out with Beck." I smile, going for casual. No big deal. Just spending time on a Saturday night with my secret crush after I let him finger me last night in the back of his 4Runner.

My cheeks threaten to go hot and I will myself not to blush.

"Beck Callahan?" Her brows shoot up.

I nod, hoping I don't have to explain myself.

"As friends?" She sounds skeptical. I've never revealed my feelings about Beck to her, because I knew I'd get the third degree.

"Sure," I say way too quickly.

"Sure?" Her brows rise even higher, if that's possible. "Is this a date?"

"He didn't call it a date. He asked if I wanted to hang out."

"I thought he had a girlfriend."

"They broke up."

"I see." That's all she says.

I see.

Yeah, she probably sees more than I want her to.

My shoulders deflate. I don't need a speech. Not tonight. "It's no big deal, Mom. We're just going to grab something to eat. Talk for a while. I might even come home early."

"Be home by eleven," she says.

"Mom." This time, I do roll my eyes, and I see her gaze flare with irritation. "My curfew on the weekend is midnight."

"When you're with your friends."

"Beck *is* my friend."

"Who happens to be a boy."

"So?" I turn my back on her and kneel down, opening the bottom drawer of the old dresser I keep in my closet, so I can go through my shorts. "It's nothing."

I'm such a liar. Tonight with Beck could be...

Everything.

"Do you like him?"

"I've liked him for years. He's a good friend. You used to invite him over for playdates," I remind her.

"When you were nine." She laughs, but the sound lacks humor. "That girl he was with before, she's a year older than you, right?"

"Yeah." I find the pair of shorts I want, but I don't hold

179

them up in front of Mom. She'd probably freak out and declare them too short, and with too big of holes in the front.

All of that is true, but I don't need to call attention to it.

"I'm sure they've had sex then."

I slam the drawer shut and rise to my full height before I whirl on her. "Stop with the sex speech, okay? I know what I'm doing. I'm almost eighteen."

In a matter of weeks, actually.

"I know you are. You're very responsible, and I'm so grateful for that, but Addie, this boy is full of testosterone and once they've already done it, they always want to do it," Mom says.

I laugh nervously, trying to play this off. "You make him sound like a sex addict."

"Teenage boys are horny. It's a known fact."

I drop my clothes on top of the other dresser in my room and cover my ears. "I hate that you just said that word."

"What? Horny? Please. You kids say far worse."

"No one wants to hear their mom say it." I open the top drawer and rifle through my underwear, slipping out a lacy thong as discreetly as possible before I quickly hide it inside my folded shorts.

I slam the drawer shut and turn like I'm going to leave my room for the bathroom across the hall, but Mom blocks me.

"Aren't you going to grab a fresh bra?" she asks.

She didn't miss a beat, did she? I'm sure she noticed the lacy thong. This is so...humiliating. "The shirt I'm going to wear...a bra doesn't work with it."

"Maybe you should find another shirt then." She rests her hands on her hips, glaring at me.

"Mom." I'm whining and I hate it, so I snap my lips shut, clear my throat and start all over again. "The shirt isn't that revealing. The top is really tight. It'll keep my boobs contained. A bra will ruin the look."

Her lips thin. "Hold up the shirt again."

I do, praying she doesn't make me switch it out. The shorts were a nice touch last night, but the T-shirt I had on was plain. Boring. Normal.

I want to spice it up tonight, though I get the feeling my mother is going to ruin my entire vibe.

"I should tell you no," she says, her gaze lifting from the shirt to meet my eyes. "But go ahead. This time, I'll let you wear it."

I break out into a smile, quietly hating on the "this time" comment. "Thanks Mom."

"But you have to be home by eleven."

"What? Come on!"

"Or you wear a different shirt."

This is blackmail. And we're wasting valuable time arguing, when I should already be halfway done with my shower.

"Eleven thirty," I bargain.

"Ten thirty."

"Mom!"

She sighs. "Fine. Eleven thirty and not a minute later."

"Thank you." I go to walk by her and drop a kiss on her cheek before I head for my bathroom.

"Don't do anything I wouldn't do," she calls after me.

I don't answer her, slamming the door before she can say something else.

No way can I make that promise. After last night...

I'm pretty positive I can be persuaded by Beck Callahan to do almost anything.

* * *

I'm RUNNING LATE and am almost done getting ready when I get a text from Beck at exactly 7:01.

181

Beck: **I'm outside your house. Want me to come to the door?**

Me: **It's okay. Give me a couple of minutes and I'll be right out.**

Beck: **No problem.**

I slip some tiny gold hoops in my ears. Put on my favorite delicate gold chain necklace I got for Christmas last year. I washed and blow dried my hair and even curled the ends a little bit, but not too much.

I don't want to look like I'm trying too hard, but I had to get that fried food smell off of me.

The top I'm wearing is a pale blue with the tiniest, most delicate floral print scattered across it. The sleeves come almost to my elbows and they're billowy, with little ties at the end. It's the square bodice in the front and back that my mother has an issue with. It dips low, but the fabric is ruched, so it clings to my chest tightly.

No bra necessary.

Sexy, sexy, sexy, which is a look I never strive for. But I want to look sexy for Beck. I want to witness that glow of appreciation in his eyes when he first sees me.

Satisfied with my appearance, I slick on some rose-tinted lip balm, grab my tiny bag and head out of my room, making my way to the front door, as quietly as possible, so hopefully my mother doesn't notice.

I couldn't be so lucky.

"Are you off for the night?" She exits the kitchen to meet me by the front door, her narrowed gaze running over my outfit.

If she says something about the shorts being too short, I'm gonna scream.

"Yeah." I raise my voice so my dad can hear me over the blare of the TV, where he sits in the living room. "Night, Dad!"

"Night, sweetheart! Love you! Have fun with your friends!"

"Love you too!" I smile at my mother, but it fades when I see the look on her face.

Mom shakes her head. "Your father is clueless. I told him you were going out with Beck and he didn't think anything of it."

"You shouldn't either, Mom. It's truly no big deal." I hug her quickly, wishing she'd stop worrying about me all the time. I'm not my sister.

I won't get knocked up at seventeen.

"Have fun," she tells me once we break apart. "Be home by—"

"Eleven thirty. I know, I know. Night, Mom." I open the front door and jet out of there, grateful when I hear her close the door without saying another word.

I make my way to Beck's 4Runner, where it sits idling next to the sidewalk in front of my house. Beck is watching me from the driver's seat, his perfect mouth curved into a faint smile, his eyes sparkling. He gets out at the last second and darts around the front of the vehicle, so he can open my car door before I reach it.

"Such a gentleman," I tease him as I climb into the car.

He shuts the door for me and heads back to the other side, slamming his car door before he glances over at me. "Hi."

The hushed quiet of the inside of his 4Runner is filled with memories of last night. I squeeze my thighs together in anticipation of what might happen later. "Hi."

"You look..." His gaze slips down, lingering on my chest. My bare thighs. "Really great."

I smile, suddenly feeling shy. "Thank you."

"If I'm being real right now, it's more like you look fucking hot."

I burst out laughing, I can't help it. "Thank you," I repeat.

"I want to kiss you." His voice is low. And deep. It makes me feel all fluttery inside.

"Later," I whisper, like I'm a tease.

Really? I don't want him kissing me while we're sitting in front of my house. For all I know, my mother is spying on us at this very moment.

"Is that a promise?" he asks, one brow lifting.

I devour his handsome features. His lush mouth and that sharp jawline. His dark blue eyes and the dark brows and all that dark hair on his head that I happen to know is extra soft, since I had my hands in it not even twenty-four hours ago.

I want my hands in his hair now. I want to touch that pretty face. Trace his jaw. His full, delicious lips. Kiss his neck and breathe him in—

"You're staring at me," he says, startling me from my thoughts.

"You're staring at me," I return.

He smiles and turns, so he can settle his hands on the steering wheel in front of him. "Where do you want to go?"

"You're the one who asked me out," I say, my voice teasing. Flirtatious. "Where do you want to take me?"

Who am I right now?

The side of his mouth quirks up as he puts the vehicle in drive and pulls away from the curb. "I've got an idea."

"Where?" I ask, curious.

His expression is mysterious as he glances over at me. "You'll see."

CHAPTER 19

BECK

We stop off at one of the local supermarkets to pick up some food and snacks to munch on, plus some drinks. I won't tell Addie where we're going, which is frustrating her, but it's fun to watch her pout and try to get it out of me.

I'm tight-lipped, though. I want it to be a surprise.

As we walk around the store, I trail after her, my gaze lingering on all of Addie's good parts. The shirt she's wearing is low in the back, revealing plenty of skin. Cluing me in that she's probably not wearing a bra.

Interesting.

Those shorts she has on are killer. She is nothing but long, tanned legs, and I swear when she bends over to grab a bag of chips in the snack aisle, I can see a hint of ass cheek.

I stifle the groan that wants to escape. This girl is killing me.

Killing. Me.

We scan our stuff at one of the self-checkout registers, and I refuse to let Addie pay. She argues with me for a little bit but eventually gives in and bags up our items, her eyes dancing with excitement.

"You're really not going to tell me where we're going?" she asks as we make our way through the parking lot toward my car. She's practically skipping beside me, and she's fucking adorable.

I shake my head, enjoying myself. "Nope."

"You're mean."

"You love it."

"No, I really don't."

"You're not one for secrets, are you?"

"I can keep a secret. I love sharing secrets too. But surprises? I loathe them," she says.

"Pretty strong words," I tell her as I hit the keyless remote so the back door lifts up.

She comes to a stop right beside me as I load the bags in the back of my 4Runner, her teeth sinking into her lower lip as her gaze scans where we were just last night.

I can tell she's having the same thoughts of the memories we now share. I want to make more of them with her.

Hopefully tonight—and every night after that.

Once everything's loaded, we're out of the parking lot and on the road, headed north. She groans as we leave town, shaking her head.

"You're not taking me to the lake, are you?"

"You have a problem with the lake?"

"I was just there, at work. And when you work at the lake, sometimes you want to avoid it," she says.

"Good thing I'm not taking you to the lake then," I say, my tone smug as hell.

An aggressive sound leaves her. Almost like...a growl. "You're so frustrating."

I chuckle. "I'm keeping this up because I know you don't like it."

For the rest of the drive, we talk about last night's party. She tells me how she had to comfort Emma and ended up taking her home. How Marcus wouldn't back down over inviting Monique to his party.

Lame. I think he likes the jealous shit these girls are pulling on him. He's in the middle of a love triangle and enjoying every minute of it, and I tell Addie that.

"I agree. He wants to keep both of them in his life," she says, a sigh escaping her. "Their drama is exhausting. Emma is exhausting."

I feel bad for her, but remain quiet. I'm not about to bad mouth her best friend. I totally agree with her though.

It does sound like Emma is exhausting.

"You slept over there? At Marcus'?" she asks.

I nod. "Yeah. I passed out on the floor, then found a couch. Got the hell out of there as soon as I woke up in the morning. It kind of sucked."

"Tori told me she had fun."

"I'm sure she did. She was with Dom the entire night."

"They make a cute couple."

"I agree." I'm quiet, thinking we make a cute couple too.

But I don't say it. I don't want to freak her out or push too hard. Not yet.

I turn onto a side road, right off the highway, driving through the quiet neighborhood until the houses become sparser, and the area becomes more wooded. I open my window, fresh air scented heavily with pine rushing in, and I quickly glance over at Addie to see her wavy dark hair is blowing across her face. She keeps batting at it.

"Want me to close the window?"

She shakes her head, smiling at me. "It feels good. Nice and cool."

"We'll get even higher in a bit. Have you been back here?"

"No. Never."

It feels good to take her someplace she's never been before.

I speed up, not wanting to miss the sunset and that giant orange ball is sinking lower and lower. By the time we make it to our destination, I'm switching my vehicle into four-wheel-drive and climbing on top of a hill that's essentially comprised of nothing but granite.

Addie clutches the handle above her, her expression wary. "You never mentioned going off-roading."

"This is as bad as it gets. Trust me." I come to a complete stop and put it in park, the car swaying from the climb. Before I shut off the engine, I open her window, and there's nothing but silence.

Pine trees.

The lake looks like a pond below us.

And the sun's going down, streaking the sky in various shades of pink and orange.

She's quiet as she stares out the windshield, her eyes going wide as she takes it all in before she turns to me. "This is beautiful."

I stare at her, overcome. "No, you're beautiful."

Her cheeks turn as pink as the sky and she looks away, staring at that disappearing sun. "Should we go outside?"

"Yeah. Let's do it."

We climb out of the car and she follows me as I lead her onto the jutting rock. I stop just before the ledge, gazing down at the ground below. We're pretty high up and when I turn back, I notice she's lingering a few feet behind me.

"Come here." I wave a hand.

She slowly shakes her head. "I don't like heights much."

I take a few steps backward, so I'm closer to her and farther away from the ledge. "I won't let anything happen to you."

Addie laughs nervously. "I'm a klutz sometimes. I could send myself right over the edge all on my own, thanks."

"Adds." I go to her and take both of her hands, giving them a squeeze. "I won't let anything happen to you."

She stares up at me, hesitation written all over her face. "I'm scared."

Damn, she could be describing so many things. She's scared of heights. Of me. Of how fast we're moving. We've been in school a whole two days. We've had our own little love triangle to contend with. Is she scared of Liam finding out about us?

Does she still like him?

No way. That's my own insecurity rearing its ugly head. If she likes him, she wouldn't have hooked up with me last night, right?

"I've got you," I murmur, never letting go of her hands as I slowly lead her to the edge of the hill. "I won't let you fall."

Her breathing starts to accelerate and she looks toward the setting sun, coming to a stop. "This is amazing."

"It is," I agree, letting go of her hands and shifting just behind her. Deciding to go for it, I slip my arms around her, pulling her snug against my body, her back to my front. She fits perfectly and everything inside of me goes hot when she melts against me.

Addie is a tall girl, but I'm taller. Her hair brushes against my jaw, soft and fragrant, and I briefly close my eyes, taking a deep breath. The woods and Addie.

An ideal combination.

"This is nice," she says, her voice so soft I can barely hear her. "Peaceful."

"Yeah," I agree, clutching her tight, showing her that I won't let her go.

I won't let anything happen to her.

We're silent as the sun lowers. Within minutes, it's gone,

and the light sky turns darker. Velvety shades of blue and purple, with the stars already starting to shine.

"I'm hungry," she admits, turning in my arms so she's facing me. "I want some of our snacks."

Unable to resist, I cup her face, tilting her head back so her lips are primed for mine. I kiss her, soft and slow at first. Learning the shape of her mouth. The taste of her lips. Savoring her as I lick my tongue against hers. "You're my snack," I murmur against her mouth at one point, and she smiles.

"I'm still hungry."

Her stomach growls as if on cue.

"Let's eat then." Keeping her hand in mine, I lead her over to the car.

We situate ourselves, much like we did last night—sitting on the back end of the 4Runner, Addie digging through the bag and pulling out all the food we bought to eat. Crackers and chips and dips. A mini veggie tray, plus a small meat and cheese tray. I even grabbed a box of chicken strips from the deli and the smell hits me when she pulls it out, making my own stomach growl.

"I think we bought enough food for four people," Addie says with a laugh as she examines the spread.

"I can eat for approximately three people, so we're good," I say with a grin as I crack open the paper container with the chicken strips and pick one up, biting off half of it.

We eat and drink and talk. About nothing. About everything. She tells me about her job. She works at one of the local resorts, and she's always busy, but she likes it and especially likes the money.

"Have you ever had a job?"

I shake my head, my mouth full of chicken. I chew quickly and swallow. "My mom and dad say school is my job."

"Plus, I'm guessing you don't really need to work?" She winces, and I'm thinking she's uncomfortable bringing up my family's wealth.

"If I wanted to, I wouldn't have to work for the rest of my life." I shrug. I'm not bragging, it's just a fact of life.

My dad comes from a wealthy family—a family he never really wants to talk about. Plus, he was an NFL superstar for years and made a ton of money playing professional football, plus endorsements. Mom got endorsements too with a couple of lifestyle companies. They were a power couple in their heyday, before I was even born.

"What do you want to do?" she asks, sounding genuinely curious.

"I don't know. I don't like to think too far ahead," I admit. "I want a league champion win this season. I want to go to state playoffs."

"I'm sure that can happen."

"I want to go to college and still play ball."

"Where do you want to go?"

"I don't know about that either," I confess.

"It's something you should be thinking about. We'll have to apply to college soon," she says as she pops a baby carrot into her mouth.

"Where do you want to go?"

She scratches the side of her head, vaguely uncomfortable —why? "I have a few places in mind."

"Like what?"

A sigh leaves her and she turns to face me. "You're going to tell me I'm being totally impractical."

"Never," I say, shaking my head. "Tell me."

"Stanford or UCLA?" She wrinkles her nose. "Impossible, right? That's what my mom says."

"You're smart," I tell her and she shakes her head.

"Not that smart. The acceptance rate at both colleges is

small, and they both have great volleyball teams. So does UC San Diego," she says. "I could get in with my grades and volleyball stats—hopefully. But the competition is fierce."

"You want to stay in California then?" I like that. I wouldn't mind staying in California too.

Yeah, totally ridiculous to think we can start planning our college futures—together. We've only being spending time with one another this past week. That's not enough time to base any major life-changing situations on.

But I feel like I've been wanting her...forever. This is all just natural progression, and it feels good.

So damn good.

"I do. Or I'd go to Washington. UW has a great volleyball team too, and I'd be close to my sister, since it's in Seattle," she says.

Seattle is so far. Too far. My sister is there too, but if Addie went there...

I'd never see her.

I have zero plans on going to Washington.

"I've heard good things about that college," I say, keeping my tone casual. Like it's no big deal.

"I toured the campus last spring," she admits. "It's beautiful. I can imagine myself there. Honestly, I could get in there, I think. Especially being out of state."

"You're going to apply?"

She nods. "And Stanford and UCLA too. Along with UC San Diego and Fresno State, because my dad wants me to."

"I'm applying there too. Ash played there. So did Eli," I say. "They have a great football team. My dad says it would be a smart move, to go there. And my mom would like it because then I wouldn't be far. She's really uh—overprotective of me."

Addie smiles, her gaze meeting mine. "It's because you're her baby."

I make a dismissive noise. "Her six-foot-five baby who towers over her."

"You are pretty tall." Addie's gaze roams over me, and my skin grows warm.

"I'm the tallest Callahan in the family." I sit up straighter, puffing out my chest. I can't help it. "Taller than Jake, which kills him."

She laughs. "I'm taller than Jos."

"How tall are you, anyway?"

"Five-foot-nine. I've always been self-conscious of my height. Guys don't like it."

"I don't mind." I grin.

"Because you're a giant," she teases, then immediately grows somber. "Jonah didn't like it. Only because he claims he's five-ten, but I don't think he is because I'm taller than him. Not by much though."

I'm quiet for a moment, hating that she brought up Jonah, but I can't blame her. He's all she has to compare me too, I guess.

"Forget that guy."

"Yeah." She laughs. "I saw him at Marcus' house Friday. Briefly. He was all over Serena, his new girlfriend."

I watch her carefully, looking for any indication that she's sad or upset. "Did that bother you?"

She shakes her head, her gaze meeting mine, steady and true. "No. Not at all. I never really…"

Addie dips her head and doesn't finish the sentence.

"You never really what?" I ask, bracing myself.

"I never really felt that—way about him, you know?" She's still not looking at me.

"No, I don't know. You never felt what way?"

"I don't want to go into too much detail, since I'm sure you don't want to talk about my ex with me, just like I really don't want to talk about your ex with you, but I wasn't in love with him," she admits. "I never felt—consumed with him. Does that make sense?"

It makes all the sense in the world, because I feel the same way about Sasha. I liked her. I cared about her. I just wasn't in love with her.

And I definitely wasn't consumed by her.

Not like I am with…

Addie.

"Makes sense," I say, as I drink her in. It's hard to believe I've got her here with me. All alone. Just the two of us. I don't have to worry about a friend walking by saying something stupid, or one of Addie's friends having a moment of crisis and needing her.

It feels like we're the only people on this planet right now, sharing food and a view and secrets.

She has no clue what she means to me, and it's not that I can tell her.

Not yet.

But I will. Eventually. Because I know…

I'm totally falling in love with her.

CHAPTER 20

ADDIE

*B*eck is watching me so closely, his gaze full of adoration. I recognize that look—it's how he used to stare at me last year, right before he got together with Sasha. Even when he was actually with Sasha, I'd catch him looking at me like this.

I was such an idiot. A complete and utter idiot who thought she had no chance with a guy like him. I was also oblivious. In so much denial that we could actually be something beyond friendship.

Well, look at us now.

Last year, I told myself it could never work with Beck. I thought he wanted Sasha, when all along he really wanted me. And I wanted him.

Why didn't he just tell me? I know we had a few shared moments—specifically that time in the bathroom at that one party, when he almost kissed me. I should've known then. I should've realized a long time ago.

But the night of the party, I was with Jonah, and I wouldn't have dared to cross that line because I never believed I had a chance in the first place with Beck.

I was Beck's friend, and he was mine.

That was it.

There is nothing friendly happening between us right now though. The air is crackling with chemistry. And tension.

So much freaking tension.

"We should put away the food," I suggest, because I need to break up all that tension. It's either we pack up our stuff or we get carried away and next thing I know, Beck rolls me over onto the veggie tray in a heated make out sesh.

I really don't want to get ranch dressing all over my shirt.

"Good idea," he says gruffly, clearing his throat. "You want to keep anything out?"

"Just a bottle of water," I say, as I reach for the plastic lid that covers the meat and cheese tray. Beck goes for it as well, our fingers brushing, and I slowly pull my hand away, suddenly overwhelmed.

I didn't lie to Beck just now. I was never consumed with Jonah like I am him. Beck looks at me in a certain way and I want to melt. He barely touches me in a casual manner and I want to fling myself at him, begging for more. It's unlike anything I've ever experienced before, the emotions he makes me feel.

Does he feel the same way? Is he experiencing the same swirling, confusing, delicious emotions within him? My entire body feels strung tight, like a wire being stretched at both ends. As if I might snap at any moment if he so much as touches me on the arm.

I was always so reluctant with Jonah. Yeah, we did a few things, but nothing major. I wanted to take it slow. I was scared.

I came up with every excuse possible.

With Beck, I'm not scared. He makes me feel safe, even when we're doing something risky, like walking too close to a cliff. Or letting him feel me up in the back of his car. It's like I don't care what happens, as long as I'm with him.

It's scary, but in a good way.

We're silent as we package everything back up as best we can. We use one bag for trash and the other for the things we're keeping. We work well together, which is no surprise.

It feels like we do everything well together.

"Want to sit in the front?" he suggests, when we're done cleaning and everything is stashed in its place. He then hands me a full water bottle. "We can listen to music. Talk."

"Sure." I keep my tone light and casual, but I'm hoping for more than us talking.

From the nervous smile he flashes at me, I think he's feeling the same way.

After he closes the back hatch, we head for the front of the vehicle, a shiver stealing through me when a cool breeze blows. It's colder up here, just as he said, and I take a deep breath of crisp mountain air before I climb into the passenger seat and close the door.

Beck climbs in at the same time, our doors slamming simultaneously. He rubs his hands together and blows on them. "That sun drops and it's cold out there."

"It is," I agree, wrapping my arms around myself.

He reaches out and rests the back of his hand on my cheek, making me yelp. He grins. "Cold, right?"

I reach for him, resting my cold hand on his warm, smooth neck. "Cold, right?" I repeat to him with a smile.

He doesn't even react, save for the way his lids lower over his eyes from what I can only assume is me placing my hand on him. "I like it when you touch me," he says, his voice like velvet, rubbing over what must be every nerve ending I have. "You don't do it enough."

"You want me to touch you more?" I scoot a little closer,

my hand sliding up and around to his nape, his silky hair trapped between my fingers.

"I want you to touch me all the time," he admits, just before he leans over the center console and presses his mouth to mine.

It's a simple kiss at first, but I can tell he's using restraint. His big body practically vibrates as his mouth moves over mine, sweet kisses that last longer.

And longer.

Until his hand is in my hair, so he can hold my head still, his tongue delving into my mouth over and over, sliding against mine. We're straining toward each other over the center console, our bodies not even touching, his fingers growing tighter in my hair as we continue to kiss.

I break away first, needing to catch my breath. Calm my thoughts. I'm breathing hard, my heart is racing and we stare at each other in the darkness, the only light coming from the moon hanging above us in the sky.

"You said you wanted to talk," I whisper, pressing my tingling lips together, discreetly licking them.

I can still taste him, and it just makes me want him more.

"I lied," he says, his expression deadly serious. "If you'd rather talk…we can talk."

"No." I shake my head, smiling faintly. "This is good too."

"Is it?"

I nod. "Yeah."

We stare at each other, the only sounds our ragged breathing. And we've just barely started tonight. Imagine what might happen when we're thirty minutes in.

Sixty minutes in.

Hopefully I don't pass out from total euphoria.

"What time is it?" I ask, and he grabs his phone from where it sits in the cup holder in the center console.

"Almost nine thirty."

"I have two hours."

His brows draw together and he sets the phone back, lifting his gaze to mine. "What do you mean?"

"My curfew. It's in two hours." I don't bother telling him it's normally midnight on the weekends. I don't need to go into detail about that stupid conversation I had with my mother earlier.

It's the last thing I want to think about right now.

"We can do a lot in two hours." He grins, and he's so adorable.

Adorably hot.

"What are we, thirty minutes from my house?" When he nods, I continue, "Then we have ninety minutes."

"We can do a lot in ninety minutes too." He glances down at the center console with a scowl. "Hate that thing. Gets in the way."

"Yeah, it does." I glance toward the back.

So does he.

"We could go back there. Or—" He reaches toward the left side of his chair and hits a button, slowly easing the seat back. "We could stay right here."

My entire body flushes at the thought of climbing on top of Beck. Of straddling him.

"O-okay."

Oh God, I'm nervous. But I've got this.

I can handle it.

I can.

Once the seat is as far back as it can go, Beck encourages me to crawl over the center console with a crook of his finger. He even helps pull me over. I fall onto him in a heap, laughing nervously as I readjust myself, his hands guiding me, situating my body, so I'm sitting on top of him.

Sitting.

On.

Top.

Of.

Him.

I rest my hands on his broad shoulders, realizing quickly that with the position I'm in, I'm looking down on him. He tilts his head back, his eyes practically smoldering as he studies my face, his lips curled into a mysterious smile.

"What?" I ask when he doesn't say anything. Do I look dumb? Is my hair a mess? Do I have something on my face or my shirt? I glance down at myself, my hair falling forward and he slips his hand in between us, his fingers just beneath my chin as he tips my head up, forcing me to meet his gaze.

"I never thought I'd get the chance to have Addison Douglas on my lap. In my car," he admits, his deep voice soft and smooth. Even a little vulnerable. "It's like my every dream come true."

"Beck. Come on," I tease, though I'm partly serious. I'm his every dream come true? He has to be exaggerating. "You can have any girl you could ever want."

"I didn't want any other girl." His thumb drifts over my chin, making me shiver. "I only ever wanted you."

A soft gasp leaves me at his confession and we stare at each other, lost in one another's eyes. I press my lips together, trying to come up with a response, wanting to say something like he's made my every dream come true with that confession, but nothing comes out.

Instead, I lean down and kiss him, melding our mouths together, breathing him in. His hand seems to hover near my waist, not quite touching me, but right there, and I bend my head down closer, shifting my entire body, so he can see that I want his hands on me.

I want his hands all over me.

Our kiss turns hungry in an instant, and we devour each other. I strain toward him, my body wanting to feel his, and he removes his fingers from beneath my chin, his hands finally settling on my waist, pulling me in. Until I'm pressed against him, my breasts pushing into his hard chest.

He breaks away from my still-seeking lips, his mouth finding my jaw. My neck. Delivering hot, wet kisses all over my sensitive skin. I tip my head back, giving him better access, and he sucks on the spot where my neck meets my shoulder. Shifting upward, he nibbles and sucks so hard, I'm worried he's going to give me a hickey.

No one has ever given me a hickey before. Emma wears them like a badge of honor. I can only imagine what my mom would think if she saw one on my neck.

She'd freak the hell out.

"Fuck, you smell so good," Beck murmurs against my neck, nuzzling me there. I shiver, tilting my head to the side, my hands sliding up and down the firm wall of his chest. His T-shirt is soft and I want to gather it in my fingers, tugging it upwards so I can touch his bare flesh.

"This shirt." He reaches between us, his fingers tracing the bodice, his touch featherlight. The tops of my breasts are basically exposed, which is totally not my style. I've never worn this shirt before anywhere. It was a total impulse buy, and once I got it into my closet, I was always afraid it was a little too revealing.

But it's perfect for this night. This date, or whatever we should call it.

With Beck.

"What about it?" I ask breathlessly.

He glances up, his smoldering, hot gaze meeting mine. "It's cut really low."

Those fingers trace back and forth.

Back and forth.

"You don't like it?" I ask, my voice shaky.

"I love it." He dips his index finger into the space between my cleavage, the very tip of his finger barely touching my skin, making me suck in a sharp breath. "Did you wear it for me?"

I'm shocked silent by his question, the commanding way he asked it. This is a side I've never seen from Beck before and it's really...

Hot.

"Yes," I whisper, deciding to be truthful.

The pleased gleam in his eyes tells me he likes my answer. "Rise up."

I do as he asks, straightening my spine as he wraps his arms around me, his hands splayed on my back as he dips his head...

And runs his lips along the same spot where his fingers just were.

My entire body feels weak at the first touch of his mouth on my skin. His lips are hot and smooth, and I tilt my head down, blatantly watching him. All the air feels like it's caught in my throat and I'm panting, as if I have no control over myself.

Beck glances up, his gaze fusing with mine, his mouth still on my skin. Never tearing his gaze away, he reaches up, a single finger curling around the front of my shirt and tugging. Gently at first.

Then harder, as he tries to pull it down. The fabric loosens and gives, gaping from my chest and he cocks his head to the side, looking down my shirt.

My nipples are hard, rubbing against the ruching, and I wait for him to do something.

Say something.

He's quiet as he reaches for my billowy sleeves, pushing the first one, then the other, off my shoulders. The fabric falls easily, gathering in the crooks of my elbows, and this helps the bodice fabric loosen as well.

The boy knows what he's doing.

Beck draws the back of his knuckles across the tops of my breasts. Goosebumps spark everywhere, covering my skin, making me shiver, and when he pulls the front of my shirt down, I'm almost completely exposed.

Only my nipples are still covered.

"Lean back a little," he whispers, and I automatically do as he says, my gaze still glued on him as he runs his mouth all over my newly exposed skin. He licks the valley between my breasts. Cups them together, his tongue tracing my cleavage.

I watch, breathless, overcome. This sort of thing would freak me out if I were with anyone else. I could barely take it when Jonah would touch my boobs, and there was no way in hell I would let him take my clothes off.

With Beck, though, I'm impatient. My thoughts are frantic, consuming—full of him and what he might do to me next. All I can concentrate on is the touch of his mouth on my skin, and how can I take this shirt off, so I can give him even better access to my body.

"I don't want to rip it," he murmurs, glancing up at me through his eyelashes. "Help me take it off, okay?"

I lift my arms and let him carefully pull the shirt up and over my head, before it falls onto the passenger seat and I'm sitting on Beck's lap, completely topless. Half-naked and exposed.

He falls back against his seat, blowing out a harsh breath, his gaze never straying from my chest. He stares at my breasts, working his jaw. Licking his lips. When he finally lifts his gaze to mine, his expression is ravenous.

Without hesitation, he reaches for me, his hand curling around the back of my neck, his fingers tangled in my hair as he consumes me with his hungry mouth. I'm greedy too, my hands sliding down, reaching for the hem of his shirt, so I can pull it off. He breaks away from me for only a second, ignoring my whimper of protest as he violently pulls his shirt off, tossing it aside. We come back together, our chests pressed close, for the first time we're skin-to-skin.

Oh God, he feels so good. Hot and smooth and firm.

I'm burning up from the inside. Going up in flames. Our mouths find each other, our tongues dancing. Mating. I'm grinding on top of him. I can feel him through his shorts. He's hard and long and oh my God, I want to touch him again. I want to see it.

I want to see all of him.

"Fuck, Adds." He tears his mouth from mine, pressing his face into my collarbone. I hold him close, my fingers tugging on his hair as I rest my cheek on top of his head. I can't stop moving. I feel restless. Needy. "We should slow down."

I go completely still when his words sink in. I can't believe he's the one who has to say it.

That's usually my line.

We sit like that for a moment, the sound of my racing heart pounding in my head, my ears. His stubble-roughened cheek brushes my sensitive skin. Skin that's never been touched by another before, and a whimper leaves me.

That one he heard. He glances up, as if he only just realized his own power, and he dips his head.

And rains kisses across the tops of my breasts.

I lean back, giving him more room, ignoring the stretch and ache of my legs. The position I'm in isn't the best, but I don't care. I want to lose myself in the sensation of his mouth on my skin. He cups one breast while kissing the other, his mouth everywhere but my nipple, where I want him the most. I wait, breathless as he drops a kiss on one. Licks it. Then sucks it into his mouth.

"Oh God," I gasp, clutching him to me. He drifts his thumb back and forth across the other nipple, alternating between the two. Giving them both equal attention. All while

I feel as if I'm about to lose my mind from his touch. His mouth.

This is what Mom worried about, I think, as my mind starts to empty from all other thoughts except this boy and how he makes me feel. This all-consuming lust filling me, driving me on. I'm restless. Squirming. I want his mouth all over my body. I want his hand between my legs. I want to feel his fingers search me. I want him naked.

I want to know what it feels like, to have this boy move inside of me. To be connected to him in the most intimate way possible.

His hand drops, resting at the front of my shorts, hesitating for only a moment before he undoes the snap.

Slides down the zipper.

The denim parts, his mouth still on my skin, his lips still wrapped around my nipple as he sucks, his fingers fumbling as he spreads the denim of my shorts wider. Those magical fingers brush against the front of my lace panties, and he releases my nipple from his mouth with an audible pop, leaning back against his seat.

"I need to see," he says, tilting his head down, his hand coming around my ass and pushing me forward on his lap. "Lace."

"White," I admit softly. He lifts his gaze to mine, his brows drawn together. "Is that what you wanted to see? What color they were?"

"I just want to see *you*." He tries to push my shorts down, and I lift my hips, knowing they're going to get hung up eventually, but looking for any kind of freedom I can get so I can move.

The shorts drop a little bit and I shimmy my hips, until the denim is wrapped tight around my thighs, completely restraining me. The position is incredibly awkward, and I'm sure I look ridiculous, but I can't even focus on that right now.

All I can see is the way Beck is staring at me with reverence. As if I'm the prettiest thing he's ever seen. He reaches out, trailing his fingers across the front of my panties and I hiss in a breath.

"Wet," he whispers.

I say nothing. There's no use denying it. This is what he does to me.

"You're trapped," he says and I nod, trying to spread my thighs farther, but they're not budging. "Should we take this to the—"

I shake my head, a muffled whimper leaving me as I collapse on top of him, my mouth seeking his. I kiss him, worried we're running out of time, wanting him to touch me in my most intimate spot. Will he do it?

Does he want me as bad as I want him?

He's a good guy. He'd never want to push me. He respects women—respects me. Maybe he'll say we're moving too fast...

Or maybe he feels like me and isn't thinking at all. He's just doing what he wants.

And what he wants to do is me.

When I feel his fingers brush against the elastic waistband of my panties without hesitation, I breathe a sigh of relief.

That's exactly what I want.

CHAPTER 21

BECK

J test the thin waistband of her panties, slipping just the tips of my fingers inside. I'm going slow, easing her into this, and she never protests. Never asks me to stop.

Addie wants this as badly as I do.

We're probably moving too fast. We confess we like each other and now I'm about to slip my fingers in her panties. Hell, I had my fingers in her pussy just last night.

It was all so spontaneous and happened so quickly...

Just like tonight.

How does someone prepare for this anyway? Watching lots of porn? That seems cheap and shitty. Talking with friends? Like those assholes would give me pointers. They'd just mock my ass for asking questions.

Google it? Jesus, I feel like an idiot...

Sasha and I were together for months, but we never had actual sex. We messed around a lot, especially when we were first together, but after a while, we weren't doing much at all.

Which tells me we really weren't meant for each other.

A horrible thought enters my mind, one I can't ignore.

Did Addie have sex with Jonah? Is that why she's so forward? So bold? Not that I'm complaining about the daring stuff because I fucking love how she's not hesitant with me at all.

But I sort of hate the idea of her losing her virginity to that asshole who marches around the field every halftime with his stupid drum set in front of him, thinking he's the shit.

Deciding I need to get over myself and just go for it, I slip my hand deeper into her panties, my fingers finding scant pubic hair. She lifts her hips, causing my hand to slide down into warm wetness.

Oh fuck.

She's so wet.

Addie bites her lip, her cheeks flushed, her head tilted down as she watches me push my fingers into her, though it's all hidden thanks to her panties. Maybe that's what makes it hotter. My busy hand stretching the fabric out. Tentatively stroking her. She's so wet I can hear my fingers slick through her pussy and my cock surges, reminding me that he's eager for some attention too.

Not sure if he's going to get his chance tonight, but the possibility is there.

I curl my other arm around her and bring her forward, my mouth landing on her nipple. I suck it deep into my mouth, pulling and licking and sucking. She thrusts her hands into my hair and holds me to her as she rides my hand, little cries falling from her lips every time I hit a certain spot.

The temperature in the car rises, making me sweat, and I wish I could kick off my shorts. My boxer briefs. I want to be naked. I want her to touch my dick. I want to bury myself inside her and feel her tremble around me. I want to fuck her until we both explode, though damn, since it'll be my first time, I'll probably shoot my wad way too early and leave her unsatisfied.

Yeah. Can't do that.

"B-Beck," she stutters, when I touch that one particular spot, "do that again."

I try to imitate what I did last time, but it's tough when I don't know how I did it in the first place. I brush my thumb against the top of her pussy, finding the little bundle of nerves there. Her clit. I press down on it, and she gasps. I circle it with my thumb, over and over, and she moves with me, a choked sound coming from her.

"S-so good," she whispers.

"Tell me where else to touch you," I whisper against the spot between her breasts, just before I kiss her there.

"Keep doing what you're doing," she encourages, and so I do. I stroke her. Kiss her. Stroke her harder.

Faster.

The circles get smaller. Tighter.

She's panting. Her hips are thrusting.

I think she's close.

I pull her head down to mine and take her lips in a savage kiss. Absolutely no finesse there. It's sloppy and dirty and has my cock leaping. I deliberately lick her lips, and she sticks out her tongue, licking me back, our tongues tangling.

Fuck me, that was hot.

Little cries fall from her lips and my instincts were correct. She rubs against me, faster and faster, and she's definitely close. I cup her pussy, my thumb working her clit, fumbling around like an idiot, but it doesn't seem to matter.

She squeezes her thighs around my hand, a gasp escaping her just before she starts to shiver and shake. I pull away slightly, so I can watch her fall apart, and fuck me, she does it so beautifully. Her entire body is flushed pink and her head is tossed back, her hair spilling everywhere. Her nipples are red and puffy from my mouth, standing straight up, and I swear to God if she clamps her thighs any tighter, I'm afraid she might break my hand.

She collapses, falling backwards, and she hits the steering wheel, the horn. The sound startles her, making her scream, just before she dissolves into giggles.

Slowly, I remove my hand from between her legs, and I can't help myself. I bring my hand to my face, breathing in her scent deeply, darting out my tongue to lick.

She tastes good. Salty. Sweet.

I'm so busy sucking on my finger, I don't notice that she's watching me carefully, her gaze heavy. Knowing. I touch her swollen lips, and she draws my index finger into her mouth, my eyes almost bugging out of my head when she begins to suck in earnest.

"Fuck, Adds," I groan. "You're killing me."

The wicked smile on her face tells me everything. She is one hundred percent aware of the power she has over me, and I'm pretty sure she likes it.

A lot.

"You like the way you taste?" I ask her, my voice sounding more like a low growl.

She releases my finger from her mouth. "I want to know what you taste like."

Fuck yeah. Let's go.

"Someday," she adds shyly.

Okay. Cool. I can work with that.

Addie yanks her shorts back on and climbs over the center console, falling into the passenger seat. I watch in mute fascination as she rids herself of the shorts, until she's sitting there in nothing but a pair of lacy white panties that look downright virginal, despite her sitting in my 4Runner practically naked.

I grab the phone and check the time—it's just past ten

o'clock. We gotta leave in less than an hour to make her curfew.

Fuck.

"Let's go to the back seat," I tell her.

"You mean the back of the car?"

I shake my head. "The back seat. If we go to the back of the car…"

Where there's more room, we could end up having sex. And stupid me, I didn't bring a condom.

My friends would be laughing their asses off at me right now.

"Climb over the console," I tell her, and I get out of the car, keeping the door open, so I can watch her climb over, her heart-shaped ass in the air as she does so. Everything inside of me clenches with need and I'd give anything to get her completely naked but…

No. I can't. Not yet.

We need to pace ourselves.

I forget all about pacing myself when I get into the back seat to find her sitting there looking like my every wet dream come to life. Her hair tousled and her eyes sleepy. Her lips swollen and her hard nipples on display. Pretty sure that's a hickey forming on the side of her neck, and I feel a swell of pride, knowing I'm the one who put it there.

We have stumbled head first into this, and it doesn't scare me at all. Or fill me with wariness.

All I want is more.

More Addie.

We reach for each other, our mouths connecting, our hands everywhere. She smooths her hand down the front of my chest as we kiss, until it rests on my stomach, making the muscles beneath her fingers twitch with need. My erection strains the front of my boxer briefs, demanding to be set free, and I mentally tell it to calm the fuck down.

I whisper her name against her lips when she settles her hand on top of my cock, a few minutes later. Everything inside of me goes completely still, laser focused on where she's touching me. Anticipating what she might do next.

"I...I really have no idea what I'm doing," she murmurs, pulling away slightly, so we can look at each other.

I stare at her pretty face, drinking her in. She's flushed and her eyes are wild. She's mostly naked and in the back seat of my car, and right now, in this moment, I feel like the luckiest man alive.

"Just—touch me," I tell her as I press my face against her neck and breathe in her delectable scent. "Like I did to you."

That's exactly what she does. She curls her fingers around my length, stroking. Her touch is tentative. Questioning. Pretty sure she can tell by my breathing that I approve. Everything she does, I'm not going to stop her or complain.

I can't even fucking believe I'm with Addie like this. Wrapped all around me, my mouth fused with hers, her hand on my dick. And when she slips her hand beneath my briefs to actually touch me, damn.

I'm worried I'm going to come all over her fingers in seconds.

I groan into her mouth when her thumb brushes the head. My skin goes tight and that familiar tingly feeling starts at the base of my spine.

I'm already close.

Like a tease, she removes her hand and curls it around my shoulder, pulling me in closer to her. We're struggling to get closer, and it's not easy in the back seat of my car, but we're making it work. Sparks light up my skin every time I brush against her and I want more.

I need more.

Until I'm pulling her on top of me, nothing stopping us or holding us back. She melts against me, her arms wound around my neck, her fingers in my hair—always in my hair, I think she likes it—it's as if she can't get enough of me.

I feel the same way.

We kiss and kiss until my jaw aches, but I still don't stop. She rubs her pussy against my cock, the only barrier between us actually touching skin-to-skin are her lace panties and my cotton boxer briefs.

Fuck. It would be so easy to get rid of them and push inside of her. Just for a second...

Can't do it. No condom, no actual penetration, I tell myself. I gotta wrap it up. No way can I risk it. This is the girl whose older sister got pregnant when she was in high school.

But I can touch her, which is exactly what I do when I slip my fingers inside her panties to find her still drenched. I slick through all that wetness, rubbing her, making her moan softly against my lips, and she reaches for me too, fumbling for my cock until we're both straining toward each other.

Exploring each other.

The moment she grips my cock beneath my boxer briefs, I'm done for. A ragged groan leaves me and I'm coming, spilling all over her fingers exactly as I envisioned only a few minutes before. Shudders wrack my body until there's nothing left and I slump against the seat, breathing so hard, my lungs hurt. My heart thumps. My head swims.

Addie's fingers are still curled around my semi-deflated cock.

"Um...I guess you liked that," she murmurs, as she carefully removes her hand and falls onto the seat beside me.

I crack my eyes open to watch her glance around, her fingers coated in cum. Leaning forward, I find a couple of napkins in the seat pocket and hand them to her, feeling...

Embarrassed?

I shouldn't feel that way. I care about this girl more than I ever realized. What we just shared...

Was something I've never experienced before.

She cleans her hand and tosses the wadded-up napkins on the floorboard before she settles right next to me, resting her head on my shoulder. We sit with each other in silence, our breathing slowly returning to normal, a little shiver moving through me here and there. She turns her head and presses her mouth to my shoulder before she glances up, watching me. I turn to look at her, noting the smile on her face. The way her eyes sparkle.

"I guess we like each other," she whispers.

I cup her cheek, staring into her dark blue eyes. "Guess we do."

Her laughter is the sweetest sound I've ever heard. "I can't believe that just—happened."

I lean down to kiss her, my lips lingering on hers. "Any regrets?"

"Oh my God, no." She moves her lips over mine, breathing into me before she slowly pulls away. "I just hope you don't think we're moving too fast."

"I hope you don't think I'm moving too fast." I smooth my thumb across her cheek, savoring her velvety soft skin.

She shakes her head, her gaze never straying from mine. "I think we've wasted a lot of time."

"Yeah." I smile at her, my heart cracking wide open, my feelings for her spilling everywhere. "Let's not waste any more time, okay?"

"Okay," she whispers. "I should—probably get dressed. I need to get home."

"Same."

We pull our clothes back on, and I get behind the wheel, checking my phone. It's a little after eleven, and when I tell Addie that, her expression shifts into full-blown panic.

"Oh my God, I need to get home. I can't be late."

She pulls her seat belt on and I start the engine, navigating carefully off the granite mountain, not wanting to drive too fast because it's dark and I'm not that familiar with the trail.

I can tell my slowness makes Addie anxious, but there's nothing I can do about it. Once I finally hit the paved road, I increase my speed, concentrating on the road, trying to ignore the uneasiness resonating off of Addie in giant waves.

The tension is off the charts—and not the good kind either. She keeps checking her phone, looking at the time and sighing. To the point that I'm a little irritated.

"I'm driving as fast as I can," I tell her, my voice tight as I turn onto the highway so fast, my tires squeal.

"I'm sorry," she says. "It's just—my mom is really strict when it comes to my curfew."

"It's pretty early." I feel her glance over at me. "Eleven thirty on a Saturday night? You're almost eighteen."

"It's normally midnight, but I had to compromise with her tonight." She doesn't explain further, and I don't ask. "What's your curfew?"

I shrug. "I don't have one."

"Seriously?"

"I don't stay out that late, and if I do, I end up staying the night wherever I'm at. A friend's house, or up at Bayshore. You know what it's like," I explain.

"My mom doesn't trust me," Addie admits. "And I never do anything, really. I mean, well..."

Addie's voice trails off and if she goes into detail about anything she's done with another guy—Jonah—I'm going to lose it.

Thankfully, she doesn't.

"We did something tonight," she finally says. "And I'm going to be late. I'm giving her reasons not to trust me for once in my life."

"Why doesn't she trust you?"

"I don't know," she says, but I can tell.

She does know.

She just doesn't want to tell me.

Which is cool. Whatever. Though it kind of hurts, that she doesn't trust me enough to confess why.

By the time we pull up in front of her house, it's eleven-thirty-five and I'm feeling pretty good that I got her home only five minutes late. I had to do it driving pretty fucking fast, which probably wasn't the smartest thing, but hey, I got her home.

"I have to go. Goodnight." She's reaching for the door handle, ready to bolt, but I stop her by placing my hand on her shoulder. She turns to look at me, her eyes wide and full of worry. "What?"

I kiss her, because I can. Because she's mine. "Text me in the morning, okay?"

Addie nods, visibly swallowing. "Okay."

"Goodnight, Adds."

Her smile is faint, but it doesn't quite reach her eyes. They're still full of worry. "Night."

She's out of my car in an instant, and I watch her head up the walkway and enter her house. Only when I know she's safely inside, do I pull away from the curb and drive home.

With a smile stretched across my face the entire way.

CHAPTER 22

ADDIE

I sneak into the house as quietly as possible, shutting the door so slowly, it barely makes a sound. I slip off my shoes and head for my room, the house so quiet it's almost eerie.

Only when I'm in my bedroom, do I feel like I've made it free and clear, and I close the door, leaning my head against it for a few seconds before I reach for the lamp on my dresser and flick it on, gasping when I see someone sitting on the end of my bed.

My mother.

"You're late."

"What are you doing?" I ask, hating how rapid my heartbeat is. How suspicious she looks. "And I was only five minutes late."

"According to my phone, you're ten minutes late." She thrusts her phone out toward me, showing the screen where it says eleven-forty at the top. "Where were you?"

"We just—hung out." I shrug one shoulder, purposely vague.

"You didn't answer my question. Where were you?" she repeats, her voice rising.

"We went up into the mountains with some friends and checked out the view."

"What friends?"

"Tori and Dom. They're dating."

"Dominic Devito?"

I nod. "Yeah. He's Beck's best friend."

"I know his mother. She's very nice."

"You know Beck's mother too. And she's very nice." Exhaustion suddenly hits me and I push away from the door. "Are you done with your questioning? Because I want to go to bed."

"I know you were up on Rattlesnake Mountain," she says.

I stop in my tracks. "What, you were spying on me?"

Stupid *Find My Phone*. I shouldn't complain. At least she doesn't have one of those tracking apps on me, so she'll know my every move, including how fast I'm driving when I'm in my car.

"I like to know where you are. That you're safe." Her gaze is intense as she watches me. "Are you sure you were with friends? Or was it just you and Beck up there?"

I try to keep my expression impassive. "We were with friends."

She rises from the bed and walks toward me, stopping directly in front of me. "You weren't alone with him, doing something you're not supposed to?"

"Mom." My cheeks go warm. "This is so freaking embarrassing. Seriously, nothing happened. We just hung out."

"I just worry about you, sweetie. I know Beck is a nice boy, and it sounds like you like him a lot. But be careful. Don't move too fast. You have all the time in the world for a serious relationship," she says.

If she only knew how fast we moved tonight. She'd freak out.

No way can I tell her. She'd put me on lockdown and I'd never be allowed to see Beck Callahan again.

"I understand," I say softly. "And don't worry. I do like Beck, but we're taking it slow."

That was probably the biggest lie I've ever told my mother.

* * *

I SLEEP LIKE THE DEAD, finally waking up around ten, feeling groggy. I grab my phone to check my notifications to see I have a text from Tori and one from Emma in our group text thread.

And a Snapchat from Beck.

I check his first, smiling when I see his photo. He's shirtless and sleep rumpled and oh my God, he's so adorable first thing in the morning. I stare at the photo for a while, drinking him in, wishing we were in bed together, so I could snuggle close to him and breathe in his spicy male scent.

His caption says, good morning.

Taking a quick selfie, I caption mine the same and send it to him, then check my other messages.

Emma: **Marcus and I worked it out. He came over last night and we had a long talk.**

Tori: **Yay! I'm so glad! Dom took me to the movies last night, but we didn't watch it.**

I ignore Emma's text because, let's be real—they're going to argue again and split up. I can almost guarantee it.

But I do respond to Tori's.

Me: **Why didn't you watch it?**

I'm playing stupid on purpose. Pretty sure I know why they weren't paying attention to the movie screen.

Tori: **Um because he wouldn't stop kissing me. We sat in the very back row and all he did was kiss me over and over.**

Emma: **Oooh Tori! Getting some action in the movie theater!**

Tori: **It wasn't that big of a deal. Just a simple make-out session.**

I smile, thinking of my Saturday night. We took it way too far, and it was worth every moment.

As a matter of fact, I can't wait to do it again.

Emma: **What were you up to last night, Addie?**

Me: **I was with Beck.**

Tori: **Ooooh do tell.**

Me: **There's nothing to tell. We had fun.**

Emma: **That's great.**

We chat for a while longer until Beck FaceTime's me.

Oh shit. I look terrible. I run a hand over my hair. Yank my camisole up so my tits aren't hanging out.

Finally, I answer him, and it takes a while for the call to connect before his face fills my phone screen.

"Mornin'." His voice is deep and sleep-roughened and I've never heard anything sexier.

"Hey." I smile at him. "And you already said that."

He holds his phone in one hand while he scratches at his chest with the other. "I did?"

"In your Snap you sent me earlier," I remind him.

"Oh yeah. I woke up, sent you that and fell back asleep." His smile is sheepish. "I was tired."

"Big night last night?"

"Fuck yeah. Was with this really hot girl who rocked my world." He grins.

I blush.

"Did you get in trouble for being late?" he asks.

"Get this." I sit up a little, ready to tell my story. "I sneak back into the house, feeling pretty confident no one heard me. I walk into my room and turn on the light to find my mother sitting on my bed."

He frowns. "No way."

I nod. "Yeah. She was mad I was ten minutes late."

"You were only five minutes late."

"By the time I got into my room, it was ten. And she was kind of mad."

"She didn't give you any shit, did she?" He frowns, seeming concerned.

"Kind of. I had to lie to her and say we were with Dom and Tori." I hesitate, feeling dumb. "She wouldn't like it if we were alone. She knew where we were."

"Does she track you with Life 360?" he asks.

I shake my head. "Just *Find My Phone*."

"My parents do the same, though they only check when they're worried about me, I think."

"My mother is always worried about me, so she checks it a lot." I tuck a few wild strands of hair behind my ear. "If we do something together again, she's going to want you to come in the house and do that whole formal introduction, *I'll take care of your daughter, ma'am* type thing."

"If we do something again? Maybe we need to get one thing straight." He brings the phone up to his face, so I can only see his mouth. His beautiful, wicked mouth. "We're definitely doing something together again, if I have anything to say about it."

My cheeks are hot. This is the sort of confirmation I always needed from him, though it's still a little hard to believe.

That Beck Callahan wants me. Wants to be with me. Wants to do things with me.

"Okay," I say weakly, because what else can I say to that?

He pulls the phone away, so I can see his entire face again. "What are you doing today?"

"Homework. Laundry. More homework." A sigh leaves me. "I know we've only had two days of school so far, but I have a math assignment due by midnight."

"I do too." He runs a hand through his hair, his biceps bulging, making a bigger mess of it. "I wish I could see you."

"You're seeing me right now," I tease.

"And while I appreciate seeing your beautiful face via FaceTime, I wish we were in-person," he says, his voice going lower. "So I could touch you."

"Beck." I burst out laughing, trying to bat down the intense feelings that threaten to take over. He called me beautiful. Again. "We'll see each other tomorrow."

"At school. Not good enough."

"We're busy people." I bite my lip. "I won't even be here this upcoming weekend. We have our annual tournament in Mammoth."

"Oh." His face falls. "That'll be fun."

"It always is."

"You'll miss my first regular season game."

"Isn't it an away game?"

"Yeah, but it still counts. I was hoping you would be there. You'll be at school, right? You can wear my jersey."

I would give anything to wear his jersey around school, but...

"We leave Friday morning, right after second period. We're taking a couple of district vans and heading over the pass, through Yosemite," I explain. "I won't be back until Sunday night."

"Oh. I won't get to see you at all over the weekend." His frown deepens.

"It'll go by fast. And you'll get to see me before school

starts Friday," I tell him reassuringly. "I bet you won't even miss me."

"I'm missing you right now," he admits, his gaze hooded. Eep, he's hot when he looks like that. Being shirtless doesn't help in downplaying his good looks either. He's just too scorching for words. "And I'll definitely miss you this weekend when you're gone."

"It's just one weekend," I murmur. "Three days."

"Three days too long."

"It's my last time playing in this tournament with my team," I say. "I'm a little sad over it."

"It's weird, knowing all of these things we're doing, which we've done for years, are now for the last time," he says.

I smile. He gets it. He knows what I'm talking about, and there's something so comforting about it.

He understands me.

And more than anything, I want to understand him too.

CHAPTER 23

BECK

*E*xcitement fills me as I arrive at school Monday morning, fully decked out in another new pair of shorts and a black Vans T-shirt, strutting up the walkway in my new Vans. I'm barely on campus and already getting compliments on my fit, which has me standing taller. Feeling even more confident.

Then I spot my friends standing in a circle, talking and laughing.

I see Liam. Addie standing right next to him.

My confidence crumbles a little bit, quickly replaced with anger.

What the fuck is that guy doing, stepping in on my territory?

I slow my pace, my gaze on Addie and no one else, looking for a sign that she's actually engaging in real conversation with that asshole. They're standing close, but there's still some distance between them. They're not touching each other, thank God.

I'd have to break his fingers if he so much as laid one on her.

Relief floods me as I draw closer. They're not even talking. She's chatting with Tori and Dom, who are hanging all over each other, Marcus standing with them and accompanied by...

Oh, fuck me, is that Monique?

I'm officially confused.

I approach my friends, putting on a broad smile when they spot me and a few of them call out a greeting. Addie sends me a shy smile before she returns her attention to Tori, who is talking a mile a minute.

"What's goin' on?" I ask Dom, as I stop to stand beside him. I don't want to interrupt Addie and Tori, whose heads are bent close as they start whispering to each other.

"Bro, major gossip. I'll fill you in later," he murmurs, glancing over at Tori with a soft smile before he returns his focus to me. "I'm this close to making it official with her."

"Oh yeah? That's great. But maybe give it a little more time," I tell him, trying to sound like a wise soul.

Really? I have no idea what I'm talking about, considering I'm the one who practically had sex with Addie Saturday night, and we're not even officially together. Are we even officially talking? I've said nothing and neither has she, though we did chat with each other via text most of Sunday.

"I'm going to. She might show her true colors quick." Dom makes a face and shakes his head. I'm sure he's trying to put up a wall with Tori, but he already seems like he's gone over her.

He hasn't had a serious girlfriend since our sophomore year. He went out with a girl—Mia—who put him through hell and back. Manipulative, conniving, Mia used my boy hard. Cheated on him too, and he ended up feeling like a fool. Angry and in love and pissed at himself about it. Their toxic relationship made him wary of all girls for a solid year.

Tori is the complete opposite of Mia. She's open and

bubbly and seems down for a fun time, always. I'm thinking she's exactly what Dom needs, but I still stand by my advice. He needs to be cautious at first. You just never know.

"He wasn't talking to her, was he?" I flick my chin toward Liam and Addie, silently fuming. I hate that he's even standing next to her. She brings out this possessive side in me I had no idea existed.

"He made an attempt, but she pretty much shut him down." Dom laughs. "He's still trying with her and I don't know why."

The anger rises. "Are you serious? He's flirting and shit?" I start for him, but Dom slaps his hand against the center of my chest, stopping me.

"It was nothing, trust me. I'll watch out for your girl when you're not around." Dom raises a brow. "You are trying to get with her, right?"

"I pretty much am with her," I confirm.

Dom slaps my chest again, a little lighter this time. "That's my boy. You see each other over the weekend?"

"Saturday night," I admit. "Things got pretty hot and heavy. That's why I'm pissed Liam is sniffing around her."

"He can be a dick, but I'm thinking he's pretty harmless. Don't worry about him." Dom glances over at Liam, who's now got Danny standing next to him, and they're talking with Marcus and Monique, which is sus as hell.

"Why is Marcus with Monique anyway?" I ask, deciding to change the subject.

"He's not. She's just trying her hardest to spend time with him since Emma hasn't showed up yet." Dom shakes his head, chuckling. "Guess I filled you in on all the gossip already—and you shared some good shit too."

"Just don't mention anything about me and Addie to anyone yet. It's not like we're official," I tell him, knowing he'll keep his mouth shut.

Plus, it feels too new, too fragile between us. Not that she's going to bail on me if she hears I'm telling everyone we're together, but...

Maybe she would. I don't know. Maybe she wants what happened between us to be kept under wraps too...

"I can keep your secret." Dom nods, a faint smile on his face.

"Emma and Marcus break up at his party Friday night?" I ask, my gaze zeroed in on Addie as she greets Emma, who's just shown up. Tori and Addie wrap Emma up in a group hug, but she pushes them off, marching right up to Marcus and basically throwing herself at him in front of Monique.

He grabs Emma's ass and hauls her in, delivering a long, tongue-filled kiss to his new/old girlfriend. And I know it was tongue-filled because we all just saw their tongues.

I look away, not interested in watching them dry hump each other first thing on a Monday morning.

"They got into an argument, but from the looks of it, they didn't break up." Dom waves a hand at Emma and Marcus. "Though I hear he took a free hand job from Monique that night too."

Oh damn. That's some bullshit. But also, it's none of my damn business. Marcus and I are friends, but I wouldn't call us close.

The warning bell rings and we all start to walk toward the buildings where our classes are. I'm heading for my English class, wincing when I already feel the back of my Vans rub against my ankles. I come to a quick stop, read-justing my shoe when I realize someone is walking directly beside me.

Addie.

"Hey, Callahan," she greets, her smile sweet.

Just for me.

"What up, Douglas?" I keep my voice casual. Like this is

no big deal, though just having her walk next to me leaves my legs wobbly.

Seriously, what the hell is wrong with me? She makes me feel like a bumbling idiot every time I get around her. I saw her pretty much naked only a few days ago. We shared something I've never shared with any girl before, and I want nothing more than to pull her into me and give her a big ol' kiss in front of everyone. But would she freak out? Push me away?

I restrain myself, just barely.

"What's your first class?" she asks.

"English."

"Mine too." Her lips turn into the smallest frown. "Too bad we don't have the same class together."

"Right. I'd be writing a paper on *To Kill A Mockingbird* if I did." I make a pained face and she laughs. "No thanks."

"Even if it meant I was in the class with you?" Her smile and tone are both flirtatious.

"You'd be the only thing that would make it worth being in that class," I tell her, dead serious.

"Aw, you are too sweet. You're telling me you don't want to overanalyze literature written over one hundred years ago?" She raises her brows as we head down the hallway side by side.

I'm ignoring all kinds of people saying hello to me. She is too. We're only focused on each other, just the way I like it.

"I'll have you know, *To Kill A Mockingbird* was published about fifty years ago," I tell Addie, like I'm full of literary knowledge.

"You're right." She frowns. "How did you know that?"

I shrug, playing it off. "I went and saw the play on Broadway with my parents a few years ago."

Her eyes widen. "Really? That's so cool. I've never been to

a play on Broadway before. I haven't been to New York City either. Was the play any good?"

"It was really good. Totally held my interest. New York was awesome too, though way too big a city for me. Too many people," I say, hating how close we're getting to my class. "Looks like we're next door to each other."

"We are. Thank you for walking me to class," she says, smiling up at me.

"Anytime." I lean against the wall, watching her. She takes a step closer, and I lower my voice to say, "I really want to kiss you right now."

"No one is stopping you." Her smile is warm.

Glancing around, I push off the wall and move in slowly, dropping a kiss on her cheek at the last second.

She mock-pouts. "That's it?"

"There's more where that came from," I say, my voice full of promise.

Addie laughs and darts into her classroom, making me laugh too.

Our flirtatious interaction takes me straight through the morning, leaving me on an Addie-fueled high. Even through lunch, when I was stuck meeting with the rest of the team and the offensive coach, who showed us tape of the team we're playing this Friday. I'm distracted as fuck, trying to concentrate on all the plays this team makes, when really, my head is full of images of Addie.

Addie straddling me. When I first pulled the front of her shirt down. The taste of her lips. The way she whimpers when she's close. How good it felt to have her fingers wrapped around my dick.

I'm also glad Liam is stuck in here with us during lunch, because it keeps him away from Addie. I'm going to have to talk to him. Tell him to back off, once and for all. I thought he got the picture that she wasn't interested on Friday, but looks like he didn't. The fucker. I don't want to have to lay hands on him—he is my friend, but not when he's pulling shit like this.

A dickish thought, but here I am, thinking like a dick. Embracing it really.

By the time I'm walking into our World Religions class, I'm eager to see her. Unfortunately, she's not at her desk and I settle into mine, checking my phone with one eye on the open doorway. Lots of people walk inside, some of them saying hi as they pass me by, and I mumble a greeting, hating how anxious I feel.

This is what she does. Leaves me twisted up inside every single time.

Finally, she appears.

With Liam looming right behind her.

I keep my eye on him, glaring the entire time. He doesn't look in my direction, too entranced with Addie. My gaze goes to her, noticing how annoyed she appears, how she's trying to get away from him. I'm about to go help her, but she must say something to him that makes him mad, and he storms off.

Good.

Addie settles into her desk next to me, irritation flashing as she plops her backpack on her desk noisily, digging into it until she pulls out a notebook and lets it drop with a slap on top of her desk.

"You all right?" I ask carefully.

She flashes me a tight smile. "I'm fine. Great."

The bell rings and Hardison immediately starts talking, ending our conversation. Which is frustrating, considering how angry Addie seems.

Is she mad at me, or Liam? I didn't ever get a chance to tell her where I was at lunch, though it's not like we made definitive lunch plans. This is where I suck in the relationship department. I should've made plans with her yesterday, when we were texting.

Instead, I have to sit here, wishing I was talking to her. Unsure of how she's feeling.

Hardison ends up lecturing the entirety of class, and the minute the bell rings, I'm on my feet, my backpack already thrown over my shoulder as I stand in the aisle between mine and Addie's desks.

"Ready to go?" I ask her.

She glances up at me, her expression blank. "Sure."

"Cool." I nod, feeling decidedly not cool.

Addie zips her backpack closed before she rises to her feet. "Ready?"

"Let's do it," I tell her, indicating she can walk in front of me.

We leave the classroom and exit the hall, until the sun is shining down upon us, making me immediately break out into a sweat. August where we live is hot as hell during the day, and I'm living for the moment we can finally get a cool down, so practice isn't such a sweaty nightmare.

"What's wrong?" I ask her when she still hasn't said anything.

A sigh leaves her. "It's Liam. He keeps trying to talk to me, and it's annoying. I'm not interested in him."

She comes to a stop and so do I.

"Want me to talk to him?" I ask, my voice tight.

"I don't want to cause any trouble. You guys are friends —" she starts, but I shake my head, cutting her off.

"If he's making you uncomfortable, I'll speak to him. He needs to back off." I clench my hands into fists, letting the anger course through my blood.

I'm not in the mood to deal with him sniffing around my girl. He needs to back the fuck off.

"Maybe I'm overreacting," Addie says, as we resume

walking toward the library. "He might be just making friendly conversation, but I don't know…"

"What exactly did he say?"

We pause just outside the library's front doors. "He asked if I would give him another chance."

What the hell?

"That is definitely not friendly," I say as I breathe through my nose. My nostrils are literally flaring, I'm so pissed. "It's a little too friendly, if you ask me."

"He doesn't know," she says, her voice soft. "About us. No one does. I mean, we hung out Friday at the party, but no one really saw us there either."

"Is that what you prefer? To keep it a secret?" That is the last thing I want. I want to shout to the world that I'm with this girl. That she's mine.

"No, I just…I don't know." Her gaze is imploring. "What are you thinking?"

"Hey guys!"

We turn to see Emma heading for us. Addie greets her, her voice weak. I don't say a word.

I'm too busy clenching my jaw and silently stressing the fuck out.

"What are you guys doing? Headed for the library?" Emma asks.

"We're Hardison's TAs, remember? She doesn't have us really doing anything yet, so we hang out here and do homework," Addie says.

"Oh. Right." Emma looks from me to Addie. "You two seemed cozy just now. Still do."

Addie rolls her eyes. "Stop trying to make something out of nothing, Emma."

She doesn't even wait for her best friend to respond. Instead, she walks into the library, never once looking back.

"Touchy," Emma says once Addie is gone.

I glare at her, not saying a word as I follow Addie into the library. She's already seated at the table we were at last week, and I settle into the empty chair directly across from her.

"Sorry about that," she mumbles as she keeps her head bent while she digs through her backpack.

"Sorry about what?" I lean across the table, lightly touching her arm, making her go still. "What just happened out there?"

Addie shoves her backpack away, her gaze finding mine. "Emma can be—a lot sometimes. I'm tired of the snide remarks she makes. She's been doing it all day."

I want to tell her I don't think Emma is a very good friend to her, but I keep my mouth shut. Instead, I smile at her, wishing I could touch her.

So I do. I grab hold of her hand and give it the barest of squeezes, my entire body reacting when we make first contact.

"Want to get together after practice tonight?"

Addie shakes her head. "I can't. I'm sorry. I have to go straight home."

"It's okay. Maybe later this week." Disappointment crashing into me, I let go of her hand and pull my math textbook and a couple of sheets of paper out of my backpack and start in on my homework.

Addie does the same, pulling out a different, far more advanced textbook, and cracking it open. I glance at it, the formulas and problems looking like a foreign language, and I'm reminded of how smart she is.

How she's probably going to some fancy college far away from here, while I'm hoping to stay in state and play college ball. I don't have much ambition beyond that.

I haven't even really thought about it either. I haven't had to. My parents don't push me about my future. They just want me to go to a good college, and I know I can do it. But what do I want beyond that? It's intimidating, how ambitious my brother and sisters are, and then there's me.

But I can't worry about my future. I need to remain in the here and now, concentrating on the pretty girl sitting across from me. The girl I'm totally falling in love with.

She slides her foot forward, and I realize at some point, she must've taken off her sandal. Her bare toes slide up my leg, startling me.

All the worry and uneasiness inside of me evaporates, and I go completely still.

She lifts her lids, her amused gaze meeting mine as she drags her toes up and down my bare leg slowly.

As usual, I feel that seemingly innocent touch all the way to my balls.

"My mom is being extra strict," she admits, her voice low as she stares at her textbook. "I think she's upset we went out Saturday, and she's taking it out on me."

"That's...irrational." I can't think of anything else to say.

"Tell me all about it." Her foot curls around my calf. "Maybe I can tell her I'm hanging with the girls after the volleyball game tomorrow. We do that a lot, so she wouldn't question me."

"You'd lie to her?" I raise my brows, but she's not even looking at me.

"When she does this sort of thing to me, then yes. I have to."

I reach for her, settling my hand over hers, so she has to stop scratching her pencil across the paper. "I don't want to make you lie to your parents, Adds. Maybe I should come over and talk to her."

Addie jerks her head up, her eyes wide. Her foot falls away from my leg. "No. That's a terrible idea."

"You really think so?"

She nods. "My mom is being really hard on me right now.

She does this sometimes. She's always afraid I'm going to veer off track."

"Off track from what?"

"My goals. My future. College."

I interlace our fingers together, sliding mine against hers. "What are your goals? Because my current one is to spend as much time with you as possible."

The tiny smile she flashes my way makes my heart feel like it just skipped a beat. "I like that goal."

"Oh yeah?" I pick her hand up with mine, about to bring it to my mouth, so I can drop a quick kiss on her knuckles. "Wait until—"

"What the hell are you two doing?"

CHAPTER 24

ADDIE

The sound of Liam's furious voice makes Beck and I jerk away from each other. "What are you doing here?" I ask him, irritated.

God, he just completely ruined that particular moment. Beck was being so sweet. Like an actual...

Boyfriend.

"What the fuck is going on here?" Liam raises his voice, turning his anger on me. "I thought we had something going."

"Liam—" I start, but he cuts me off.

"You playing us both? Really?"

Anger rises within me, plus a healthy dose of embarrassment. "No, I'm not playing you both. I'm not playing anyone."

"We were talking. You and me." Liam taps his chest with his finger. "Not him. I know I screwed up, but I asked you to give me another chance. It's the least you can do."

He says it like I owe him.

He's wrong.

"Can we talk about this later?" I glance around, noticing

that more than a few people are watching us. Doesn't help that Liam is being so loud. "How about after practice?"

"I thought you had to leave right after practice," Beck says to me.

Feels like he's trying to stir the pot.

But is he?

I turn to see him watching me with confusion clouding his blue eyes. "I do."

"So you're just saying that, but you really don't want to talk to me?" Liam snaps, his tone hostile. "Great."

"Liam—"

"Come outside with me," Liam demands.

"No." I gesture toward where my backpack sits on the table. "I'm busy, Liam. We can talk later."

I thought we already resolved this. Liam didn't reach out to me at all this weekend. I assumed he knew I wasn't interested and moved on.

But maybe I was wrong. I guess that's what I get for assuming.

"Too busy for me, but not too busy for that asshole." Liam gestures toward Beck, who sits up straighter, his expression turning fierce.

"Hey, what the hell, Thatcher?"

"You've been sniffing around her since you realized I had a thing for her," Liam continues, his face contorted into an angry snarl. "Back off, Callahan. She's mine."

"I'm not a piece of property you can claim—" I start, but Liam swings all that anger onto me.

"Shut the hell up, Addie. I don't need your input."

Beck rises to his feet. All six-foot-four—or is it five?—of him. "Don't talk to her like that." His voice is deep and way too calm.

Like...scary calm.

I'm in shock over what Liam just said to me. As if my opinion doesn't matter, when I'm just as involved in this situation as he is.

Like seriously, what the hell? No one has ever spoken to me like that before.

"Yeah? What are you going to do about it?" Liam goads, his gaze flicking to Beck's feet before he scans the entire length of him. "You're all bark and no bite. Slow as fuck too."

Beck's jaw hardens. He didn't like the slow remark. Boys. "Watch what you're saying, man. You might not be able to walk back from it when this conversation is over."

Liam makes a dismissive noise. "Please. You don't scare me. You never have. Rich asshole who thinks he's above everyone else with your daddy coddling you every chance he gets. You're just a so-so football player with an 'aw-shucks' attitude that everyone falls for. I'm the only one who sees through you. It's a bunch of bullshit."

"Liam, come on." I don't want them to get into a fight, though I think it's too late for that. But these guys are friends. I don't want to come in between them. I jump to my feet and reach for my backpack. "Let's go outside and talk."

The last thing I want to do is continue this conversation with Liam, but I also don't want things to get worse between him and Beck.

They completely ignore me, though. Too busy having a staring match to listen to what I have to say.

"Yeah, well, at least I'm not a mediocre player who spends the majority of his game time standing on the sidelines," Beck tosses back at him like a bomb.

Uh oh.

I back up just in time.

Liam lunges for him, his arm swinging out and only grazing Beck's chin when he jerks back at the last second. It's

Beck who makes contact first, his fist colliding with Liam's eye.

"Fuck!" Liam roars.

That gets everyone's attention.

I'm shrieking, begging them to stop. The librarian is behind her desk and on the phone, calling administration, I'm sure. The librarian assistant is running toward us, demanding that they break apart. One of the guys from the football team joins in the fray, getting in the middle of them and pushing Liam away from Beck, who's rubbing at the side of his mouth, his chest heaving.

I stare at him in shock. I can't believe they were fighting.

Over me.

Beck cradles the side of his face, his knuckles red and raw from hitting Liam. His eyes are wild and when they meet mine, he flashes me a closed-mouth smile.

Oh shit. That was kind of…

Hot.

I go to Beck, my hand curving around the spot where Liam hit him, making him wince.

"Are you okay?"

"I'm fine. Are you all right? You didn't get hurt, did you?" Beck runs his hands over my shoulders, down my arms, shocking me.

He just got into a fight, and he's making sure I'm all right?

Mrs. Adney chooses that moment to bustle into the library, and everything immediately calms. Adney has been the vice principal at our high school for years. No one messes with her. She's a freaking institution at this place.

"What in the world is going on here?" she asks, when she comes to a stop at our table. Her gaze finds mine. "Addison Douglas, please don't tell me you're in the middle of this?"

I am one hundred percent in the middle of this. The only reason they're arguing is because of me. I'm about to open my mouth and tell her exactly that when Beck speaks over me.

"She's not, Miz Adney. This is just between Liam and me."

Oh God. He just totally protected me. I can't even look at him right now, not with the way Mrs. Adney is watching me, her shrewd gaze telling me she's on to us.

"Boys, in my office. Now," she demands, taking a couple of steps closer to me. "I'll want to talk to you as well, Addison."

I swallow hard, fighting the nerves swarming inside me. I've never been in trouble before, like ever. This is a total first.

"Let's go," Adney commands before she heads toward the doors. Liam and Beck fall into step behind her, keeping their distance, and I grab my backpack, ducking my head as I walk through the library. Everyone's eyes on us as we exit.

The gossip is going to be absolutely rampant. It'll be all over school by the final bell, just watch.

I trudge up the hill toward the administration building, grateful when Beck stops to walk beside me.

"You sure you're okay?" he asks, his voice low.

"I should be asking you that," I murmur. "How's your jaw?"

"His fist barely made a connection, but it still kind of hurts." He touches the side of his face, wincing. "I'm going down."

"What do you mean?"

"We're both going to get suspended. They don't tolerate fighting on campus," Beck says, worry filling his eyes. "My dad is gonna kill me."

My heart aches for him. "I'm so sorry."

"It's not your fault. He shouldn't talk to you like that." He sends me a quick glance, his brows drawn together. "He's rude as fuck, Addie. Tell him to leave you alone, or I'll tell him for you."

Beck doesn't say this quietly and, of course, Liam turns, fury in his features. "Fuck off, Callahan. You're asking for it."

"No, *you're* asking for it, Mr. Thatcher, by threatening another student in my presence." Mrs. Adney stops and turns to face us all, standing above us since we're on a hill. "Beck, do not speak to Addison. You're only making things worse. Addison, come up here and walk with me."

I do as she says, sending an apologetic look in Beck's direction as I walk past him.

I don't even look at Liam. I'm too mad at him.

Way too mad.

We walk the rest of the way to Adney's office in complete silence, her walkie-talkie crackling with activity every few seconds, I swear. It's hot outside, the sun bearing down on us, and I can feel the sweat start to form on my hairline.

Just another fun Monday afternoon in high school.

Adney ushers Liam and Beck into her office and makes me wait outside in the chairs next to the front desk, where the school secretary, Kelli, sits. She smiles at me, her eyes full of worry.

"Everything okay, hon?"

"I'm fine," I say with a nod, grabbing my phone from my backpack, not surprised to see I have text messages.

From Tori:

Uh, I just heard there was a fight in the library between Liam and Beck????!!!!! I need deets!!!!

From Emma:

Did I just see you head up to the office with Adney and the boys?

From Reagan, another girl on my volleyball team:

Girl, what happened? You got caught up in the middle of a fight in the library?

I don't bother answering any of them. My fingers are too shaky to type anything out anyway.

Shoving my phone back into my backpack, I slump in my seat, my mind filled with all of the things Adney could say to my mother when she calls her.

Will she call her? Will I get in trouble? I didn't instigate this fight, but I am squarely in the middle of it, just as Adney suspects. Mom is upset with me already for staying out five freaking minutes late with Beck. The guilt I feel over hooking up with him when I know that's her biggest fear doesn't help.

When she finds out Beck fought another boy over me, she's really going to lose it.

They're in there for so long. I'm freaking out by the time the boys finally exit Adney's office, Beck hanging his head, and Liam's head held high so everyone can look at the black eye forming, I assume.

It's going to be a nasty one too.

Beck stops at the counter of Kelli's desk, glancing over his shoulder to offer me a quick smile. Liam walks straight past him and heads for the exit. He pauses next to me to say, "Hope you're happy with your choice."

Then he's gone, pushing through the double doors so hard, they slam back into place, rattling the window.

"Addison, you can come in now," Mrs. Adney says from behind me.

I turn to face her and slowly approach her office doorway. She's already seated behind the desk, and I walk inside, looking around at the various Badger memorabilia lining the walls. The photos and the artwork span at least twenty years.

I've been in her office before for leadership-related stuff, but never like this.

"Have a seat," she says, indicating the chairs on the other side of her desk.

I settle in, my back ramrod straight, my heart pounding so hard I swear it's going to break free and fly out of my chest.

"Beck completely denied you had any involvement in their altercation," Mrs. Adney says, getting right down to business as she leans back in her desk chair. "Liam didn't say a word. But I'll have you know, I'm not blind, Addison. I see everything that happens on this campus, as does the rest of my staff. And while you're not in trouble, I would advise you not to put yourself in situations where two boys could end up fighting over you. Not that you have any control over their actions. I'm definitely not blaming you for any of this."

I say nothing. To deny it would be a lie. To protest would get me nowhere.

"I would also advise you to watch who you're spending your time with," she continues. "I cannot divulge any information, but sometimes, things aren't what they seem."

My shocked gaze finds hers. Which one is she talking about?

I can only assume she's referring to Liam.

"Are they in trouble?" I ask, my voice barely above a whisper.

"They'll both be suspended for three days. No football practice this week, and no game this Friday," she announces, resting her arms on top of her desk, her hands clasped. "You have a volleyball game tomorrow, correct?"

I nod, terrified she's going to suspend me, so I can't play.

"I look forward to watching you and the rest of the team." She levels me with a look. "Now go on. Get to practice."

I'm speechless as I grab my backpack and stand, eager to get out of there.

"Thank you," I rasp before I walk out of her office, hurrying back into the front lobby.

Disappointment crashes over me when I realize Beck is already gone.

* * *

PRACTICE FEELS ENDLESS. If people aren't asking me questions about the fight, they're sending me questioning looks. The whispering among clustered groups when we take water breaks, the way they glance over their shoulders in my direction, tells me they're talking about what happened between Liam and Beck.

Talk about embarrassing. This is not how I expected things to play out.

Tori and Emma are practically bursting with the need to ask me what happened, but I told them I would talk to them about it after practice. No way am I going to share details about what went down between the boys in front of our entire volleyball team.

Though maybe that would ensure the truth will be spread versus stupid rumors.

What I really want is for all of this to disappear. I don't want people knowing Liam and Beck were literally fighting over me. It's so embarrassing. Plus, I feel bad about coming in between them.

Did I ruin their friendship completely?

Regret and worry hang over me like a dark, heavy cloud, and I feel terrible. Distracted. I keep making mistakes throughout practice, dumb errors I would normally never make. By the end of our two-hour practice, I'm angry with myself.

Disappointed too.

"Let's grab dinner," Tori suggests as we're exiting the gym.

"I can't," I protest. "My mom said I had to come straight home."

That doesn't sound so bad. I could hide away in my room and crawl into bed, bury myself under the covers. But my friends want to know what's going on, and I want to tell them.

I need to talk about it with someone, and I know I can trust them to keep everything quiet.

"Oh, come on. I was hoping you'd give us all the deets," Tori says.

"Yeah, you need to tell us what happened," Emma adds.

Sighing, I pull my phone out and send a quick text, asking if I can stay after practice to talk with Emma and Tori.

Mom: **You sure you aren't spending time with Beck Callahan?**

I think of what I said to Beck earlier, how I would lie and say I was hanging out with my friends.

Mom knows me better than I realized.

Me: **I'm with Emma and Tori. Really.**

"Take a selfie with me," I tell my friends, and they crowd around me, staring into the camera as I snap a quick photo and send it to my mother.

Mom: **Fine. Come straight home when you're done.**

Me: **I will. Promise.**

Mom: **Be home by eight.**

Me: **Okay.**

"I can go," I say.

"Yay!" Tori claps.

"You sure you don't want to go to the football field first?" Emma asks us with a little pout on her face.

Tori rolls her eyes. "Uh, no, Emma. I'm sure that's the last place Addie wants to be, right?" She looks at me, her gaze imploring.

I nod. "Yeah, no. Though I get it if you guys want to go down to the field and see your boys."

"Is *your* boy going to be there?" Tori asks me.

You mean Beck, is what I want to ask, but I keep my mouth shut.

"They were both suspended," I admit, glancing around to make sure no one else is near us as we walk toward the parking lot. "For three days."

"Holy shit," Tori breathes.

"That's crazy. Were they really fighting over *you*, Addie?" Emma sounds skeptical as always.

Why does she doubt everything that comes out of my mouth? Why does she treat Tori and I like such garbage all the time? And worse...

Why do we let her get away with it?

I'm so used to always rushing to her defense, or dealing with her bad moods, I guess it's become a habit.

A group of girls are suddenly behind us, all of them suspiciously quiet, and I can't help but wondering if they're trying to spy on our conversation. "I'll tell you later."

We end up going to a burger place on the lake—a solid choice since no one comes to this place after school, considering it's so far. There are a few people from our school who work at the restaurant, but none of them are on duty right now, so we're good.

I can speak freely.

Once we're settled at a table outside and we've placed our order, I launch into my story about what happened in the library. I don't spare a single detail and the more Tori gasps and makes those wide-eyed shocked faces, the more into it I get.

"Liam sounds like an asshole," Tori says when I'm finished. "He actually told you to shut up? No wonder Beck rushed to your defense."

"Yeah, and what's up with him doing that anyway?" Emma asks, playing with the wrapper from her straw. "What does he care how Liam talks to you?"

"Emma," Tori says, disappointment tinging her voice. "It wasn't cool, how Liam treated her. Of course Beck is going to defend her. Besides, they've been friends for a long time."

Oh, we are definitely more than friends now, is what I want to say.

But I don't.

"Liam was totally rude. I don't want to be with a guy who treats me like that," I add. My mother always told me a boy should respect me. She really hammered that home after what happened between Jos and Diego. At least Diego eventually redeemed himself in my parents' eyes. "And while I didn't mean for them to get in a fight and get suspended, I'm sort of glad it happened, only because Liam showed me who he really is."

"Harsh, girl. Don't forget you were the one who went to dinner with him only a few nights ago," Emma reminds me.

All true, I know.

"It was just dinner," I retort, a little annoyed.

"Whatever. You two were into each other," Emma says.

"For like a minute." I roll my eyes.

I hate how she keeps trying to make Liam and me into something when we're not.

Beck is the one I like. The one I messed around with all weekend. Not Liam.

Yeah. No. Definitely not Liam.

"Let it go, Em. Liam and Addie aren't a thing, and they never will be."

I appreciate Tori trying to squash whatever Emma's trying to get at.

"Really?" Emma's brows rise. "That's not what I heard."

The table goes quiet and the longer my supposed best friend keeps silent, the more irritated I get.

"Just spit it out, Emma," I finally say. "Whatever you heard, it's definitely not true."

A sigh leaves her before she leans across the table, causing Tori and me to do the same. "Liam told the guys you two hooked up Thursday night."

An uneasy feeling forms in the pit of my stomach. "What? After Marisco's?"

She nods. "That's what Marcus told me."

Tori can only blink, her expression full of shock.

"Did Dom say anything about that to you?" I ask her.

Tori quickly shakes her head. "No way. He told me Beck's completely into you. We think it's cute. We're team Beck."

A sigh leaves me and I take a sip of my Coke, wishing it was something stronger.

And I rarely want to drink.

"I'm team Beck too," I admit. "I like him. A lot. And he likes me. I think—no, I'm pretty sure we're a thing," I admit.

"Oh my God, really? That's so great!" Tori's practically bouncing in her chair, she's so excited. I smile at her and she beams in return. "I knew you two would end up together! Forget Liam. He sucks."

Emma doesn't say anything at all. Typical.

Why can't she support me like Tori? She's my best friend. She's supposed to be there for me no matter what, just like I am for her.

Lately, she's not there for me at all.

"And what you heard about Liam and me? It's a lie." I keep my gaze on Emma, my voice strong and clear. "I haven't done *anything* with Liam. Not a single thing. You saw me leave that night. I didn't go anywhere with him."

"Yeah, Liam is definitely trouble," Tori says firmly. "You should be glad that's over, Addie."

"You're right. I am." I'm reaching for my phone when Emma says something, making me pause.

"I've always liked trouble," she says with a wicked smile. "It could be fun, dating the bad boy."

"He's a bad boy I'm definitely not interested in," I say firmly, remembering the fierce look on Beck's face after he hit Liam. His entire body tense and ready to fight, his eyes blazing with fury.

Hot.

Hot, hot, hot.

Pretty sure Emma's got it all wrong.

Good guys who rush to your defense are fun too.

CHAPTER 25

BECK

*F*uck my life.

I spend the last however many years being a good student and avoiding trouble as much as possible, and the first week of my senior year, I get into a physical fight with a guy I thought was my friend and get suspended.

Mother fucking *suspended.*

Can't practice, can't play in this Friday's game. Our season opener.

At least it's an away game, but damn.

Adney made me feel like absolute shit with her lecture. Liam seemed completely unaffected by her little speech, but her words and the look on her face just about did me in. All this talk about our last year of high school and how we needed to end it in a positive way. We have college hopes and dreams, and while she didn't want to dole out the suspensions as punishment, she had no choice. We forced her hand.

No violence on campus. That is the rule. And while I wasn't the one who started the fight, I didn't stop it either. In fact, I got a solid punch in, from what I saw of the black eye forming on Liam's face.

The asshole.

That's what makes it worse. I feel terrible about getting in trouble, and the suspension on my record could potentially ruin my college hopes, but damn, it felt pretty fuckin' good to dole out that punishment. Liam was a complete dick, and he treated Addie terribly. She didn't deserve it. Even though no one really knows, she's my girl now. I had to defend her.

It was the right thing to do.

Sucks that I haven't seen her since it happened. Or talked to her. I have no idea what she's thinking or how she's feeling. I tried calling her, but she didn't pick up.

She's at volleyball practice, so I don't know what I expected.

I'm definitely texting her later though and checking up on her. Maybe we could even FaceTime. I just want to see her, hear her voice. Talk to her and make sure she's okay.

Make sure *we're* okay.

I have no idea what happened between her and Adney after I left. Hope to hell she didn't get in trouble too, though there's no reason she should, since she did absolutely nothing. She might've got a speech from Adney, but those are punishment enough.

I went straight home after Dad showed up outside the office to talk to me. He could barely look at me, he was too busy pacing back and forth, thrusting his hands in his hair as he kept repeating a variation of, "I don't expect this sort of behavior from you, Beck. Not you. Never you."

Yeah. Me either, Dad.

That was more Jake's deal. My older brother has a temper and used to pop off here and there, especially in high school. As he's gotten older, his emotions are more under control.

I thought mine were too. I'm pretty easygoing. I always have been. But something about Liam and the shitty things he said to Addie sent me over the edge.

I'm chilling at the kitchen counter eating a brownie and trying to concentrate on my math homework when Mom enters the house from the garage, her arms full of reusable bags loaded down with groceries. She stops short when she sees me.

"What are you doing home?" She glances at the clock on the wall.

I should be at practice, and she knows it.

"Dad didn't tell you?"

"He called me earlier, but I missed it. Tried to call him back, but he didn't answer. I assumed he was busy with practice. Like you should be." She sets the bags on the counter. "Come help me unload the car and tell me why you're here."

I explain everything to Mom as we unload her Range Rover, Mom listening and never interjecting, which I appreciate. It feels like I need to get everything off my chest all at once, and by the time I'm done telling her, I feel emotionally exhausted. I slump back onto the barstool at the counter and devour the rest of my brownie while Mom puts the groceries away.

"I can't say I'm not disappointed in you, baby, because I am." She puts a few things in the fridge and shuts the double doors before turning to face me. "Violence is never the answer. But...I get why you did it. You were defending Addison. I can't believe Liam said those horrible things to her. He's always been so nice. Or so I thought."

I nod, misery coursing through me. "I never meant to disappoint you, Mom. Or Dad. I didn't mean to get into a fight either."

Her smile is gentle. "I know. How was your father when he found out?"

"In shock, I think." I'm going to hear it from him tonight, I'm sure.

"Yeah, I bet." She stops and leans against the counter, close to where I'm sitting. "How's Addison?"

"I don't know. We didn't get a chance to talk." I shrug. "I'm going to text her later, after volleyball practice."

"Beck." I glance up when she says my name. "Are your feelings...serious about Addie? I know you've liked her for a long time."

I hang my head and tell the counter, "Yeah. Kind of."

"Does she know how serious you feel?"

"No." I shrug. "I don't know. We hung out this weekend and I figured she knew what I wanted from her, but she acted like nothing really changed between us when I got to school today."

"Hmm." I glance up when she remains quiet. "Do you think she's interested in Liam?"

"No." I shake my head, thinking of the way Addie looked Saturday night when I made her come with my fingers. "No way."

"Then what's going on between the two of them?"

"I think he's pissed that she's more interested in me. He believes I swooped in and stole her from him, when that's not the case. I've been halfway in love with her for years," I admit.

Mom smiles. "That is so sweet. No wonder you did what you did."

I ignore her sweet comment. I can't believe I just told her that I was halfway in love with Addie for years.

"He was an asshole to her, Mom. I couldn't let him get away with it." I wince at the curse word flying from my mouth, but she doesn't mind. Everyone in this house has had a filthy mouth at one point or another. I'm probably the cleanest out of all of them, even my sisters. "He had no right talking to her like that. You taught me to always treat women with respect."

Did I throw her words back at her on purpose?

Oh yeah.

Did I say it to make me look like slugging Liam in the face is justifiable?

You bet.

"I forget. Does Liam have sisters?" Mom asks.

"No."

"Figures. I think that helps, growing up with sisters. Teaches you how to respect them—and females in general." A sigh leaves her as she takes a couple boxes of crackers into the pantry. "Your father and I will discuss what happened, but I see no need to punish you any further. I'm thinking you're being punished enough."

Relief courses through me, and I slump against the counter. "I can't go to school for three days."

"Perfect time for you to catch up on whatever reading and homework you need to do," Mom says as she exits the pantry with a smirk.

"We've barely started school. My assignment load isn't that bad," I protest.

"I'm sure you have some reading to catch up on. You always do."

She's not wrong.

"Can't play football either. For the *entire week*," I stress.

"Plenty of time on your hands for you to do all sorts of things around the house." She glances toward the giant French door that leads to our back yard. "You can help me do yard work."

I withhold a grimace.

She taps her fingers against her pursed lips. "I'm sure I can find plenty for you to do. If not, your dad will step in and come up with something."

This time I let the groan out. "Great."

"You'll be fine." Her smile is almost evil as she reaches for me and musses my hair, like I'm still a little kid. I duck away from her. "Not that happy about it, though. Colleges don't like it when students get suspended."

Her words stay with me as I go up to my room. As I try and concentrate on the rest of my math homework. I might've screwed myself out of getting into a good college. I was hoping to go to a D1 school and play football, but now...

That might not happen.

All because of that prick, Liam.

I can't stop thinking about Addie either. How she came to me after the fight, not Liam. I know she doesn't like him, but the things he said to me...he definitely thinks she's still interested in him, which is weird.

She's not playing us both like my mom said. Is she?

Around six o'clock, my dad shows up, barging into my room without knocking. I'm still at my desk, scrolling through my phone when I still have a few math problems to solve and I fumble with my phone when I see him, dropping it onto the floor.

Dad bends over to grab it, setting it on my desk next to me.

"Beck."

Him just saying my name and nothing else fills me with fear. Not like I'm scared of my father or anything. I just don't want to disappoint him.

Or my mom.

"I know," I finally say when he remains quiet. "I'm sorry."

"Explain to me exactly what happened," he says, settling on the edge of my bed.

I turn to face him and lay it all out, just like I did for Mom earlier. I tell him how Addie and I were just hanging out in the library, doing our homework and talking. How confrontational Liam was with me when he suddenly showed up, and how he lunged for me first.

"You still put hands on him," Dad says when I finish. "That's why you got suspended."

"Yeah," I croak, feeling stupid for the entire thing. "I messed everything up, huh?"

"What do you mean?"

"Football. College. My entire future." I look down, my emotions trying to get the best of me. It's hard to face him about this. Especially when I fucked everything up over an impulsive, stupid mistake. "I know you and Mom are disappointed in me."

He sighs, the sound ragged, and I peek at him from beneath the hair that hangs in my face, grateful to see he doesn't seem that upset. "We're definitely disappointed, son. A suspension on your school record doesn't look good, and I don't know what'll happen in regards to college. But I—I understand why you did what you did in defense of Addie. Liam has no business talking to her like that."

"I wish I hadn't hit him," I admit.

"You can't take it back now. What's done is done. Considering Liam's been your friend for a while, you should try and work it out with him. Though you two probably need to simmer down first," Dad says, pragmatic as always.

"Yeah, you're right," I agree morosely.

"Team looks good," Dad continues, changing the subject. "We missed you out on the field though."

Feels like he's rubbing it in, my not being there.

"Everyone must think I'm an asshole," I groan.

"No, more like they're upset with Liam for starting shit with you," Dad says. "You'll definitely be missed Friday night."

"It's killing me that I can't be there," I admit.

"You'll be back next week," Dad says firmly, rising to his feet. "Mom and I will have chores for you to do while you're suspended. Plus, you'll need to keep up on your schoolwork."

"No problem," I say, watching him as he goes to my door. "I'm sorry."

Pausing, he turns to face me, a grim smile on his face. "I'm sorry too, son. But we'll help you figure everything out."

"Do you really think it'll hurt my chances to get into college?"

He shrugs. "I don't know. But I'm going to look into it."

I watch him go as he slowly closes the door behind him, and when he's gone, I grab my phone and go into Snapchat, checking out the SnapMap.

Addie's turned her location off, when it's normally on.

Damn. Is that because of me? Or Liam? Or everything that's happened in general?

Deciding I need to get over myself and reach out, I send her a quick message on Snap.

Me: **Hope you're okay.**

She doesn't respond right away, so I set my phone down and try to read a chapter from my American Government textbook, but I can't concentrate for shit, so I give up. I go to my bed and scroll through my phone, wishing she would answer me.

But she doesn't.

My phone rings and I answer it immediately when I see Jake's name flash on the screen.

"Heard you caused a little trouble," is how he greets me.

I groan. "What? Did Mom call to tell you about it?"

"Nah, it was Dad, and he texted me all the details." He hesitates for only a moment. "What the hell, little brother? Getting in fights on campus? Getting suspended? I bet Adney was furious."

My brother had a few run ins with Adney when he was in school so he knows what she's like.

"More like disappointed. They all are." My voice lowers

and I grip my phone tight. "That's the worst part. I feel like I disappointed everyone."

"Tell me what happened."

I give him the full rundown, not leaving out a single detail. I even tell him how much I like Addie, and what she means to me, and what Liam said to her that sent me right over the edge.

"I get why you did it," he says after I'm finished.

"It was dumb though, right?"

A sigh leaves him. "Look, you gotta stand up for what you believe in, and protect those who you care about. And I get the sense you really care about Addison Douglas."

"I do," I admit, trying to shove aside the worry that gnaws at me since she hasn't responded to my earlier text. "She probably thinks I'm some muscle head asshole now."

Jake chuckles. "I doubt that. Sometimes, girls really love that shit."

"You think so?"

"For sure. You ran to her defense. You socked your friend in the face for being rude toward her. That's kind of a big deal. Not just anyone would do that."

I would for her. Every time.

"I guess," is what I mumble to my brother instead.

I don't want him thinking I'm an idiot either. My entire life, I've looked up to Jake, always seeking his approval. I don't want to lose it now.

Or ever.

I let him change the subject and he tells me about his football schedule and how much he wants us to come out and watch him soon. We somehow always make the hectic schedules work. Dad doesn't give a shit how much a plane ticket costs. He's there for my games and Jake's, and when he can, even Ash's and Eli's too.

Meaning he is on the move a lot, and most of the time, I am too.

Would Addie mind that? Could I convince my parents to let her come with us sometimes? Would she even want to go?

Shit, I don't know.

After I eat a somber dinner with my mom and dad, I'm in my bathroom, about to take a shower, when my phone chimes, indicating a Snapchat text from Addie.

Finally.

Addie: **I'm fine. A little shaken up over it. I should be asking you if you're okay.**

I could play games and answer her after I take a shower, but screw it.

I've been dying to talk to her since it all happened.

Me: **I'm all right. Jaw hurts a little.**

Addie: **I didn't think he actually hit you.**

Me: **More like his knuckles brushed against my jaw. He didn't get a solid punch in. Still hurts tho.**

Addie: **Adney told me you were both suspended.**

Me: **Yeah. Sucks. Can't play in our first game Friday night either.**

Addie: **I'm so sorry.**

Me: **Hey, it's not your fault.**

Addie: **I know. I just feel bad. You got in a fight over what Liam said to me.**

I don't regret what happened.

I only regret that I lost control and we got busted.

Me: **Don't feel bad. Liam has been shitty toward me for a while. I don't know what his problem is.**

She doesn't respond for a while and I go to my room, grabbing some clothes to take into the bathroom with me. Exhaustion hits me hard and I've already started the shower and am stripping when I finally get a text from her.

Addie: **Thank you for defending me, Beck. It means a lot, how you watch over me.**

Damn, if she only knew how much more I want to watch over her. Take care of her. The need to protect her fills me to the point that I can't think of anything else.

Pretty sure she's completely unaware just how much my feelings for her consume me.

Me: **I'll always defend you, Adds. You know this. I've got your back.**

I stand in the middle of my bathroom in my boxer briefs and nothing else, my phone clutched in my hands as I wait for her response like a little kid who just admitted to his crush that he likes her.

Addie: **I'll miss seeing you at school. Want me to ask your teachers for your homework assignments?**

They're all just going to email me my assignments anyway, but okay. I like that she's coming up with an excuse to see me.

Me: **Yeah, that would be great. Thank you.**

Addie: **Maybe I can bring them by for you tomorrow? Won't be until later in the night though because we have a game.**

Disappointment crashes over me. I won't be able to go cheer her on. When you're suspended, you're not even allowed on campus. And Adney will be at that game tomorrow night—she's at most activities at school a lot of the time since she lives so close to campus. She's just always there. And she'd kick my ass right out the moment she spotted me.

Me: **Wish I could go to your game.**

Addie: **Me too.**

She adds a red heart with her response.

Emojis were a heavy commodity back in middle school. They meant something. A push forward, a way to share your feelings without blatantly stating I LIKE YOU. Guess it's still the same now, and we're both practically eighteen, for the love of God.

Seeing that heart emoji gives me hope.

Me: **You don't have to bring my assignments over tomorrow. I'm sure my teachers will email me.**

Addie: **I don't mind. I want to see you.**

Again, I'm open with my feelings to her. No game playing this time around.

Me: **I already miss you.**

Addie: **I miss you too.**

I smile. Despite everything that happened today, those four words light me up inside.

Addie: **I'll text you when I'm on my way to your house, okay?**

Me: **Okay, sounds good. Good luck on your game tomorrow.**

Addie: **Thank you. Goodnight, Beck.**

Another red heart emoji accompanies her words.

I take a deep breath, realizing the room is filling with steam, thanks to the hot spray of the shower.

Me: **Night Adds.**

I send her a red heart emoji too.

Fuck it.

Let's go.

CHAPTER 26

ADDIE

*O*ur first game of my last volleyball season went well. We won the first two sets and even finished earlier than normal.

Basically, we crushed them.

School was rampant with rumors when I first arrived this morning. The fight between Liam and Beck was far bloodier and dragged on much longer. I was shoved out of the way by Beck because Liam was actually going to hit me. We're caught up in a supposed love triangle and everyone is talking shit.

It's literally the fourth day of school and this is what's happening to me. So bizarre.

I told the truth to anyone who asked, not caring who knows—and not that many people actually asked. Our school is small and the rumors spread so fast, everyone already knows what happened in the library yesterday, including teachers and staff. I get a lot of stares when I first arrive, but by lunch, everyone is pretty much over it, thank goodness.

I wasn't lying when I told Beck I would miss seeing him

at school, but it was almost a relief that he wasn't here today, as well as Liam. Especially Liam.

He's the last person I want to see. If he never came back, I'd be okay with it.

Though I missed him, Beck is also a distraction I didn't need today, especially with our first game looming. I was nervous all day, working myself up. Freaking out that I might make a mistake or play like crap.

But now the game is done and we played fabulously. Coach was happy and I'm in a good mood as I drive to Beck's house.

I'm also nervous.

Going to see Beck at his house to drop off his homework is such a flimsy excuse, and I'm pretty sure he knows it. He has to. He's the one who pointed out his teachers would most likely email him his assignments. A few of his teachers said exactly that to me when I asked.

I don't even care. I want to see him.

Pretty sure he wants to see me too.

I texted him before I left the high school to let him know I was on my way. The moment I pull in front of his house, the front door is opening, and there he is, waving at me from the front porch.

Once I put my car in park and shut off the engine, I sit there for a moment, staring at him, my heart starting to race. He's so freaking gorgeous. With the handsome, all-American good looks and the big, muscular body that I had my hands all over only a few nights ago. Despite his size, he moves with an almost graceful ease, ambling toward me wearing a gray Badgers football T-shirt and a pair of navy gym shorts, his feet in Nike slides.

I climb out of the car, smiling at him. "Hey."

"Hey." He stops directly in front of me. The sun has mostly set, the sky streaked with vivid pink and orange, thanks to a fire somewhere above us, and it casts Beck's face in the perfect light.

Golden hour indeed.

"Heard you guys won," he says, slipping his hands in his pockets, an easy smile stretching his lips. "Congrats."

"Thank you. It was an easy game." I shrug.

"You kicked their asses." When I frown, wondering how he knows so quickly, he explains, his expression sheepish, "I watched your game on my phone."

"Oh right. They broadcast them sometimes." How sweet that he watched.

"Yeah. It was kind of shit reception, but I saw most of it. You did great." His gaze slides down me, nice and slow, making me tingle. "I really like the new uniforms."

I'm still a little sweaty and I can feel tendrils of hair coming undone from the extra tight French braids Tori did for me before the game, but I feel freaking beautiful under Beck's watchful gaze. "Thanks. I like them too."

Our uniform shirts are white with blue stripes on the arms and our mascot and number on the front of them. I glance down at myself, hating how my sports bra minimizes my boobs. I practically look flat-chested right now. "I like the shirts."

"Me too," he says, taking a step forward, his arm stretching out. His finger brushes against the small Badger strutting on my shirt, just below my left collarbone. His touch burns through my shirt, as if his finger actually presses against my skin. "I especially like the Badger."

"Studly?" That's our mascot's name. Silly, right?

"Yeah." He smiles. Taps Studly the Badger a couple of times before his hand drops. I already miss his touch. "Studly."

We smile at each other like idiots for a moment before I

realize I came here for a reason, beyond seeing his pretty face and basking in his presence. "I brought your homework." I gesture toward my car where my backpack sits in the passenger seat.

"My teachers already sent me everything," he says, his smile growing. "You didn't need to drive all the way over here. I probably should've texted you."

"Oh." My heart falls a little and I feel dumb. Maybe he didn't want me to come to his house?

No. He definitely wanted me to come over. I know he did. He could've said no.

"Guess I didn't need to bring it over, huh?" I say with a shrug.

"I'm glad you did. I've been lonely all day. Everyone's busy while I'm sitting at home, bored out of my mind," he admits.

"You actually miss school?" I'm teasing him, but he nods, his expression solemn.

"Yeah. I miss seeing my friends. Football." He hesitates for the briefest moment. "Definitely you."

My heart trips over itself at his admission and I try to play it off. It's so hard, though, because I don't know where we stand right now. We hook up Friday and Saturday night, and then nothing else happens. He acts like the same ol' Beck at school yesterday, too. Meaning, he doesn't necessarily treat me like a girlfriend, so I don't know what he wants from me.

This last week has been incredibly confusing.

"Well, guess you can't miss me because here I am," I say, my voice light and casual.

Hmm, maybe that's what he wants.

My heart literally hurts at the thought.

"Yeah. I'm glad you're here, Adds," he says, his voice low, making me warm.

My throat is dry and I don't know what to say next. Swallowing hard, I'm scrambling to come up with something when he beats me to the punch.

"Tell me what happened at school today."

I lean against my car, thinking over today's events.

"They were talking about the fight, I'm sure," he adds.

"Oh yeah. The rumors were crazy." I roll my eyes and he chuckles. "They were saying you shoved me out of the way at the last minute because Liam was going to hit *me*. Can you imagine?"

He grows somber. "I would've killed him if he did that."

From the serious tone of his voice, I half-believe him.

"They also made it seem like the fight was a lot bloodier. You were both horribly beaten. Blood everywhere. I'm surprised you didn't have to go to the hospital." I'm teasing, trying to make him smile, which he does.

"I hope you know I'm not a violent person," he says, his tone solemn. "I don't know what came over me yesterday."

"Liam was being a jerk," I remind him.

"Yeah. Talking shit. I didn't like what he said to you. That was my biggest problem. He told you to shut the hell up." Beck rubs his jaw, wincing slightly.

"Does it still hurt? Where he hit you?" I ask, pushing away from the car, so I can move closer to him. In the waning light, it's hard to see if there's a bruise on his face.

"A little bit. I can't imagine how bad it would've been if he actually got a good hit in," Beck says irritably.

"Let me see it."

He turns his head to the side and I step even closer, rising up on my tiptoes, so I can examine the spot where Liam punched him. I peer up at his jaw, seeing the faintest shadow of a bruise there, beneath the light stubble.

He hasn't shaved today and it sends a prickle of awareness through me. He's so...masculine. As in, he's built like a

266

man. Big and broad and so ridiculously good looking, it almost hurts to look at him.

Hurts even more when I know what he feels like beneath my hands. What he looks like when he comes…

"Right there?" I ask, giving in to temptation and touching his jaw lightly.

He flinches but doesn't pull away from my fingers. "Yeah. There. The asshole. Felt like he barely hit me at the time though."

"It's a very light bruise," I say as I continue to touch it. His skin is so warm. A little sharp thanks to the faint growth on his chin and jaw. "Might even be gone by the time you come back to school."

"Or the bruise will be worse." His gaze finds mine, turbulent and intense, and I stand there with my lips parted, my fingers still on his jaw, struck dumb by his nearness.

"Makes you look tough," I tell him with a faint smile as I lean in and inhale his warm, spicy scent, gently pressing my mouth to the bruise, like my kiss will heal him.

He sucks in a sharp breath when my lips make contact with his skin, and before I can pull away, his hand is on my face, steering me to his mouth.

He kisses me and I give in, my fingers clutching the front of his shirt as his mouth moves over mine. His other hand settles on my waist, his fingers sliding beneath my uniform shirt to touch bare skin, and I take a step closer, needing to feel him as well.

It's as if I can't resist him—and he's drawn to me too. It's as if we can't resist each other. Anyone who would see us right now would probably notice nothing. Just two people sharing a kiss outside in front of a giant house on a pretty late summer night. It's cooler up here near the lake, and the air is heavy with the fragrance of pine.

But it's so much more than a kiss—at least for me. This boy means something to me.

I'm completely falling for him.

Actually, I've already fell for him.

His fingers slide to the back of my head, angling me to deepen the kiss. My skin prickles with awareness when his tongue touches mine, and I'm already throbbing between my legs.

That's all it takes. One kiss in front of his house and I want him. That chemistry that's always simmering between us, it's undeniable. We've managed to ignore it for years, and now that we've finally given in, there's no going back.

"You like it when I look tough," he murmurs against my lips, making me smile as we end the kiss.

"I must." I lean into his hand when he strokes the side of my face, his gaze warm as he drinks me in. "You were kind of hot, punching Liam like you did."

"You thought I was hot?"

I nod slowly, turning my head, so I can drop a kiss on his palm. "Totally."

His eyes darken. "Maybe I should get into fights more often."

"Um, you better not." I grin at him.

He grins at me in return.

"Did you get in trouble?" I ask. "With your parents?"

"Not really." He chuckles. "Mom had me cleaning up around the yard this afternoon. She said tomorrow I get to help her reorganize the pantry."

He makes a horrified face and I giggle. "I love reorganizing stuff."

"I definitely don't. It's a form of punishment for me and she knows it." A sigh leaves him and he loosens his hold on me. "Mom also said it's punishment enough that I can't practice or play in the game this Friday. She knows it's making me crazy that I can't be there, and she's pretty positive I've learned my lesson."

"Is there a lesson to learn?" I can't help but ask.

"Yeah, don't let rude pricks talk down to your girl." He clamps his lips shut, his cheeks turning ruddy. "Uh, I didn't mean to say that last part."

My heart is tripping over itself at his choice of words, but I remain calm, despite the giddiness rising within me. "Or did you?"

His expression turns sheepish. "I didn't mean to say it out loud."

"And I didn't mind hearing you say it," I admit, barely able to contain my smile.

He pulls me back in close, dropping another kiss on my lips before he murmurs, "We're probably moving too fast."

I slide my hand up his chest, silently marveling, yet again, at the warm, firm muscles I feel beneath my palms. "Probably."

"I sort of don't care." He kisses me again, his lips lingering.

"Me either," I breathe into his mouth, wrapping my arms around his neck.

A car approaches, the lights flashing across us, and as it passes, the driver honks the horn, causing us to spring away from each other.

"Constantly interrupted," Beck says with a chuckle.

"All the time," I agree, swallowing hard. He barely touches me and I'm instantly rattled. Not like we can do anything out here on a public street.

I'm kind of glad that car drove by just now. I might've let Beck have his way with me on the hood of my car.

"You know what's going on with Liam?" Beck asks out of nowhere, his voice clipped.

I frown at him. "If you're asking if I've talked to him, the answer is absolutely not."

"I didn't think you were talking to him. I just—wondered if you'd heard anything at school."

"Not at all."

"From what I've been told, he's super pissed at me. And in big trouble with his dad," Beck admits. "He got his phone taken away."

"Oh." I feel sort of bad for Liam, but then again, I don't.

He's the one who started all of this.

"Guys on the team have kept me updated," Beck says, explaining his source of information. "They're mad at Liam because I can't play this week."

"I feel partially responsible for all of this, you know?" I tell him, before I blow out a harsh breath. "It's my fault you got in a fight with Liam in the first place. And you guys are friends. I don't understand what happened."

"Hey, you're not responsible for the fight." He takes a step closer, his big hands settling on my shoulders and giving them a squeeze as he peers down at me. "You didn't ask for him to say that shit to you, and I'm the one who inserted myself into the situation. It definitely isn't your fault."

His hands feel so good on me, even like this. "Okay." I exhale softly, trying to let the guilt leave me. "Thank you again for rushing to my defense."

"Anything for you, Adds." The way he says that just does something to me. Makes me feel all fluttery inside. Everything he does to me makes me feel that way. "You know that, right?"

I nod, my mouth dry, and I let him pull me in closer. Until he's got me wrapped up in a solid, warm hug, his arms around me, his hands splayed across my back. I do the same, slipping my arms around his waist, clinging to him, my face pressed against his chest. I take a deep breath, inhaling his clean, masculine scent and...

Yeah. I don't want this moment to ever end.

Not sure how long we stand there in each other's arms, but I hear a noise. A door opening. A woman's voice.

"Beck? Are you still out here?"

We let each other go, Beck turning to face his house. His mom.

"I'm still out here with Addie, Mom." His voice is tinged with the faintest irritation.

I cover my mouth to muffle the laugh.

"Oh." The front porch lights blaze on, casting their massive lawn in golden light. "Hey, Addie."

I see her wave from the porch.

"Hi, Mrs. Callahan," I say to her, waving back.

"We've known each other a long time, Addison. You can call me Fable," she says.

Beck sends me a look, rolling his eyes. Another giggle escapes me.

"Go back inside, Mom," he tells her, but it's not in a mean way. His voice is full of affection, though with a hint of annoyance still. I know he's close to his mom.

"Come in soon, okay? Bye, Addie!" She shuts the door, but leaves on those bright lights, which I don't mind because at least I can see Beck.

The sky has darkened, turning a velvety black and purple shade, and I sit on the street curb, staring upward. A few stars are twinkling, but not many, and I hold my breath when Beck settles onto the curb next to me, his shoulder brushing mine.

"Are you sure your parents aren't mad at you about the fight?" I ask. "I didn't tell my mom about it."

She would lose her mind if she knew Beck got suspended because he was fighting another boy over me. It all falls into her *serious relationships are nothing but trouble* theory and she'd most likely ban me from seeing Beck ever again.

I can't risk it.

He glances over at me. "It's more like they're disappointed. No one has been suspended before. It's a first in the Callahan house. My mom said she never suspected I'd be the one to get in trouble like this."

My role in this situation makes me feel bad. "Your mom is right. You've never been problematic. You don't get in fights."

"Until yesterday," he reminds me.

"Right. Until yesterday." I gaze up at the sky, spotting a few new stars twinkling. "Are your parents mad at me? I mean, they might be, since I'm the reason you got into a fight with Liam in the first place."

He chuckles, the warm sound settling low in my stomach. "Nah, they're not mad at you. I'm my own person who can make my own decisions. They don't blame you for anything."

Relief floods me and I smile at him. "Okay. Good."

"Yeah." He smiles at me.

I smile back, my mood lighter, and I decide to change the subject. I'm tired of talking about the fight, and I'm sure he is too. "Not much else happened today at school. By lunch they'd stopped gossiping about you guys. They were talking about Marcus and Monique."

I feel him stiffen slightly. "What about them?"

"Monique keeps chasing after him and Marcus claims he's not interested. It's making Emma so mad. She said she's going to knock Monique out like you did Liam, if she doesn't watch it."

It was all Emma could focus on today, and I got tired of hearing her complain, so I eventually tuned her out.

Does this make me a crappy friend? She knew what she was getting into, trying it again with Marcus when he was still occasionally hooking up with Monique. That has complete disaster written all over it.

"What a mess," Beck mutters, shaking his head before tipping it back to stare at the sky like I still am. "Lots of drama going on."

"And it was only the fourth day of school."

"Maybe we're getting it all out at the beginning of our senior year. Then it'll be smooth sailing until we graduate," he suggests.

"Huh. Maybe." A girl can wish, but maybe he's on to something. I don't want any drama in my life. It's stressful, and while I know I can't avoid it completely, I do think the main problem I have right now is Liam.

And Emma.

My mom.

Okay, fine. That's a lot of drama.

We're quiet as the sky rapidly darkens, until the stars are twinkling high above us. The moon is a thin sliver, allowing the stars to shine brighter, and there's a cool breeze off the lake that washes over us.

"Can you go to the game Friday?" I finally ask.

"Yeah, I just can't play. Sucks. Dad spoke to Adney and asked if I can be on the sidelines. She said yes." He sighs. "At least it's an away game."

"Too bad it's not a scrimmage." I'm teasing him. I hope he realizes it.

From the smile on his face when he looks over at me, he does. "Yeah. Should've smashed Liam's face in last week."

"I wish I could go." I'm excited for our last Mammoth tournament though. Every year our coach reserves camping spots for us and the entire team stays there in tents. It's a great bonding experience for us and I always feel closer to the girls afterwards. It's how Emma and I got so close to Tori last year.

"I'll miss seeing you there," Beck admits.

"I'll miss watching you." I press my shoulder against his and he glances down at me with a gentle smile.

My phone rings from inside my car. I can hear it since the driver's side window is still rolled down. The ringing stops, then immediately starts back up again.

"Someone's trying to find you," Beck says.

"Maybe I should go look at who it is." I hate that they've interrupted our moment, but what else is new?

Moments with Beck are always getting interrupted.

I go to my car and check my phone to see it's Emma calling. When I answer, she's already talking.

Crying.

"I hate you! Oh my God, get away from me!" she screams at someone.

"Emma? What's going on?" Concern fills me when I hear her sobs, and I lean against my car.

"I j-just caught M-Marcus with that w-whore!" she wails.

My stomach sinks. She doesn't even have to say a name. "Oh my God."

"He had his hands all o-over her!" The sobs dry up and she screams. I pull the phone away from my ear. "He is such an asshole! He told me they were done."

Clearly, he was lying.

"I'm so sorry, Em. Where are you?"

"Still at the school! We've been arguing in the parking lot."

"Where's Monique?"

"Her shady ass took off the minute I caught them. She didn't stick around." Emma laughs, but she sounds borderline hysterical. "She's lucky. I would've beat her into a pulp if she stayed."

Why is everyone so blood thirsty? "Emma, you need to calm down."

"NO. Fuck that. I don't need to calm down for anyone.

Marcus is a lying heap of shit. Monique is a giant whore who'll spread her legs for every guy at school. I *hate* her. I hate him too," Emma says bitterly.

I turn to face Beck, who's watching me with a questioning gaze. I place a hand over my phone. "It's Emma," I whisper to him.

"Marcus is the one you should be mad at," I tell her. "He's the one who said he wasn't with her anymore."

"Only because she keeps chasing after him! She's relentless!"

She's not going to hear anything I have to say to her, so I stop trying to convince her. "Do you want me to meet you somewhere?"

"No, it's okay. Marcus just got into his car. He's leaving. I'm going home too." She exhales loudly. "I guess there's no point in yelling at him for the rest of the night. He'll just get madder at me."

Oh geez. This probably means if he sweet talks her later and promises he won't get with Monique ever again, my friend will most likely take him back.

"Go home, take a shower and try to get some sleep. Things will become clearer in the morning," I tell her, wanting to roll my eyes at my lame advice.

But it's true, right? She's pissed right now. Some sleep and distance will help her see what Marcus did to her. And how she needs to end things with him, once and for all.

"You're right. Thanks, Addie. I'll text you later," she says, sounding exhausted.

"Drive safe." I end the call with a sigh and glance over at Beck. "She caught Marcus with Monique in the school parking lot."

Beck's brows lift. "Doing what?"

"Not sure, but it was definitely something they shouldn't have been doing." I shake my head, already reaching for the door handle to climb into my car. "I should probably go."

"Thanks again for coming by." He smiles at me.

I smile at him in return, trying to ignore the nagging worry that's hanging over me.

Not about Beck, but my best friend. She's changed. Slowly but surely.

And I'm worried about her.

CHAPTER 27

BECK

I finally return to school on Friday, enthusiastically welcomed back by my friends the moment I exit the parking lot and head up the sidewalk. They're clustered together as usual, standing in a group near the edge of the cafeteria and I can't help it...

Disappointment hits me when I realize Addie isn't with them.

That's probably because Marcus is standing there with Monique draped all over him, her arms looped around his neck while he completely ignores her and talks to everybody else. He's not even looking at her, but her attention is totally on him and no one else.

It's kind of pathetic, her behavior. Sasha was affectionate with me, but not like that. We weren't big on PDA, and I wasn't filled with the need to publicly claim her at school.

I feel different about Addie though. Even though we haven't one hundred percent confirmed it, I do think of her as my girl...

And I want every motherfucker on this campus to know it.

"Callahan! You're back." Dom breaks free of the group and approaches, extending his hand toward me. I grab it, performing one of those complicated handshakes we love to make up, grinning at him. "We've missed you."

"Glad to be back." I glance around before I ask, "Have you seen Liam yet?"

Dom nods, his expression turning serious. "He was hanging out by the gym after we got out from conditioning."

Hate that I had to miss a conditioning session, but I'll be back at it next week. As will Liam. Shit. "How was he?"

"Pretty much fuming, but when is he not? I guess his dad made his time off from school fuckin' miserable. And I guess Addie hasn't reached out to him at all, which pisses him off even more."

I keep my expression neutral, secretly relieved that she hasn't talked to him. Not that I thought she would.

She's been too busy talking to me. We've been texting pretty much nonstop since Tuesday night, when she stopped by with the excuse of bringing my homework. That kiss we shared...I had to restrain myself from jumping her out in the road.

Neighbors probably wouldn't have liked that. They're kind of snooty.

The car that drove by caused us to separate. And then my mom...

Cockblocked by my mother. Unbelievable, but also typical.

I'm a patient man. I will make Addie completely mine, and soon.

No doubt about it.

I'm pulled into the group by Dom, all of them happy to see me with the exception of Monique, who watches me with a faint sneer on her face. Not that I care, considering I don't really like her much. She's trouble. She and Marcus eventually wander off, and I'm glad.

I'd rather just hang with my bros and catch up.

We're talking about tonight's game and how they think it's going to be an easy win. I smile and nod and agree with them, secretly wishing I could play. It's going to kill me, standing on the sideline, watching it all go down, and not being able to do anything.

Freaking sucks.

The bell is about to ring when I spot Addie walking toward us, Tori beside her, wearing Dom's jersey. Without hesitation, I break away from the group, falling into step right beside Addison, the smile on her face making me grin in response.

"Morning, Adds." I flick my chin toward Tori. "Nice jersey, Victoria."

Tori scowls at me right before she starts laughing. "What's up with the full name, Mr. Callahan?"

"Don't know. Guess I'm in a good mood." I shrug, my gaze on Addie. She's the reason I'm in a good mood. Seeing her is the perfect way to brighten my day.

Dom approaches, grabbing Tori by the arm and pulling her in for a quick hug and a smacking kiss on the lips. Guess they're pretty much official.

Helps that he pulled Tori away though, because it gives me a chance to talk with Addie alone while we head for class. The bell rings, causing people to spring into action, but we're walking slowly, lagging behind everyone else heading to their first period.

"I should've asked you to wear my jersey," I say, my voice quiet as we walk side by side. "But I'm not even playing…"

"I still would've worn it," she admits, and I send her a quick look, noticing how pink her cheeks are.

"But I'm not playing, so I didn't want you—or me—to

hear a bunch of shit from people." I'm half-tempted to take her hand, but I don't. "Next week for sure. If you want to wear it."

"I want to," she says quickly, laughing nervously. "Um, yeah. I should've probably played it cool just now."

"You don't have to do that with me, Adds," I say easily, confidence making me stand taller.

This girl wants me. Maybe even as badly as I want her.

"I'm glad you're back," Addie says after we're quiet for a few seconds. "It's been weird, not having you around."

"That used to me already?"

She nods, a little smile curling her lips. "Maybe."

"Hope that's not a bad thing. Don't want you to get bored with me." I'm teasing. Flirting. Fumbling a little with it, but fuck it.

This is happening. Addie and I are turning into a thing.

Fucking finally.

"You don't bore me, Beck Callahan. Not even close." Her smile is knowing as we enter the massive hallway where our English classes are. "I was bored in the library the last couple of days without you there. Got all my homework done though."

"Are you saying I'm a distraction?" She completely distracts me, I know that.

"Definitely," she says with a firm nod, stopping near her classroom door. "I'm leaving after second period for Mammoth."

Disappointment hits me. "Oh, right. Now it's my turn to miss you," I say, my smile faint, my hands itching to touch her.

"Yeah." Her voice is soft and she glances around before taking a step closer. "I'll miss you too."

I give in to my need and pull her in for a hug. She feels

good. Smells better. I drop a kiss on her temple before I pull away. "Be safe."

"You too," she says, looking a little dazed. "Bye."

"See ya." I get it, is what I want to tell her. I understand that dazed look and the feelings that come with it.

But I don't say anything at all. Instead, I leave her where she's standing and walk into my class, settling at my desk with a big ol' smile on my face.

My morning classes pass by quickly, and by lunch, I'm leaving campus with Dom, hopping into his car and heading for the local pizza place that always has a Friday special he likes to take advantage of.

"Already missing Tori?" I ask as we're driving.

"Yeah, but it's cool. I hope she has fun in Mammoth," Dom says.

"You and Tori official yet?"

"I mean, we've not said anything to each other. I haven't asked her to be my girlfriend. But we talk all the time. We went out after her volleyball game Tuesday. And we're not talking to anyone else," Dom explains.

"Sounds official to me."

"We're not into labels."

I laugh. "No one is lately. I guess that's why Marcus is trying to get with two different girls?"

"Now there's some drama." Dom shakes his head. "Marcus is playing with fire. I wouldn't mess with Emma or Monique."

"Monique will just find someone else. I think she's getting off on the fact that she still has power over Marcus," I say. "Addie told me Emma is super pissed at him, yet they still meet up after school."

"Right, because Marcus is fucking around with Emma *and* Monique. He's crazy," Dom mutters.

"Yeah, he is." I can't imagine playing two girls. First, I would feel like absolute shit. The guilt would be tremendous. And second, that's a hell of a lot of work. I'd be exhausted, keeping my lies straight. Eventually I'd mess up and ruin it all.

"What's really going on between you and Addie?" Dom asks me, changing the subject.

"We're like you and Tori. We've—hung out." Hooked up. "We talk all the time. Text each other a lot." I glance down, picking at a loose string on the hem of my shorts. "Guess I'm finally taking my shot."

"About fucking time," Dom says, making me glance up and glare at him. But he's grinning at me, so my glower can't last too long. His smile fades fast though. "I saw something happen after second period you should know about."

"What did you see?" I ask, hating the worry that's suddenly filling me.

"Liam and Addie talking. Didn't look like he was being a dick to her or anything, but they were definitely having a conversation," Dom says.

Asshole. I guess I can't blame him for trying to talk to her since they haven't spoken since the fight Monday in the library, but still.

He needs to stay away from her.

"Did she tell you about it?" Dom asks me.

"I haven't talked to her since before first period, and they've already left." That's probably why she hasn't mentioned it. She sent me a couple of texts and selfies after she left, but nothing major.

We can't have a conversation like that while I'm in school and she's trapped in a van with half the volleyball team.

"Tori keeps sending me selfies," Dom says. "With Emma sitting right next to her, scowling into the camera."

"That girl is always in a bad mood," I say irritably.

"I'd be in a bad mood too if my supposed boyfriend was getting with another girl." Dom shakes his head.

When we arrive at the pizza place, it's packed with students all coming for the same lunch deal, including Marcus and Liam, who are at the end of the line.

No girls in sight, thank God, which means no shitty Monique to deal with. Not sure how I feel about seeing Liam for the first time after the fight, though.

"You can't avoid him forever," Dom says, pulling open the door. "You'd be having this conversation with him either after school or right now."

"Off campus means he can throw another punch and not get suspended," I say, wary as we enter the restaurant.

"Off campus also means someone can call the cops and Liam will get tossed into jail," Dom says. "He's already eighteen, remember?"

"I will be soon too." My birthday is in September, only a few weeks away.

"Yeah, but as of right now, you're not, which means he could go down for assault on a minor." Our voices lower as we draw closer to the line. "Just be cool."

Like he needs to tell me that. I'm the level-headed one of the bunch, though I went against type by getting in that stupid fight.

Marcus spots us first, nudging Liam's side with his elbow before they both turn to face us. "Fancy meeting you dicks here."

Dom rolls his eyes. "Fuck off, loser."

I say nothing.

Marcus is the biggest shit-stirrer on the planet, swear to God.

"We gonna pretend that fight never happened or are you two going to talk this out?" Marcus asks, his gaze going from Liam to me.

I say nothing. I refuse to apologize. I'm not the one who started this shit.

Liam fully faces me, the shiner I gave him a vivid combination of yellow and purple bruises, with a streak of red. "Callahan," he says through tight lips.

"Thatcher," I return, tempted to call him Snatcher like Dom always does. I always thought that shit was hilarious.

Right now, there is nothing funny about Liam.

Dom groans. "Please. No standoff in the pizza line. I just want to get my lunch in peace."

"Same, bro," Marcus adds.

Deciding to be the bigger man, I thrust my hand out toward Liam. "We good?"

Liam eyes my hand like it might be a snake ready to strike. He slowly lifts his gaze to mine. "Sure."

He shakes my hand, giving it one pump before he lets it go.

No apology, but it's a start.

We make our order and Marcus calls us over to their table when we're finished. Reluctantly, we sit with them, and I'm grateful when Marcus takes over the conversation.

"We're gonna miss you tonight, Beck," he says, shocking me. Marcus is not one to give me any kind of compliment. More like, he loves to give me endless shit.

"I hate that I won't be on that field," I admit, stirring my straw in my Dr. Pepper, jostling all the ice. "But I'll be back next week. You guys got this tonight."

"Yeah," Liam adds, his expression sullen.

"Forget football," Dom says, waving his hand. "This game is a no-brainer. What I want to know is what's up with you and Monique?"

Marcus smirks, looking pleased with himself. "I can't help it if she wants my body."

We all groan and throw our straw wrappers at him while he just laughs. He's eating this up.

"What about Emma?" I ask, bracing myself. He's going to say something that I should probably report back to Addie. Emma is her best friend.

She'd want to know, so she could tell her what's going on.

"That girl wants my body too, but I don't know." Marcus leans back in his chair. He's a big boy. Not as tall as me but broader. Heavier. He could mow anyone down, including me. "Emma started sniffing around me again, and Monique was playing hard to get when Emma wasn't, so I decided to give Emma a shot because why not? Girl was down last time we were together, and nothing has really changed."

Marcus laughs, as does Liam.

I can't imagine talking about Addie like that. What we experienced was…special. And I respect her. Kind of disgusts me, to think of talking about her so callously.

"Are you just playing them both?" Dom asks.

"Well, at first, yeah. But I actually want Monique back. Right now, she seems into me too, but that girl changes her mind like she changes her underwear. At least once a day, maybe more. Depends on if I made her cream them or not." Liam high fives Marcus, their laughter so loud people are staring at them.

Jesus, these two.

"Emma is a little crazy," Liam says, his smile knowing. As if he speaks from experience. "She has a temper. It's kind of hot."

He would think her temper is hot. He has one too.

"She's fucking mean if you ask me," Dom says, shaking his head. "She treats Tori like shit sometimes."

I sit up a little at that admission. I wonder if she treats Addie bad too?

"She treats everyone like shit sometimes," Marcus says. "That's just her way."

"Just because it's her way doesn't mean it's right," I point out.

"Oh, high and mighty Callahan, always the golden boy." Marcus rolls his eyes and he and Liam laugh.

"You're a dick," Dom says, not holding back. "Get off his case."

"He did get a good punch in," Liam admits, pointing at his eye.

I wince, feeling bad for it, though I shouldn't. "You got me too." I turn my head to the side and point to the fading bruise on my jaw.

"Gotta have a microscope to see that shit," Marcus says, giving his friend grief. Liam just scowls. "You need to work on your accuracy, my friend."

Damn, Marcus is being harsh.

"With girls too, man," Marcus adds. "You fucked everything up with Addie."

My hackles rise. Liam has zero chance with Addie. I'll make sure of it.

"I'm not interested in her anymore," Liam mutters. "He can have her."

He inclines his head toward me.

"Oh, thanks. Appreciate you giving her to me," I say sarcastically.

"Like you'll snag her up," Marcus says. "If you two haven't sealed the deal by now, you're never going to."

Anger rises within me. What is it about this guy that gets under my skin? "What the hell do you mean by that?"

"Come on, like you haven't noticed she's been dying to ride your jock for years." Marcus leans across the table. "She's hot for you."

"She has not," I protest. More like I'm the one who wanted to get with her, and she always friend-zoned my ass.

Well, not anymore. Not that I'm telling these assholes anything.

"She has," Dom adds, bumping his shoulder against mine. "I've noticed it. I also noticed you staring at her like you're trying to figure out what she looks like naked pretty much the entirety of our junior year."

Great. So we've been obvious to everyone. And Liam still tried to get with her.

The dude is a shit friend.

"You'll never hook up with her," Liam says assuredly. "She's not into that."

Two employees come over to our table and deliver our individual pizzas to us, dropping off a pile of red peppers and parmesan cheese packets in the center of the table before they leave us to eat.

My appetite disappears as I glare at Liam. "She's not into what?"

"Hooking up. Listen, I'm friends with Jonah. Her ex." He glances around like he's afraid someone can hear him and leans over the table, his voice lower. We all draw closer to him. "He tried hard to get in her pants, but she kept denying him. That's why he broke up with her. Girl is scared of sex or whatever."

Scared of sex? She didn't seem too afraid when she was touching my dick Saturday night.

And what the hell is her ex doing, talking about her like that with this asshat?

"She's not scared of sex," I say firmly, because fuck it. I know. "Maybe she just wasn't into him."

"Hundred bucks says you can't bag that," Marcus says.

I glare at him. "What the fuck? You want to make a bet about me and Addie?"

"Sure, because it's easy money, Callahan. You won't do it. You can't pull the trigger either. Look at you and Sasha," Marcus says. "That girl is fine as hell and I know for a fuckin' fact you didn't bang her."

"How the hell do you know that?" I ask, infuriated.

"You told us, dumbass."

Shit. I did. After the disaster that was prom night, I told them how I wouldn't do it with her because she was so shit-faced. I wanted her to actually remember the moment, you know? And I was trying to be respectful. Of course, these assholes—every single one of them at this table, even my best friend—told me I was crazy for turning her down.

"Which leads me to believe you've had zero pussy in your life so far," Marcus adds, a shit-eating grin on his face.

I say nothing because to deny it would be a lie. To act like I get all kinds of girls would also be a lie. It's easier to remain quiet.

And I sure as hell am not telling them about hooking up with Addie last weekend.

"Leave him alone," Dom says, right before he takes a big bite out of his pizza.

"Why? You know it would blow people's minds that Mr. Big Man on Campus still hasn't done it," Liam adds with a sneer. His gaze finds mine. "Maybe you two fumbling virgins could figure out the whole sex thing together."

I brace my hands on the edge of the table, ready to lunge, when Dom grabs my arm, stopping me. "He's not worth it."

Liam grins.

I scowl.

"Let's make a bet then. Think of it like a goal, Callahan. An end date to work toward," Marcus says, sounding pleased with himself. "I bet you can't fuck Addison Douglas by Halloween."

I blink at him, mentally counting the days. I could definitely fuck her by Halloween. Hell, I could probably fuck her by my birthday.

Wait a minute. What the hell am I thinking? I should not fall into this trap. I can't. Addie means way too much to me.

"What if he doesn't?" Liam asks, goading his friend as he slides his gaze toward me.

"Then he owes me...two hundred bucks," Marcus says.

"I want in on this," Liam adds.

"You guys are fuckheads," Dom practically growls. "What the hell? He can't make a bet like that."

"No, I'll take the bet," I say without thinking, my gaze on the two idiots sitting across from us. "You're on."

My voice is weak, and my heart is pumping wildly, like I just ran across the entire football field at full speed.

What the fuck did I just agree to?

Liam high fives a surprised Marcus. "Easy money, just like you said."

The subject is dropped, thanks to Dom talking about the game, and we eat our pizza, the occasional group of girls stopping by our table to say hello. Dom doesn't pay attention to any of them and neither do I since I'm sulking and feeling like a goddamned idiot. Besides, the girls we want to talk to are on their way to a volleyball tournament.

Marcus and Liam though? They flirt with every single one of them.

The more I think about it, the more I can't believe I agreed to that stupid bet. I feel like shit for even agreeing to it. Why the hell did I say yes? It's like I didn't even think. But I also really hate it when they give me shit. I can't help but agree to whatever they're saying just to shut them up.

This could turn messy quick. If Addie ever found out— and knowing these two and their big fucking mouths, she probably will—she's going to hate me.

And with good reason too.

"What the hell were you thinking, agreeing to that bet?" Dom asks me after we've finished eating, and Liam and Marcus are refilling their cups at the soda machine.

"I don't know," I say morosely. "I wasn't thinking at all."

"Clearly." Dom snorts.

"They were running their mouths and it pissed me off," I admit.

"That's their plan. It worked. Now you've agreed to have sex with Addie by Halloween and tell them all about it, or you're out *four hundred bucks*." Dom shakes his head, reminding me of a disappointed father. Something I've been used to seeing lately.

If my dad ever found out about this? And he could, he hears everything in that locker room, and man, he'd be pissed. Angrier than Dom.

"She'll never find out." I sound way more confident than I feel.

I don't trust those fuckers. Not even close.

"Oh, she might, and if she does..." He whistles low. "She's going to hand your ass to you on a plate. You made a bet. With *Liam*. The guy who tried to steal Addie from you."

"I don't own her." Though I feel like I do. And I want to. In my head, she's already my girl.

She's been my girl for a while.

Dom shakes his head, clearly aggravated. "Listen, bro. You're contradicting yourself right now. You throw down for her. Get suspended for her, then claim you don't own her, yet make big dollar bets with two dickwads who can't wait to see you epically fail. Guys who are supposedly your friends."

"They're your supposed friends too," I remind him, irritated with Dom for making me feel like a dumb shit.

"Yeah, they're my friends, but they're guys I don't really trust. I keep them at arm's length. You usually do too. Until now."

"What am I supposed to do? If I back out, they'll give me endless shit."

"You back out and pay them their money, they won't say anything. They'll feel rich," Dom says.

Liam and Marcus both come from families who don't have a lot of money. They're not hurting, but they don't come from wealth like I do. And while I know I'm lucky and I'm grateful for what my dad can do for us, I also didn't necessarily ask to be born into this family. Just luck of the draw, I guess.

My two supposed friends love to give me shit about it. Like I'm some privileged asshole, which I suppose I am. I could give them their money and it wouldn't hurt me. Not one bit.

I'm coming up with a convincing speech in my head when Marcus and Liam return to our table, clutching their refilled cups in their hands.

"Ready to go?" Liam asks, seemingly impatient.

"Look guys." I blow out a harsh breath, hating that I have to do this. Mad at myself that I agreed to their stupid bet in the first place. "I can't agree to that bet."

"You already backing out?" Marcus lifts his brows. "You'll owe us money."

"That's fine." Tension eases from me at his words. Guess Dom was right. That's all they want.

"Nope," Liam says, earning a quick look from Dom. "I'm not letting you back out. A bet's a bet, Callahan. And I think I can make it more interesting."

"What do you mean?" I ask warily.

"I bet *I* can bag Addie by Halloween." A little smile plays upon Liam's lips. "Double or nothing."

"No fucking way," I say firmly. "You can't get involved in this."

"Who says I can't? Let me be the challenge you need." He

grins as Marcus nudges him in the ribs. "Either way, we both win a prize, don't you think?"

"Fuck that," I start but Liam just laughs, cutting me off.

"Naw, fuck you, Callahan."

They walk away from the table, laughing together as they leave the restaurant, and I clench my hands into fists, pounding them on top of the table and making everything jump.

"You asked for that," Dom says with a sigh.

I don't need him to remind me. "I'm fucked, aren't I?"

Dom nods. "For sure."

"I can't let him win. I don't want him coming after Addie."

"Then you need to stake your claim, bro," Dom says. "Don't mess around any longer. Go for it. Make that girl yours."

Yeah. Dom's right. I thought that's what I was doing all along, but I need to step it up.

Fuck that bet. I need to tell her about it. If she hears it from me and I explain myself, she won't be mad.

Hopefully.

God, I'm such a fuckup. I gotta make this right.

And then I need to make that girl mine.

Once and for all.

CHAPTER 28

ADDIE

*W*e're in the van on the way back home after the tournament and I'm exhausted. We played hard Friday night and most of Saturday, and sleeping in a tent both nights in the freezing cold wasn't ideal, but I had a great time.

I'm eager to get home though. To sleep in my own bed.

And hopefully see Beck.

We've texted sporadically throughout the weekend, and he asked if I could get together with him when I got home late Sunday afternoon. I told him I could, but I never asked my mom and she might...

Tell me no.

She probably will tell me no, because that's how she rolls. I don't understand why she's so anti-Beck. He's a good guy, despite the fight and the suspension, which she, of course, found out about and did not approve of.

Whatever. I'm going to see him. Whether she likes it or not.

Tori, Emma, and I are all sitting in the middle bench seat in one of the vans, Emma on her phone the entire drive so far, while Tori is snoozing, her head falling onto my shoulder. I texted with Beck earlier to let him know we were on our way home, but we haven't texted for at least a half hour. Eventually we're going to be deep in Yosemite Park where the service is abysmal. I guess that's why Emma is texting so furiously.

From the look on her face, I'd guess it's with Marcus. And they're most likely fighting.

As if she can feel me watching her, Emma glances up, frowning at me. "What?"

"Are you texting Marcus?"

"So what if I am." She shrugs. "He keeps saying he missed me."

I'm sure he was with Monique the entire weekend. Without Emma around, he has free rein to do whatever he wants. And now that she's coming back, he's trying to keep the peace.

Why can't she see what he's doing to her?

"Just—be careful, Em. I don't want him to hurt you," I tell her.

"He's already hurt me. Multiple times," she says. "Maybe I like the pain."

I don't bother arguing with her, and I envy Tori being able to fall asleep anywhere, so she doesn't have to deal with this. "It's so easy for you to judge me, isn't it?"

My gaze is sharp as it returns to Emma. "I'm not judging you."

She actually scoffs, which makes Tori shift away from me in her sleep. "Please. You're always judging me. Little Miss Perfect while I'm over here making countless mistakes and endless bad choices."

I'm gaping at my best friend, shocked she'd say this to me. "I don't judge you for anything you do, Emma. And I definitely don't think I'm perfect."

"You keep everything locked up tight. You're practically untouchable. Did you know that Jonah came to me when you two were together for advice? He wanted to know what could get you to loosen up," she says, her voice rising.

I glance around, noting how most everyone in the van is seemingly asleep, but I'm thinking some of them are pretending. Meaning that they're listening. "Emma."

"What? You don't like me airing your dirty little secrets? Mine are blasted all over school, so it's only fair yours are too."

"I'm not the one who puts you on blast around school," I insist. "That's everyone else." And Marcus.

Oh, and Monique.

"Whatever. At least people don't think I'm stuck up. Like the guys. All of them think you are, except for Beck, but that's only because he's stuck up too. Though I'm just waiting for the day when he comes to me and asks what he can do to get you to warm up to him. You're a bit of an ice queen, Addison. All the boys know it," Emma says, crossing her arms in front of her and slumping in her seat.

I'm speechless. How cruel can my best friend get?

Much worse. I know she's capable of it. She's vicious when she wants to be, which is often.

Like now.

And the more I think about it, the more infuriated I become.

"They think I'm an ice queen? At least people don't think I'm stupid for turning a blind eye toward my cheating so-called boyfriend."

The words fly out of my mouth before I can stop them and some of the girls in the van actually gasp.

Sleeping my ass. The only one who is actually asleep is Tori.

Emma's face turns about ten shades of red and her gaze

narrows. "See? You just proved my point. Judging me as usual. Well, fuck you too, Addison."

Before I can say a thing in my defense, before I can apologize or take it all back, she turns so her back is toward me, popping her AirPods into her ears. She rests her head on the edge of the seat, completely ignoring me.

I do much the same, angling my body toward the window, my knees drawn up, my lip trembling. I'm on the verge of tears, and I suck in a sharp breath, trying to suck it up. An ice queen? Really?

And Jonah came to her for advice about me? That sounds like a lie.

Maybe it's not though. I was pretty cold toward Jonah when we were together. Always pushing him away and telling him no. At the time, I liked the idea of *having* a boyfriend, but I didn't want to actually *do* anything with Jonah. And that eventually drove him away.

I can't blame him.

With Beck, I don't feel that way at all. The word *yes* runs through my mind on a constant loop. He could ask me to have sex in public and I'd probably ask him what time I should meet him.

I close my eyes, trying to calm my swirling emotions, the guilt that's sweeping over me and making me miserable. I feel terrible for what I said to Emma, but she's been mean to me for months. Always snapping, so demanding all the time. She doesn't listen to what I have to say, making me feel like she doesn't care what's happening in my life, yet I always come running when she needs me.

It's unfair.

Does that justify what I said to her though?

No. Not really.

Grabbing my AirPods, I put them in my ears and listen to one of my favorite playlists, which eventually helps me fall asleep. Only for me to have a dream that I catch Emma with Jonah—their arms around each other and their mouths locked. When Jonah lifts away from Emma, he smiles.

Then somehow it turns into Beck.

I jolt awake, glancing to my right to find Tori watching me, her hand on my shoulder. She lets me go and I pull one AirPod out. "What?" I ask her, my voice shaky.

"You were talking in your sleep." Her brows are lowered as she studies me.

"What was I saying?"

"No. On repeat." She rubs my shoulder again, leaning in close to whisper, "I talked to Emma. She's so mad at you."

Stubbornness streaks through me. I'm still mad from the dream and clinging to it. "I'm mad at her too."

A sigh leaves Tori and she glances in Emma's direction before returning her attention to me. "She told me what you said."

"Did she tell you what she said to me?" I raise a brow.

"Yes. Look, I know you two are heated right now, but you can work this out. She just...the truth hurts, you know? Lizzo doesn't lie."

I don't even know how Tori can say that with a straight face, but she is right. Lizzo isn't a liar with her song. The truth does hurt. And that's all I did—was tell Emma the truth.

"Did Jonah really talk to her about me?" I ask.

Guilt flits in Tori's eyes and I realize she knew. She always knew. I bet Emma told her. But why wouldn't they tell me. "He didn't do it to be mean. He asked because he didn't know what to do."

I stare out the window, the landscape familiar. We're getting closer to home, thank God. "And you guys kept it from me?"

"Emma swore me to secrecy," Tori says, tugging on my shoulder so I face her. I see the worry in her expression and also filling her gaze. She didn't want to upset me. "Emma thought she was being a good friend, giving him advice about you. She wasn't doing it in a malicious way."

A sigh leaves me. I know Tori is speaking the truth, but it still hurts that they never told me. "Do the boys really say I'm an ice queen?"

Tori tilts her head, her brows scrunching together. "I've never heard that before."

"Emma says they do," I whisper, glancing around. Though I guess I shouldn't care who overhears me. The worst part of our earlier conversation was already heard by pretty much everyone in this van.

"So what if they do? Who cares what they think?" Tori says with a kind smile.

"I do. I care what Beck thinks." My voice cracks and I press my lips together.

"And has he called you an ice queen?"

"No." I rest my head on the back of the seat, staring at the van's ceiling. I have been anything but an ice queen with Beck. He looks at me and I immediately melt. He touches me and it's as if his fingers set me on fire.

"Then it doesn't matter what anyone else thinks about you and Beck. Or what we think about Emma and Marcus. It's your own business." Tori's eyes are wide as she watches me. "I confessed to her that she puts all of her drama on us and it's exhausting."

"You did?" I'm shocked.

Tori nods. "I think she's a little irritated with me too, but she'll get over it. We can rectify this friendship, don't you think?"

"Of course we can," I say absently, rubbing my arms. I don't want Emma angry with me, but I'm also tired of her putting her drama on me.

Tori's right. It's exhausting.

* * *

BY THE TIME I'm walking into my house, all I want to do is take a warm shower and collapse into bed. Maybe sleep the rest of my Sunday away. Even though I know Beck wants to see me, and I definitely want to see him, I need to clear my head first.

Take a nap.

Put the argument between Emma and me out of my mind for at least a few hours.

"There you are," Mom says in greeting, stopping short in the middle of the living room when she sees me. "Have fun this weekend?"

I nod, dropping my duffel bag onto the floor next to me. "I'm so tired."

"I bet." She comes to me and pulls me in for a hug, which I return halfheartedly before she lets me go. "We missed you. This is the first year we didn't go to your tournament with you, and it's your last one."

She wanted to come, but my little brother had a cross country meet all day Saturday and she needed to be there for him more than I needed her. And Dad was too busy working, as usual.

"You didn't miss much, but yeah. I had fun. I need a shower and a nap." I grab my bag again and start for my room when she stops me, her fingers wrapping around my upper arm.

"Your grandparents are coming for dinner so don't nap for too long," she tells me.

"Oh God. They are?" I'm whining like a baby, but a Sunday family dinner is the last thing I want to deal with tonight.

"They want to see you and hear all about your tournament." Mom beams.

It takes everything I've got not to collapse and start crying. Instead, I mutter, "Okay," and head down the hall to my bedroom, where I toss my bag on the floor, grab a few things and then lock myself in the bathroom, so I can take a shower.

My phone dings before I even turn on the water and I check to see it's a text from Beck.

Beck: **We still on for tonight?**

Everyone wants something from me, I swear. Though I know Beck isn't like that. Not really. He just wants to see me. Be there for me.

And I want to see him. I really do. Mom's not going to make it easy though. If I ask, she'll tell me no, I can almost guarantee it.

Me: **I don't know. My grandparents are coming over for dinner.**

Beck: **After dinner then? I just want to see you for a few minutes. I've missed you.**

My heart swells. He really is the only one who can make me feel good right now.

Me: **Maybe after they leave?**

Beck: **I can swing by. We can just sit in my car for a few minutes.**

Me: **Things happen when we're in your car...**

I chew on my lower lip, surprised at myself that I mentioned it, but I had to. We're up to no good when we're in the 4Runner and he knows it.

Beck: **Only good things.**

He sends me three blushing emojis and I laugh.

Me: **Don't act like you're embarrassed.**

Beck: **I'm not. I still can't stop thinking about what happened last Saturday in my 4Runner.**

Now I'm blushing. Everywhere.

I have to see him. I just...

I have to.

Me: **I'll text you when my grandparents leave. Then you can come over and we can hang out for a bit.**

Beck: **In my car?**

Me: **Definitely in your car...**

CHAPTER 29

BECK

*A*ddie didn't text me to come over to her house until almost nine, and her message was cryptic.

Head over now, but park around the corner from my house and text me when you get there, okay? I'll come out and meet you.

I do exactly as she asks, parking my 4Runner before I send her a quick text letting her know I'm here. Rolling down the window, I stare out, my knee bouncing, nerves erupting in my stomach.

Not sure why we're sneaking around. Maybe because of her mom? She mentioned she could be kind of strict.

Within a couple minutes of my sending the text, she's right in front of me, popping her head through my open window. "Hi."

"Hey."

We lean toward each other automatically, our lips meeting in a too-quick kiss. She pulls away just as fast, glancing left, then right, before she goes around the front of my car and climbs into the passenger seat.

"Want to get out of here?" she asks.

"Sure." I put the car in drive and pull away, heading out of her neighborhood. "Did you sneak out?"

She's quiet, and when I chance a look at her, I see a sneaky smile on her face.

"You did," I accuse her, shaking my head. "And here I thought you were a good girl."

Her mood shifts, turning somber. "I have a question to ask you."

"What is it?" Apprehension tries to grip me and I tell myself to chill.

"Have you ever heard any of your friends call me an...ice queen?"

I frown, hating how worried she sounds. "No. Why? Who told you that?"

A sigh leaves her and she explains how she had an argument with Emma on the van ride home this afternoon.

"...she said that I have a reputation as an ice queen among the guys in our class," she finishes, sounding sad. "I had no idea."

"Me either, and I'm friends with a lot of guys in our class." I turn right and head north on the highway. "I don't believe it."

"You think Emma was lying to me?" She sounds shocked.

"I don't know. Kind of hard to believe it when I've never heard that rumor ever."

"Were you ever friends with...Jonah?"

What the fuck? "No," I bite out.

"I guess when we were together, he went to Emma and asked for advice about what would get me to...loosen up, are the words she used," Addie admits, dipping her head.

I grip the steering wheel tight, fighting the anger that courses through me. Feels like Emma is trying to make her best friend feel like shit, which is all sorts of fucked up. "Do you believe her?"

"Tori confirmed it, so yeah. It's almost like Emma is lashing out because she's upset over Marcus," Addie says to her lap.

"She's acting like a bitch," I say, not holding back.

"Yeah." Addie lifts her head, staring out the window. "She is."

"I'm sorry she upset you. And I probably shouldn't have called your best friend a bitch," I say.

"No, it's okay. She is acting like one." Addie flashes me a quick smile, but it doesn't quite reach her eyes. "I don't want to talk about her anymore. Or me. How was your weekend?"

"It was all right. Kind of boring. We won Friday, like I told you. The team did good. I hung out with Dom Saturday. We played video games like…all day," I admit.

"Sounds fun," she says.

"We should go out with him and Tori sometime. It'll be fun. Just the four of us," I say as I turn onto a road that takes us to the other side of the lake—the tourist side, where all the campgrounds, resorts and restaurants are, plus a few giant badass houses that sit practically on the water.

"Like a double date?" she asks.

"Definitely like one." I pull into a mostly empty parking lot that's a day-use area. No one is really around. The sun has already set and it's pretty dark outside. I park in a space that faces the water and roll down the windows before shutting off the engine, turning so I can look over at Addie.

"Beck…" Her voice drifts, and she looks away, staring out her open window, her back to me. Her hair is perfectly straight and she's wearing a simple white tank that makes her skin look tan.

I want to touch all of that skin. Explore her with my hands and my mouth. What she said Emma told her just sounds like an insult slung by a jealous friend. Addie isn't cold. At least, she's not with me.

She's the farthest thing from an ice queen.

"What?" I ask, when she still hasn't finished whatever she wanted to say.

Taking a deep breath, she turns to face me. "What exactly are we doing?"

I frown. "What do you mean? We're just hanging out."

"Is that how you view this…whatever it is we've got going on? Hanging out?" She raises her brows.

"I was talking about right now," I say with a chuckle. "But if you're talking about us, and how I feel about you…"

It's hard to put into words my feelings for Addie, when my emotions for this girl are so vast. From the moment I met her, I felt connected to her, even when we were little and playing together at recess. When she'd come over to my house for playdates and my friends would make fun of me for hanging out with a girl.

I think I loved her, even back then.

It's turned into something bigger than that. Better. Far better than anything I've ever experienced. I knew there was a reason I was so stuck on her. Even when we were just friends. Even when I was with someone else.

This girl is just it for me.

The only one.

"Adds…hold on." I climb out of the car before she can say a word and jog over to the other side, opening her door. "Come with me."

She's watching me with wide eyes as she steps out of the 4Runner, her expression wary. I take her hand and lead her over to an empty picnic table, settling on the bench so my back is against the table and I'm facing the lake. I pull Addie's hand so she has no choice but to sit on my lap, and she releases my hand so she can slip her arm around my shoulders.

Our faces are so close, it would be easy to kiss her. Instead, I search her gaze with mine, hating how nervous she looks.

She has to know how I feel about her, right?

Maybe not.

"I've wasted enough time when it comes to you," I admit, reaching up to touch her cheek. Her eyes never leave mine, and I swear she's holding her breath. "I'm falling in love with you, Adds."

She doesn't even blink. "What?"

"Yeah, there's no falling." I brush her mouth with mine before I pull away. "I'm in love with you."

"Beck..."

"I know what you're going to say, that we haven't been together long enough or whatever, but I feel like I've been falling in love with you for years. I was just too much of a dumbass to do anything about it." It's all true. Even when I was with Sasha, I wanted to be with Addie.

Last year, like a complete idiot, I truly believed Addie didn't want to be with me. That she only saw me as a friend. But I was wrong.

And I'm so glad we figured this out before we lost our chance to be together for real.

I drift my fingers down her cheek, emotion surging inside of me when her eyes fall closed, her lips parting. I trace her jaw, her bottom lip with shaky fingers. "I love you, Adds. And I want you to be my girlfriend."

Her eyes slowly open, and they're fucking glowing. "Okay. I'll be your girlfriend."

I wait for her to say something else. The most important thing. And from the smile curling her lips, I think she might be dragging it out on purpose. Fucking with me. "And?" I raise a brow.

She laughs, and it's the most joyous sound. "I love you too, Beck."

I kiss her because I'm tired of wasting time with this girl. Knowing that she loves me, that she wants to be with me...

Nothing is better than this moment, right here. Right now.

We kiss until our mouths are tired and our clothes are rumpled. Until it's close to midnight and we're shivering from the cold breeze blowing off the lake and our over-whelming emotions. She's snuggled so close to me, I don't know where I end and she begins, and when I tilt her face up, taking in her swollen lips and sleepy expression, I know I'll never forget this night for as long as I fucking live.

"I need to get you home," I whisper, kissing the tip of her nose before I press my forehead to hers. "It's late."

"My mom is going to kill me, and I don't even care," she whispers, a giddy smile on her face. "This was such a bad day, and you turned it into my most favorite day, ever."

I cup the back of her head, my fingers threaded in her silky dark hair. "I love you."

It's like I can't stop saying it. And when she grins and says, "I love you too," I can't get enough of hearing her say it either.

Fuck, I'm in deep.

And I don't mind. Not at all.

"Come on." I lightly smack the side of her bare thigh, making her yelp. It was torture, having her sit on my lap the entire time in those little cotton shorts she's wearing. She even straddled me at one point, her knees digging into the wood bench, until it got too painful for her.

If she only knew how much pain I've been in the entire time, having her hot body rub against mine.

"Let's get you back home," I tell her as she leaps to her feet.

The drive back to her house happens way too fast. I hold her hand the entire time, not wanting to break contact with her. She keeps playing with my fingers, interlocking them. Letting them go. Over and over.

I don't mind. I don't want her to ever stop touching me. It's going to be difficult, watching her walk back into her house. Knowing I won't be able to see her again until tomorrow.

She has me park around the corner, same as when I arrived earlier and I protest.

"I won't be able to see you walk into your house and know you got inside safely," I say, being the overprotective boyfriend.

Which is what I am now. I'm full-on embracing it.

"I'll text you." She leans over that damn center console and kisses me. It's full of tongue and a soft little moan, and I capture her face with my fingers before she breaks away, keeping her there as I continue drinking from her lips until she finally murmurs, "I have to go."

Reluctantly, I let her go, watching as she reaches for the door handle. She hesitates, turning to look at me one more time. "No one makes me feel as good as you do, Beck."

My heart thunders in my chest, threatening to break free. "I love you, Addie."

"I love you too." She kisses me one more time. A quick one, and then she's opening the door. "Goodnight."

"Night."

I sit there, waiting until she texts me that she's inside. Two minutes go by and I don't hear from her, so I turn around and do a slow drive by her house.

The light is on in the living room, and my heart stops for a beat. Maybe even two.

I bet her mom was up.

I bet she caught her sneaking in.

Coming to a stop in the middle of the road, I grab my phone and text her.

Everything okay? Did she catch you?

No reply.

Fuck.

CHAPTER 30

ADDIE

I'm extra careful as I sneak back into the house, going through the side door of the garage my father always forgets to lock, then through the door that leads into the kitchen. I took off my flip flops in the garage, entering the house in my bare feet and I walk practically on tiptoe through the kitchen and past the living room. I'm about to turn down the hall toward my room when a light snaps on in the living room.

I freeze, squeezing my eyes closed as a soft sigh leaves me.

Busted.

"Where have you been?"

My mother sounds cold. Furious.

Slowly I turn around to face her. She's perched on the edge of the couch, her hands clutched together as if she's been wringing them for the last three hours since I snuck out.

For all I know, she has.

I stand up taller. "I met up with a friend."

"And didn't bother to tell any of us. You snuck out of the house. You know we have a rule that you always tell us where you are. And you have a curfew. It's almost one in the morning and it's a school night." She studies me, her gaze hard. "Who were you with? And don't lie and say it was Emma. I know for a fact it wasn't."

I frown. "What do you mean?"

"I mean, I called her and she was at home. Said she hadn't seen you since you guys returned from Mammoth. So don't bother telling me you were with Emma or Tori or some other made-up female friend. I want the truth. Who were you with at the lake?" Her voice rises, and I know she checked *Find My Phone* to see where I went.

"Beck. I was with Beck," I admit, my voice weary, my mood ruined. She's about to say something, but I rush toward her, falling to my knees in front of her, ready to plead my case. "I had a terrible day, Mom. Emma and I fought and she said such awful things. We've been having a hard time for a while and I just needed someone to listen to me. Someone who would let me talk and not interject their feelings."

"I listen," Mom starts but I shake my head.

"You listen and you always defend me, which I appreciate. Beck does too, but...it's different with him. I can tell him anything." My voice goes soft and I think about what he said to me earlier. The look on his face when he said that he was in love with me. The most momentous night of my life. "I'm in love with him."

"Oh, Addison." I don't think I've ever heard my mother sound so disappointed in me before. "It's not love. It's just surging hormones."

I jump to my feet, immediately offended. "It's not just hormones. We're in love. He told me he loved me tonight."

"Was that before or after you two had sex?" The fear on her face, that she's experiencing, is downright palpable, and something snaps inside of me.

"Mom!" The word explodes past my lips, startling her.

"We didn't have sex. We went to the lake and we talked." I leave out the kissing part. "That's it. He told me he loved me. That he's been falling in love with me for years. And I—I feel the same way about him. I'm in love with Beck Callahan. And he's in love with me. There's nothing wrong with that. I want to be with him. He means everything to me, and it's okay if we're in a serious relationship, because we love each other."

It's like she doesn't hear a word I say. The disappointment on her face is still clear. "It's not love, Addie, it's—"

"It's not hormones!" I'm screaming. I don't care if I wake up my dad and brother. I don't care if I wake up the entire neighborhood. She's not hearing me and I need her to listen for once. "I'm not Jocelyn, okay? I'm not going to get pregnant my senior year and screw everything up. I'm not her, and I never will be. I'm me. Oh, and guess what? I'm still a virgin! Beck and I haven't had sex yet, I swear to God!"

Mom blinks at me, surprised by my outburst. "You can't talk to me in that tone, young lady."

"Did you even hear a word I said? Or are you too focused on the fact that I'm in love with a boy and ooh, I might have sex with him?" I throw my hands into the air. "I'm almost eighteen. You can't control my life forever!"

"What the hell is going on out here?"

We both turn to find my dad standing there in a white T-shirt and blue plaid pajama pants, his hair a mess as he squints at us.

"Go back to bed. I'll explain it later," Mom tells him.

He ignores her. "You okay, Addie?"

"No." The tears started the moment he asked me that question. "No, I'm not okay. I'm never going to be okay as long as she tries to control my every move."

"I don't control your—"

"I'm not a baby, Mom. I'm almost eighteen. I'm graduating from high school and I'll be going to college. I can figure this stuff out on my own. I will probably make mistakes, and have my heart broken, but I can handle it. Just —support me, okay? That's all I ask from you. To just support me." The sob escapes me and I can't take it any longer.

I run down the hallway past my father and into my room, slamming the door so hard I swear the entire house rattles.

I don't even care.

I throw myself on the bed and cry into my pillow so no one can hear me. This has been the wildest day ever. My emotions are all over the place. I shouldn't have snuck out to see Beck.

But if I hadn't, then we would've never had that magical moment by the lake when he confessed his love for me.

Sniffing, I lift my head and wipe at the tears still streaming down my cheeks, pulling my phone out of my pocket so I can check my messages.

I have a bunch.

All from Beck.

Everything okay? Did she catch you?

ARE YOU ALL RIGHT?

Adds, I need you to text me. Or call me.
I'm worried.
Are you in trouble?
I'm sorry I kept you out so late.
But I'm not sorry for what happened.
I love you.
Please let me know you're okay.

I smile through my tears, loving that he cares so much. That he's checking on me and worried that I'm going to get in trouble.

Composing myself, I type out a response to him.

Me: **I'm okay. My mom was waiting up for me. We got into a huge argument.**

He replies immediately.

Beck: **Oh shit. I'm sorry Adds. Is everything okay?**

Me: **I don't know. I yelled at her. She never listens to me. She's always afraid I'm going to end up pregnant like my sister.**

Beck: **Considering we haven't done it yet, that's impossible.**

His string of laughing/crying emojis make me smile. I know he's trying to cheer me up.

Beck: **Not for lack of trying though.**

I bite my lower lip, wondering if I should ask him the question that's been lingering in my mind since we started spending time together.

I decide to go for it.

Me: **Can I ask you a question?**

Beck: **Sure.**

Me: **Did you have sex with Sasha?**

Beck: **No.**

I lean back against my pillow, in shock. I thought for sure…

Me: **Really?**

Beck: **Really. Did you have sex with Jonah?**

Me: **No.**

Beck: **Huh.**

I'm smiling.

Me: **Yeah, huh.**

There's a knock on my door and then it opens, Mom peeking her head around it. Her expression is contrite, and her eyes are full of sadness. "Can I talk to you for a minute?"

I give her a tight nod, not speaking.

A sigh leaves her. "I didn't mean to put all of my worry on

you. I guess I can't help it after what happened with your sister."

"I'm not Jocelyn, Mom," I whisper. "Though I don't think she turned out so bad. Do you?"

Mom actually laughs. "She's married to a good man who just so happens to be an NFL superstar and is living the dream with their sweet family in Seattle. No, I don't think she turned out so bad at all."

I watch as she walks into my room and settles on the edge of my bed, contemplating me. "I just want the best for you, Addison, and I've always been a little overprotective of you. You're my dreamer. The one who believes everyone is good, even when they're not."

I think of how I let Emma take advantage of me. How Liam tried to push me around. How frustrated Jonah would get with me when we were together, always trying to tell me what to do.

"I need to stand up for myself more," I admit.

"And I need to back off more, because you're right. You are almost eighteen and you can make your own choices. For the most part. I just—I look at you, and still see my baby. My little girl with the big blue eyes and sticky face because you were always sneaking candy when I told you no." Mom's eyes fill with tears and mine do too. "I love you, Addie. And I'm sorry if I've been comparing you to Jocelyn too much. I worry about you, that's all. It's hard to see your babies grow up."

"I'm sorry I snuck out," I admit. "I just—I knew you'd tell me no, and I really wanted to see him."

She wipes at the tears on her face. "You really care about Beck?"

"I'm in love with Beck." My heart soars at the thought of him. "And he's in love with me."

Her expression is thoughtful. "You two always shared a connection, even when you were little. I wondered if it would turn into this. Then he started dating Sasha and I figured you weren't interested in him either."

"I've always cared about him. And he's always cared about me. I guess we just weren't ready to be together yet," I confess.

"But now you are."

I smile faintly. "Now we are."

I think...

I think she gets it.

"You've never given me or your father a reason to distrust you. I've just been so worried about you having a serious relationship with a boy and having him break your heart, that I kept the shackles on you. When all that does is force you to sneak around and be secretive," Mom explains. "So it's time for some new rules, I think."

"Okay," I say warily.

"You will always be honest with us in regards to who you're with and where you're at."

I nod. "I can do that."

"Curfew stands at midnight on the weekends and eleven o'clock during the weekdays," she continues.

"That's fine."

"If you want to have Beck over for dinner sometime, we would like that. We want to get to know him better."

My heart expands. "I would like that too."

We sit in silence for a moment, watching each other.

"I'm not in trouble?" I whisper.

Mom slowly shakes her head. "Not this time. I needed the wakeup call, I think. You're right. I need to let you make your own mistakes, and trust you to do right."

I throw myself at her, giving her the biggest hug. She holds me tight, squeezing me to her, and I bury my face in her shoulder, breathing in her familiar mom smell. "I'm sorry, Mama. I didn't mean to scare you or make you mad."

She runs her hand over my hair. "It's okay. I love you, Addie. So much. Sometimes maybe too much."

I let her hold me for a long time, knowing she needs it.

Knowing I need it too.

CHAPTER 31

ADDIE

I show up at school the next day apprehensive, staying in my car once I park in my regular spot. Tori is knocking on the passenger side window almost immediately and I unlock the door so she can climb in.

"Why do you look so scared?" she asks after she shuts the door, her eyes wide.

"I haven't talked to Emma since our big blow-up yesterday," I admit. "I have no idea how she's going to act toward me."

Tori rolls her eyes. "She texted me last night, complaining nonstop about Marcus, and I told her if she had nothing positive to say, then I didn't want to hear it."

My mouth hangs open. I can't believe Tori did that. "And what did she say to that?"

"She told me that I was a shit friend and so were you." Tori shrugs. "And I told her we're the best friends she has because at least we keep it real with her."

"Emma isn't a huge fan of keeping it real when it comes to her life." Relief floods me. I don't want Tori to take sides. That's not what this is about.

But it's nice knowing she agrees with me when it comes to Emma—and is standing by me.

"Oh, I know. And she said pretty much the same thing. I FaceTimed her later and we worked it out." Her smile is small, but I can tell she's pleased with herself. "I told her she needed to apologize to you for being so rude and taking out all of her frustration on you. She totally agreed and said she'd talk to you today."

My mouth falls open again. What is even happening right now? I feel like I'm living in some sort of alternate universe. One where I don't get in trouble for sneaking out of the house to see my boyfriend, Beck Callahan.

One where I hear Emma feels bad for treating me terrible all the time.

It's so weird.

And so great, all at once.

"I have something to tell you," I announce.

Tori's expression turns eager. "Ooh, what is it?"

I tell Tori everything that happened last night between Beck and me, and how my mother caught me sneaking into my room. The argument, and the eventual compromise. By the time I'm finished, Tori is bouncing in her seat with excitement.

"You and Beck are official-official?"

I nod, barely able to contain my smile. "We are officially official."

"Oh my God!" She grabs hold of me and gives me a hug, squealing in my ear and making me wince as I pull out of her arms. "I'm so excited for you! You two are the cutest couple *ever*. Now we can go on double dates! Dom and Beck, you and me."

I laugh. "So Dom and Beck are dating now?"

"Ha! You know what I mean." She shoves at my shoulder. "Let's go find our dudes."

We find them hanging with the usual group in front of the school, the warm sun glinting off of Beck's hair, making the threads of gold shot through the dark strands look even brighter.

I come to a stop for a moment, blatantly admiring him. My boyfriend is really good looking. Like heartbreakingly so.

When he glances in my direction, he does a double take, his lips curving into a secretive smile. He leaves the group to meet me halfway and I forget about Tori. I forget about everyone as he holds out his arms and I walk straight into his embrace.

"I missed you," he murmurs, kissing my forehead.

I press my face into his shirt, inhaling his clean, masculine scent. "I just saw you a few hours ago."

"I know. Still missed you." He drops another kiss on my forehead, pulling away so he can smile down at me. "Good morning."

I beam up at him. "Good morning."

"Hello, Mr. Callahan," Tori says teasingly as she approaches us.

"Victoria." He nods in her direction. "Dominic is waiting for you."

"You're showing him up, greeting your girl like you just did," Tori says, just as Dom comes over to where we're standing.

"Stop making me look bad," Dom says to Beck, slinging his arm around Tori's shoulders.

"Can't help it," Beck says, positioning me so my back is to his front. "Can't get enough of her."

Dom rolls his eyes. Tori actually applauds.

I can only smile, my entire face going hot.

Liam chooses that moment to walk past us, Danny by his side. They both sneer at us, Liam calling out, "Guess you win, Callahan."

I go still, frowning. I can feel Beck stiffen behind me too, and not in a good way. "What was that about?"

A rough exhale leaves Beck and he dips his head, his mouth at my ear as he murmurs, "I need to talk to you."

Without a word, we leave everyone, my hand in Beck's as we head to a more private spot behind a giant bush.

"I need to tell you something, and you need to know it now before you hear it from someone else," Beck says, his expression downright nervous. "Like Liam."

My stomach swims with dread. "What is it?"

He glances to the side, allowing me to stare at his profile. He's so pretty it hurts. The strong jaw, the sharp cheekbones and that mouth. A sigh leaves him and he returns his gaze to mine. "Dom and I went to lunch last week and we sat with Marcus and Liam."

I frown. "Okay…"

"And Liam was talking shit, as usual. He made a bet with me that I couldn't get with you by Halloween. And then he included himself in that bet and said he was going to try and get with you too," he explains.

"Oh." Well, that's kind of shitty. "I'm guessing this was Liam's idea?"

"And Marcus' too." Beck seems absolutely miserable. I can see it in his eyes. And it's written all over his face. "I don't know why I agreed to it. Dom said I was a dumbass."

"You kind of were," I agree.

He smiles, shaking his head. "Liam just pissed me off. I found myself agreeing to it even though everything inside of me was screaming not to."

"Well, guess what?" I say, purposely keeping my voice light.

His brows draw together. "What?"

"You won, Beck Callahan. Guess it's time for you to

collect your prize." I take a step closer, wrapping my arms around him.

"Are you saying you're my prize?"

I tilt my head back to smile up at him, a sigh leaving me when he wraps me up in his arms. "Yes. It's your lucky day."

"Yeah, it is." He dips his head, his mouth finding mine. "You're not mad?"

"I'm glad you told me," I whisper against his lips. He kisses me again. "If I found out from someone else, I probably would've been mad. And hurt."

"Yeah. That's the last thing I want to do—hurt you. It's been killing me, knowing I agreed to that stupid bet, and I didn't want Liam to be the first one to tell you. Or Marcus. I'm sorry," he says.

"You're forgiven."

Beck kisses me again, his lips lingering. "I love you, Adds."

I don't think I'll ever get sick of hearing him say that to me.

"I love you, too," I tell him, just as the warning bell rings.

He grabs my hand and we head for the building together, a big smile on my face as people walk past us, most of them noticing our clasped hands.

Yep, we're official.

Finally.

* * *

I'm about to head out to lunch with Tori when Emma approaches us, a guarded look on her face. "Hey guys."

Tori and I come to a stop, standing side by side.

"Hey," Tori says.

"Hi."

We stare at each other, and it's kind of awkward, but I'm

waiting for something from Emma. An apology maybe? Though I need to give her one too.

"You going off campus for lunch?"

Tori nods. "We're grabbing sandwiches at Raley's."

One of the local supermarkets in town makes the best sandwiches in their deli.

"Where are the guys?" Emma asks, glancing around.

"They're reviewing tape," I say. It's their Monday lunch ritual to view the opposing team's most recent play tape to prepare for the week's upcoming game.

"Ah. I called it quits with Marcus last night so I forgot." Emma shrugs. "I won't have to worry about the football team anymore, I guess."

"I'm sorry, Em," Tori says.

"It's for the best. We aren't good for each other. More like, he's not good for me," Emma says.

We offer up no reply because she's right. Their relationship was toxic, every time.

"I heard you and Beck are a thing," Emma says to me.

I nod, smiling like I can't help myself. "We are."

"That's awesome. You two look good together." She hesitates only for a moment. "I want you to know I'm sorry, Addie. For what I said yesterday. For dumping all of my problems on you lately. It was unfair, and I feel bad."

Everything within me lightens. That's all I wanted to hear, and even if it took Tori to remind her that she needed to say something, I don't care. At least she apologized. "I feel bad too and I want to apologize for what I said. It was rude." The words gush out of me with relief. "I didn't mean to fight with you in the van."

"I did." Emma laughs, shaking her head. "I was mad and I wanted someone to hurt like I was, so I lashed out. And that sucks because you're my best friend and you've done nothing but be sweet to me and take all my bullshit for years."

"No kidding," Tori mutters.

Emma glares at her, but I can tell she's not too upset. "Again, I'm sorry. To the both of you. Can you guys forgive me?"

"Oh my God, yes," I say, Tori saying pretty much the same thing.

In seconds, we're wrapped up in a group hug, squeezing each other before we all pull apart.

"I'm starving," Emma says. "Can I go to lunch with you guys?"

"Duh! Of course you can," Tori says as we all hook arms and start heading for the parking lot. We take Tori's car to go to Raley's and she cranks the music extra loud as we leave campus, the three of us singing along to a Taylor Swift song from her latest Spotify playlist. The windows are down and our hair is blowing across our faces.

I don't think I've ever felt this happy.

After a few struggles and some bumps along the way, everything has come into place. I can't complain. School has only just started. I'm on good terms with my best friend, and I've gained another one since I've gotten closer to Tori. My mom and I are okay. And then there's Beck...

My boyfriend.

Senior year is going to be epic.

CHAPTER 32

BECK

Friday night lights and I'm sweatin'.

The team we're playing has been a challenge since the first quarter, but we're holding them back, and our offense is scoring. We're up by ten late in the fourth quarter and the game is almost finished.

I'm out on the field, bent into position, when I hear the female voice call from the stands, "Lookin' good, Callahan!"

That was definitely Addie.

And I can't help but grin.

I lunge forward, blocking the opposing player when there's a whistle from the referee, a yellow flag thrown onto the field. False start against the other team, and the onlookers roar their approval.

Including my girl.

I spot her in the stands, sitting in the student section with her friends, my number not only on her chest, thanks to her wearing my jersey, but she's also got it painted on her cheek. Her hair is in a high ponytail that bobs as she talks and she's about the cutest thing I've ever seen.

"Stop daydreaming over your girlfriend." One of my

teammates knocks me in the back of my helmet as he walks by me, and I can only laugh.

How can I protest? He caught me. It's a known problem, me getting caught up watching my girlfriend in the stands, but Adds is never a true distraction.

I just love knowing she's sitting there, watching me. Supporting me. I do the same for her. I go to every volleyball game I can, rooting her on, wearing her number on my cheek. All the guys made fun of me at first, but at the next game, Dom showed up with Tori's number on his cheek *and* the number painted in white on a navy T-shirt and I just shook my head.

Guess I started a trend.

The rest of the quarter goes by quickly and we win, the band playing the fight song as we form into a line in the center of the field and high five the opposing team, as is the ritual after every game. We walk over to the sidelines to face the bleachers, our helmets in our hands as we hold them over our heads and yell together, "Thank you, fans!"

The crowd, as usual, goes wild.

Within minutes, the field is flooded with people. Family members and students. Girlfriends with signs, ready to pose with them while they stand next to their boyfriends.

Like my girlfriend.

Addie's sign says, "#64 tackled my heart," with "Go Callahan," painted below it.

She waves it at me, a giant smile on her face.

I head straight for her, pulling her into me, so I can drop a quick kiss to her lips. "Nice sign."

"I knew you'd love it." She rises up to press her mouth to mine before she pulls away and stands next to me. "Tori, take a photo! Quick, before he starts griping."

I roll my eyes and sling my arm around her shoulders as she holds the sign up in front of us. I never gripe, and she knows it. We pose for a few photos and then she does the same for Tori and Dom. Emma is usually the photographer, but she just got a job and had to work tonight.

Maybe it's better. Currently Monique and Marcus aren't too far away from where we're standing out on the field, and it still stings for Emma, seeing them supposedly happy. It's only been a month since she broke it off with him, so it makes sense.

From what I can tell, Marcus and Monique argue all the time, but I don't delve too deep into their business.

It's easier that way.

Dom and Tori are going strong, just like me and Addie. We hang out together a lot, which I know Addie and Tori love. Dom acts like it's no big deal, but he's so gone over Tori, it's not even funny. They make a good couple. Addie and I do too.

Just as Addie recently told me, our senior year is pretty perfect so far.

"Beck!"

I turn to see my mother walking toward me and when she gets close, I pull her in for a hug, squeezing her tight. She's come to watch pretty much every single one of my football games over the years. Through the heat and rain and cold weather. That one playoff game in the eighth grade when it was so cold, they worried it might snow. Through my games *and* Jake's, she's always there, smiling and cheering us on.

I've got the best mom in the world.

"You played so good tonight," she says once I release her. "I still can't believe this is our last high school football season. Every game that goes by reminds me that it's almost over."

She's pretty nostalgic right now, which I guess I can't blame her. Soon she won't have to go to any high school football games on Friday nights, and she's feeling it.

"Thanks, Mom. And you can always come watch me play in college." I smile at her.

"Oh I will. And speaking of that." She tips her head toward me. "We have something special planned for your birthday. And Addie's."

I frown. "What are you talking about?"

"You'll see." Her tone is mysterious, as is the expression on her face.

Much later, when the game is long over and I've got Addie half-naked in the back of my 4Runner, her legs wrapped around my hips and my mouth on her neck, she whispers, "Your parents are planning something for us."

I pull away from her neck, scowling at her as I slowly thrust my hips against hers. "You can't mention my parents while we're doing this, Adds. Kind of ruins the mood."

She laughs, not bothered by my comment whatsoever. "I can't help it. Your mom was dropping some hints during halftime when I talked to her and I'm dying to know what's up."

"I know nothing." I run my mouth along the length of her throat, making her sigh. The sound goes straight to my dick, as usual. "And I don't care what they're planning. All I care about is you."

Her legs tighten around my hips and I wish we were completely naked. But I don't want our first time to be in the back of my car. I want us to have sex on a bed, but right now that feels impossible. My mom is always home. Her mom is always home. And I'm not going to have sex with Addie at some random party in someone else's bed.

I want it to be special. My friends would make fun of me, but Addie gets it. Deep down, I think I'm a romantic at heart.

Actually, I know I am.

But only for Addie.

"I did something," she says, her hands on my shoulders, gently pushing.

I lift away from her neck to stare down at her pretty face. Her eyes are sparkling and her cheeks are flushed, as is her chest. Her hair is a complete mess and I push a few strands away from her forehead, dropping a kiss there. "What did you do?"

"I went on birth control." Her expression is solemn as she stares up at me. "I've been on it for the last week."

"Are you saying you want to have sex with me, Adds?" I'm teasing. It's kind of obvious. I literally just had my fingers between her thighs not even a few minutes ago.

"Yes. Maybe even...tonight?" She raises her brows, hopeful.

"I'm not fucking you for the first time in the back of my car," I say firmly. "Besides, isn't it close to your curfew?"

Her shoulders fall a little. "Yeah. It's just—I *really* want to have sex with you, Callahan. Like, bad."

I laugh. "I'm dying to have sex with you too, Douglas. But I want to do this right."

"Always talking about doing what's right." She rolls her eyes, though she's also grinning. "Such a saint, Beck."

"You like me this way." I kiss her, my tongue thrusting against hers. I'm not feeling so saintly right now, and from the way she's moaning and shifting beneath me, I can tell she's not feeling too saintly either. "Soon, Adds. I promise."

"Oh my God, it feels like I've been wanting this forever." Her hands are in my hair and she gives it a hard tug.

"You're not scared?" She used to say that, when we first started messing around on the regular, but I haven't heard her use that word in a while.

"Not with you. Not anymore." She touches my cheek. "I love you."

"I love you too." I kiss her nose. She reaches for my cock,

and while I definitely don't mind, I know what she's trying to do. "But we're not doing it back here."

She pouts. "We need to make this happen. Soon."

"We will." I pull away from her, wondering where all of this restraint is coming from. Maybe all that talk from my mother growing up about respecting women actually sunk into my brain.

"In the meantime, since you didn't come…" Her voice drifts, and next thing I know, I'm lying flat on my back, my boxer briefs long gone and Addie's warm, wet mouth is wrapped around the head of my dick, her fingers curled around the base.

I push her hair away from her face so I can watch, because damn, there is nothing hotter than watching my girl give me a blow job. The back of my car has witnessed all sorts of scandalous shit since we've been together.

We're hungry for each other all the time. Overly affectionate. I want to touch her always. Kiss her almost as much. I am so gone for this girl some might call it pathetic.

I just consider myself lucky. I finally got my dream girl.

And she's all mine.

CHAPTER 33

✣

ADDIE

The surprise Beck's parents put together included flying all of us for Beck's eighteenth birthday to... Seattle.

We arrived early Saturday morning and we're staying at Eli and Ava's house. A perfect storm of Callahans was brewing—the Seattle Seahawks are playing the Arizona Cardinals Sunday afternoon. Bennett versus Callahan. Beck's brother-in-law Ash plays for the Raiders and the team has a bye-week.

This means all of the Callahans are in Seattle. As is my sister and brother-in-law.

Talk about meant to be.

The moment we arrived at SeaTac Airport, we went to the rental car area and picked up an SUV and drove to Eli and Ava's to drop off our stuff. We played tourist for the afternoon, walking around downtown Seattle, visiting the Public Market, and enjoying a long lunch by the water. After lunch, we went to the University of Washington and walked around the campus. It's a school we're both contemplating, but I'm not sure what we're going to do yet.

Considering we need to start applying soon, it's something that's in the forefront of our minds. It's unspoken, but I think we're going to try to go somewhere together.

When we finally arrived back at Ava and Eli's, they'd put together a birthday party for Beck—and for me. The entire family was already there.

Ava arranged to have the party outside. The weather was crisp and cool—absolutely perfect. Happy birthday and our names were spelled out in golden balloon letters and strung on the wall. There was so much food and more than a few kids running around with adults chasing after them. The only couple—besides Beck and me—who don't have kids is Jake and Hannah and I think they're still okay with that decision, though I did see Hannah cuddling Ava and Eli's son Rhett in her arms, smiling down at him as he slept.

The only time that kid is calm, I swear.

Within a few minutes, he woke up, reached for a strand of Hannah's long red hair and tugged so hard, she yelped and immediately set him down. He took off running like the little terror he is.

He's basically Eli junior, which is more than a little terrifying.

Everyone talked over each other at dinner. Eli, Diego and Jake got into an argument over NFL stats and Beck's dad had to interject his opinion here and there. To the point that they were all yelling at each other, insisting they were right. Even Beck got in on the action, looking up stuff on his phone to prove whoever was wrong.

Most of the time, it was Diego who was right. This infuriated Jake and Eli.

I thought it was funny.

The women talked about kids and their men and how football rules their lives. I don't think they're upset about it, though. They all seem pretty content. My sister is the happiest I've ever seen her with her two kids and doting husband. Diego would often ask her if she needed help with the baby, since Axel is one and a handful. They'd trade off watching him and I helped out too, chasing Axel and Rhett around the yard.

Those little boys are already best buds. Rhett will grab hold of Axel around the neck and give him a big kiss on the cheek. It's so cute.

Another generation of friends in the making.

"You seem really happy," Jocelyn says to me at one point, coming to sit beside me after we've all cleared the table and Beck's parents forced us outside so they could clean the kitchen. "With Beck."

"With everything," I admit, smiling at her. "It's been a good senior year so far."

"Are you in love with him?" Jos asks, her brows shooting up.

I offer a shy nod, ducking my head. I don't know why I'm embarrassed to admit this to my big sister, but I am. It still feels so fresh and new between Beck and I.

"He's really sweet to you. And he watches you everywhere you go." When I glance up at her, I find my sister smiling at me. "Pretty sure he's obsessed with you."

We both laugh. It's actually something Beck said to me a few nights ago, after a particularly hot and heavy make out sesh in his 4Runner.

"You still like it here in Seattle?" I really do want her opinion. Washington is an option for college, and it would be great to live closer to my sister. We've grown distant, which I think is normal. She's busy raising a family while I'm in school, but I want us to get closer.

I think she does too.

"I love it. I don't mind the weather. It's beautiful here, and when Diego isn't playing, we spend a lot of time outdoors.

We both worry he'll get traded though." She shakes her head. "But that's okay. Wherever Diego and our children are, is where I want to be. We can make a home anywhere."

"That's actually the sweetest thing ever," I admit, and Jos smiles.

"Wait until you find it someday. Your forever person. Maybe you already have."

My smile is small, my thoughts filled with Beck.

Yeah.

I think I've found him.

By the time the cake is brought out, I'm tired. Ava added candles to the three-tiered cake that are more like fireworks, and they give off sparks everywhere as everyone sings Happy Birthday to us. We eat cake and open presents, and I find myself leaning back in the stuffed chair I'm sitting in, closing my eyes as people chat around me.

"Hey, Sleepyhead. Don't pass out on me now," Beck whispers to me.

I crack my eyes open to find him kneeling beside my chair, his direct gaze warming me up. "I'm so tired."

"Guess you should nap then. I have plans later." He leans in closer, his mouth brushing against my ear as he whispers, "I'm gonna sneak into your room."

Oh.

When he pulls away, that sly smile on his face, I can't help but laugh.

"You're bad," I tease him.

"You like it." He kisses me.

Anticipation fills me. If it all comes together, I know what's going to happen tonight.

And I can't wait.

Jos and Diego leave first, their kids in tow.

"You sure you don't want to stay the night with us?" Jos asks me as they're about to walk out the front door.

"I'm so tired. I hope you don't mind if I stay here instead." I offer her a sleepy smile, which is real, but let's face facts. I'm not leaving this house. Not after what Beck told me.

"We can talk more at the game tomorrow," I add.

"Sounds good." She hugs me. Gigi does too.

And then they're off.

Ash and Autumn are staying at a hotel. So are Jake and Hannah. They all leave together, Jake promising he's going to destroy the Seahawks tomorrow out on the field.

"Bring it, Callahan!" Eli shouts at him as they're leaving. "We're going to kick your asses!"

"Yeah! Kick their asses, Daddy!" Kenzie crows, which makes Eli crack up.

Ava, not so much.

It's pure chaos leading right up to bedtime, but soon enough, I'm tucked away in one of the guest rooms, running my hands over the soft comforter before I pull it back and snuggle in. I already took a shower and I'm warm and sleepy, clad in my favorite sleep shorts and tank top. The pillow is so fluffy and comfortable, I can't resist closing my eyes for just a second.

"Adds." Gentle fingers grip my shoulder, shaking me. "Adds, are you awake?"

My eyes flutter open to find my shirtless boyfriend sitting next to me on the bed. I immediately push up onto my elbows, looking around. "What time is it?"

"Just past eleven." He smiles. "You fell asleep."

"I was so tired." I collapse on the mattress, glancing over at him. "Chasing all those little kids wore me out."

"We did a lot today." He leans over, delivering a chaste kiss to my lips before he pulls away slightly. "Are you too tired?"

"For what?"

"You know."

I do know.

"No. I'm not too tired." I smile at him.

He grins back.

"Did you lock the door?" I ask.

He nods.

"Do your parents know where you're at?"

"Uh, no." He makes a face. "Want me to text them? Let them know what's up?"

I giggle. "Of course not. I just—you don't think we're going to get caught, do you?"

"My sister's house has wings, Adds. My parents are on the other side of the house. The complete other side. You really think they're going to catch us?" He stands and I quickly take in what he's wearing as he walks around the bed. Black basketball shorts slung so low there's no way he's wearing underwear beneath them.

My body catches fire at the realization, my gaze snagging on his flat stomach as he pulls back the covers, so he can slide into bed with me. "They're probably already asleep," he reassures me as he tugs the comforter back over the two of us.

Excitement bubbles up inside of me, with a healthy dose of apprehension as well. I'm not too scared about having sex, especially with Beck. But I really don't want us to get caught.

Talk about embarrassing.

"This mattress is hella comfortable. I think my sister gave you the better guest room," he grouses as he grabs hold of me and pulls me in close.

I love how physical he is, and how easy it is for him to pick me up, drag me around, whatever. I'm not a delicate little girl. I'm tall and I've got some muscle on me. But Beck makes me feel downright dainty.

I sneak a leg around his, rubbing my toes against his calf as he starts nuzzling my neck, his lips pressing into my skin.

"I am the guest, so I guess I deserve it. Besides, you're just her baby brother."

"Hmm, do I feel like a baby right now?" He rolls me over, so I'm on my back and he's hovering over me.

And I can already feel that he's hard.

"Not quite," I tease him, sucking in a breath when his mouth finds mine. His kiss is insistent, hungry and I open to him, our tongues dancing, his hand already slipping beneath my tank. His fingers graze the underside of one breast, sending shivers...

Everywhere.

"Fuck, you smell so good," he whispers as he drops little kisses along my jaw. Down my neck. On my ear, biting the lobe. I suck in a soft breath, a sigh leaving me when he slips farther down, his mouth mapping my collarbones, my chest, along the neckline of my tank.

"Should I turn off the light?" I ask him, my eyes popping open to stare at the softly glowing lamp on the nightstand.

"Fuck no," he practically growls. "I want to see you."

He's right. I want to see him too.

I don't want to miss a thing.

Impatiently he shoves my tank up, revealing my breasts to his gaze. He stares at my chest for a moment, like it's the first time he's ever seen me, before he dips his head and draws a slow circle around my left nipple with his tongue. He does the same thing to my right nipple, and I arch into his mouth, wanting more.

Wanting him to suck them.

He knows what I want and he delivers, and I can feel the rhythmic pull of his mouth, matching the throbbing between my legs. I spread my thighs and he settles in between them, scooting down, his mouth on my ribs. My stomach. Until he's pulling my shorts off, exposing me completely.

"No panties?" He glances up at me, his brows up.

I shake my head. "Lucky you."

"Lucky me," he drawls as he rises up and pulls them all the way off, tossing the shorts over his shoulder and making me giggle. A smile curves his perfect lips, just as he dips down and presses them below my belly button.

He's gone down on me before—exactly once, and while I enjoyed it, and he made me come, it was also awkward because every sexual experience we have is either in my car or the 4Runner. It's never fully comfortable, especially for him because he's so tall.

That's why it's absolute bliss, being with him in a bed, and a giant one at that.

His hands are on my hips as he shifts farther down, his mouth landing on the inside of my thigh. Anticipation races through my veins as I watch him, a shuddery breath leaving me and he glances up, his blue eyes meeting mine before he drops his head, his mouth finding me exactly where I want him.

I close my eyes, a breathy sigh leaving me as his tongue slicks through my folds, searching, finding my clit. He sucks on it, sliding a finger inside of me at the same time, and I spread my thighs farther apart, eager for more.

He lavishes so much attention on me, until I'm thrashing beneath him, my fingers in his hair, my hips thrusting as I basically rub my pussy against his face. I'm chasing after my orgasm, the one that hovers just on the surface, threatening to wash over me at any minute. His tongue works some sort of magic on my clit, making me tremble, making me cry out, and I immediately slap my hand over my mouth, not wanting anyone to hear me.

And just the thought of someone hearing me somehow sends me over the edge, my body quaking with the force of my orgasm as I arch my back. Beck holds onto me, his mouth still working me, even as I keep coming until I'm trying to push him away from me, his mouth too much on my sensitive flesh.

I'm breathing hard, my heart racing so fast I rest my hand against my chest, closing my eyes as I try to calm myself. Beck shifts so he's sliding up my body, his face suddenly right there, his mouth on mine. He kisses me deep, his tongue in my mouth, tasting like me, and I kiss him back, purposely slowing down the rhythm of our mouths as I try to steady my thumping heart.

"You were a little loud," he whispers against my lips. "I don't think I've ever heard you scream like that."

"I didn't scream."

"Oh yeah, you did." He grins, looking proud. "It was hot, babe."

"You're going to have to be quiet too," I remind him. Sometimes he likes to shout when he comes.

Tonight shouldn't be one of those times.

"I can handle it," he says with far too much confidence. "I, uh, I brought condoms. Just in case."

"Do we need them?" I wrinkle my nose.

"To be extra safe. If it makes you feel better."

He's respectful of that, the worry that lingers in the back of my mind about pregnancy, thanks to my mom's constant nagging through the years. I'm on the pill, the statistics are in my favor I won't get pregnant.

"I don't want to use a condom," I tell him, my voice soft. "I want to feel you."

His entire expression shifts into complete and utter excitement. "Yeah, okay. Cool. I want to feel you too."

He starts fumbling around, trying to take off his shorts and my chest goes tight at how cute he is. How nervous he suddenly is too.

I love this boy so much. Man. He's eighteen now. So am I. And since we got together and became a real couple, I can't imagine my life without him.

I don't want to. He's always been there, waiting in the shadows.

And now he's mine.

He belongs to me.

The shorts are gone and now, it's just the two of us, skin-to-skin. He feels good. Hard and smooth, solid as a rock. He's so careful as he hovers above me, not wanting to rest all of his weight on top of me and I want to feel him. I wrap my arms around his middle, my hands skimming his back as I push on him until he's pressing into me.

"You feel so good," I tell him just as he kisses me. Devours me. The kiss goes from sweet to dirty in a matter of seconds, our mouths wild, biting and tugging, his tongue thrusting against mine. I reach between us, my fingers brushing against his erection, and he hisses in a breath.

I touch him again, curling my fingers around him, giving him a squeeze. He's thick and long and perfect. Maybe even a little intimidating because I wonder how that's going to fit, but I know it's going to work. People do this all the time.

We've got this.

He positions himself above me, one hand on the mattress next to my head, the other wrapped around his erection as he guides it inside of me. I lift my hips, wincing when just the head of him fits inside of me and I close my eyes, swallowing hard.

"Am I hurting you?" He sounds worried.

I shake my head. Take a deep breath. "No. Just—be slow."

Beck does exactly as I request. He sinks into me slowly, inch by inch, pausing every few seconds as he tries to control his breathing. I stare up at him, marveling at how thoughtful he is, and how much I love him. At just how connected we are.

There's no going back. He is mine.

Forever.

CHAPTER 34

BECK

Goddamn, she feels so good. Tight and hot, wrapped snug around my dick. I won't last long, not like this. That's why I went down on her and gave her that orgasm. Besides helping her loosen up for me, I was worried I'd be a two-pump chump and come in her within two seconds of being inside her body.

Looks like my worry was valid. I'm this close to coming and I've barely done anything but slip inside her. I close my eyes and think of football. Stats. My brother shouting at Eli and Diego. That was some stupid shit at dinner, but also fun. I love hanging out with those guys.

My family.

Addie runs a hand down the center of my chest, leaving me shaky. I open my eyes to find her smiling up at me. "You okay?"

"I should be asking you that."

Her smile grows. "I am more than okay."

Slowly, I start to move, restraining myself. Trying to make this last. Trying to make it good for her. We're awkward together at first, attempting to get in sync and find a rhythm, but after a while, it's as if it comes naturally. I thrust inside of her, increasing my pace and she moves with me, her hips lifting to meet mine. She throws her head back, her eyes closed, her lips parted and that's it.

That's all it takes.

The orgasm slams into me, a guttural groan sounding from deep inside my chest as I spill inside of her. Her legs rise up, her thighs pressing against my hips as she winds them around me and fuck, that makes me come even harder.

I collapse, still careful not to rest all of my weight on top of her. She wraps her arms around my neck, pulling me down for a long, tongue-filled kiss.

"I love you," I whisper against her lips.

"I love you too," she murmurs.

"Was I too loud?" I pull away slightly so I can stare at her pretty face.

She frowns. "I don't know. I sort of...lost myself in the moment. I wasn't paying attention."

We both swivel our heads toward the door.

"No one's trying to bang it down," I say.

"The only one doing any banging right now is us," she says, making me chuckle.

"I want to do it again," I whisper, stealing a kiss.

She laughs. "Okay."

I roll over so we're lying on our sides, facing each other. I trace her face with my fingers, staring at her, letting all of my emotions sweep over me. How much this girl means to me. How glad I am that we finally got our heads out of our asses and figured out how much we care for each other.

I love her. So damn much. I think I always have.

"What are you thinking?" she asks. It's a question she asks a lot, and I always answer truthfully.

"How much I love you."

Her smile is gradual. Beautiful. Has she ever been this gorgeous? I don't think so. "I love you too."

I slip an arm around her waist, pulling her to me, until there's nothing between us. She's warm and smooth and every inch of her is mine. "Are you ready for the next round?"

"Now that we've finally done it, have we created a monster?" She angles her head to the side, giving me more room to kiss her neck.

"Hell yes," I growl against her throat, making her giggle. "Though I'm figuring you want it just as bad as I do."

"I do," she says on a sigh as I rise above her. "I so do."

EPILOGUE

Beck

Two months later...

THE BADGERS ARE STILL in the playoffs and tonight's game is...

Really freaking cold.

Because we won league, we have home field advantage, which is a bonus, but it also means we're playing at a high elevation thanks to our mountain town. At the end of November.

The day after Thanksgiving, to be exact.

Offense is currently on the field and I'm on the sideline with the rest of my teammates, glancing over my shoulder to look for my family in the stands. Mom is sitting up pretty high with Hannah and Jake, and I make eye contact with my brother, who smiles his encouragement.

I realize a bunch of guys from my school are sitting on the other side of the aisle across from my brother, watching Jake in complete awe. I can't even imagine what might happen if he brought the rest of the football playing family members with him.

They'd probably all cause a riot.

My gaze finds my girlfriend next, who's sitting on the other side of my mother with her friends, Tori planted right in the middle between Emma and Addie, and I can tell Tori is talking nonstop. Addie offers me one of those small smiles of encouragement and I break out into a grin, lifting my hand into a wave.

"Callahan!" My father is screaming for me and I go to him, noting the serious expression on his face.

"What's up, Pops?" We've been calling him that since Jake showed up late Wednesday night to spend the Thanksgiving holiday with us. Dad puts on an act like it irritates him, but deep down, I think he likes it.

Even though he's currently scowling at me.

"You need to watch it when you get back out on the field. I think they've got you figured out." He means the opposing team.

"I've got this. I'm not worried," I tell him confidently, meaning every word I say.

Sometimes you just know when things are going to work out, and tonight is one of those times. I haven't been nervous all day, despite everyone asking me if I'm ready for this game, even Jake. I understand the entire game doesn't rest on my shoulders, and shit can go sideways in an instant, but something tells me we're on top of it. Our team is solid, both defense and offensive. Our quarterback Dylan has been so accurate the last few games, it feels like we've been down-right untouchable.

But I can't get too cocky yet. It's only the bottom of the first half, and while we're leading by ten, things can change fast.

When it's my turn to run out onto the field, I keep my eye on all the dudes surrounding me, ready to bring my A game. And by halftime, we're up by thirteen. Once we're back in the locker room, Dad leads a short by rousing speech, saying the usual stuff to keep us motivated. I'm only half listening, thinking about the conversation Addie and I had earlier this afternoon, when we talked about applying for college, which we just did a few days ago.

We want to go somewhere together. And while we haven't mentioned it to our parents yet, they have to realize that Addie and I? We're the real deal.

Someday, I'm going to marry that girl.

"Callahan! You listening?"

I blink, realizing it's my freaking brother who's standing in front of the team, taking my dad's place. "Uh, yeah," I tell Jake, sitting up straighter.

"Okay then." Jake nods before his gaze scans the room, his face serious. "I've been in your place not too long ago, and I know exactly what this feels like. This game tonight is every-thing. If you win it, you go on to the state championships, and if you lose…"

It's so quiet, I don't think any of us are breathing.

"It's over. You're finished."

His words hang in the room like a bad mood, heavy and somber.

Fuck that.

From the grumbling I hear coming from my teammates, they feel the same damn way.

347

"I know deep in my heart, you guys aren't finished. You are the farthest thing from being finished. Am I right?"

We all roar a variety of answers, the majority of them being 'fuck yeah!'

"Are you going to show the Blue Raiders who's in charge?"

Now we're all screaming 'hell yeah!'

Those freaking Blue Raiders have been our number one competitor when it comes to the division championship for the past couple of years. We win it, then they win it. For a couple of years, they won the title consecutively.

Now we want the trophy back.

Jake keeps talking, pumping us up until our locker room feels like it's filled to bursting with testosterone and adrenaline. We all go running out onto the field with a roar, getting into position on the yard lines so we can run through jumping jacks together, counting them in unison, our voices ringing loud.

The crowd in the stands cheer and whistle their encouragement, and my gaze goes to Addie, who's watching me with pride shining in her eyes, a permanent smile on her face.

We're going to win this game. I'm going to do it for my family. My brother.

My girl.

The second half whips by in a blur and it's a complete blow out. We never let them score again. At one point, I even intercept the ball and gain some major yardage, which makes my dad as giddy as a little girl, hopping up and down on the sidelines as I'm running past him. We end up totally owning the Blue Raiders, with the final score 41-12.

We won our entire division. It's official—now we're on to state playoffs.

When the buzzer rings and the announcers call the game,

the floodgates open. The crowd leaves the stands in droves, all of them spilling out onto the field, eager to congratulate us.

"We fucking did it," Dom says before he pulls me into a hug, slapping my back extra hard as he pulls away. "Can you believe it?"

"Yeah actually, I can." I sound like a smug dick, but I mean every word I say.

I had faith in us. I knew we could do it.

Jake approaches us, a giant smile on his face. "I think my speech worked."

"You can't take all the credit," I tell him just before we hug.

"You were amazing out there," he says, his voice low and just for me. "Good job tonight, brother."

It means everything to me that Jake thinks I played well.

Everything.

There are more congratulations offered. I'm taking photos with my teammates, all of us holding up our index finger as in we're number one. My brother takes photos with us too, and the sports reporter from the local news is so nervous talking to Jake, her voice actually shakes.

"Listen, you don't want to talk to me," he says into her microphone, flashing the cameraman a charming smile. "You need to talk to these guys." He waves a hand at all of us and we pump our fists and yell in answer.

The reporter laughs. "You're right, you're right."

Once we're finished speaking to the reporter, I'm talking to my dad and the rest of the coaching staff when my entire body sparks with awareness. Glancing to my right, that's when I see her headed my way.

Addie.

"There you are." I open my arms to her and she walks

right into them, sliding her arms around my waist and resting her head against my chest. "Where have you been?"

"I wanted to give you time to talk to everyone else first and bask in the limelight." She pulls away slightly so she can smile up at me, her eyes sparkling. "You played so good!"

"I didn't do so bad." I shrug one shoulder.

"You caught an interception! It was great."

Her enthusiasm always puts me in a good mood.

"Now that was dope as hell." I bend down, dropping a quick kiss on her lips. "We won."

I know she knows, but I felt the need to say it again and let it sink in.

We won.

We motherfuckin' won.

"I'm so proud of you," she murmurs.

"I'm proud of all of us." I glance around the field at all of my teammates, pulling Addie to my side, my arm draped over her shoulders. All the families and friends intermingling with us out here, as well as people from our school. Staff and administration. Mom's hugging on Jake and Hannah is laughing at something my dad is telling her.

My heart...is fucking full tonight.

"Hannah told me something," Addie says.

I look down at her. "What was it?"

"They've finally set a wedding date." Addie's brows shoot up. "It's next spring, right before we graduate."

"No kidding? That's great. Why didn't they tell us yesterday, during dinner?" Practically the entire family was there. It would've been the perfect time.

"I don't know. I asked her the same question and she just shrugged and said Jake is weird. I kind of have to agree."

I burst out laughing. Leave it to Hannah and Addie to blame Jake. "I'm excited for them."

"Me too. Hannah says they've been engaged forever."

"They have," I agree, my mind going forward, to the future when I ask Addie to marry me.

It's gonna happen.

Just wait and see.

"Hey Adds."

Her brows shoot up when I just grin at her for a few seconds. "What's up?"

"Thanks for always being there for me. And supporting me." She's the most supportive person I know. I try to be the same to her, but sometimes I feel like I fail.

I'm working on it though. I want to be a better man for her.

A man she deserves.

Because my girl deserves the world.

Her smile is soft, as is the glow in her eyes. "I love you so much, Beck Callahan."

"I love you too." I pull her back into my arms, my hands landing on her butt, making her laugh. "I'm so glad you're mine."

Her eyes are glowing. "I'm glad I'm yours too."

ACKNOWLEDGEMENTS

Ah Beck and Adds. You know, these two surprised me because they rushed it. As in, once they knew, they really went for it - as in each other. The timeline of this book is whiplash fast, and at one point I worried about it, but these two have been longing for each other for years. So in a way it makes sense that they'd waste no time.

If you've read any of the **When Bae...** installments in my newsletter, then you know this already. I hope you enjoyed their story, and those little glimpses of other peeps too. PLUS, if you read the epilogue (you really should LOL), then you know who's getting married in A Callahan Wedding. And I'm so excited! I hope you are as well.

A big, huge thank you to the readers, reviewers, bloggers, etc. who read the **Callahans** and the **College Years** series. Yes, I write these books for me, but I also write them for you. And it thrills me every time I hear from one of you, letting me know which one is your favorite. I also want to thank everyone at Valentine PR for taking care of me - Nina, Kim, Daisy, Kelley - you ladies are the best!

Also want to thank my editor Rebecca and proofreader

Sarah for slapping this book into shape. Thank you Nina, for the solid notes - y'all got more Jake Callahan in this story because of her! I also want to thank Hang Le for the amazing cover, as always.

I said Beck Callahan is the last Callahan I'm writing about BUT! You still have A Callahan Wedding to look forward to! I'm going to do my best to have everyone (and I mean everyone) show up for that wedding. It's going to be a blast!

p.s. - If you enjoyed **MAKING HER MINE**, it would mean the world to me if you left a review on the retailer site you bought it from, or on Goodreads. Thank you so much!

ALSO BY MONICA MURPHY

BILLIONAIRE BACHELORS CLUB (REISSUES)

Crave & Torn

Savor & Intoxicated

NEW YOUNG ADULT SERIES

The Liar's Club

KINGS OF CAMPUS

End Game

LANCASTER PREP

Things I Wanted To Say

A Million Kisses in Your Lifetime

Birthday Kisses

Promises We Meant to Keep

I'll Always Be With You

You Said I Was Your Favorite

New Year's Day

Lonely For You Only (a Lancaster novel)

LANCASTER PREP: NEXT GENERATION

All My Kisses for You

THE PLAYERS

Playing Hard to Get

Playing by The Rules

Playing to Win

WEDDED BLISS (LANCASTER)

The Reluctant Bride

The Ruthless Groom

The Reckless Union

The Arranged Marriage boxset

COLLEGE YEARS

The Freshman

The Sophomore

The Junior

The Senior

DATING SERIES

Save The Date

Fake Date

Holidate

Hate to Date You

Rate A Date

Wedding Date

Blind Date

THE CALLAHANS

Close to Me

Falling For Her

Addicted To Him

Meant To Be

Fighting For You

Making Her Mine

A Callahan Wedding

FOREVER YOURS SERIES

You Promised Me Forever

Thinking About You

Nothing Without You

DAMAGED HEARTS SERIES

Her Defiant Heart

His Wasted Heart

Damaged Hearts

FRIENDS SERIES

Just Friends

More Than Friends

Forever

THE NEVER DUET

Never Tear Us Apart

Never Let You Go

THE RULES SERIES

Fair Game

In The Dark

Slow Play

Safe Bet

THE FOWLER SISTERS SERIES

Owning Violet

Stealing Rose

Taming Lily

REVERIE SERIES

His Reverie

Her Destiny

BILLIONAIRE BACHELORS CLUB SERIES

Crave

Torn

Savor

Intoxicated

ONE WEEK GIRLFRIEND SERIES

One Week Girlfriend

Second Chance Boyfriend

Three Broken Promises

Drew + Fable Forever

Four Years Later

Five Days Until You

A Drew + Fable Christmas

STANDALONE YA TITLES

Daring The Bad Boy

Saving It

Pretty Dead Girls

ABOUT THE AUTHOR

Monica Murphy is a New York Times, USA Today and international bestselling author. Her books have been translated in almost a dozen languages and have sold millions of copies worldwide. Both a traditionally published and independently published author, she writes young adult and new adult romance, as well as contemporary romance.

facebook.com/MonicaMurphyAuthor

instagram.com/monicamurphyauthor

bookbub.com/profile/monica-murphy

goodreads.com/monicamurphyauthor

amazon.com/Monica-Murphy/e/B00AVPYIGG

pinterest.com/msmonicamurphy

tiktok.com/@monicamurphyauthor

Printed in Great Britain
by Amazon

44809159R00209